zero day

David Baldacci is a worldwide bestselling novelist. With his books published in over 45 different languages and in more than 80 countries, and with over 110 million copies in print, he is one of the world's favourite storytellers. His family foundation, the Wish You Well Foundation, a non-profit organization, works to eliminate illiteracy across America. Still a resident of his native Virginia, he invites you to visit him at www.DavidBaldacci.com, and his foundation at www.WishYouWellFoundation.org, and to look into its programme to spread books across America at www.FeedingBodyandMind.com.

ALSO BY DAVID BALDACCI

The Camel Club series

The Camel Club
The Collectors
Stone Cold
Divine Justice
Hell's Corner

Sean King and Michelle Maxwell series

Split Second
Hour Game
Simple Genius
First Family
The Sixth Man

Shaw series

The Whole Truth
Deliver Us From Evil

Other novels

True Blue
Absolute Power
Total Control
The Winner
The Simple Truth
Saving Faith
Wish You Well
Last Man Standing
The Christmas Train
One Summer

David
Baldacci

zero day

PAN BOOKS

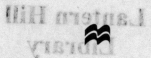

First published 2011 by Grand Central Publishing, USA

First published in the UK 2011 by Macmillan

This edition published 2011 by Pan Books
an imprint of Pan Macmillan, a division of Macmillan Publishers Limited
Pan Macmillan, 20 New Wharf Road, London N1 9RR
Basingstoke and Oxford
Associated companies throughout the world
www.panmacmillan.com

ISBN 978-1-4472-1338-3

1 3 5 7 9 8 6 4 2

A CIP catalogue record for this book is available from
the British Library.

Printed and bound in India by Replika Press Pvt. Ltd.

Visit www.panmacmillan.com to read more about all our books
and to buy them. You will also find features, author interviews and
news of any author events, and you can sign up for e-newsletters
so that you're always first to hear about our new releases.

To the memory of my mother

And to Charles "Chuck" Betack, my friend

zero day

1

THE CLOUD OF COAL DUST driven deeply into his lungs nearly caused Howard Reed to pull his mail truck off the road and throw up onto the stunted, burnt grass. But he coughed and spat and tightened his gut. Reed worked the accelerator and raced past the haul roads where dump trucks lumbered across, spewing black grit into the air like burning confetti. That same air was filled with sulfur dioxide because a coal waste pile had caught on fire, as they often did. These elements would drift up into the sky, react with oxygen to form sulfur trioxide, and then clamp onto water molecules to create a potent compound that would later fall back to earth as toxic acid rain. None of it was a trusty recipe for environmental harmony.

Reed kept his hand tightly on the special mechanism, and his eighteen-year-old Ford Explorer with the rattling tailpipe and shuddering transmission stayed on the cracked asphalt. His mail truck was his personal vehicle and had been modified to allow him to sit in the passenger seat and pull up flush to the mailboxes on his route. This was accomplished in part by an apparatus that looked like the fan belt in a car. It allowed him to steer, brake, and accelerate from the right side of the car.

After becoming a rural mailman and learning to drive from the "wrong" side of the vehicle, Reed had wanted to travel to England and try his newfound skill on the roads there, where every motorist drove on the left. He had learned that this dated back to the days of the jousters. Most folks were right-handed, and back then a man wanted to keep his sword or jousting pole closest to his enemy. His wife told him he was an idiot and would most likely end up dead in a foreign land.

He moved past the mountain, or where the mountain had once been before the Trent Mining and Exploration Company had blown it up in order to get to the buried rich coal seams. Large tracts of the area looked like the surface of the moon now, cratered and denuded. It was a process called surface mining. To Reed a better term was surface annihilation.

But this was West Virginia, and coal provided the bulk of the good-paying jobs. So Reed didn't make a fuss about his home being flooded by a fly ash sludge storage pond giving way. Or about well water that turned black and smelled like rotten eggs. Or about air that was routinely full of things that did not mix well with human beings. He didn't complain about his remaining kidney or his damaged liver and lungs from living around such toxic elements. He would be viewed as anti-coal and thus anti-jobs. Reed just didn't need the added grief.

He turned down the road to make his last delivery of the day. It was a package that had to be signed for. He had cursed when he'd picked up his load of mail and seen it. A signature meant he had to actually interact with another human being. All he wanted right now was to scoot over to the Dollar Bar where every mug of beer on Monday cost a quarter. He would sit on his little worn-down perch at the end of the mahogany slab and try not to think about going home to his wife who would smell the alcohol on his breath and spend the next four hours lecturing him about it.

He pulled into the gravel drive. This neighborhood had once been fairly nice—well, if one went back to the 1950s. Now it was not so nice. There wasn't a soul around. The yards were empty of kids as though it were two in the morning instead of two in the afternoon. On a hot summer's day the kids should be out running under the sprinkler or playing hide-and-seek. But kids didn't do that anymore, Reed knew. They sat inside in the AC and played video games so violent and gory that Reed had forbidden his grandchildren to bring them into his house.

Now the yards were filled with trash and dirty plastic toys.

Ancient rusted Fords and Dodges were up on concrete blocks. The homes' cheap siding was popping off, every surface of wood needed painting, and roofs were starting to collapse as though God above were pressing down on them. It was all sad and rather pathetic and made Reed want that beer even more, because his neighborhood looked exactly the same as this one. He knew a few privileged folks were making a fortune off the coal seams. It was just that none of them happened to live around here.

He pulled the package from the postal bin and trudged toward the house. It was a tired-looking two-story with vinyl siding. The door was hollow-core wood, white and scarred. A sheer glass door fronted it. A plywood wheelchair ramp bled off the stoop. The shrubs in front of the house were overgrown and dying; their branches had pushed against the soft siding, buckling it. There were two cars parked in the gravel in front of his black Ford: a Chrysler minivan and a late-model Lexus.

He took a moment to admire the Japanese car. Something like that would probably cost him more than a year's salary. He reverently touched the blue metallic paint. He noted a pair of aviator sunglasses hanging from the rearview mirror. There was a briefcase in the backseat and a green jacket next to it. Both vehicles' license plates were from Virginia.

He continued on, bypassing the ramp, hit the bottom step, trekked up the three squared-off logs of poured concrete, and rang the bell. He heard the sound pealing back at him from inside.

He waited. Ten seconds. Twenty. His irritation grew.

He rang again.

"Hello? Mailman. Got a package needs a signature." His voice, virtually unused throughout his workday, seemed strange to him, as though someone else were talking. He glanced down at the eight-by-eleven-inch flat package. Attached to it was the receipt that needed signing.

Come on, it's hot as hell and the Dollar Bar is calling my name.

He glanced at the package label and called out, "Mr. Halverson?"

Reed didn't know the man but did recognize the name from previous deliveries. Some mailmen in rural areas became friendly with their customers. Reed had never been that kind of mailman. He wanted his beer, not a conversation.

He rang again and then knocked on the glass, two sharp raps with his knuckles. He swiped at a bead of sweat that trickled down the back of his burnt red neck, an occupational hazard from sitting next to an open car window all day with the sun beating down on him. His armpits were oozing sweat, staining his shirt. He wasn't running his car AC with the window down. Gas was expensive enough without wasting it.

He raised his voice: "Hello, it's the mailman. Need a signature. If it goes back you probably won't see it again." He could see shimmers of heat in the air. He felt slightly dizzy. He was getting too old for this.

He aimed his gaze at the two cars. Had to be somebody home. He stepped away from the door and tilted his head back. There was no one peering at him from the dormer windows. One was open, making them look like mismatched eyeballs. He rapped again.

Finally, he heard someone approaching. He noted that the wooden door was cracked open a few inches. The sounds grew nearer and then stopped. Reed was hard of hearing or he would've noticed the odd sound of the footfalls.

"Mailman, need a signature," he called out.

He licked his dry lips. He could see the quarter beer in his hand. Taste it.

Open the damn door.

He said, "Do you want your package?"

I could give a rat's ass. I could just chuck it down a ravine, like I've done before.

The door finally inched open. Reed tugged back the glass portal, his hand extended, the package in it. "You got a pen?" he asked.

When the door opened more, he blinked. There was no one there. The door had opened all by itself. Then he glanced down. A miniature collie looked back up at him, its long snout and furry hindquarters swaying from side to side. It had obviously nosed the door open.

Reed was not the stereotypical mailman. He loved dogs, had two of his own.

"Hey there, buddy." He knelt down. "Hey there." He scratched the dog's ears. "Anybody home? You want to sign for this package?"

When Reed's hand hit the wetness in the animal's fur he at first thought it was dog pee and he jerked back. When he looked down at his palm he saw the red, sticky substance that had been transferred from the collie.

Blood.

"You hurt, boy?"

He examined the dog. More blood, but no wound that he could see.

"What the hell?" Reed muttered.

He stood, one hand on the knob. "Hello? Anybody here? Hello?"

He looked behind him, unsure of what to do. He glanced down at the dog; it was staring up at him, its features now seemed melancholy. And something else was strange. The dog hadn't barked once. His two mutts would raise the roof if someone came to his door.

"Shit," Reed said under his breath. "Hello?" he said in a loud voice. "Everybody okay?" He edged inside the house. It was warm. His nose wrinkled at the unpleasant smell. If his head hadn't been stuffed with allergies, the odor would have been far more unpleasant.

"Hello. Your dog has blood on him. Everything okay?"

He took a few more steps forward, cleared the small vestibule, and peered around the corner into the tiny living room set off the hall.

An instant later the wooden front door was thrown back, the knob punching a crater in the drywall. The glass door was kicked open so hard that it hit the metal banister on the left side of the porch, shattering the glass. Howard Reed jumped from the top step to the dirt. His heels dug in, he gave one shudder, sank to his knees, and threw up what little was in his stomach. Then he rose and stumbled to his truck, coughing, retching, and yelling in terror like a man suddenly deranged.

And he was.

Reed Howard would not make it to the Dollar Bar today.

CHAPTER

2

JOHN PULLER STARED out the window at the great state of Kansas a few thousand feet below. He leaned closer to the plane's window and looked straight down. The flight path into KCI airport took them over Missouri and west into Kansas. The pilot would do a protracted series of banks and head back to the Show-Me State to land. The jet was now flying over federal property. In this case that federal property was a prison, or rather several of them, both federal and military. Down there several thousand inmates sat in their cells and brooded over having lost their liberty, many of them forever.

He squinted, putting up one hand to block the glare from the sun. They were passing over the old USDB, or United States Disciplinary Barracks, also known as the Castle. For over a hundred years it had housed the worst of the armed forces' lawbreakers. Whereas the old Castle looked like a medieval fortress made of stone and brick, the new USDB looked like a community college. That is, until you noted the twin fourteen-foot fences that ringed the facility.

Leavenworth Federal Prison for civilians was four miles to the south.

Only men were incarcerated at USDB. Female military prisoners were housed in the San Diego naval brig. The inmates here had been convicted at court-martial of violations of the Uniform Code of Military Justice. USDB only housed prisoners who were sentenced to five years or more or those convicted of national security offenses.

National security.

That was why John Puller was here.

The jet's landing gear came down and the plane descended into the Kansas City airport, touching down smoothly on the tarmac.

Thirty minutes later, Puller slid into his rental car and drove out of the airport, steering his ride due west toward Kansas. The air was still and hot. The hills were green and rolling. Puller didn't turn on the car's AC. He preferred real air, hot or not. He was exactly six feet three and seven-eighths inches in his bare feet. He knew this because his employer, the United States Army, was very good at measuring its personnel. He weighed 232 pounds. On the Army's height-to-weight-to-age standards he would be deemed, at thirty-five, to be about ten pounds overweight. But no one looking at him would have thought that. If there was an ounce of fat on the man it would take a microscope to locate it.

He was taller than most infantrymen and almost all other Army Rangers he had served with. That had its advantages and disadvantages. His muscles were long and ropy and his limbs carried the advantage of extraordinary leverage and endurance. The downside was he was a far bigger target than the typical grunt.

He had been a decent tight end in college and looked like he could still suit up on Saturday. He had always lacked the super-normal speed and agility to make it into the NFL, but that had never been his ambition. There was only one career John Puller had ever wanted. And that was to wear the uniform of the United States Army.

He was not in uniform today. He never wore it when he came to USDB. More miles went by. He passed a sign for the Lewis and Clark Trail. Then the blue bridge came up. He crossed it. He was now in Kansas. More specifically, he was now at Fort Leavenworth.

He cleared the main checkpoint, where the military examined his ID and wrote down his license plate number. The guard saluted Warrant Officer Puller and said a crisp "Thank you, sir. You may proceed." Puller drove on. With an Eminem tune playing on the radio, he passed along Grant Avenue and eyed the remains of the old Castle. He saw remnants of the wire canopy that had covered the former prison. It had been placed there to prevent escape by chopper. The Army tried to think of everything.

Two miles later he arrived at the USDB. Somewhere in the background a train's horn sounded. A Cessna lifted off from nearby Sherman Army Airfield, its bulky snout and sturdy wings battling a crosswind. Puller parked and left his wallet and most of his other personal possessions in the car, including his standard-issue SIG P228, which the Army designated the M11. He had checked his sidearm and ammo in a hard-sided case for the flight here. He was supposed to carry his gun with him at all times. Yet walking armed into a prison did not seem like a good idea to Puller, authorized or not. And he would have to secure the gun in a locker anyway once inside. For obvious reasons, no weapons could go in where the prisoners were.

There was one bored young member of the Military Police manning the scan gate. Though Puller knew it wasn't possible, the soldier looked like he'd been pulled straight from boot camp to hold this post. Puller presented his driver's license and his cred pack.

The burly, chubby-cheeked MP stared at the badge and ID card identifying John Puller as a Criminal Investigative Division, or CID, special agent. The crouching eagle with its head turned to the right was the centerpiece of the badge. It had large claws that gripped the top of the shield. Its one revealed eye looked menacing, the large beak poised ready to strike. The MP saluted and then gazed up at the tall, wide-shouldered man.

"You here officially, sir?"

"No."

"John Puller Jr.? You related to—"

"My old man."

The young MP looked awed. "Yes, sir. Give him my best, sir."

The United States Army had many fighting legends, and John Puller Sr. was right near the very top of that list.

Puller stepped through the magnetometer. It beeped. He was wanded. Like always. The device screeched at his right forearm.

"Titanium rod," noted Puller. He rolled up his sleeve to show the scar.

The wand went off again at his left ankle.

The MP looked up inquiringly.

Puller said, "Screws and plate. I can lift my pants leg."

"If you will, sir."

When Puller let his pants leg drop back down the guard said apologetically, "Just doing my job, sir."

"I would've given you hell if you didn't, MP."

Wide-eyed, the soldier said, "Did you get those in combat, sir?"

"I didn't shoot myself."

Puller grabbed his car keys out of the bowl he'd put them in and slid his license and cred pack back into his shirt pocket. He signed the visitor's log.

The heavy door was buzzed open and he walked a few paces to stand in the visitor's room. There were three other inmates receiving visitors. Young kids played on the floor while husbands and their wives or girlfriends talked quietly. Kids were forbidden from sitting on their daddies' laps. One hug, kiss, or handshake at the beginning and end of the visit was allowed. No hands could dip below the waist. In between, a visitor and the inmate could intertwine fingers. All conversations had to be conducted in normal voices. You could only converse with the inmate you'd come to see. One could bring in a pen or pencil but not paints or crayons. That rule, thought Puller, had come from a big mess that someone had made, probably a child. But it was a stupid rule, he thought, since a pen or pencil could easily be turned into a weapon whereas a crayon wouldn't be much of a threat.

Puller stood there and watched as a woman who looked to be the mother of an inmate read the Bible to him. You could bring books in, but you couldn't give them to the inmate. Neither could you give them a magazine or newspaper. You couldn't bring in any food, but you could buy your inmate food from the nearby vending machines. They were not allowed to buy things themselves. Perhaps it would have seemed too much like normal life, thought Puller, which was not something prison was designed to provide. Once a visitor entered the room, leaving it instantly terminated the visit. There was only one exception to this rule, of which Puller would never be able to take advantage: breastfeeding. There was a room for that upstairs.

The door at the opposite end of the room opened and a man in an orange jumpsuit walked through. Puller watched him come forward.

He was tall but an inch shorter than Puller, and possessed a more slender build. The face was similar, though the hair was darker and longer. There was a touch of white in places that Puller did not have. Both men's jaws were square, the line of the noses narrow and slightly off to the right, and the teeth large and even. There was a right-side dimple and eyes that appeared green in artificial light and blue in the sun.

Puller also had a scar across the left side of his neck that angled down toward the back. There were other distinguishing marks on his left leg, right arm, and upper torso both front and rear. They all represented unwelcome intrusions of foreign objects fired with violent velocity into his person. The other man had none of these, and his skin was white and smooth. No suntanning in here.

Puller's skin had been roughened by brutal heat and wind and equally debilitating cold. He would be described by most as rugged-looking. Not handsome. Never cute. On good days he could perhaps be attractive, or more likely interesting-looking. It would never occur to him to even think about those things. He was a soldier, not a model.

They did not hug. They shook hands briefly.

The other man smiled. "Good to see you, bro."

The brothers Puller sat.

CHAPTER

3

"LOST WEIGHT?" asked Puller.

His brother, Robert, leaned back in his chair and draped one long leg over his opposite knee.

"Chow here's not as good as the Air Force."

"Navy does it the best. Army's a distant third. But that's because the wings and the water guys are wimps."

"Heard you made warrant officer. No longer an SFC."

"Same job. Little bump in the pay."

"Way you want it?"

"Way I want it."

They fell silent. Puller looked to his left, where a young woman was holding hands with her inmate and showing him some pictures. Two little towheads played on the floor at Mom's feet. Puller gazed back at his brother.

"Lawyers?"

Robert Puller shifted his weight. He too had been watching the young couple. He was thirty-seven, had never been married, and had no children.

"Nothing left for them to do. Dad?"

Puller's mouth twitched. "The same."

"Been to see him?"

"Last week," he said.

"Docs?"

"Like your lawyers, not much they can do."

"Tell him hello for me."

"He knows."

A spark of anger. "I know. I've always known that."

Robert's raised voice drew a long, hard stare from the burly MP stationed against the wall.

In a lower voice Robert said, "But still tell him I said hello."

"Need anything?"

"Nothing you can provide. And you don't have to keep coming."

"My choice."

"Younger brother guilt."

"Younger brother something."

Robert slid his palm across the tabletop. "It's not that bad in here. It's not like Leavenworth."

"Sure it is. Still a prison." Puller leaned forward. "Did you do it?"

Robert glanced up. "Wondered why you never asked me that before."

"I'm asking now."

"I've got nothing to say on that," replied his brother.

"You think I'm trying to sneak a confession out of you? You've already been convicted."

"No, but you are CID. I know your sense of justice. I don't want to put you in an untenable conflict of interest or of the soul."

Puller leaned back. "I compartmentalize."

"Being John Puller's son. I know all about that."

"You always saw it as weight."

"And it's not?"

"It is whatever you want to make it. You're smarter than me. You should have figured that out on your own."

"And yet we both joined the military."

"You went officer route, like the old man. I'm just enlisted."

"And you call me smarter?"

"You're a nuclear scientist. A mushroom cloud specialist. I'm just a grunt with a badge."

"With a badge," repeated his brother. "I guess I'm lucky I got life."

"They haven't executed anybody here since '61."

"You checked?"

"I checked."

"National security. Treason. Yeah, real lucky I got life."

"Do you feel lucky?"

"Maybe I do."

"Then I guess you just answered my question. Need anything?" he asked again.

His brother attempted a grin, but it failed to hide the anxiety behind it. "Why do I sense a finality with that query?"

"Just asking."

"No, I'm good," he said dully. It was as if all the man's energy had just evaporated.

Puller eyed his brother. Two years apart in age, they had been inseparable as young boys and later as young men in uniform for their country. Now he sensed a wall between them far higher than the ones surrounding the prison. And there was nothing he could do about it. He was looking at his brother. And then again his brother was no longer really there. He'd been replaced by this person in the orange jumpsuit who would be in this building for the rest of his natural life. Maybe for all of eternity. Puller wouldn't put it past the military to have somehow figured that one out.

"Guy was killed here a while back," said Robert.

Puller knew this. "Installation trusty. Baseball bat to the head on the rec field."

"You checked?"

"I checked. Did you know him?"

Robert shook his head. "I'm on 23/1. Not a lot of time to socialize."

That meant he was locked up twenty-three hours a day and then allowed out for one hour of exercise alone in an isolated place.

Puller did not know this. "Since when?"

Robert smiled. "You mean you didn't check?"

"Since when?"

"Since I belted a guard."

"Why?"

"Because he said something I didn't care for."

"Like what?"

"Nothing you need to know about."

"And why is that?"

"Trust me. Like you said, I'm the smart brother. And it wasn't like they could add any more time on to my sentence."

"Anything to do with the old man?"

"You better get going. Don't want to miss your flight out of here."

"I've got time. Was it the old man?"

"This isn't an interrogation, little brother. You can't pump me for info. My court-martial is long since over."

Puller looked down at the shackles on his brother's ankles. "They feeding you through the slit?"

There were no bars at USDB. The doors were solid. For prisoners in solitary their food was delivered three times a day via a slit in the door. A panel at the bottom of the door allowed the shackles to be put on before the door was opened.

Robert nodded. "Guess I'm lucky they didn't stamp me NHC. Or else we wouldn't be sitting here."

"Did they threaten No Human Contact status?"

"They say lots of things in here."

The men sat in silence.

Finally Robert said, "You better get going. I've got stuff to do. Keep real busy here."

"I'll be back."

"No reason. And maybe a better reason not to."

"I'll tell the old man you said hello."

The men rose and shook hands. Robert reached out and patted his brother on the shoulder. "You miss the Middle East?"

"No. And I don't know anybody who served over there who does."

"Glad you came back in one piece."

"A lot of us didn't."

"Got any interesting cases going?"

"Not really."

"You take care."

"Right, you too." Puller's words were empty, hollow, before they even left his mouth.

He turned to leave. On cue the MP came to get his brother.

"Hey, John?"

Puller looked back. The MP had one big hand on his brother's left upper arm. Part of Puller wanted to rip that hand off and knock the MP through the wall. But just a part.

"Yeah?" He locked gazes with Robert.

"Nothing, man. Just nothing. It was good to see you."

Puller passed the scan MP, who jumped to attention when he came by, and hit the stairs, taking them two steps at a time. The phone was ringing when he reached his rental. He looked at the caller ID.

It was the number for the 701st MP Group out of Quantico, Virginia, where he was assigned as a CID special agent.

He answered. Listened. In the Army they taught you to talk less, listen more. Much more.

His response was curt. "On my way." He checked his watch, swiftly calculated flight and drive times. He would lose an hour flying west to east. "Three hours and fifty minutes, sir."

There was a slaughterhouse in the boonies of West Virginia. One of the victims had been a full colonel. That fact had triggered CID involvement, although he wasn't sure why the case had landed in the lap of the 701st. But he was a soldier. He'd gotten an order. He was executing that order.

He would fly back to Virginia, grab his gear, get the official pack, and then it was burnt rubber to the boonies. However, his thoughts were not on the murder of a colonel, but rather on that last look on his brother's face. It perched in a prominent corner of Puller's mind. He *was* good at compartmentalizing. But he didn't feel like doing it right now. The memories of his brother from a different time and place slowly trickled through his thoughts.

Robert Puller had been a fast-track major in the Air Force who had helped oversee the nation's nuclear arsenal. He was a lock for at least one star, and possibly two. And now he was a convicted traitor to his country and would not be leaving USDB until his last breath had been drawn.

But he was still his brother. Not even the U.S. military could change that.

Moments later Puller fired up the engine and smacked the car into gear. Every time he came here he left a bit of himself behind. There might come a day when there would be nothing left to take back.

He had never worn his emotions on his sleeve. He had never cried when men around him were dying on the battlefield, often horribly. But he had avenged them, in equally horrible ways. He had never walked into combat carrying uncontrolled anger, because that made you weak. And weakness made you fail. He had not shed a tear when his brother was court-martialed for treason. Men in the Puller family did not cry.

That was Rule One.

Men in the Puller family remained calm and in control at all times, because that raised the odds of victory.

That was Rule Two.

Any rules after that were largely superfluous.

John Puller was not a machine, but he also could see that he was awfully close to becoming one.

And beyond that he refused to engage in any further self-analysis.

He left USDB far faster than he'd arrived there. A far speedier wing ride east would take him headlong into another case. It was welcome to Puller, if only to take his mind off the one thing he had never come close to understanding.

Or controlling.

His family.

CHAPTER

4

"You're on your own with this one, Puller."

John Puller sat across the desk from Don White, his SAC, otherwise known as the special agent in charge at the Criminal Investigative Division's headquarters in Quantico, Virginia. For years the headquarters had been farther north at Fort Belvoir, Virginia. Then the base realignment and closure folks had decided to consolidate CID offices across all branches at Quantico, which was also home to the FBI Academy and the Marine Corps.

Puller had made a quick stop at his off-base apartment to pick up a few things and check on his cat, a fat orange-and-brown tabby he had named AWOL, since it was always going off without getting clearance from him. AWOL meowed and then snarled at him before brushing against his leg and letting Puller run his hand over its arched back.

"Case, AWOL. Be back sometime. Food, water, and litterbox in the usual places."

AWOL meowed his understanding of this and then glided away. He had wandered into Puller's life about two years ago, and Puller figured the cat would wander out of it at some point.

There had been several phone messages on his apartment hard line, which he only kept in case the power went out and his cell phone went dead. There was only one message that he listened to in full.

He had sat down on the floor and played it through two more times.

His father.

Lieutenant General "Fighting John" Puller was one of America's greatest warriors and the past commander of the Screaming Eagles, the Army's legendary 101st Airborne Division. He was no longer in the Army and he was no longer a leader of anything. But that did not mean the old man accepted either of those points of reality. In fact, he did not. Which of course meant he was not really living in reality.

He was still ordering his younger son around as though he was at the top of the stars-and-bars chain and his boy at the bottom. His father would probably not remember what he had said on the message. He might not even recall that he had phoned. Or the next time Puller saw him he might bring it up and chastise his son for not executing the given order. The old man was as unpredictable in civilian life as he had been on the battlefield. That made him the toughest of opponents. If there was anything a soldier feared, it was an adversary you could never read, a foe who might be more than willing to do whatever it took, however outrageous, to win. Fighting John Puller had been such a warrior. Consequently he had won far more than he had lost and his tactics were now a fixture in the Army training methodology. And future leaders learned about him at the War College and spread the Puller fighting tactics to all sectors of the Army universe.

Puller erased the message. His father would have to wait.

Next stop was CID headquarters.

The CID had been started by General "Black Jack" Pershing in France during World War I. It had become a major Army command in 1971 and was headed up by a one-star. Worldwide, nearly three thousand people were assigned to it, nine hundred of them special agents, like John Puller. It was a centralized stovepipe command structure with the Secretary of the Army at the top and special agents at the bottom, with three layers of bureaucracy in between. It was a lasagna dish with too many noodle beds, Puller thought.

He focused on the SAC. "With an off-post homicide we usually go heavier than a one-man team, sir."

White said, "I'm trying to get you boots on the ground in West Virginia, but it's not looking good at this point."

Puller now asked the question that had been puzzling him ever since learning of the assignment. "The 3rd MP Group has the 1000th Battalion at Fort Campbell, Kentucky. West Virginia is their area of responsibility. They can investigate a colonel's homicide as well as we can."

"Murdered man was with the Defense Intelligence Agency. Sensitive slot calls for the 'quiet professional' of the 701st." White smiled at the description often given to the highly trained field investigative personnel of the 701st CID.

Puller didn't smile back.

White continued. "Fort Campbell. That's where the 101st is stationed. Your father's old division, the Screaming Eagles."

"Long time ago, sir."

"How's the old man doing?"

"He's doing, sir," Puller replied tersely. He did not care to talk about his father with anyone other than his brother. And even with his brother it was usually only a few sentences at most.

"Right. Good. Anyway, the 701st's FIUs are the best of the best, Puller. You weren't assigned here like other MP groups. You were *nominated.*"

"Understood." Puller just sat there wondering when the man would get around to telling him something he *didn't* know.

White slid a file across the metal desk. "Here's the prelim. Duty officer took down the initial info. Check with your team leader before you head out. An investigative plan has been formulated, but feel free to ad-lib based on conditions on the ground."

Puller took the offered file but kept his gaze on the man. "Thumbnail, sir?"

"Dead man was Colonel Matthew Reynolds. As I said, he was with DIA. Stationed at the Pentagon. His local address is in Fairfax City, Virginia."

"West Virginia connection?"

"Unknown as yet. But he's been positively identified, so we know it's him."

"His duties at DIA? Anything that could connect to this?"

"DIA is notoriously tight-lipped about its people and what they

do. But we have learned that Reynolds was in the process of retiring and going into the private sector. If we need to get you read in
for purposes of the investigation we'll do so."

If? Puller thought.

"What were his official duties at DIA?"

The SAC wriggled a bit in his seat. "He reported directly to the
J2's vice chair."

"The J2 is a two-star, right? Gives the daily intel briefing to the
Chairman of the Joint Chiefs?"

"That's right."

"Guy like that gets murdered, why isn't DIA all over this? They
have badged investigators?"

"All I can tell you is that the task has fallen to us. Namely,
to you."

"And if we catch the person, does DIA or more likely the FBI get
to swoop in and do the perp walk?"

"Not my call."

"So DIA is sitting this one out?"

"Again, I'm just telling you what I know."

"Okay, do we know where he was heading to after he left the
service?"

White shook his head. "Don't know yet. You can check directly
with Reynolds's superior at DIA for specifics. A General Julie
Carson."

Puller decided to say it. "Looks like I'll have to be read in to do
the investigative work, sir."

"We'll wait and see."

That answer was nonsensical and Puller noted his SAC didn't
look at him when he said it.

"Any other victims?" he asked.

"Wife, two kids. All dead."

Puller sat back. "Okay, four dead, probably complicated crime
scene in West Virginia with the investigation also extending to
DIA. We would normally send out at least four to six people with
major tech support on something like this. Even calling up some
bodies from USACIL," he added, referring to the Army's Crimi-

nal Investigation Lab at Fort Gillem in Georgia. "We'd need the manpower just to properly process the evidence. And then another team to hit the DIA angle."

"I think you just hit on the operative word."

"What's that?"

"Normally."

Puller sat back up. "And *normally* in an office as large as the 701st I'd be getting my assignment from my team leader, not the SAC, sir."

"That's right." The man did not seem inclined to expand on that response.

Puller dropped his gaze to the file. He was obviously expected to figure this out on his own. "Phone call said slaughterhouse."

White nodded. "That's how it was described. Now, I don't know how many homicides they have out there in West Virginia but I guess it was pretty bloody. Whatever it is, you'll have seen far worse in the Middle East."

Puller said nothing to this. Much like the subject of his father, he did not talk about his tours of duty in the desert.

White continued. "The local police are in charge of the investigation since it's off-installation. It's rural, and from what I understand they do not have an official homicide detective; uniforms will lead the investigation. Finesse will be called for. We don't really have grounds for full involvement unless it's determined the killer was military. And because of Reynolds's position I want us involved at least on a collateral investigation basis. To do that we need to play nice with the locals."

"Is there a secure facility in the area where I can store evidence?"

"Homeland Security has a secure site about thirty miles away. Second person stationed there to witness opening and closing the safe. I've gotten you authorization."

"I assume that I can still have access to USACIL?"

"Yes, you can. We also did a quick phone call to West Virginia. They voiced no objection to CID involvement. The Army lawyers can paper it later."

"Lawyers are good at paper, sir."

White studied him. "But we're the Army, so together with finesse the occasional hammer will also be necessary. And I understand that you are equally capable of providing either one."

Puller said nothing. He'd spent his entire military career dealing with commissioned officers. Some were good, some were idiots. Puller had not made up his mind about this one.

White said, "I've only been here a month, got posted here after they moved the operation from Fort Belvoir. Still feeling my way. You've been doing this five years."

"Going on six."

"Everyone who counts tells me you're the best we've got, if a little unorthodox." He leaned forward, rested his elbows on his desk. "I'm sure I don't have to tell you that there's a lot of interest from up top on this one, Puller. I'm talking past even the Secretary of the Army and on to the civilian corridors in D.C."

"Understood. But I've investigated cases involving Defense Intelligence that were handled within normal parameters. If there is that much interest at those levels, Colonel Reynolds must've had some extra juice in his post at the Pentagon." He paused. "Or maybe more dirt."

White smiled. "Maybe you are as good as advertised."

Puller stared back at the man. He thought, *And maybe I'd make an excellent fall guy if this all goes to hell.*

White said, "So you've been doing this nearly six years."

Puller remained silent. He thought he knew where this was going, because others had gone there before. The man's next words proved him correct.

White continued, "You're college educated. You speak French and German and passable Italian. Your father and brother are officers."

"*Were* officers," corrected Puller. "And the only reason I speak those languages is because my father was stationed in Europe while I was a kid."

White didn't seem to be listening. "I know you were a star of your training class at USAMPS," he began, referring to the United States Army's Military Police School at Fort Leonard Wood in

Missouri. "As an MP you bounced the drunken heads of grunts all over the globe. You've cracked cases pretty much everywhere the Army has a footprint. And you've got your Top Secret and SCI clearances." He paused. "Even though what your brother did nearly blew that for you."

"I'm not my brother. And all my clearances were renewed."

"I know that." The man fell silent and tapped the arm of his chair. Puller said nothing. He knew what was coming next. It always did.

"So why not West Point for you, Puller? And why CID? Your military service is solid gold. Top scores at Ranger School. Hell of a combat record. A leader in the field. Your father earned forty-nine major medals over three decades and he's an Army legend. You garnered nearly half that in six tours of combat in Iraq and Afghanistan. Two Silvers, one of which landed you in rehab for three months, three Bronzes with V-devices, and a trio of Purples. And you bagged a guy on the fifty-two-card most wanted deck in Iraq, right?"

"Five of spades, sir," said Puller.

"Right. So you've got more than enough stars and scars. Army loves that combo. You're a stud with an impeccable military pedigree. If you'd stayed with the Rangers you'd be a shoo-in for the top enlisted spot. If you'd gone to West Point you'd be a major or maybe even a lieutenant colonel by now. And you could've earned at least two shoulder stars before you left the Army. Hell, maybe three like your old man if you played the political games right. At CID an enlisted man tops out at command sergeant major. And my predecessor told me the only reason you filed your warrant officer application was because sergeant first classes sit their butts behind desks at CID while WOs can still get out in the field."

"I don't much like desks, sir."

"So here you are, at CID. On the low side of the bars and clusters. And I'm not the first to wonder about that, soldier."

Puller let his gaze drop to the other man's row of ribbons. White was dressed in the Army's new blue Class Bs that were over time replacing the old greens. For anyone in the military the chest of ribbons and/or medals was the DNA of a person's career. It told all to the experienced eye; nothing of significance could be hidden. From a combat perspective there wasn't anything in the SAC's history worthy of note, not a Purple or valor device in sight. Certainly the ribbons were many in number and would look impressive to the layperson, but it told Puller that the man was basically a career desk-humper, who only fired a weapon for recertification.

Puller said, "Sir, I like where I am. I like the way I got there. And it's a moot point now. It is what it is."

"I guess it is, Puller. I guess it is. Some might call you an underachiever."

"Maybe it's a character flaw, but I've never cared about what people call me."

"Heard that too about you."

Puller eyed the man steadily. "Yes, sir. I guess the case is getting cold out there."

The man glanced over at his computer screen. "Then get your gear and head out."

When White looked back moments later, Puller was already gone.

He'd never even heard the big man leave. White leaned farther back in his squeaky chair. Maybe that was why he had all those medals. You couldn't kill what you couldn't see coming.

CHAPTER

5

SITTING ON THE TRUNK of his black Army-issued Chevy Malibu, Puller drank one extra-large cup of coffee while he scanned the file under the arc of a streetlight outside CID headquarters. Clustered around here were all the criminal investigative divisions of the military, including NCIS, which had become a hugely popular television show. Puller wished he could solve crimes in sixty minutes each week as his TV counterparts did. In the real world it often took a lot longer, and sometimes you never did get to the truth.

In the background the sounds of gunshots were relentless. The FBI's Hostage Rescue Team and the Marines trained around the clock with live ammo. Puller was so used to the gunfire that he barely noticed it. He would only react if he hadn't heard it. Ironically, no shots fired at Quantico meant something was seriously wrong.

He turned the page in the file. The Army was as methodical and precise about recordkeeping as it was about everything else: the size of the file, the number of pages stapled to it, right-side info versus left-side, what dot and dash and triple slash went where. There were volumes of field manuals devoted to every last detail. Just the regulations that went along with maintaining the Military Police Blotter were legendary in their exactness. But the important thing to Puller would always be what was on the page, not where in the folder it was supposed to go.

Matthew Reynolds and his wife Stacey and their two teenage kids, one girl, one boy, had been murdered at a house in rural West Virginia. Mailman discovered the bodies. Local police on the scene. Husband was a colonel at DIA. He was in the process of rotating out and flipping to the private sector after pulling his twenty-six years in uniform. He was stationed at the Pentagon and lived in Fairfax City, so Puller didn't know what the man and his family were doing in a house in West Virginia. That would be one of many questions he would have to find answers to. Maybe the locals already had answers. He would take any they had and then verify them independently.

He put the file in his briefcase and checked his gear pack in the trunk. It was contained in a customized infantry rucksack with over a hundred compartments. It held pretty much everything he would need in the field: light blue latex gloves, flashlights, paper bags, body bags and tags, 35-millimeter and instant cameras, green biohazard suits complete with hood and air filtering gear, white field evidence collection scrubs, tape measure, ruler, evidence tape, departmental file forms, latent print kit, GSR analysis kit, barrier sheeting, digital recorder, crime scene notebook, medical equipment kit, shoe covers, body thermometer, purification mask, reflective vest, pocketknife, and nearly six dozen other items. He had two M11 pistols, and extra thirteen- and twenty-round mags. Puller also carried in his trunk an MP5 submachine gun. He had spare combat duds neatly packed in another bag. For now with the heat still at eighty-five degrees this late at night, jeans and a short-sleeved white shirt and Nikes would do.

Puller had never taken on a case like this solo. There was usually at least one other CID agent with him, usually more, plus tech support. And this case begged for more resources. But he had his assignment. And in the Army once you had your assignment the next step was to execute it. Otherwise you would find yourself in front of a military tribunal with perhaps prison your next career post.

He programmed the address where he was heading into his GPS, closed the Chevy's door, punched the gas, and left Quantico behind.

He stopped once to take a leak and grab another cup of black coffee. He hit Drake, West Virginia, population 6,547 as the sign said, at three in the morning. Sunrise would be in a little over three hours. He had gotten lost once, when the GPS led him down a two-lane road on the outskirts of Drake.

His headlights had hit on a neighborhood of abandoned houses. There must've been at least a hundred of them, maybe far more. They looked to be prefabricated and mass-assembled on site. There was a string of electrical and telephone poles down one side of the street. Yet as his car glided down this little "detour," Puller had changed his mind. The houses weren't abandoned; at least some of them were occupied. There were old cars parked out front. But the lights that glowed in a few of the windows didn't seem to be electrical. Maybe gas or battery-operated. He kept going, and then his lights hit on something else peculiar. It was a huge dome-shaped mass formed out of concrete that rose up out of the woods.

What the hell is that?

Despite his natural curiosity he had driven on, anxious to get to where he was going. The GPS had recalibrated and he soon found himself on the right path. When he arrived he wasn't tired. In fact the long ride had both relaxed and energized him. He decided to get to work.

He'd called ahead and reserved a room at the only motel in the area. It was a few notches below a Motel 6, but Puller didn't care. He'd spent years of his life in tin cans in swamps and deserts with a bucket for a shower and a hole in the earth for a bathroom, so this particular crevice in the wall was like the Ritz.

The door to the office was locked, but on the third ring of the buzzer, the door opened. Later, after she checked him in, the sleepy old lady in hair rollers and ratty robe standing behind the counter asked him what he was in town for.

As he palmed the room key Puller said, "Vacation."

That had made the old woman laugh.

"You're a slick one you are," she said, her voice lisping through a large gap between her front teeth. She smelled of nicotine, garlic, and salsa. It was an impressive combination. "And big." She gazed up at him from her five-foot-one-inch perch on earth.

"Any place you'd recommend to eat at?"

Army Rule Number One: Find a dependable place for chow.

"Depends," said the woman.

"On what?"

"On whether you mind coal dust in your eggs."

"Can't be any worse than depleted uranium in your morning coffee. And I'm still standing."

She cackled. "Then any place in town will do. They're all about the same, honey."

As he turned away she said, "You married?"

"You looking?" he replied, turning back to see her gap-toothed grin.

"If only, honey. If only. Get a good night's sleep."

Puller headed out. Sleep was not on his agenda.

CHAPTER

6

PULLER HAD CALLED the police officer in charge of the investigation a number of times on the drive to West Virginia and left multiple messages. He hadn't received a response. Maybe the locals were not going to be as cooperative as his SAC had suggested they would be. Or maybe they were just overwhelmed with four bodies and a massive forensics puzzle. Puller could hardly blame them if they were.

The motel was a one-story courtyard configuration. On the way to his room Puller passed a young man lying unconscious on a strip of grass near a Pepsi machine that was chained to a metal post thirty feet from the motel office. Puller checked the man for injuries and found none. He made sure he had a pulse, smelled the liquor on his breath, and kept going. He carried his bag into his twelve-by-twelve room. It had a bathroom so tiny he could stand in the middle and easily touch the opposite walls simultaneously.

He made some coffee from his own stock and using his portable percolator, a habit he'd picked up while on assignment overseas. He sat down on the floor with the file spread in front of him. He eyed the numbers, slid out his cell, and punched them in.

The voice was female, groggy. "Hello?"

"Sam Cole, please."

"Speaking."

"Sam Cole?" he asked again in a louder voice.

The voice became rigid and more alert. "Short for Samantha. Who the hell is this? And do you have any idea what time it is?"

The local accent thickened with the level of anger, Puller noted.

"It's 0320. Or twenty after three for civilians."

Long pause. He could see her wheels spinning, translating this to something comprehensible.

"Damn, you're Army, right?" Her voice was now husky, attractive.

"John Puller. CID special agent from the 701st MP Group out of Quantico, Virginia." He recited this in staccato fashion as he had a million times before.

He envisioned her sitting up in bed. He wondered if she was alone. He didn't hear any male mumbles in the background. But he did hear the percussion of a Zippo followed by a few seconds of silence. Then there was an intake of breath followed by an elongated exhale of smoke.

"You miss the surgeon general's warning, Ms. Cole?"

"No, it's right here on the side of my smokes. Why the hell are you calling me in the middle of the night?"

"You're listed in my file as the officer in charge. I just got into town. I need to get up to speed. And for the record, I called you four times over the last six hours and left messages each time. Never got a call back."

"I've been busy, haven't even checked my phone."

"I'm sure you have been busy, ma'am." He thought, *And I'm sure you did check, but didn't bother to call me back.* Then his SAC's admonition came back to him.

Play nice.

"I'm sorry to roust you out of your sack, ma'am. I thought you might still be at the crime scene."

She said, "I've been working this thing all day and most of the night. My head just hit the damn pillow an hour ago."

"Which means I have a lot of catching up to do. But I can call back later."

He heard her get up, stumble and curse.

"Ma'am, I said I can call back later. Just go back to sleep."

"Will you just shut up a minute?" she snapped.

"What?" Puller said sharply.

"I have to pee!"

He heard her drop the phone on the floor. Footsteps. Door closed, so he didn't actually hear Cole relieving herself. Another minute went by. He wasn't wasting time. He was reading through the report again.

She came back on. "I'll meet you there at seven o'clock—excuse me, oh zero seven hundred o'clock a.m. or whatever the hell it is you say."

"Zero-seven-hundred Juliet."

He listened to another long inhale and then exhale of smoke.

She said, "Juliet? I told you my name is Sam."

"Means local daylight saving time. If it were the winter and we were in eastern standard time it would be zero-seven-hundred Romeo."

"Romeo and Juliet?" she said skeptically.

"Contrary to popular belief, the United States Army has a sense of humor."

"Goodbye, Puller. Oh and just so you know, it's *Sergeant* Samantha Cole, not ma'am, or Juliet. Romeo!"

"Got it, Sergeant Cole. I'll see you at zero-seven. Look forward to working with you on this case."

"Right," she growled.

He could visualize her throwing the phone across the room and falling back into her bed.

Puller put the phone down, drank his coffee, and went through the report page by page. Thirty minutes later he gunned up, slipping one M11 into his front holster and the other into a holster attached to his belt in the rear. After fighting his way through the Middle East, he never felt as though he had enough weapons on his person. He put on a windbreaker and locked his motel room door on the way out.

The young man who'd been lying in the bushes was now sitting up and gazing around in bewilderment.

Puller walked over and looked down at him. "You might want to think about cutting back on the booze. Or at least pick a place to pass out that has a roof."

The man blinked up at him. "Who the hell are you?"

"John Puller. Who are you?"

The man licked his lips as though he was already thirsty for another round.

Puller said, "You got a name?"

The man stood. "Randy Cole." He wiped his hands on the front of his jeans.

Puller reflected on the last name and wondered about the obvious possibility but chose to keep it to himself.

Randy Cole was good-looking and appeared to be in his late twenties. About five-ten with a lean, wiry build. Under his shirt he probably had six-pack abs. The hair was brown and curly, the facial features strong and handsome. There was no wedding band on his finger.

"You staying at the motel?" asked Puller.

Randy shook his head. "I'm local. You're not."

"I know I'm not."

"So what are you doing in Drake?"

"Business."

Randy snorted. "Business. You don't look like no coal man to me."

"I'm not."

"So why, then?"

"Business," Puller said again, and his tone indicated he was not going beyond that description. "You got a car? You okay to drive?"

"I'm cool." Randy climbed out from the bushes.

"You sure?" asked Puller. "You need a ride somewhere I can give you a lift."

"I said I'm cool."

But he staggered and grabbed at his head. Puller helped to right him.

"I'm not sure you're all that cool yet. Hangovers are a bitch."

"Not sure it's just a hangover. I get headaches."

"You ought to get that checked out."

"Oh yeah, I'll go get me the best docs in the world. Pay 'em in cash."

Puller said, "Well, next time I hope you can find a bed to sleep in."

Randy said, "Hell, sometimes bushes beat the shit out of beds. Depends on who you're sharing the bed with. Right?"

"Right," said Puller.

Puller aimed his ride west, following the GPS, but really listening to his own internal compass. The high-tech stuff was good, but your head was better. High-tech sometimes failed. The head didn't unless someone had put a bullet through it, and then you had far bigger problems than just being lost.

He again wondered briefly if Randy Cole was related to Samantha. Cop and drunk. Not an unheard-of situation. Sometimes the cop was also the drunk.

Forty minutes later, after winding in and out of surface roads barely a car wide and fighting switchbacks and becoming lost once, he reached the street he wanted. By his internal compass it had taken him forty minutes to go about seven miles, and he noted that the GPS agreed with this. There were no straightaways in the mountainous terrain, and he had never once cranked the Malibu above forty.

He slowed his car and eyed the surroundings. One of the CID's credos came to him.

Look. Listen. Smell.

He took a deep breath. It was all about to begin.

Again.

CHAPTER

7

Puller eased his car to the side of the road and looked out the window. This would be the only time on this case his senses would not be dulled by prior observation.

He stepped out and leaned against the Malibu. He took another deep breath. In the air currents he could smell the mining operation he had passed a couple of miles back. His ears picked up the distant sounds of rumbling trucks. He looked to the west and saw a searchlight crisscrossing the sky; why, he didn't know.

He studied the neighborhood. His night vision was excellent and the moonlight and lightening skies allowed both large and small details to be revealed. Small, dilapidated cookie-cutter houses. Toys in yards. Rusted trucks on blocks. A stray cat sneaking by. The place was tired. Dying. Maybe already dead. Like the Reynoldses. Wiped out.

However, what Puller wasn't seeing was the most disturbing of all.

There was police tape hanging in front of the door telling everyone to keep the hell away. And someone had fashioned a jury-rigged barricade to the driveway using two five-gallon buckets turned upside down and more yellow police tape strung between them.

But there wasn't a cop in sight. No perimeter guard and yet the scene was barely fourteen hours old. Not good. It was unbelievable, in fact. He knew the legal chain of evidence could be blown out of the water by leaving a crime scene unsecured.

He didn't really want to do this, but not doing so would be derelict and might cost him and others their careers. He took out his phone and hit the numbers from memory.

She answered on the second ring. "I swear to holy God I am going to shoot whoever this is."

"Sergeant Cole, it's Puller again."

"Do you have a death wish?" she shouted into the phone.

"There's no guard here."

"Where?"

"At the crime scene."

"How the hell do you know that?"

"Because I'm parked outside the house."

"You're wrong. There's a patrol car with a deputy in it on duty. I ordered that myself."

Puller gazed around. "Well, unless he's hiding in the woods and ditched his ride, he must've turned invisible. And isn't the point of a perimeter guard to be *visible*?"

"Shit. Are you really out there?"

"I really am."

"And there's really no patrol car there?"

"There's really not."

"I'll be there in thirty-five minutes."

"Not faster than that?"

"If I tried to drive faster than that on these roads in the dark, I'd end up wrapped around a tree or off a mountain." She paused and Puller heard her clomping around in her bare feet, opening drawers, pulling out clothes, no doubt.

"Look, Puller, can you do me a favor and temporarily secure the crime scene? I'm going to call the deputy who's supposed to be there and chew his ass out."

"I can secure it. Are the bodies still inside?"

"Why?"

"If they are I want to see them."

"The bodies are still in there."

That was a long time to keep the bodies at the scene, but Puller decided not to comment on why that was. In a way he was glad. He wanted to see everything just as the killer had left it.

"I don't want to screw up your crime scene. Have you dusted for prints? Searched for trace?" he asked.

"Pretty much. Going to do more this morning."

"Okay. Was there forced entry?"

"None that we could see."

"So I can go in the front door?"

"It's locked. At least it should be."

"Then I'll go in the front door."

"Puller—"

"Thirty-five minutes."

She said slowly, "Okay, see you then. And…thanks for the assist."

Puller closed the phone and looked around. There were eight houses on the short dead-end street. Each one was dark. That was unremarkable at this time of the morning. Cars in the driveways of each of them. Woods at the rear of the houses on both sides.

He grabbed some items from his rucksack and put them in a collapsible backpack he always carried with him. He slipped on an ear mic and connected it to a recorder that he dropped into a pouch on his belt. He slapped on his light blue gloves.

He walked to the front of the house, glanced down at the gravel shoulder, and hit it with his Maglite. Tread marks. Could be any of the vehicles that had come here to investigate. He went over the chronology in his head.

Mailman found the bodies at about 1400 and called it in. First responders showed up at half past. The call to the Army had come in ten minutes later. That was fast. Someone out here was on the ball. He wondered if it was Cole. He'd gotten the heads-up in Kansas and hopped his flight back. The plane had had a hell of a tailwind and they'd gotten in forty minutes early. After a brief stop at home he'd pulled in to CID at 1840. He was wheels out at 1950. He'd driven like a rocket and hit Drake a bit after three; it was now going on 0500.

Puller eyed the wheelchair ramp. Matthew Reynolds was in his late forties and in good enough shape to be in the Army. His wife was five years younger with no health problems. Her insurance records were clean. The kids were sixteen and seventeen with clean health records. They weren't using the ramp. This wasn't their house. They were here for another reason. A reason that might have cost them their lives.

He studied the tread mark on the shoulder again, and then his gaze traveled to the dark patch. Right where the engine would be if the car were pointed to the east. Careful not to impact the tread mark, he squatted, touched the liquid. Warm. Oil. Recent. The perimeter cop? Probably. If so, where was he?

He moved swiftly up to the front door, noted the broken glass. He slipped on his shoe covers. The front door was locked but it wasn't a deadbolt. It took him all of three seconds.

He moved forward, shining his light around with one hand, the other gripping his front-side M11 pistol.

Puller figured you go into a house where four people had been murdered and the guard who's supposed to be out front isn't, certain possibilities come to mind. He reached the living room and his light hit them.

On the couch.

Lined up in a row.

Four bodies, the weight of one holding up its neighbor.

He holstered his weapon and, keeping well back, spoke into the mic, recording everything he was seeing.

Dad to the far right, teen daughter to the far left. Mom and brother in the middle. Mom next to Dad. He hit the carpeted floor in front of them with the Maglite. No blood spatters. He glanced up, aimed his beam at the heads.

Dad had taken a heavy ordnance load right in the face; a near contact wound.

Mom's face was relatively intact but her torso was destroyed. Puller glanced down at the dead woman's hands and saw that they were nearly obliterated. She'd held them up, he surmised, right before they shot her. The hands had no chance of protecting her from the blast, but it was just instinctive to block whatever part of the body the gun was aimed at.

The two teens' kill wounds were not evident. Maybe they'd taken it in the back. The parents had not been killed here. The spatters would have covered the room. Killed somewhere else in the house, moved here, lined up like a family watching TV together.

Pretty sick. But then you had to be pretty sick to take out a family.

Sick or a professional without a conscience.

And maybe it was the same thing.

He drew closer, careful not to step on anything marked with an evidence number on the carpet. Dad was in his old green Class Bs that could be officially worn for a few more years. The right side of his face was mostly gone, his spine exposed through the gaping wound in the neck. Bone and a hollow eye socket looked back at Puller. No wounds in his torso. He'd taken it all in the face and neck at close range.

A shotgun was pretty much the only firearm that did damage like that.

He could see bits of white in the wound tracks. Wadding from the shell. Hopefully they'd be able to tell the gauge from measuring the diameter of the wadding or by the name of the maker on top of the wad, if it was still readable.

Mom's eyes stared back at Puller. For an observer given to melodrama it would have appeared that the woman's look was pleading.

Find my killer.

Puller illuminated her chest with the Maglite. Dozens of punctures, randomly distributed. Shotgun as well, but different in the way it had been deployed.

He drew a ruler from his pocket and measured the distance between the punctures on Mrs. Reynolds's blouse that had once been white but was now mostly crimson. He did the calculation in his head and put the ruler away. He felt the man's arm and then the woman's. Still in rigor, though it was well on its way down and the muscles were relaxing. The bodies were the temperature of the room or lower. He pulled his air thermometer and took a reading. Blood had pooled to the lower extremities. Bowels and bladders long ago emptied. Skin greenish blue, rotting smell, faces dissolving. In death everybody was ugly.

He turned his attention to the teens.

Then he stopped, swiveled. A noise. From somewhere in the house.

Apparently he wasn't the only living person in here.

CHAPTER

8

THUMP-WHOOSH-THUMP. Thump-whoosh-thump.

Down the stairs, basement level.

Of course it is.

Puller eased to the doorway.

He sniffed the air. The scent of decomposing bodies was heavy, but Puller was not focusing his nose on that. He was trying to detect something else. Sweat. Cologne. Cigarettes. The molecular signature of bad breath. Anything that would give him an edge.

Nothing.

He moved the door open with his foot. The passageway down was dark.

Of course it is.

Thump-whoosh-thump.

The mechanical nature of the sound did not cause Puller to relax.

If he were leading someone to his death he would employ deception. In fact, in Iraq and Afghanistan he'd done it many times, just like the other side had been trying to do to him.

He pulled a pair of night optics from his knapsack, slipped them on his head, flipped down the eyepiece, and fired them up. The tunnel of darkness immediately flamed to life, albeit a green, somewhat hazy life. He squatted and pulled his other pistol from its holster. Both handguns were double-single action, racked and ready. Ordinarily he would not use two pistols at the same time, for the simple reason that his aim and accuracy could be diminished if he fired at two targets simultaneously. However, in a contained space like this, where accuracy was not so critical, he needed as much firepower as possible.

Two of the main differences between MPs and CID special agents were that MPs carried their weapons without a round chambered. CID agents went through life with racked guns at all times. MPs turned in their weapons when their shift was done. CID agents didn't draw a breath without their guns in easy reach.

When Puller applied twelve pounds of pressure on the trigger and fired, the slide would push the hammer back and his weapon would become a single-action pull. Twenty-round mags, so forty shots total, though he normally only needed one. He had never been a spray-and-pray kind of guy. But he could empty both pistols in about ten seconds if need be and lay down a man-sized target at fifteen meters with no problem. Now he just needed to acquire a target, preferably before it acquired him.

With his silhouette narrowed and lowered he began to proceed down the carpeted stairs. He squinted along the iron sights of the right-hand pistol. He did not like being in an enclosed space. The "fatal funnel," the Army called it. He had decent firepower, but they might have more.

Thump-whoosh-thump.

Mechanical. But someone had to hit the start button.

The file had mentioned a dog. Cole and her folks had to have confiscated the animal. They wouldn't have been so stupid as to leave a dog alone to mosey through the crime scene, particularly with bloody dead bodies around. Dogs, though domesticated, were carnivores after all.

Thump-whoosh-thump.

He hit the bottom step and crab-walked over to a far corner and did a recon.

Unfinished space.

Poured concrete floor, both studded-out and concrete foundation walls, exposed ceiling. Wires snaking up the naked walls. Mildew hit his nostrils. It was far better than the smell upstairs.

Against one wall he saw the marks. And on the floor in front.

Blood. The killing had been done down here. At least for Mom and Dad.

Thump-whoosh-thump.

He scanned the area once more. The room doglegged at the other end. There was a space he couldn't see because of a jutting concrete load-bearing wall.

Thump-whoosh-thump.

Of course the sound is coming from there.

Both guns aimed at this spot, Puller advanced, keeping low and his torso turned to the side.

He reached the corner, backed away parallel to the wall. Corners were problematic. "Dynamic corners" were how the Army referred to them, because situations could change quickly once you stepped around one. He said, "Federal agent."

Nothing.

"Federal agent."

He eyed the wall. Concrete. If it were wood or drywall he would have fired some shots through it, to get the attention of anyone on the other side waiting to ambush him. With concrete his rounds were more than likely going to ricochet right back at him.

"Slide any weapon out, then follow it with hands on head, fingers interlaced. I count to five, noncompliance will get you a flash-bang right up your ass."

He counted off, wishing he had a flash-bang with him.

Thump, whoosh, thump.

He holstered one pistol, slipped off his backpack, aimed, and tossed it in front of the opening.

Thump, whoosh, thump.

Either there was no one there, or he was one cool customer. Puller crouched, tensed, and did a quick turkey peek. In that momentary flash he took in a lot. None of it was good.

He edged around the corner. Following the sound, he looked down. The floor fan was on its side. The whoosh sound was the fan. The thump was the fan oscillating from side to side where the frame made contact with the concrete on each revolution.

But something had turned it on. And now he knew what that was.

Puller glanced up. The man was in uniform. He was hanging from the ceiling. The strap used to hold him there had loosened. His body had dropped down, though it was still suspended. It had hit the fan, knocking it over and turning it on.

Puller had just discovered what had happened to the perimeter guard.

He eyed the man through his optics. Clearly dead. Eyes bugged out and glassy. Body hanging limp. Hands bound. Feet the same. Puller approached, touched the man's skin. Somewhat warm but rapidly cooling. Hadn't been dead all that long. He checked for a pulse, just to be sure. There was none. Heart had stopped beating and everything else had stopped working instantly. He was past the point of no return, but not by much.

They had taken his police wheels. Warm oil, warm body.

The dead guy looked young. The low man on the totem pole, he'd drawn the crap post assignment. Guarding stiffs in the nighttime, and now he was a stiff too. Puller eased his gaze over the uniform. Looked to be a deputy sheriff. Drake County, the shoulder badge said. He eyed the holster. No gun. No surprise. Man has a gun he's not going to let you string him up without a fight. The face was swollen enough from the strangulation to where Puller couldn't tell if he'd been beaten.

He reached down and turned the fan off.

The thump-whoosh-thump symphony ceased.

Puller drew closer to the body and used his optics to read the nameplate.

Officer Wellman.

That was ballsy, thought Puller. To come back here and kill a cop. To come back to a murder scene once you'd done the deed.

What had they missed? Or left behind?

The next moment Puller was sprinting up the steps.

Someone else was coming.

He glanced at his watch.

It might be Sergeant Samantha Cole.

Or it might not.

CHAPTER

9

THE WOMAN CLIMBED out of her ride. It wasn't police wheels. It
was a plain, decades-old pickup truck with a four-speed stick drive
and three transmission antennas drilled in the cab's roof. It also
had a white custom camper with side windows and a flip-top gate
on the back with the word "Chevy" stenciled on it. The truck's pale
blue was not the original color.

Samantha Cole was not in uniform. She was dressed in faded
jeans, white T-shirt, a WVU Mountaineers windbreaker, and
worn-down calf-high boots. The butt of a King Cobra double-
action .45 revolver poked from inside her shoulder holster. It was
on the left side, meaning she was right-handed. She was a sliver
under five-three without the boots, and a wiry one-ten with dirty
blonde hair that was long enough to reach her shoulders. Her eyes
were blue and wide; the balls of her cheekbones were prominent
enough to suggest Native American ancestry. Her face had a scat-
tering of light freckles.

She was an attractive woman but with a hard, cynical look of
someone to whom life had not been overly kind.

Cole stared at Puller's Malibu and then up at the house where
the Reynoldses sat dead all in a row. One hand on the butt of her
gun, she advanced up the gravel drive. She passed the Lexus when
it happened.

The hand was on her before she realized it. Its grip was iron. She
had no chance. It pulled her down and then over to the other side
of the car.

"Shit!" Her fingers closed around the long, thick fingers. She could not break the grip. She tried to pull her gun with her other hand, but it was blocked by her attacker's arm pinning hers against her side. Cole was helpless.

"Just stay down, Cole," the voice said into her ear. "There might be a shooter out there."

"Puller?" she hissed as she turned to him. Puller released his grip and squatted next to the right front fender of the Lexus. He flipped up his night optics. He had one M11 in hand. The other pistol was parked back in its rear holster.

"Good to meet you."

"You nearly gave me a heart attack. I never even heard you."

"That's sort of the point."

"You about crushed my arm. What, are you bionic?"

He shrugged. "No, I'm just in the Army."

"Why did you grab me?"

"Your guy named Wellman?"

"What?"

"The cop on guard duty tonight?"

"Yeah, Larry Wellman. How'd you know that?"

"Somebody strung him up in the basement of the house and then stole his ride."

Her face collapsed. "Larry's dead?"

"Afraid so."

"You said there might be a shooter?"

He touched his optics. "Saw a flash of movement through a window of the house when I heard you pulling up."

"From where?"

"The woods behind the house."

"You think they...?"

"I don't presume. Why I grabbed you. Already killed one cop, so what's another to them?"

She gave him a searching glance. "I appreciate that. But I can't believe Larry's dead. No wonder he didn't answer my call." She paused. "He's got a wife and a new baby."

"I'm sorry."

"You sure he's dead?"

"If I weren't I would've cut him down and tried to resuscitate him. But trust me, it would've been pointless. He hasn't been dead long, though. Body's still warm."

"Shit," she said again, her voice shaky.

He drew in her scent. Her breath smelled of mints with the tobacco lapping right underneath. No perfume. She hadn't taken time to wash her hair. He glanced at his watch. She had gotten here two minutes ahead of her own deadline.

He saw her eyes start to glisten; a wobbly tear freed itself and slid down her cheek.

"You want to call it in?" he asked.

She answered in a dull, tired voice, "What? Oh, right." She hastily wiped her eyes and pulled out her phone. She drilled in the numbers. She spoke fast but clearly, also putting out a BOLO on the missing police cruiser. The woman had gone from emotionally paralyzed to professional in a few seconds. Puller was impressed.

She closed the phone.

"How many officers do you have available?" he asked.

"We're a rural county, Puller. Lot of space, not a lot of dollars. Budget cuts have wrecked us; cut our force by a third. And three of my guys are reservists who are currently in Afghanistan. So that translates into us having a total of twenty-one uniforms to cover about four hundred square miles. And two of them are banged up from a car crash last week."

"So nineteen. Including you?"

"Including me."

"How many are coming now?"

"Three. And that's a stretch. And it won't be fast. They're nowhere near here."

Puller looked toward the woods. "Why don't you stay here and wait for them and I'll go check out whatever it was I saw in the woods."

"Why would I stay here? I'm armed. Two's better than one."

"Suit yourself." He eyed the woods, did the run-through logistics in his mind. It was so ingrained in him that he thought about it thoroughly without seeming to think about it at all.

"You ever been in the military?" he asked.

She shook her head. "State police for four years before I came back here. For the record, I'm a hell of a shot. Got the ribbons and trophies to prove it."

"Okay, but you mind if I take the lead on this search?"

She looked out at the dark woods and then at his large, muscular physique.

"Works for me."

CHAPTER

10

A FEW MINUTES LATER Puller glanced behind him to see Sam Cole struggling to keep up with him in the dense brush. He stopped and held up his hand. Cole froze. He swept the area in front of him with his night-vision optics. Trees, brush, the dart of a deer. Nothing that was looking to kill them.

He still didn't move. He thought back to what he'd seen in the woods through the window. A shape, not an animal. A man. Didn't necessarily have to be connected to the case, but probably was.

"Puller?"

He didn't look back at her but simply waved Cole forward. She crouched next to him a few seconds later.

"You catch anything with that fancy gear of yours?"

"Just a deer and a whole lot of trees."

"I don't hear anything either."

He eyed the lightening sky. "There was a searchlight on when I arrived. To the east, couple of miles away."

"Probably mining operation."

"Why a searchlight?"

"Chopper landing most probably. Giving the bird a target to hit."

"Chopper landings at a coal mine in the middle of the night?"

"No law against it. And it's not a mine. They do mountaintop extraction here. Which means they don't tunnel under, they just blow up the mountain instead."

Puller kept scanning ahead and on the peripheries. "Were you the one who contacted the Army about Reynolds?"

"Yes. He was in uniform. That was our first clue. And we checked his car, found his ID." She paused. "You've been inside obviously. You saw he didn't have much of a face left."

"Did he have a briefcase or a laptop?"

"Both."

"I'll need to see them."

"Okay."

"There could be classified material in and on them."

"Right."

"Are they secure?"

"In our evidence room back at the station."

Puller thought for a moment. "I need you to make sure no one tries to access them. Reynolds was DIA, Defense Intelligence. It could be a big issue if an unauthorized person gets into that stuff. A real headache you don't need."

"I understand. I can make a call."

"Thanks. File said you printed him?"

"And faxed it off to the Pentagon to a number they gave us. They confirmed his ID."

"How many crime scene techs you have?"

"One. But he's pretty good."

"Medical examiner?"

"Chief's way over in Charleston along with the state medical lab."

Puller kept scanning while he talked. Whoever had been out here was gone. "Why are the bodies still in the house?"

"A number of reasons, but mostly because we didn't really have an appropriate place to put them."

"Hospital?"

"Closest one is a good hour away."

"Local ME?"

"We're in between."

"What does that mean?"

"It means the one we had moved out of town. And he wasn't a doctor. He was an EMT. But under state law that was good enough."

"So who's going to do the posts on the victims?"

"I'm trying to work that out now. Probably a local doc I know who has some forensics background. How many crime scene techs did you bring with you?"

"You're looking at him."

"Tech and investigator? That's a little unusual."

"It's actually a smart way to do it."

"What do you mean?"

He said, "That way nothing gets between me and the evidence. And I've got the Army's Criminal Investigation Lab to fall back on. Let's head back to the house."

A minute later they stood in front of the four bodies. It was growing light outside but Cole turned an overhead on.

Puller said, "The integrity of the crime scene has been blown. The killers came back. They could have screwed with the evidence."

"They could have screwed with it before too," shot back Cole.

"Even if we get a suspect to trial, his attorney can trash the entire prosecution based on this."

Cole said nothing. By her angry features Puller could tell that she knew this to be true.

"So what do we do about it?" she finally said.

"Nothing for now. We keep working the scene."

"Will you have to report this back?"

He didn't answer her. Instead he looked around and said, "The Reynoldses didn't live here. So what were they doing here?"

"Home belongs to a Richard and Minnie Halverson. They're Mrs. Reynolds's parents. They live in a nursing home. Well, he does. Mrs. Halverson was living here, but she suffered a stroke recently and is at a specialty hospital over near Pikeville. Not that far as the crow flies, but on our back roads it'll take you a good hour and a half to get there."

"I saw some of that getting here."

"Apparently Mrs. Reynolds was staying here temporarily to take care of things, oversee her father's care, get the house ready for sale, and have her mother admitted into the same nursing home since she can no longer live alone. It was summer, so the kids were staying with her. Mr. Reynolds was apparently coming out here on weekends."

"Where'd you get all this info?"

"Local sources. Nursing home and the hospital. And from poking around here. And we talked to some of the neighbors on the street."

"Good work," said Puller.

"I'm not here to do crappy work."

"Look, I'm only here because one of the victims is wearing a uniform. And my SAC said you guys were cool with a collateral arrangement."

"My boss was."

"And you?"

"Let's just say the jury's still out."

"Fair enough."

"So he was with DIA?"

"Didn't they tell you that when you faxed the prints in?"

"No. They just confirmed for me who he was. So military intelligence? Was he some sort of spy? Is that why someone killed him?"

"Don't know. He was getting ready to retire. Might just be a paper-pusher with eagle leaf clusters looking to punch the private-sector ATM. Pentagon is full of them."

Puller had decided not to fill her in on what Reynolds had really done at DIA. She wasn't cleared for it, and he wasn't looking to get busted down in rank for letting something slip he shouldn't.

"That doesn't really help us all that much, then."

Puller's honest side got the better of him. "Well, it might be he wasn't just a paper-pusher."

"But you just said—"

"I said *might*. It's not confirmed. And I'm just coming to the investigation too. Lot I don't know."

"Okay."

Puller drew closer to the bodies. "You found them like this. All seated in a row?"

"Yes."

"The adults' causes of death are pretty obvious. What about the kids?" He pointed to them.

When she didn't answer, Puller turned to her.

She'd pulled her Cobra and was aiming it at his head.

"WAS IT SOMETHING I SAID?" asked Puller quietly, his gaze on her face and not the muzzle of the Cobra. When someone drew down on you, you watched her eyes; that told you intent. And her intent clearly was to shoot him if he said the wrong thing or made the wrong move.

She said, "I must be punch-drunk because of lack of sleep."

"Not following."

"I have no idea if you are who you say you are. You're the only one who said you were with CID. I should never have given you permission to enter the crime scene. For all I know you killed Larry Wellman and made up a story about seeing somebody. Maybe you're a spy looking to steal what was in that man's brief-case and laptop."

"My car outside has Army plates."

"Maybe it's not your car. Or maybe you stole it."

"I've got ID."

"That's what I wanted to hear." She flicked the .45. "Show me, real, real slow."

Cole backed slightly away. Puller noted she used a standard Weaver firing stance, named after a county deputy in California who'd revolutionized shooting competitions back in the late 1950s. Feet shoulder width apart, knees locked. Gun-side foot slightly back of the other foot. She would employ the classic push-pull to control recoil when she fired. He could tell she had locked her dominant arm, but had not done the same with the hand. She would suffer grip tremble when she fired because of this. But she held the Cobra like she knew it well. And while her form might not be perfect, it was more than good enough to take him down with one shot at this distance.

He three-fingered his cred pack from his shirt pocket.

"Flip it open for me," she instructed. "Badge first, and then ID card."

He did so. She studied his picture and then glanced back at him. She lowered her weapon. "Sorry about that."

"I would've done the same."

She holstered the Cobra. "But you didn't ask for my ID."

"I called you to come here. Name and number was in the official Army file. Army doesn't make mistakes like that. I saw you climb out of your ride. Badge on your belt. When I grabbed you and you cried out, I recognized the voice I'd heard on the phone."

"Still got the drop on you," she reminded him.

"Maybe not as much as you thought."

He showed her the black KA-BAR knife he was holding in his other hand, concealed by his forearm. "You probably would've still gotten your shot off just by reflex. Then maybe both of us would've gone down." He slipped the knife into its holder on his belt. "But it didn't happen."

"I never saw you pull the knife."

"I did it before you took your gun out."

"Why?"

"I saw you look at me, then at the Cobra, and then at the bodies. Not too hard to figure what you were thinking."

"So why didn't you pull your gun on me instead?"

"When I pull my gun I intend on using it. Didn't want to make an awkward situation worse. Knew you'd ask for the cred pack. I had the knife in reserve in case you had something else on your mind." He looked back at the bodies. "The kids?"

She stepped forward, pulled a pair of latex gloves from her windbreaker, slapped them on, gripped the back of the boy's neck, and tilted the corpse forward about ten degrees. With her free hand she pointed to a spot near the base of the neck.

Puller hit the area with his Maglite. He saw the large purplish bruise. "Somebody crushed his brain stem."

She leaned the body back to its original position. "What it looks like."

"Same with the girl?"

"Yes."

"From the condition of the bodies they've been dead over twenty-four hours, ballpark, but less than thirty-six. Your CST have a better read?"

"Roughly twenty-nine hours, so you were close."

Puller checked his watch. "So they were killed around midnight, Sunday night?"

"Right."

"And the mailman found them on Monday in the early afternoon. So rigor would've just started by then. Can you confirm that as a supplemental benchmark?"

"Yes."

"Did the mailman notice anything suspicious?"

"You mean after he dry-heaved on the front lawn for the fourth time after we got there? No, not really. Killers long gone by then."

"But they came back tonight. Killed a cop, in fact. Any other wounds or marks?"

"As you can see, we haven't undressed them, but we did a pretty good look around and found nothing. But you crush the brain stem, the person's dead."

"Yeah, that one I get." He was looking around the room. "You have to know what you're doing, though. Precise hit, otherwise you incapacitate instead of kill."

"Professional, then."

Puller thought, *Or military. And if this is a soldier-on-soldier killing?*

He said, "Maybe, or lucky." He looked at the girl. "But not lucky twice. They weren't killed here, at least the colonel and his wife."

Cole stepped back away from the couch, looked at the carpet. "Right, blood spatters. None up here. Basement is a different story."

"I noted that when I was down there."

"Speaking of, I need to go see Larry."

Puller thought he heard her voice catch even though she had tried to say this in a casual tone.

"Do me a favor first?"

"What's that?"

"Make the call to the station and put the seal on the colonel's briefcase and laptop."

She did as he asked. As soon as she closed the phone he said, "Follow me."

She trudged after Puller down the stairs. He led her over to the spot where the cop was hanging. The dead man had dropped still lower, his black leathers almost touching the concrete.

Puller studied her while she was studying the dead guy. No tears this time. Brief shake of the head. Woman was internalizing it. Probably embarrassed to have already teared up in front of him. And then the voice catch. She shouldn't have been embarrassed. He'd seen friends die, lots of them. It never got any easier. It only got harder. You thought you became desensitized to it, but that was just an illusion. The hole in your mind just got deeper so more shit would fit inside it.

She stepped back. "I'm going to get whoever did this."

"I know you are."

"Can we get him down? I don't want to leave him up there like a damn slaughtered hog."

Puller checked the back of the man's neck. "We can cut the noose loose opposite the knot in the line to preserve it. But give me a sec."

He hustled out to his car and grabbed his rucksack.

Back downstairs, he took out some plastic sheeting and a portable stepladder. "I'm going to wrap this around the body to safeguard any trace, then hold him up while you climb on the stepladder and cut him down. Remember, cut on the opposite side of the knot. You can use my knife."

They accomplished this without a hitch and the plastic-wrapped dead man leaned into Puller's strong arms. He laid him down on the floor on his back while Cole climbed down.

Puller said, "Turn on that light over there." He motioned to a wall switch.

The light came on and Puller examined Wellman's neck. "Carotid and jugular compressed. Hyoid bone's probably fractured. Post will confirm that." He pointed to several spots around the dead man's neck. "Blood vessels ruptured, means he was alive when they strung him up."

Puller carefully edged the cop up on one side so they could see his bound hands. "Check for defensive wounds or trace under the nails. If we're real lucky we got some DNA leave-behind."

Cole used Puller's Maglite to do this. "Nothing that I can see. Don't understand that. Larry should've fought back. Or maybe the killer scrubbed it afterwards."

"I think this probably explains it." Puller pointed to matted blood in the man's hair. "They knocked him out before hanging him."

He pulled a skin thermometer from his rucksack, ran it over Wellman's forehead, and checked the reading.

"Little under five degrees down from normal." He swiftly did the required calculation in his head. "Dead about three hours. So about half past two."

They heard cars pulling to a stop outside.

"Cavalry's here," said Puller.

Cole looked down at her colleague. "You seem to know what you're doing," she said softly, staring down at the dead man.

"I'm here to help, if you want it. Your call."

"I do." She turned and walked toward the steps.

Puller said, "I know you've already processed the scene, but I'd like to do it again." He added, "I'm not looking to step on anyone's professional toes, but I've got people I have to report to. And they expect our investigations to be processed in a particular way."

"I don't care so long as we get the son of a bitch who did this."

Cole headed up the stairs.

Puller looked down at the dead cop and then over at the far walls where the collection of blood and flesh against the studs revealed where the adult Reynoldses had been executed.

Executed was really the only way to look at it.

Head shot for him, torso for her. He wondered why the different treatment. And then the kids not shot at all. Usually with mass killing the same method of murder was employed. Changing weapons took time, precious time. And killing and then moving the bodies took still more time. But maybe this killer had all the time in the world.

Puller glanced back down at Wellman's body.

Every murder was the same in that someone was dead from a violent cause. Yet other than that factor, everything was always different.

And solving it was like treating cancer. What worked in one case almost never worked in another. They all required their own unique solution.

He walked off to join Cole upstairs.

CHAPTER

12

THE THREE DRAKE COUNTY COPS stood in a row looking down at their fallen colleague. As they did this Puller studied them. All about six feet tall, two lean, one chubby. They were young, the oldest in his early thirties. Puller spotted an anchor tattoo on the hand of one.

"Navy?" he asked.

The man nodded, drawing his gaze briefly from Wellman's body. The tattoo, Puller knew, had been done after the man had left the service. No tattoos that were visible with your uniform on were allowed in the military.

"You're Army?" said Anchor Man.

"I'm with the 701st CID out of Quantico."

"Marines train down there, right?" said the chubby cop.

"That's right," said Puller.

"My cousin's a Marine," said Chubby. "He said they're always first in the fight."

"Marines covered my butt many times in the Middle East."

Cole came down the stairs. "A miner on his way to work found Larry's cruiser about two miles from here, down in a ravine, and called it in. Sending our tech over to scrub it down."

Puller nodded. "And then he can come here? I need to talk to him."

"I'll let him know." She turned to her men. "Considering what happened to Larry, we'll need two officers to post here at all times."

"Sarge, that really cuts into our patrol. Pulled thin as it is," said Anchor Man.

She pointed down at Wellman. "Maybe Larry thought that too, and look what happened to him."

"Yes, Sarge."

"And, Dwayne, I want you to head over and secure Larry's cruiser," she told him.

"Yes, Sarge," said Dwayne.

Puller observed the other cops for any visible reaction in dealing with a female superior. If West Virginia was anything like the Army it was still tough going for the girls even in the twenty-first century. From the looks of them it was still tough going for the ladies in the Mountain State.

"Special Agent Puller here will be assisting us in this investigation," said Cole.

The three cops looked at him with stiffened expressions. This didn't surprise Puller at all. In their shoes he would've felt resentment too.

He didn't say anything as patently clichéd as that they were all looking for the same thing, justice. In fact he didn't say anything at all. While he was being polite and professional, the truth was he had no authority over these folks. It was left to Cole to keep her men in line.

"Where's the crime scene log?" he asked, glancing at Cole. She'd zippered up her windbreaker—perhaps, Puller thought, to cover the sheerness of the T-shirt underneath in the presence of her deputies.

"In my pickup."

She got the log and Puller added his name to it, recording the date and time of entry. He studied the names of the other people on the list. Cops and the one tech. And a medical professional who had no doubt officially proclaimed the four corpses to be lawfully dead.

He waited for Cole to give Dwayne the location of Wellman's ride and send him off.

"Any media on this yet?" he asked Cole. They were on the front porch. Dawn had broken and it was light enough for him to see the dark circles under her eyes. She pulled a cigarette from her pack.

He held up his hand and lowered his voice so the cops who were still inside the house couldn't hear. "Let's put together a break area in the side yard over there. This scene is going to take a while to process. You can smoke, and we can eat and pile our trash up there. And we'll need a portable john."

"There're two bathrooms in the house."

"We don't change the crime scene in any way. Don't touch the thermostat, use the john, smoke, eat, drink, or chew tobacco. Our stuff gets mingled with what's here it makes things more complicated."

She put the smoke away and folded her arms over her chest. "Okay," she said grudgingly.

"Media?" he said again.

"We only have one weekly newspaper. The nearest TV and radio stations are a ways away. So no, not much in the way of media, and I won't be holding a press conference, just in case you're wondering. We're hard to get to. You have to really want to get to Drake. And right now, no one in the media seems to want to."

"Good." He paused, looked at her.

"What?" she finally said under his scrutiny.

"You related to somebody named Randy Cole?"

"My younger brother. Why?"

"Ran into him earlier."

"Ran into him where?" she asked sharply.

"Place I'm staying."

She assumed an uninterested air that Puller saw right through. "And how was he?"

"What do you mean?"

"I mean drunk or drunker?"

"He was sober."

"What a shock."

"But he said he gets headaches."

"Yeah, I know," she said in a more worried tone. "For the last year or so."

"Told him to get that checked out."

"I told him the same thing. Doesn't mean he's going to do it. In fact, it means he probably won't."

"I'm going to grab my gear and get to it."

"You need any help?"

"You're in charge. That's lackey work, isn't it?"

"Not much around here is lackey work. We all pitch in. And even if it were, Larry getting killed changes things. At least for me. Never lost a man on my watch. Now I have. Changes things," she said again.

"I can see that. I'll let you know if I need a hand."

"You lose many of your guys over in the Middle East?"

"Even one was too many," replied Puller.

CHAPTER

13

PULLER HAD SKETCHED preliminary drawings of the main floor and the basement. He had put together his loose-leaf notebook with his name, rank, and the date, weather, and lighting conditions on each page, as well as compass north designated. Measurements had been done to all relevant landmarks and other objects in the rooms.

Cole, who was watching him finish the drawing, asked, "Army taught you that?"

"Army taught me a lot of things."

"Why do you think they came back, Puller?"

"To get something. Or leave something. I just don't know which one."

Cole let out a long breath filled with frustration. "Never thought that could happen. Coming back and killing the cop guarding the crime scene."

He put the sketchpad aside and drew from his rucksack a 35-millimeter camera, tripod, flash, and flash extension cord. He also stuck a device that looked like a flashlight into a holder on his belt.

"My guy already took pictures," Cole said.

"I like to take my own. Procedures we have to follow, like I said."

"Okay. But he's good and you're welcome to what we have."

"I appreciate that. Where is he, by the way? Shouldn't have taken him that long to scrub the car."

Cole went to the window. "Speak of the devil," she said.

"Landry Monroe," said Puller.

"How'd you know?"

"Saw his name on the log."

"We call him Lan."

"Tell me about him."

"Twenty-four years old. WVU grad. Criminal Justice. Certified in CS processing. Been with the department for two years."

"Where'd he get his certification?"

"State runs a program."

"Okay."

"It's a damn good program, Puller."

"Didn't say it wasn't."

"I could tell by the look on your face."

"What's your goal here?"

"What?"

"Your goal."

"To catch whoever did this," she said grimly.

"Mine too. And if we work together and follow each of our protocols the odds are a lot better that we'll find the people responsible."

They stared at each other for an uncomfortably long few moments.

Cole turned, went to the door, and called out to the man, who had his head buried in his car's trunk. "Lan, get your stuff and get in here. Got somebody who's *really* looking forward to working with you."

She turned back to Puller and pointed a finger at him. "Let's get one thing straight. He's a kid. You can rough him up some, show him stuff that'll make him better, but you are not to crush his confidence. You'll be leaving West Virginia after this, but not me. I have to work with him and he's all I've got. Understood?"

Puller nodded. "Understood."

Lan Monroe came in about thirty seconds later juggling bags and knapsacks. He was black and wearing green scrubs. He stopped at the front door and dropped his gear to put on booties and latex gloves. He signed the on-site log held by one of the officers on perimeter security and stepped inside.

Monroe was not much taller than Cole, with narrow shoulders and the bulk of his weight carried in his gut, hips, and butt. His legs were thick and short. His head was shaven and he wore wire-rimmed glasses that had slid halfway down his nose.

Cole said, "Lan, meet CID special agent John Puller."

Monroe smiled and looked up at Puller, who was nearly a foot taller than he was. He put out his hand. They shook.

"Nice to meet you, Special Agent Puller."

"Just make it Puller." He glanced at the bags. "Your equipment?"

"Yep."

Cole said, "Did you do Larry's car?"

Monroe nodded. "The prelim didn't turn up anything. There was no blood in the vehicle. I had it towed back to the station. I'll do a more thorough scrub there."

Puller said, "Sergeant Cole said you'd taken pictures. Can I see them?"

"That's a big ten-four, good buddy."

Monroe dug into one of his bags while Puller glanced over at Cole with hiked eyebrows. She shrugged and attempted a smile.

Monroe got his camera out, powered it up, and showed the range of pictures on the flip-out viewfinder.

"Thirty-five mil SLR?" said Puller.

"Yep. That's what they had us use at school. Now, I did three shots of everything, one in relation to nearby objects, one with ruler, and one close-up without."

"Good. What aperture setting did you use?"

Cole shot Puller a hard glance. He ignored it.

Monroe remained oblivious to these exchanges. He said, "F/16 with everything three feet or more away, f/28 for the close-ups."

Puller nodded approvingly. "What were your angles of photography?"

"I did everything from eye level."

"Did you do a three-sixty overlap?"

Monroe suddenly looked uncertain and shook his head. "Uh, no."

Puller glanced at Cole and found her still staring intently at him, hands on hips, lips pursed. For a moment he thought she might go for her Cobra again.

Puller said, "No problem. Just Army overkill. Look, I need an experienced hand to help me with that, Lan. And you obviously know your way around a camera."

"No prob," said Monroe, his good spirits restored. "Glad to do it." He pointed at the tripod and other equipment Puller had taken from his rucksack. "Is that a flash extension?" he asked.

Puller nodded. "We'll use it to photograph fingerprints, tire marks, and any tool marks. We'll use the synch cord to engage the flash."

"How far away do you Army guys hold it?" asked Monroe eagerly.

"Ideally three feet. And at a forty-five-degree angle. Two shots from all four directions."

"What's the big deal with the extension thing?" asked Cole.

Puller replied, "Prevents hot spots of light. Causes overexposure to the top of the photos."

"Cool," said Monroe.

Puller pointed to the four members of the Reynolds family. "Since they haven't been moved, we need to photograph them properly. All four sides, including the rear. Five shots of the face, all wounds, and other marks. With and without rulers, livor mortis patterns, and all gunshot powder and stippling. You got a video camera?"

Monroe nodded.

Puller said, "You video everything but you don't rely on that for fine detail. Defense attorney will blow you out of the water with that."

Cole said, "And did that happen to you?"

"It happens to everybody," said Puller.

Puller was about to set up his tripod to start taking pictures of the bodies when he looked down at the carpet and stopped. He knelt and took a closer look at the medium-pile carpeting.

"What do you see there?" he asked.

Monroe and Cole came over. The tech dropped to his knees and studied the spot. "Not sure," he said. "An impression of something."

"*Impressions*, actually. Three of them, circular, but in a triangular pattern." Puller hefted the tripod and set it down a few feet from the others. Then he picked it back up. "What do you see?"

Monroe looked at the spot. So did Cole. They both started and looked back over at the original spot. The impressions were nearly identical.

Cole said, "Somebody already set up a tripod here. Why?"

Puller looked at the spot and then over at the bodies all lined up. "Bodies in a row, on a couch. Tripod in front, camera mounted on it."

"They were filming the Reynoldses?" said Cole.

Puller took several shots of the impressions. "No, they were *interrogating* them."

CHAPTER

14

Hours later they had finished photographing the four bodies and processing other parts of the crime scene. Puller and Monroe had laid the bodies next to each other on white plastic sheeting spread on the floor. Larry Wellman's body had been brought up and was lying in a zippered body bag in the dining room. There were no defensive wounds on Wellman or the Reynoldses. They had all apparently been taken by surprise.

Puller had recorded his observations and used the device he'd previously stuck in his belt to help him organize the investigation. Monroe had excitedly asked him what the tool was.

"Army calls it a CSED, or Crime Scene Exploitation Device. It's a camera with a bar coder, digital screen, labeler, and printer all rolled into one. It's got a flip-out USB so I can down- and upload from my laptop. My digital recorder has the same capability. And it has an electronic transcriber so it'll automatically type out what I've recorded by voice. I'm not great on the keyboard."

"That is beyond cool," said Monroe.

"Don't get too excited, Lan," said Cole. "Doubt there's money in the budget for us to get one of those."

Puller glanced at Cole. "Tell me about the dog that was here."

"Collie. Got a colleague taking care of it. Friendly thing."

"Okay, but any of the neighbors report hearing any barking?"

"Dog can't bark," replied Cole. "Probably the only reason they let it live."

"A dog that can't bark?"

"Well, it hasn't once barked for us. Might've had an operation done. That can sometimes screw up the bark. At least according to a vet friend of mine that I asked."

Looking down at the lined-up bodies, Cole said, "You said they were interrogated but didn't really explain what you meant. They obviously weren't being interrogated after they were killed. So why line them up on the couch after they were dead?"

"I think the person wanted to see them being interrogated. And they also wanted to see on the video that they were dead."

"So they were broadcasting the video out to someone else?"

"That's how I read it."

Cole slowly nodded. "So if we can get our hands on the video, there might be some clues. One of the killers might have stepped in front of the camera, for example. Or maybe it might have caught a reflection of one or more of them."

"That's true. But odds are if we find the video, we'll find the killers too. That's not something they'll leave lying around."

"Well, let's hope that happens."

"We need to get the bodies to a refrigerated environment soon and then have the posts done," said Puller as he stared down at the decomposing bodies. "At some point courtroom evidence starts falling apart. How's it coming with your doctor friend?"

"Should know something definitive later today."

Puller knelt down next to Matt Reynolds. "Shotgun to the face. Less than three feet away, minimal pellet dispersal, wadding in the wounds. If the muzzle was choke-bored it could muddy that analysis." He indicated the wadding. "Lan, have you taken a sample yet to verify gauge?"

"Yeah. Haven't done the test yet, but I hope once I compare the diameter with sample wads it'll give us an answer."

Puller turned to the wife's body. "I measured the distance between pellets, and that together with no central wound or wadding means she was probably shot from farther away than ten feet."

"But down in the basement," said Cole, who knelt next to him.

"Presumably. But serology results will confirm it," said Puller.

"Why the basement?" asked Cole.

"Quieter," said Puller. "But you still have problems."

"Like what?"

"Shotgun blast even in a basement in the middle of the night might attract attention. And you have to control the other captives. They hear the shot, they panic, start screaming, trying to get away, knowing they'll probably be next."

Monroe snapped his fingers, unlocked a metal evidence box he'd previously brought into the house, and pulled out some sealed, labeled evidence bags.

"I was wondering why I found these things in those places. But what you just said may explain it."

Puller took up the bags one by one. "Tell me what you've got here."

"That bit of gray fuzz came from the girl's left ear. The white thread I found inside the boy's mouth. Found a similar one hung up on the mom's left molar."

Cole looked at them over Puller's shoulder.

Puller said, "The white thread in the mouth? Gag?"

"And the thing in the ear?" asked Cole.

Monroe said, "I'm thinking it's a piece of an ear bud. Like from headphones to an iPod or MP3 player."

Puller said, "They were blasting music into their ears when they were shooting people. So they couldn't hear it."

"That's pretty hardcore," added Monroe.

Puller said, "But that doesn't explain the shotgun use. Maybe they couldn't hear it, but some of the neighbors might have."

Cole rose and went over to the window and looked out. She whirled back around.

"You said blasted."

Puller handed the bags back to Monroe and turned to her. "Yeah. So?"

"Trent Exploration. They might've *blasted* on Sunday night. And this neighborhood is only a couple miles away from where they're doing it."

CHAPTER

15

PULLER WAS STARING at Cole. "Okay, but would the blast be loud enough to cover a fired shotgun from being heard in another house?"

"From a basement, I'd say so. If you're close enough to them, some of those explosions can lift you right out of your bed."

"You say they *might've* blasted. You don't know for certain?"

"No, I live pretty far from here. But the sound of a blast reaching this neighborhood had to come from a Trent operation. It's the only one nearby."

Monroe said slowly, "Wait a minute. I was out late that night with my girlfriend. About two miles from here but in another direction. I remember hearing it."

Puller said quickly, "Do you recall the time of the explosion?"

He thought for a few moments. "Between midnight and one, I'd say."

"That mirrors the timeline established by the body deterioration," said Puller. "But having a tighter time window helps us in one respect."

"Alibis, or lack thereof," noted Cole, and he nodded in agreement.

Puller said, "But then we have to wonder why they shotgunned the parents and not the kids. Or why not blunt force to all of them and you don't have to worry about the sound of a gun?"

Neither Cole nor Monroe had a ready answer to those queries.

Puller looked at the tech. "You get elimination prints from the victims and the wife's parents?"

"Yeah. That's where I was early this morning before I went to scrub the car."

"You didn't tell them what had happened, though?" Cole said quickly.

"Well, the mom's had a stroke. I just printed her while she was unconscious, so I couldn't tell her anything. The dad goes in and out. I made it a game so he wouldn't catch on."

"Dementia?" said Puller, and Cole nodded.

"Does he have lucid moments?"

She said, "I think so, sometimes. You think he might be helpful?"

Puller shrugged. "Well, if somebody local killed these folks he might know something. Here're the possibilities as I see them. One, they were killed because of Colonel Reynolds's employment with DIA. Two, something connected to the mom. Three, something connected to the kids. Four, something connected to the wife's parents. Or five, something we don't see as yet."

"Could be a random burglary," noted Monroe.

Puller shook his head. "They left a late-model Lexus, a laptop computer, and the wife's wedding ring. No other valuables known to be missing. And random burglars seldom take the time to interrogate their victims."

Cole added, "The wife's parents probably don't have an enemy in the world. And the wife and kids were just here for the summer. I doubt they had time to make any enemies. That leaves Colonel Reynolds."

"Maybe. Still have to check it all out." Puller rose. "Any other prints here that didn't match the eliminated ones from the first responders?"

"The mailman's. A caregiver who works at the nursing home. Got her latent on the fridge. She was here to help Mr. Halverson before he went in the nursing home. And two EMTs who were called here when the old lady had her stroke."

"No others?"

"There were two. On the living room wall and one on the kitchen counter. I'm running the prints through our database."

Puller said, "Let me have copies and I'll get them run through the federal databases too."

"Thanks."

Puller said, "How did the killers know when the mine blasts would take place? Is that public knowledge?"

"Yes," said Cole. "There's a bunch of regulations about surface mining blasting. You have to get proper permits and have a blasting plan in place. You have to post blasting schedules in the local papers well in advance. People close to the blast get personal notification. You have to use a certified blaster. There are limits on noise, so they have to monitor the decibels of the blast. They also have to measure ground vibration. And they often separate the blast charges by eight milliseconds."

"Why?" asked Monroe, who looked fascinated by the discussion. He caught Puller gazing at him. "Went to WVU but I'm not from around here."

Cole said, "The eight milliseconds allow enough separation to keep the air blast noise and ground vibration under control."

Puller gazed at her. "You obviously know a lot about all this. How come?"

She shrugged. "West Virginia gal. Whole state's one big mine. At least that's what it feels like sometimes."

"And didn't your dad work for Trent Exploration?" asked Monroe.

Cole shot a quick glance at Puller, who was staring at her even more intently. "He did," she said quietly. "Not anymore."

"Why not?" asked Puller.

"He's dead."

"Sorry to hear that." He paused for a few moments. "What explosives do they use to do the blasting?"

"Usually ANFO, combination of ammonium nitrate—fertilizer, really—and diesel fuel. They scrape the topsoil and subsoil layers and then drill holes in the rock to lay their charges. The goal is to fracture the rock layers. Then they bring in heavy equipment to expose the coal seam."

"Why do they blow it up instead of digging tunnels?"

"Decades ago they did tunnel. But getting to the coal that's left won't allow tunneling. Softness of the rock. Or so they claim. It's funny, though."

"What?" asked Puller.

"Typically blasting has to take place between sunrise and sunset, Monday through Saturday. Trent must've gotten a special permit to blast at night and on a Sunday."

"So the blasting schedule is public knowledge," said Puller. "Doesn't help narrow down the list of possible suspects. But tell me about Trent Exploration."

"Trent is by far the biggest employer in the county."

"Well-liked outfit?" asked Puller.

Cole pursed her lips. "Nobody loves coal companies, Puller. And the way Trent does it has resulted in entire valleys being filled up with debris. It causes flooding and a host of other environmental issues, not to mention that blowing the tops off mountains leaves the countryside pretty damn ugly. But it's a hell of a lot cheaper for the company to do it that way. They're enormously profitable."

"But it still provides jobs," added Monroe. "My cousin works at Trent as a geological engineer. Makes a decent living."

Cole continued. "Roger Trent is sole owner of the company. He's had his share of code violations and accidents where people have died. And it doesn't help that he lives in a big mansion behind big gates and gets his water piped in nice and clean because his operations have screwed up the water tables."

"And folks around here just let that happen?"

"He has junkyard-dog lawyers on retainer, and even though the state's trying to clean up the judicial sector, he's still bought up half the judges in the state. But he keeps people employed, pays fair, and gives to charities, and so he's tolerated. But a few more mining accidents and a few more cancer diagnoses because of all the pollution, and he might get ridden out of here on a rail."

Puller looked over at the bodies. "How long had the Reynoldses been staying here?"

Cole said, "About five weeks according to folks we talked to."

"And the colonel was coming and going from D.C.," added

Puller. He looked out the window. "You've canvassed the neighbors?"

Cole said, "Seven other homes and we've talked to everyone. Got zip."

"That's a little hard to believe," said Puller. "Killers right next door and nobody sees or hears anything? And then a cop gets killed and someone drives off in his cruiser and again, nothing?"

"All I can tell you is what they said."

"Then I think it might be time to check with everyone again."

CHAPTER

16

PULLER WALKED DOWN the front steps and kept going until he was in the middle of the yard of fried grass. Cole had followed him outside. Lan Monroe had stayed inside to finish bagging evidence.

Puller looked right, left, and then forward again. The day had passed rapidly. The sun had long ago begun its descent, but it was still uncomfortably hot. There was no wind. The humidity pressed in from all sides like solid walls of water.

"Puller, you want to split up the houses?" she asked.

He didn't answer.

What he was seeing had to be deciphered and put into its proper perspective. There were eight homes on the street, four on each side, including the one where the murders had occurred. At six of the houses there were people out front. A few men, several women, and some little kids. They were all ostensibly doing everyday activities—washing a car, cutting the grass, getting the mail, playing ball, or just chatting. What they were really doing was satisfying their morbid curiosity by surreptitiously staring at the house where violent death had occurred.

Puller's immediate task was to separate the obvious and normal from its antithesis. He focused on the house directly across the street. Two cars and a big Harley highway bike were in the driveway. But no one was outside. No gawkers at all.

He pointed. "Did you talk to the people in that house?"

Cole looked at where he was indicating. She called over her shoulder to one of the uniforms standing guard at the crime scene. "Lou, you talked to those folks, right?"

Lou came forward. He was the chubby cop. His leather belt squeaked as he walked.

Puller knew that to be a rookie mistake. Oil the belt. Squeaks got you killed.

Lou pulled out his notebook and leafed through it. "Spoke to a man who identified himself as Eric Treadwell. He lives in that house with a lady named Molly Bitner. He said she'd gone to work early that morning and didn't mention hearing or seeing anything suspicious. But he said he'd check with her when she got home. And Treadwell said he hadn't seen or heard anything either."

"But he might've seen something last night when Larry got killed," said Cole. "I want every one of these folks questioned again. Someone drove off in Larry's cruiser. Somebody in one of those houses might've seen or heard something."

"Okay, Sarge."

Puller said, "Did this Treadwell guy show you any ID?"

Lou, who had been about to walk off to execute Cole's order, turned to him.

"ID?"

"Yeah, to prove he actually lived there."

"No, he didn't show any ID."

"Did you ask for it?"

"No, I didn't." The tone was now defensive.

"How did it go down? Did you approach him?" asked Puller.

"He was standing at the front door when I came up," said Lou. "That's probably why I didn't ask for ID. Because he was in his house."

That was bullshit, Puller knew. The guy was backpedaling, building in a justification for his lack of professionalism and even common sense.

"But you didn't know Eric Treadwell by sight?" he asked.

Cole looked over at her deputy, who was scowling at Puller. "Answer the question, Lou."

"No," Lou admitted.

"Any of the other deputies know him?"

"Not that they mentioned to me."

"What time was it?"

Lou checked his notes once more. "Little after three in the afternoon. We'd really just gotten here after the call came in."

"Any other neighbors around then?"

"No, that time in the afternoon wouldn't expect it. People in Drake work. Both husbands and wives."

"But apparently not this guy."

"What are you getting at, Puller?" asked Cole. "Are you trying to say this guy was the killer? Pretty stupid for him to hang around and talk to the cops, then."

In answer he pointed at the house. "It's after five in the afternoon. There are two cars in the driveway. They were there when I got here at about 4 a.m. And they've been here all day. So even though you said everybody works around here, it doesn't seem to apply to that house. And at every other house you've got people outside watching us. That's normal. There's no one in that house even peeking out the windows. Under the circumstances, that's not normal." He turned to Lou. "When you were talking to the guy on Monday were those two cars and the Harley parked in the driveway?"

Lou tipped his hat back and thought about this. "Yeah, I think they were. Why?"

"Well, you said the guy told you his wife was still at work. How many vehicles do they have?"

"Shit," muttered a ticked-off-looking Cole as she glared at Lou. "Come on."

She strode across the street with Puller and Lou trailing. She knocked on the door, got no answer, and knocked again.

Nothing.

She said, "Problem is we don't have a search warrant. And we've got no probable to bust in. I can try to get something—" She broke off. "What are you doing?"

Puller had leaned over the front banister and looked in the front window.

"Getting us probable cause."

"What?" asked Cole sharply.

Puller drew his M11.

"What are you doing?" exclaimed Cole.

Puller slammed his size thirteen shoe against the wood of the door and it buckled inward. His shoulder finished what his foot had started. He stepped inside, keeping low and doing visual sweeps, his gun running parallel to his gaze. He turned the corner and disappeared from view.

"Get in here," said Puller. "But keep alert. Place isn't cleared yet."

Cole and Lou pulled their weapons and followed him inside. She peered around the corner to find Puller staring at it.

"Son of a bitch," exclaimed Cole.

17

A MAN AND A WOMAN. Both heavyset and possibly in their forties. It was hard to tell with the state they were in. The man had a heavy beard, and tat sleeves ran down both bare arms. There was also an eagle tattoo across his bare pecs. The woman's hair was bottle blonde and she was dressed in hospital scrub bottoms, but no top.

They were sitting on the couch in the living room.

They were clearly dead, but it wasn't obvious how they had died.

Cole stood next to Puller, who stared down at the corpses.

Puller looked down at the floor. No visible tripod indents, because it was hardwood and not carpet. Still, his gut was sending him a clear message.

They were interrogated too.

They were both turning green. CPR was not called for. A grave was.

The man had a Virginia Tech ring on his right hand. The woman had a bracelet on her left wrist along with a Timex wristwatch.

Puller said, "Look to be dead about the same time as the Reynoldses. We'll need someone to pronounce them deceased officially."

"Okay, but how did they die?" asked Cole.

Puller checked the floor again. No blood spatters. He slapped on a fresh pair of gloves pulled from a fanny pack on his belt and tilted the man's head forward. No obvious gunshot entries or exits. There were no brain stem bruises. No knife wounds. No ligature marks on the neck. No evidence of blows to the abdomen.

"Suffocation?" said Lou, who was standing farther back and looking queasy, probably from the smell.

Puller carefully opened the man's left eyelid. "No sign of pete-chial hemorrhage." He glanced at the man's torso and then at the woman's.

"What?" asked Cole, who'd noted his quizzical look.

"The bodies have been moved. And their shirts were taken off."

"How do you know that?" asked Cole.

He pointed to some pale marks on the arms and around the necks of both. "Those are vibices. Pressure on the capillaries from tight clothing keeps them from filling. That means they had shirts on for a while after death. And after death blood pools by gravity to the lowest parts of the body."

"Lividity," said Cole.

He said, "Right. Six hours after death the capillaries coagulate. Then you have permanent postmortem staining."

"Why would they take their shirts off *after* killing them?"

Lou said, "Well, we don't know anybody killed them, do we? Maybe they committed suicide. Took poison or something and took their shirts off before they croaked."

Puller shook his head at this suggestion. "Tox screens will tell for certain. But in most poisoning cases the hypostatic areas have dis-tinct colorings, cherry red, red, red-brown, or dark brown. Don't see any of that here."

Cole examined each of their hands. "No sign of defensive wounds. Nails look relatively clean. But why take off the shirts? Especially her. I mean, if I'm a woman and I kill myself, I sure as hell don't want to be found topless."

She drew her gaze away from the woman's heavy, veined breasts, which sagged nearly to her belly button.

Puller said, "The killers took off the shirts because they wanted us to work a little harder to find out how these people died."

"Meaning?"

"Meaning the shirts had bloodstains on them."

"How do you know that?"

He pointed to a spot where the woman's right breast attached to her chest. "Blood soaked through the shirt and some of it got lodged in that crevice. Killers must've missed it, but they did a good job cleaning up everything else, because there would have been blood and tissue spatters."

"Okay, but from where and what?" exclaimed Cole.

Puller bent down and carefully lifted up the man's right eyelid. "Would've seen this earlier, but I opened the wrong one."

Cole leaned in closer. "Damn."

The eye was gone. In its place was a dark, blistered hole. "Contact wound," said Puller. "We'll find powder in the wound track. Small caliber. Check the woman."

Cole slapped on gloves. The woman's left eye was just a hole too. Gray brain matter clustered around the opening.

"Only seen that once before," said Puller. "In Germany. Soldier on soldier. Special Forces. Their knowledge base on killing people runs pretty deep."

Cole straightened up and put her hands on her hips. "Why the subterfuge? Even if we didn't catch it here, the post would have."

"The post *might* have. Maybe they were counting on you having to get a paramedic to do the cutting and missing it. Or no X-ray so they don't see the bullet in the brain. Happens all the time, unfortunately, and they probably thought it was worth a shot here. The good news is there's no exit wound on either one. That means the rounds are still in them." He eyed Lou. "This is obviously not the guy you spoke with yesterday."

"No. He was a lot thinner and was clean-shaven," conceded Lou a bit lamely.

"Give us a full description of him."

Lou did so.

Puller said, "We'll have to check for ID here."

Cole spoke up. "And this guy was obviously already dead when that guy was pulling a slick one on you, Lou. Get his description to dispatch and put out a BOLO. Go do it now, although the guy's probably long gone."

Lou left and she turned to Puller. "Now we've got two crime

scenes to work. This is going to drain my resources fast. Think the Army can spare some more people?"

"Don't know," said Puller, who thought, *They could only spare me initially. Does that change now or not?*

"Well, they have to be connected. At least we know that. Way too big a coincidence to have two murders on the same street at the same time by two different sets of killers."

When he didn't respond to this she said again, "They have to be connected, right?"

"Nothing has to be anything. It has to be proven."

"But you got any early theories as to why they might be tied together?"

Puller eyed the window. "That looks directly across to the Reynolds place."

Cole went to stand by the window and looked out. "So you're thinking these folks saw something over there and had to be silenced?"

"But if you reverse it the Reynoldses' front window looks right back at this place."

Cole nodded, seeing where this line of reasoning was going. "So it's chicken and egg? Who saw what first?"

"Maybe."

"Well, it really has to be one or the other."

"No it doesn't," said Puller.

CHAPTER

18

THE BODIES YIELDED FEW CLUES.

The basement was far more interesting.

Puller and Cole had searched the lower level and come to a door that was locked. With Cole's okay, Puller opened the door using a tire iron he found in an old storage bin set against one wall. The revealed room was ten feet wide and twelve feet deep.

On a long folding table were propane tanks, bottles of paint thinner, a can of camp stove fuel, Mason jars, rolls of tubing, gas cylinders, pill bottles and rock salt, funnels and clamps, coffee filters, pillowcases, coolers, and thermos bottles.

"You got a biohazard team?" asked Puller, putting a hand over his mouth and nose to shield his lungs from the smell of solvents and chemicals.

"Meth lab," said Cole.

"Meth lab," repeated Puller. "You got a biohazard team?" he asked again. "This thing could blow up. And take the crime scene upstairs with it."

"We don't have a biohazard team, Puller."

"Then I'll make one."

Twenty minutes later, with the neighbors and Cole and her deputies watching, Puller reentered the house dressed in a hooded green biohazard suit with an air filter, red shoe coverings, and green gloves, all of which he kept packed in his rucksack. Puller methodically pored over the site, dusting for and lifting prints, separating potentially volatile substances from each other, and photographing and tagging all of it. Two hours later he stepped outside and noted the sun was nearly down. He took off his hood. His body was drenched with sweat. The house had been hot. Inside the suit added at least another twenty degrees.

Cole saw the beads of sweat on his face, the flattened wet hair. She handed him a bottle of cold water. "You okay? You look whipped."

He drank down half the liquid. "I'm good. Lot of stuff in there. I worked a bunch of drug lab cases in the Army. That lab was pretty rudimentary but effective. They could turn out some decent product, just not that much."

"While you were working that I found a place to take the bodies."

"Where?"

"Local funeral home. They have refrigeration facilities."

"It needs to be secure."

"I'm posting two deputies here and one there. Rotate 24/7."

Puller stretched out his back.

"You hungry?" she said.

"Yeah."

"There's a good restaurant in town. It's open late."

"Late enough for me to grab a shower and change my clothes?"

"Yes. I plan on doing the same. Try to get the stench out."

"Tell me how to get there."

"Where are you staying?"

"Annie's Motel."

"Restaurant's only three minutes from there, two blocks to the east. Hang a right on Cyrus Street. Can't miss it. Hell, everything here is only three minutes from each other. That kind of town."

"Forty minutes to the hotel. Ten minutes to shower and dress. Five minutes there. I'll see you in sixty minutes."

"But the minutes only add up to fifty-five."

"I need five minutes to communicate with my boss. I should've done it before now, but things got a little busy."

"A little busy? You have high standards, then. I've got my stopwatch. Don't disappoint me."

He drove back to the motel, passing the restaurant where they would be eating, showered, and changed into fresh jeans and a

T-shirt. He pulled out his mini laptop, plugged in his communication fob, and sent an encrypted email back to Quantico. Then he spent two minutes on his secure phone filling in the SAC on what he had discovered and his progress so far. Don White wanted detailed reports sent out the next day by email with more formal ones in the snail mail shortly thereafter.

"Lot of eyes on this, Puller."

"Yes, sir. You made that very clear."

"Any theories yet?" White asked.

"As soon as I have them, so will you. The colonel's laptop and briefcase are secure. I'll try to get them released from police custody and drop them off at the DHS site."

"Have you readied anything to be sent to USACIL yet?"

"In the process, sir. Should go out tomorrow. At least the first batch. There's a lot to process. Two crime scenes instead of one." He paused to allow the SAC to offer more manpower to assist him. The offer never came.

"Lines of communication open, Puller," the man said instead.

"Yes, sir."

Puller closed his phone and slipped his mini laptop into an inner pocket of his jacket. He didn't like leaving things like that behind in a motel room that anyone could break into with a jackknife or credit card. He gunned up, one front, one back.

He passed his car on the way out and double-checked that it was locked. He decided it would be faster to walk to the place than drive.

So Puller walked. He'd get a better lay of the land that way. And he might just see the person who had wiped out two households. He had a feeling this killing was local. But not necessarily in all respects.

CHAPTER

19

THE PLACE WAS like a million others Puller had eaten at in rural towns. Plate glass windows overlooking the street with the name "The Crib Room" stenciled on the main window in letters that looked older than Puller. Another smaller sign promised breakfast all day. Inside there was a long counter with swivel seats topped in cracked red vinyl. Behind the counter were rows of coffee pots that, despite the late-night heat, were in continuous use—although Puller saw many bottles and drafts of cold beer circulated to the thirsty patrons too.

Through a serving window connecting the front to the kitchen, Puller could see columns of ancient Fry Daddies, racks of wire cook baskets ready to be dropped into vats of hot, bubbly oil. And there were big blackened pots over flaming burners. There were two short-order cooks with little white hats, stained T-shirts, and weary faces manning the kitchen. Throughout, the place smelled of decades-old grease.

Past the counter stools were four-person booths in the same checkered vinyl set in an L pattern against two walls, and tables with checkered tablecloths perched between the counter and the booths. The place was three-quarters full. Sixty-forty men to women. Many of the men were lean, almost gaunt. They were mostly dressed in jeans and work shirts, steel-toed boots, hair slicked back probably from a recent shower. Maybe mining employees, Puller thought, just off their shift. Cole had said they didn't dig here for the coal. They blew it out of the mountain and then hauled it away over treacherous roads. It was still dangerous, hard work. And these men looked it.

The women were halved between matronly types in wide knee-length skirts and modest blouses and younger wiry females in cutoff shorts and jeans. A few teenage girls wore skintight outfits short enough to reveal glimpses of panties or pale bottoms, probably much to the delight of their rugged-looking boyfriends. There were a couple of men in jackets and slacks, button-down shirts, and scuffed wingtips. Maybe mining executives who didn't have to get their hands dirty or their backs ruptured for their daily bread. But apparently they all had to eat in the same place.

Now that was democracy for you, thought Puller.

Cole was already there, at a booth near the rear. She waved and he headed over. She had on a jean skort that revealed muscled calves and a white sleeveless blouse that showed off firm, tanned arms. Her sandals revealed the woman's unpainted toes. Her large shoulder bag was next to her and inside it Puller figured she kept both her Cobra and her badge. Her hair was still damp from the shower. The coconut smell of it cut through the grease as Puller approached. All eyes in the place were on him, a fact he recorded and recognized as perfectly normal under the circumstances. He doubted many strangers found their way to Drake. But then again, Colonel Reynolds was one of them. And now he was dead.

He sat. She handed him a plastic menu. "Fifty-eight minutes. You didn't disappoint."

"I scrubbed fast. How's the coffee?" he asked.

"Probably just as good as the Army's."

His lips twitched at her comment as he scanned the menu. He put it down.

"Already made up your mind?" she asked.

"Yes."

"I guess quick decisions are a necessity for someone like you."

"So long as they're the right ones. The Crib Room?"

"Coal miner slang. Means the area designated at a mining operation for miners to eat and take a break."

"Looks like it does a brisk business."

"Pretty much the only place in town open this late."

"Cash cow for the owner."

"That would be Roger Trent."

"He owns this place too?"

"He owns most of Drake. Got it cheap. Place is so polluted people just want to sell and get out. Those that remain he gets coming and going. Groceries, vehicle repair, plumbing, electrical, this restaurant, that gas station, bakery shop, clothing place. List goes on and on. They ought to rename the place Trentsville."

"So he profits from creating environmental nightmares."

"Life's a bitch, ain't it?"

"How about Annie's Motel? Does he own that?"

"No. Owner wouldn't sell. Barely makes ends meet. Doubt Roger was really all that interested in buying it."

She scanned the other customers. "People here are curious."

"About what specifically?"

"About you. About what's happened."

"Understandable. Word travels fast?"

"It's like an old-fashioned viral. Mouth to ear."

"Media inquiries yet?"

"It finally hit. Messages waiting for me on my phone. Newspaper. A radio station. Got an email from a TV station over in Parkersburg. Expect to get one from Charleston too. Something bad happens they all want to jump on it for about fifteen minutes."

"Executive-lag them all for now."

"I'll hold them off as long as I can, but the last word's not up to me."

"Your boss?"

"Sheriff Pat Lindemann. Good guy. But he's not used to media inquiries."

"I can help with that."

"You handle lots of press relations, do you?"

"No. But the Army has folks that do. And they're good at it."

"I'll let the sheriff know."

"I'm assuming everyone has heard about the second house?"

"You probably assume correctly."

They had found ID in the house. The dead man was Eric Treadwell, forty-three years old. The lady was Molly Bitner, thirty-nine.

"So the imposter used Treadwell's name when talking to my guy. That was still a big risk. If Lou had asked for ID, or wanted to get in the house. Or what if one of my guys knew Treadwell? Drake is not that big a place."

"You're right. It was a big risk. A calculated one. But it worked out in their favor. And guys willing to take those kinds of risks and play them out successfully make for tough opponents." What Puller was actually thinking was that the imposter had some special training. Maybe military. And that would make things very awkward very fast. He wondered if the Army had had an inkling of that, and whether that was the reason he'd been sent out here solo.

The waitress, a short, crusty type with gray hair, dark eye circles, and a raspy voice, came to take their order.

Puller had decided on breakfast: three eggs over light, bacon, grits, hash browns, toast, and coffee. Cole had a Cobb salad with oil and vinegar dressing and an iced tea. When Puller moved to hand back the menu, his jacket opened and his M11 was revealed. The waitress's eyes flickered and then she gripped the offered menus and walked off. Puller noted this and doubted it was the first time the lady had seen a gun.

"Breakfast?" asked Cole.

"Didn't have one yet today. Figured I'd get it in before I go to sleep."

"So did you check in with your boss?"

"I did."

"Is he happy with the progress?"

"He didn't say. And there wasn't much progress, frankly. Just lots of questions."

Her iced tea and his coffee came.

Cole took a sip of hers. "Do you really think those people were interrogated before they were killed?"

"It's somewhere between a guess and a deduction."

"Meth lab in the basement?"

"I'd like to keep that one under wraps."

"We're doing our best. I put a seal on everything with my guys." She hesitated, looked away.

Puller read her mind. "But this is a small town and sometimes things slip?"

She nodded. "What would they have been interrogating them about?"

"Let's say the folks who killed Treadwell and Bitner were working with them in the drug business. One or more of the Reynoldses sees some suspicious activity. They're caught doing that. The druggies want to find out how much they've seen, who else they might have told."

"And put it on a video for someone else to see? Why, if this is local?"

"May not be local or entirely local. Mexican drug cartels have set up shop all over the country. Metro and rural areas. Those guys don't play around. They want to see everything. And they have first-rate equipment, including communications gear. And it could have been a live feed."

"But you said it was just a simple meth lab, with not much product coming out."

"That may have been a sideline for Treadwell and Bitner. They might have been working for a distribution ring in another capacity. You have drug problems here?"

"What town doesn't?"

"More than most?"

"I guess we have more than our share," admitted Cole. "But a lot of it is prescription drugs. So go on with your theory. Why kill Bitner and Treadwell?"

"Maybe they drew the line at murder and they had to be killed too, to keep them silent."

"I don't know. I guess that works," Cole said.

"It only works with what we know so far. That can change. There weren't wedding bands on either of their fingers."

"From what I was able to find out they were just living together."

"How long?"

"About three years."

"Planning on tying the knot?"

"No, according to what I found out, they were just doing it for expenses."

He looked at her curiously. "What?"

"Makes the paychecks stretch further if you have just one mortgage or rent payment. Common enough practice around here. People have to survive."

"Okay. What else do you know about them?"

"Did a quick and dirty while you were playing biohazard boy. I didn't know them personally, but it's a small town. He went to Virginia Tech. He started up a business in Virginia that failed. Went through a series of jobs pretty quickly. He'd been a machinist here for years, but got laid off a while back. He's been working at a chemical supply store on the western edge of town for about a year."

"Chemicals? So he'd know his way around the equipment for a meth lab. And he might also be sticking his hand into the inventory if he is in the drug business. Any scuttlebutt that he was involved with drugs?"

"Not that I could find out. But that basically means he was never charged with any drug-related crimes. He was clean on our books."

"Which means he might've been smart enough to not get caught. Or his meth business was a recent start-up. Like you said, hard times, trying to stretch the paycheck. And Bitner?"

"She worked in an office at the local Trent Mining and Exploration operation."

Puller studied her. "So our mining mogul pops up again."

"Yeah, I guess so," Cole said slowly, not meeting his gaze.

"That a problem?" he asked.

She eyed him coolly. "The way you say it you must think there is."

"This Trent guy obviously has a lot of local pull."

"No problems there, Puller, trust me."

"Good. What did she do in the office?"

"Clerical and some related stuff, as far as I know. We'll check it out more thoroughly."

"So they both worked and had a meth lab on the side and lived together to save money and they still lived in a ratty house? Didn't think the cost of living was that high around here."

"Yeah, well, neither are the wages."

Their food came and, ravenous, they plunged into their meals. Puller had two more cups of coffee.

"How are you going to be able to sleep?" asked Cole as he lifted the third cup to his mouth.

"My physiology is a little backwards. The more caffeine I consume the better I sleep."

"You're kidding."

"Actually, the Army just teaches you to sleep when you need it. I'll need it tonight, so I'll sleep just fine."

"Well, I know I can use it too. Only got a couple hours sack time." She eyed him with a mock angry expression. "Thanks to you, Romeo."

"Won't happen again."

"Famous last words."

"Are the bodies being transported?"

"Already there."

"You said Deputy Wellman was married?"

She nodded. "Sheriff Lindemann has been to see Larry's wife. I'll go tomorrow. I don't know Angie that well, but she'll need as much support as possible. I guess she's a wreck. I would be."

"She have family in the area?"

"Larry has. Angie moved here from southwest Virginia."

"Why?"

She scowled. "I know it seems like people would just be moving out of here, not the other way."

"Didn't mean that. And you told me that people were trying to get out. I'm just trying to figure out the landscape."

"Larry went to community college over in Virginia. It's not that far as the crow flies. That's where they met. He came back here and she joined him."

"What about you?"

She set her glass of iced tea back down. "What about me?"

"I know you have a brother here and your dad's dead. Anybody else in the area?"

He glanced at her hand. No wedding band. But maybe she didn't wear one on the job. And maybe she was still on the job.

"Not married," she said, catching this glance. "Both my parents are dead. My sister lives here too. What about you?"

"I have no family in the area."

"You know that's not what I meant, smartass."

"Father and brother."

"Are they in the military?"

"They were."

"So they're civilians now?"

"You could say that." Puller put some cash down on the table. "What time do you want to meet tomorrow?"

She stared at the money. "How about 0700 again. Juliet."

"I'll be there at 0600. Any chance I can get the Reynoldses' laptop and briefcase tonight?"

"It's technically evidence."

"It technically is. But I can tell you that there are folks back in D.C., and not just the ones in uniform, who are very anxious to have those items back."

"Is that a threat?"

"No. As I alluded to before, I don't want you inadvertently to do something that'll get you in trouble later. I can tell you that anything not classified and having to do with the investigation will be turned over to you."

"As determined by who?"

"The appropriate parties."

"I'd like to determine that for myself."

"Fine. Do you have Top Secret or SCI clearance?"

She moved a strand of hair from her face and glowered at him. "I don't even know what SCI means."

"Sensitive Compartmented Information. It's a bitch to get. On top of that the DoD has SAPs, or special access program clearances.

Reynolds was fully charged with TS/SCI and SAPs for his compartment and program areas. Consequently, if you try and access the laptop or check the colonel's briefcase without proper authorization you could be charged with treason. I don't want that to happen and I know you don't. I realize all these acronyms probably sound stupid, but people in the government arena take them very seriously. And the consequences of running afoul of these parameters, even by accident, are pretty severe. It's just a big headache you don't need, Cole."

"Strange world you operate in."

"No disagreement on that."

All around them the good folks of Drake were shooting curious glances in their direction. Two suits in particular were taking a special interest. As was a table of four beefy guys outfitted in corduroy pants and short-sleeved shirts that showed off their burly arms. One had on a Havoline cap. Another wore a dusty cowboy hat with a sharp crease on the right side. A third quietly drank his beer and studied the air in front of him. The fourth, smaller than the rest, but still weighing in at about two-ten, watched Puller and Cole via a large mirror on the wall.

Cole moved her gaze to look at the cash. "The police station is only—"

"Three minutes from here, like everything else."

"Actually it's about eight."

"Can I get the stuff?"

"Can I trust you?"

"I can't make that decision for you."

"So maybe I can." She put some dollars down to pay for her share of the meal.

"I think my cash covered them both with a tip," said Puller.

"I don't like owing people." She rose. "Let's go."

Puller left his money right where it was and followed her out as the town of Drake continued to stare.

CHAPTER

20

THEY WALKED down the street. The few people there stared at Puller and his blue jacket with the gold CID lettering. It didn't faze him. He was used to being the outsider. He only showed up in towns like this when something bad had happened. Nerves were tight. People were often dead by violent means. A stranger snooping around just added to the misery, the suspicion. Puller could deal with all that, but he also knew there was at least one killer out there, probably more. And something told him they were still here. Maybe a mere three-minute walk away from here, like everything else. Except the police station.

Cole nodded to some of the passersby, and said hello to one old woman using a walker to slowly amble along. The woman said in an admonishing tone, "Young lady, you haven't been to church in a while."

"Yes, Mrs. Baffle. I'll do better."

"I'll pray for you, Sam."

"Thank you. I could use it, I'm sure."

As the woman shuffled on Puller said, "Small town?"

"With all its thorns and rose petals," she replied.

They walked some more.

Cole said, "At least we know whoever killed the Reynoldses wasn't after his military stuff. Or else they would have taken the laptop and briefcase with them. Maybe that rules out the spy angle."

Puller shook his head. "You can download a laptop's hard drive onto a flash drive. So you don't have to take the hardware. Did you happen to see if anything was in the briefcase?"

She feigned astonishment. "My God, Puller, and me not having an SCI or an SAP? I wouldn't think of it. I could be charged with treason."

"Okay, I deserved that. But did you see anything?"

"It was locked with a combo code. I didn't want to break into it, so it's in pristine condition."

Keeping his gaze straight ahead he said, "Someone's on our seven. Last three blocks. Twenty meters back."

Cole kept her gaze straight too. "Could be they're going in the same direction we are. What do they look like?"

"Older man in a suit. Twenty-something big guy in a cutoff shirt with a tat sleeve down the right arm."

"Walking together?"

"Appear to be. They were in the restaurant eyeballing us the whole time, but from different tables."

"Follow me."

Cole cut to her left and started to cross the street. She let a car pass and took a look in both directions, ostensibly to check for more traffic. She proceeded on and Puller followed. She turned right and kept going in the same direction they had been heading, but on the opposite side of the street.

"Know them?" asked Puller.

"The man in the suit is Bill Strauss."

"And what does Bill Strauss do?"

"He's an exec with Trent Exploration. Like the number two guy after Roger."

"And the beef in the cutoff?"

"His son, Dickie."

"Dickie?"

"I didn't name him."

"And what does Dickie do? Something with Trent Exploration?"

"Not that I know of. He was in the Army for a while."

"Know where?"

"No."

"Okay."

"What now?"

"Well, we're about to find out what they want."

"Why?"

"They're catching up to us," Puller said.

From habit, Puller turned slightly and let his right arm dangle loosely. He lowered his chin, turned his head forty-five degrees to the left, and deployed his peripheral vision. He walked on the balls of his feet, dispersing his weight evenly so he could strike out in any direction with a balanced effectiveness. He wasn't concerned about the older man. Bill Strauss was in his fifties, flabby, and Puller's hearing told him the guy was wheezy just from a brisk walk.

Dickie the tat boy was a different story, but Puller wasn't all that concerned about him either. He was late twenties, an inch over six feet, scaled about two-sixty. Puller noted that he'd gotten fat after leaving the Army, but he'd kept the infantry brush cut and some of the muscle.

"Sergeant Cole?" said Strauss.

They turned, waited.

Strauss and his son walked up to them.

"Hello, Mr. Strauss, what can I do for you?" she asked.

Strauss was about thirty pounds overweight and a sliver under six feet. He wore a Canali pinstripe with a loosened solid blue tie and white dress shirt. His hair was mostly white and longer than his son's. His face was overly wrinkled, especially around the mouth. His voice was husky and edging toward ravaged. Puller noted the red-and-white pack of Marlboros sticking from his breast coat pocket and the nicotine fingers.

Lung cancer cometh, Mr. Wheezy.

His son's face was filled out, the cheeks reddened from too much sun. His pecs bulged from too many bench presses, but he'd grown light in the quads, hammies, and the all-important calves from neglecting his lower body. Puller seriously doubted the man could run the Army two-mile in the allotted time. His tat sleeve also caught Puller's attention.

Strauss said, "I heard about the bodies being found. Molly Bitner worked at my office."

"That we know."

"It's just awful. I can't believe she was killed. She was a very nice woman."

"I'm sure she was. Did you know her well?"

"Well, just from the office. She was one of a bunch of gals who worked there, but we never had any issues with her."

Puller said, "And would you expect to have had issues with her?"

Strauss shifted his gaze to Puller. "I understand you're with the Army. An investigator?"

Puller nodded but said nothing.

Strauss eyed Cole again. "If you don't mind my asking, why aren't you handling the case?"

"I am. It's a collaborative investigation, Mr. Strauss. One of the victims was in the military. That's why Agent Puller is here. It's standard procedure."

"I see. Of course. I was just wondering."

"Did she seem normal over the last few days?" asked Puller. "Anything seem to be bothering her?"

Strauss shrugged. "Again, I didn't have a lot of contact with her. I have my personal secretary and Molly worked out in the main office area."

"Doing what exactly?"

"Doing whatever was needed around the office, I suppose. We have an office manager, Mrs. Johnson, who could probably answer your inquiries. She would have had more contact with Molly than I would."

Puller was listening but no longer watching the older man now. His gaze was on the son. Dickie was eyeing his work boots, big hands stuffed in his worn corduroys.

"Heard you were in the Army," Puller said.

Dickie nodded but didn't look up.

"What division?"

"First Infantry."

"Mechanized man. Fort Riley or Germany?"

"Riley. Never been to Germany."

"How long were you in?"

"One stint."

"Didn't like the Army?"

"Army didn't much like me."

"BCD or a DD?"

Strauss broke in. "Well, I think we've taken up enough of your time. If we can help in any way, Sergeant Cole."

"Yes, sir. I'm sure we'll be by your office to talk."

"Certainly. Let's go, son."

As they walked off, Puller said, "Know the man well?"

"One of Drake's leading citizens. And one of the wealthiest."

"Right. Number two guy. So in the same league with Trent?"

"The Trents are in a league by themselves. Strauss is just one of his peons. But a very well-compensated peon. His house is smaller than Trent's but gargantuan by Drake standards."

"Strauss from Drake?"

"No, he moved here with his family over twenty years ago. He was from the East Coast, at least I think."

"Don't take this the wrong way, but what brought him here?"

"Work. He was a business guy and in the energy field. Drake may not look like much, but we do have energy in the form of coal and gas. He started working for Trent and the business really took off. Now what was that DD stuff you mentioned?"

Puller said, "A BCD means Big Chicken Dinner. That stands for a bad conduct discharge. A DD is worse, a dishonorable discharge. Since Dickie's still walking around free, I'm guessing it wasn't a DD. They kicked him out for a reason that didn't involve a court-martial. That's what he meant when he said the Army didn't much like him."

Cole gazed in the direction of the Strausses. "I never knew that."

"The only reason it might be relevant is that lots of BCDs are tied to drug use that the Army just doesn't want to screw around with. So they choose kicking guys out instead of prosecuting them."

"And maybe that ties to the meth lab we found?"

"You noticed it, right?" asked Puller.

She nodded. "Dickie's tat sleeve is identical to Eric Treadwell's."

CHAPTER

21

Puller snagged the laptop and briefcase from the Drake Sheriff's Office's evidence room. He had to fill out the necessary paperwork to maintain proper chain of custody.

As they walked out Cole yawned and stretched.

He said, "You should head home and get some sack time. I promise not to call and wake you up."

She smiled. "I appreciate that."

"The tat sleeve? Is that a gang deal? Or do people around here just like that particular arm design?"

"I suppose I've seen it on Dickie before but never really focused on it. I can ask around."

"Thanks. I'll see you tomorrow."

"You really going to be there at 0600?"

"I'll give you a break, I'll make it 0630."

"Oh, I found a doc to do the posts."

"Who is he?"

"Walter Kellerman. He's first-rate. Even wrote a textbook on forensic pathology."

"When is he going to do the posts?"

"Starting tomorrow afternoon. At his office in Drake around two. You want to be there?"

"Yes." He turned to head back to the motel.

"Hey, Puller, why do I think you're not really going to bed yet?"

He glanced back. "You need me, you've got my number."

"So I can call and wake you up?"

"Anytime."

Puller fast-walked back to Annie's Motel. Cole had been spot-on. He wasn't going to bed yet. He checked the little traps he always put in his room to make sure no one had been there. Annie's Motel did not offer maid or room service. One had to police his own space and find his own grub, which suited Puller just fine. He found nothing amiss.

He was on the road within five minutes, his destination the designated DHS drop site. He could kill two birds with one stone with this maneuver. He made a call and arranged for the agent stationed there to meet him. It took fifty minutes on the curvy roads. Normally the drop site was for evidence storage when a CID agent was in the field with no access to secure facilities. It took two agents to log in or log out any evidence, for obvious reasons.

When he got to the site Puller and the agent on duty packaged the laptop and briefcase in special boxes to be sent to the Army's criminal lab in Atlanta. Puller did not have the technical expertise to break the passcodes and access the laptop. And though he possessed both TS and SCI clearances, he probably didn't have the specific authorizations to look at what might be on there anyway. Because the laptop and briefcase potentially contained national security information, a commercial shipper could not be used. A special military courier was being summoned to accompany the sealed boxes down on a morning flight out of Charleston, West Virginia. They would be in Atlanta later that day. Puller could have taken the stuff down to Georgia himself, which he'd actually done in the past, but he thought it was more important to remain at the scene.

In the Army you always covered your ass. Thus he'd gotten approval for this plan from his SAC, who had covered *his* ass by getting necessary approvals all the way up to the one-star level. How the one-star covered her butt Puller didn't know and didn't really care.

On his drive back to Drake, Puller phoned USACIL in Atlanta and spoke with a supervisor he knew there who was working late on a rush case. She was a DA civilian named Kristen Craig. They had worked on many cases together, though they'd only met a few times in person. He gave her a thumbnail of what was coming.

"Kristen, I know you guys are cleared for most stuff. But you'll need to be read into this by DIA. And the stuff has to go in your secret safe. I marked everything appropriately."

"Got it, Puller. Thanks for the heads-up."

The CIL had multiple branches depending on what evidence was being processed. Latent prints, firearms and tool marks, drug chemistry, DNA, serology, paint, cars, digital evidence and computers, and the list went on and on.

"And, Kristen, it's a complicated crime scene. I'll be sending down a batch of different things across most branches. So be prepared. I'll try to be as specific as I can on the accompanying docs, but I'll probably need to clarify things by email or phone. And I think the Army is real anxious on this one."

"I'm surprised they didn't call on us for tech support. How many agents you have with you?"

"It's just me."

"You're joking?"

"Just me, Kristen."

He could hear her take a deep breath. "Hey, Puller?"

"Yeah?"

"What you just told me is starting to make sense based on what happened here today."

"What happened?"

"We got a call from the Secretary of the Army's office."

Puller kept one hand tightly on the wheel while the other pressed the phone to his ear. "SecArm?"

"Yep. That's not an everyday thing."

"I know. What did they want?"

"To be kept in the loop on everything. And then we got another call."

"You're a popular place. Who from?"

"FBI. The Director's office. Same thing. Be kept in the loop. Just thought you should know."

Puller mulled this. His SAC had said there were many eyes on this, and he hadn't been exaggerating. Maybe the answer did lie with Colonel Reynolds and whatever he was doing at DIA. But then why was the FBI involved?

"Thanks, Kristen."

"Hey, how's your father?"

"Hanging in there."

No one ever asked him about his brother.

He closed the phone and drove on.

He got back to the motel and carried his rucksack in with him. The trunk on his Malibu had a special alarm and a few surprises that were definitely not put there by the manufacturer. But Puller had also felt *he* was the best security for important items, and thus they always came in with him.

He slept with one M11 under his pillow. The other one was perched in his right hand. The only deference to safety had been no round in the chamber. He would have to wake, rack the slide, acquire his target, and fire. And not miss. He would do all of that in three seconds and trust that it would be fast enough.

He needed to go to sleep. And in ten seconds, just as the Army had taught him, he did.

CHAPTER

22

It is the fire he remembers, really. Always that. In some ways maybe *only* that. Rubber, metal, and human flesh ablaze all together give off a smell like no other. It is a scent that is burned right into your DNA. It becomes a part of you forever. It is a part of him forever.

His right forearm shattered, he fires with the left, the butt of his assault rifle wedged into his armpit. Left-hand trigger pull for a righty would normally be problematic, but he's trained for this very moment. Sweat, blood, and guts for this very second. He's become ambidextrous, can fight off both sides with nearly equal skill.

Diesel fuel soaks his combat uniform. His combat assault helmet is gone, blown off by the blast's concussive force. The strap burned his chin on the way out of the Humvee. He tastes salty blood.

His and others'.

There are scraps of human tissue on his face.

His and others'.

The sun is so hot that it seems possible it could alone ignite the fuel, burn him to cinders. He is perhaps a few degrees away from being a walking conflagration.

He assesses the situation. Up, down, out, in. All relevant compass points. Doesn't look good. Actually, it never looks good. Two heavy-as-hell Humvees blown onto their sides like downed rhinos. Despite the underside armor four of his men are dead or mortally wounded. He's the only one mobile. There's no good reason why this is the case. It's luck, nothing more. None of the dead and dying men had done anything wrong. He had done nothing particularly right.

The IED had packed some serious punch. The terrorists were getting better. Americans armor up, so the turbaned bombers make a bigger boom to compensate.

He sprays the area with his assault weapon, empties two mags, drops it, shakes free his pistol, and fires off the extended mag on that. He's not really looking to kill the enemy with the barrage, only to get their attention. To let them know he's still around. To let them know that they can't come and just take him and his men. That it won't be easy. Or smart to try.

The next weapon he pulls from the wrecked Humvee is his favorite. The Army bolt-action sniper rifle. This time he will fire with more deliberation, with far more care. He uses the metal skeleton of the Humvee as his support. He wants them to know he is serious.

He fires off one round merely to warm his rifle barrel. No matter how good a shot you were, a bullet traveling down a cold barrel often misses its target. Snipers normally had spotters, but he doesn't have that luxury right now. Thus he counts his mil dots, gauges angles, distance, ordnance drop, ambient temp, and wind among other factors and dials in the necessary adjustments on his scope. He does this automatically, without really thinking, like a computer executing a tried-and-true algorithm. The longer the shot, the greater small mistakes in calculations add up. An inch off here or there meant you missed your target by yards over a great distance. He is chasing breathing figures performing horizontal sprints across the street. These men are all lean and can run all day. Not an ounce of Western fat on them. They are brutal, hardened; mercy is not in their lexicon.

Yet he is also brutal, hardened, and mercy has been absent from his vocabulary since the day he put on the uniform. The rules of engagement are clear and have been ever since men first took up arms against each other.

He relaxes his breathing and then lets out a long exhale, reaching his cold zero point of physiological perfection for a sniper. Between heartbeats to minimize barrel motion, he executes a long, sure, and unhurried trigger pull using the ball of his finger to avoid a sideways pull on the weapon. The shot impacts its targets and spins the Taliban runner like a ballerina. He hits the Afghan soil at the mid-street point. He lies still for all time, his brain disintegrated by Corporal John Puller Jr.'s heavy round.

He exercises the bolt on his weapon and slides home another 7.62 shell.

A split second later comes another run by an even taller, leaner Taliban.

Puller performs his kill algorithm at lightning speed, his synapses traveling far faster than even the bullet he's about to deliver. Another trigger pull and then there occurs a second spin of Afghani flesh and bone with essential brain parts missing. The target twirls with grace, with utter finality. There are no second acts on the desert stage. This Taliban, like the first, doesn't even realize he's dead, because the brain is slow on the uptake in such situations. The howls of his comrades rip the air. Racks on weapons pull back.

They are pissed.

His preliminary mission is accomplished. Upset people never fight well.

Yet there will be some caution, for they know he is a force to be reckoned with. He looks at his men. He triages from a distance as blood pours out of his own body from multiple points. Three of his guys are dead, already burned nearly beyond recognition because the fuel and ammo loads have blown up in their laps. No chance for any of them. One man has been thrown clear of the fire but is dying nonetheless. A chunk of his chest and right leg are missing and as Puller watches something bursts inside the wounded man and superoxygenated arterial blood sprays over him like a horrific fountain of red. He'll be dead in seconds. Yet there are four injured men he can still save. Or die trying.

Shots come his way. The Taliban aren't running anymore. They take cover, raise their weapons—often their American-made weapons, from the Russian invasion decades ago—and do their best to end Puller's life.

They are determined.

So is he.

They have fellow warriors they are fighting for.

So does he.

There are many more of them. He has called in for backup. It will take longer to get here than he probably has to live. To get out of this he will have to kill them all.

John Puller is prepared to do just that. In fact, he expects to do just that.

All extraneous thought is banished. He focuses. He doesn't think. He simply employs his training. He will fight until his heart stops.

Total focus. This is it. All those years of sweat, of agony, of having someone screaming that you can't do something but actually expecting that you will do it better than anyone ever has. All for the next three minutes. Because that's probably how long it will take to declare a winner in this one encounter between desperate men. If you multiply all these individual fights to the death by a factor of a million it will add up to something called a war.

He lets their gunfire pass. The rounds ping off American Humvee armor. Others rip past his head sounding like miniature jet fighters. One grazes his left arm, a totally unremarkable wound among all the others. He will find out later that another rifle round whipsawed off the armor plates on his flak jacket, ricocheted off the toppled Humvee, reversed course, and found purchase in his neck after losing most of its juice. To the docs it will look like a big metal zit, right underneath the surface of his skin. Right now, he doesn't even notice. Doesn't care.

And then John Puller raises his weapon once more...

CHAPTER

23

As always, Puller didn't jerk awake. He simply eased off his thin mattress at Annie's Motel. He was in control, his movements measured, steady. He was not on the outskirts of Kandahar fighting turbaned killers. He was in American coal mining country looking for perhaps homegrown killers.

He didn't have to check his watch. His internal clock told him what he needed to know: 0430. He showered and took an extra thirty seconds under the hot water to lift the stench of a years-old memory. But it didn't work. It never did. He was just going through the motions. He dressed in what had quickly become his uniform here: jeans and CID polo shirt, but he substituted an old pair of his beige Army jump boots for the sneakers. It was already hot outside. It likely never grew cool overnight. But no matter how hot it ever became, nothing could come close to Afghanistan or Iraq in summer. That was a heat that was impossible to forget. Especially when it was fueled by diesel fire. By the screams of men burning to death. Turning black and raw and then disintegrating right in front of you.

His cell phone rang. The office. Or maybe Cole. Maybe something else had happened. He checked the ID on the screen. His expression changed from one of alertness to something else, something diminished.

"John Puller."

"You never called me back, XO."

"Out on a mission." He paused, but only for a second. "How you doing, General?"

John Puller Sr.'s voice was like the bark of a large, big-chested dog. It was an Army myth that the man could kill men simply with his voice, by making their hearts seize up with fear.

"You never called me back, XO," he said again, as though he hadn't heard Puller's reply.

"Was going to today, sir. Problems?"

"My command is going to shit."

Puller's father had had his sons later in life. He was seventy-five now and in failing health.

"You'll whip them back into shape. Always do. And they're good men. They'll respond. Rangers lead the way, General." Puller had long since given up trying to reason with his father, tell him that he no longer had a command of any kind. That he was old and sick and dying far faster than he believed. Or it might be the old warrior didn't think he was ever going to die.

"I need you down here. You can get them in line. Always count on you, XO."

Puller had joined the military on the tail end of his father's illustrious career. They had never served together. But the old man had kept a close eye on his youngest son's accomplishments. Things had not been made easier for him because of his connection to the lieutenant general. In fact, they had been made infinitely harder.

"Thank you, sir. But as I said, I'm on another mission." He paused again, checked his watch. He was behind schedule. He didn't like to use this card, but he did when he had to. "I saw Bobby the other day. He told me to tell you hello."

The line immediately went dead.

Puller closed the phone and slipped it into its holder on his belt. He sat there for a few more seconds, gazing down at his boots. He should go, he really should. Instead, he slid his wallet out of his pocket, flipped the photo out.

The three Puller men were all in a row. All tall, but John Jr. was the tallest, beating his old man out by a bare half inch. The general's face was carved from granite. The old man's eyes had been described as hollow-point ordnance with max loads. You could do pull-ups on his chin. He looked like Patton and MacArthur rolled into one, only bigger, meaner, and tougher. He'd been a son of a bitch as a general, and his men had loved him, died for him.

As a father he'd been a son of a bitch too. And his sons?

I love him. I would've died for him.

Senior had been the captain of the Army basketball team at West Point. They'd never won the championship during his father's four years. But every team they played went home bruised and battered. And those that ended up beating his father's team still probably felt like they'd lost. "Getting Pullered" was an expression often used back then. On the basketball court. On the battlefield. To the old man it was no doubt the same thing. He simply kicked the shit out of you until the buzzer sounded.

Or the armies ran out of ammo and bodies to throw at each other.

Puller's gaze held briefly on the spot in the photo just to the left of his father. There was no one there, though there should have been.

There should have been.

He put the photo away, gunned up and slipped on his CID jacket, and locked the door behind him.

The past is just that.

Gone.

CHAPTER

24

Outside, as Puller started to get in his ride, he saw the light on in the motel office. Being naturally curious, he decided to check. He eased the door open. The old lady was sitting in a chair in front of the counter. Her right hand gripped her chest. She looked scared, her chest heaving, her face reddening, with tinges of gray skirting the edges.

He closed the door and moved closer. Her lips and the skin around her nose weren't blue. So no cyanosis.

Yet.

Puller slipped his phone from his pocket and thumbed 911 without looking at the pad.

"How long you been this way?" he asked her.

" 'Bout ten minutes," she mumbled back.

He knelt beside her. "Happened before?"

"Not this bad in a long time. Then I had my quadruple at the hospital."

"Bad ticker, then?"

"Pretty bad, I think. Yeah. Surprised I lasted this long." She moaned, gripped her chest harder.

"Like a heavy weight there?"

She nodded.

"Any shooting pain in your arms?"

She shook her head. Tears dribbled out of her eyes.

A big sign of myocardial infarction was an elephant on the chest. Next big sign: sharp pain along the left arm. Not always the case and not always the left, particularly with women, but Puller wasn't going to wait for it to happen.

The dispatcher came on the line. Puller described the situation in staccato sentences containing precise details and closed the phone.

"They're on their way."

"I'm scared," she said, her voice breaking.

"I know. But you're going to be okay."

He felt her pulse. Weak. No surprise there. Bad pump meant reduced blood flow, and that equaled a crappy pulse. A stroke was also possible with someone her age. She felt cold, clammy. The veins in her neck were bulging. Another bad sign. She might be clotting.

"Just nod or shake your head. You nauseous?"

She nodded.

"Can't catch your breath?"

She nodded again.

He said, "You on any meds for your heart?"

She nodded again. He could see beads of cold sweat lining her brow like a nearly invisible pearl necklace. "I got some nitro too. But couldn't get to 'em."

"How about aspirin?"

"Same place."

"Tell me where."

"Bedroom nightstand." She pointed with a shaky finger to her left.

Puller was back in ten seconds with the bottles of pills in hand.

He gave her aspirin with some water. If she had a clot, aspirin was a good way to prevent platelet clumping. And it kicked in fast. And it didn't screw with your blood pressure.

The problem with nitro was that it only treated symptoms, not the underlying coronary disease. It would help with her chest pain, but if her blood pressure was already low the nitro would push it lower still; that's just the way it worked. That could significantly worsen the heart problem and also cause organ shutdown. He couldn't risk that. He had to know first.

"You have a blood pressure cuff here?"

She nodded, pointed to a shelf behind the counter.

It was one of those battery-operated devices with a digital read-out. He grabbed it, slipped it on her right upper arm, hit the on switch, and watched the cuff inflate. He read the results.

Not good. Pretty low already. Nitro might kill her.

He looked her over. No sign of retaining fluids, swollen feet, or vascular problems. "You on any diuretics?"

She shook her head.

"I'll be back in ten seconds," he said.

He raced to his Malibu, popped the trunk, grabbed his first aid bag, and ran back, his long legs chewing up the distance.

When he got back she looked worse. If the heart crashed now, the EMTs, instead of saving her, would pronounce her dead when they arrived.

He opened the kit, readied his equipment. He talked to her the whole time, trying to keep the old woman calm. One ear listened for the ambulance.

He had done triage in the middle of nowhere with guys who looked like red chunks of meat. He had saved some, lost others. He had made up his mind he was not going to lose her.

Puller swabbed her arm with alcohol, found a good vein, and inserted the needle, taping it securely to the inside of her forearm with white medical adhesive. He screwed the other end of the line into the IV bag of saline he'd pulled from his kit. Fluids got the blood pressure up. Same method the docs used to save Reagan after he'd been shot. It was a liter bag with an eighteen-gauge line. It was a gravity feed. He held it above her head and opened the feed wide. It would take twenty minutes to empty the bag. She had five liters of blood total. A liter of saline would boost her by twenty percent.

When the bag was half empty he punched the on button on the cuff again. He read the numbers. Both were up to safer levels. Whether safe enough he didn't know, but he didn't have much choice. She was gripping her chest tighter. Her moans both deepened and lengthened.

He said, "Open your mouth." She did and he slipped the nitro tablet under her tongue.

The nitro pop worked. A minute later she was calming; her chest stopped heaving. She took her hand away from it. With heart distress, your artery was undergoing spasms. The nitro knocked that out. With the spasms gone lots of good things could happen, at least until the ambulance arrived.

"Take long, deep breaths. Paramedics are on the way. Aspirin, nitro, and fluids have helped. You're looking better. You're going to be fine. Not your time yet."

He hit the cuff button again. Read the numbers. Both up. Both better. Her color was improving. It was a mini-miracle in the middle of coal country.

"Hospital is a long way away," she gasped. "Should've moved closer."

He grinned. "We all have regrets."

She smiled weakly, took his hand. He let her squeeze it as hard as she wanted. Her fingers were tiny, weak. He barely felt the pressure, like a rippling breeze. He could see her face relax. Her teeth were yellowed, black in places, gaps in other places, and nearly all the remaining teeth were crooked. And yet it was a nice smile. He appreciated seeing it.

"You're a good egg," she said.

"Anything you need taken care of around here? Anybody I should call for you?"

She shook her head slowly. "Nobody but me left."

Up close Puller noted the heavy cataracts. It was a wonder she could even see him. "Okay. Deep, steady breaths. I hear the siren. They know it's cardiac. They're coming prepared."

"I thank you, young man."

"What's your name? Annie, like on the sign?"

She touched his cheek, thanked him again with a shaky smile, her lips curling in pain with each beat of her creaky heart.

"My name is Louisa. I can't really tell you who Annie was. Name was there when I bought the place and I didn't have the money to change it."

"You like flowers, Louisa? I'll send you some in the hospital." He held her gaze, willing her to keep calm, breathe naturally, and not think about her heart trying to stop forever.

"A girl always likes getting flowers," she replied, her voice weak.

He heard the engine, followed by the crunch of gravel, doors opening and closing, feet running. The paramedics were swift, efficient, and well trained. He told them about the aspirin, nitro, the fluids, and her blood pressure. He listed her symptoms, because she didn't have the strength to talk now. They asked all the right questions, spoke calmly, and had her masked on oxygen and on a fresh drip within a few minutes. Her color improved even more.

One EMT said to him, "You a doc? Did all the right things."

"Not a doc, just a soldier with a few tricks. Take good care of her. Her name's Louisa. We're buds."

The short man stared upward at the massive former Ranger and said, "Hey, dude, a bud of yours is a bud of mine."

Louisa waved to Puller on her way to the wheels. He followed. She slid her mask off.

She said, "Got a cat. Could you—"

Puller nodded. "I got a cat too. No problem."

"What's your name again, honey?"

"Puller."

"You're a good egg, Puller," she said again.

The doors clunked behind her and the ambulance zoomed away, its siren firing up as night began seriously turning into day.

A good egg.

He'd have to find a florist.

He looked for the cat, found it in the woman's living space reached by a door behind the office counter. The tabby was under the bed, fast asleep. The old woman's "home" constituted two rooms and a six-by-six bath with a shower almost too small for Puller to even get into. Stacks of things people her age often collected lay everywhere. It was like they were trying to stop time in its tracks by holding on to all that had come before.

Stopping their march to death. As if any of us could.

Four of his men had died in that ambush. He had saved the other four. He'd gotten a slew of medals for doing what any of them would have done for him for free. He went home. Half of the eight did too. In shiny coffins draped with the stars and stripes.

An all-expenses-paid ride to Dover Air Force Base. Then six feet under at Arlington. A white headstone to show where you were amid all the other white headstones.

Helluva deal, thought Puller. *For the Army.*

The cat was old and fat and apparently unaware of its owner's medical distress. Puller made sure the food and water pails were full and the litterbox clean. He found the office key, locked the door behind him, and went to get breakfast.

He was suddenly hungry. And right now food would have to suffice.

CHAPTER

25

HE PARKED THE MALIBU on the street directly in front. The Crib Room was open and already half full. People rose and ate early here, obviously. Puller snagged a seat at a table in the corner, his back to the wall. He never sat at the counter unless there was a mirror so he could watch his rear flank. The Crib had no such mirror behind the counter. Hence that was not an option. And from here he could see his ride clearly.

He ordered the same meal for breakfast that he'd had for dinner the night before. Once you found something good you stuck to it.

He let his gaze wander over the other customers. Mostly men. Dressed for work or maybe coming home from it. No suits at this time of morning. Only working stiffs like him. He eyed the clock on the wall.

Zero-five-thirty.

He sipped his coffee. Twenty minutes to get his food and eat it. Forty minutes to the crime scene. Zero-six-thirty. Just like he'd told Cole.

He sipped more coffee. It was good, it was hot, and the mug was big. He cupped it with his hand, felt the heat sink into his skin.

The thermometer outside was already at eighty. It was also muggy. He had felt the sweat form on his body when he'd run to his car for the first aid kit. But when it was hot outside, you drank something hot. That made your body cool itself. When it was cold, the opposite. Simple science. But, frankly, regardless of the temperature, Puller liked his coffee. It was an Army thing. Puller knew

exactly what it was. It was a few moments of normalcy in an otherwise abnormal world where people were trying to kill each other.

"You John Puller?"

He looked to his left and saw a man about sixty standing next
to his table. He was about five-nine and rotund, with sunburned
skin. Fringes of gray hair hung out from under his hat. He was also
wearing a police uniform. Puller eyed the nametag.

Lindemann. The good sheriff of this fine hamlet.

"I am, Sheriff Lindemann. Please, have a seat."

Lindemann wedged himself across from Puller. He took off his
broad-brimmed hat and set it down on the table. He swept a hand
through his thinning hair that was sticking up at odd angles from
the encounter with the hat. He smelled of Old Spice, coffee, and
nicotine. Puller began to wonder if everyone in Drake smoked.

"Won't take up too much of your time. Figure you're busy," said
Lindemann.

"Figure you are too, sir."

"No need to sir me. I'm Pat. What do I call you?"

"Puller will work just fine."

"Cole tells me you're good at what you do. I trust her. Some say
she's a gal and shouldn't be wearing the uniform or carrying no
gun, but I'll take her over any man I have in the department."

"From what I've seen of her I would too. You want some coffee?"

"Tempting, but I have to say no. Well, at least my kidneys have
to say no after three cups already. And my prostate, which Doc
tells me is the size of a grapefruit. Not too many places to pee in a
patrol car."

"I can see that."

"Tricky damn business, all this."

"Yes, it is."

"Not used to this stuff around here. Last murder we had was ten
years ago."

"What happened then?"

"Hubby caught his wife cheating with his brother."

"He killed her?'

"No, she beat him to it. Shot him. And then shot the brother

when he came after her for shooting his brother. Got a little con-
voluted, to say the least." He paused and looked around before set-
tling his gaze back on Puller. "We don't ordinarily collaborate with
outsiders on police matters."

"I can understand that."

"But the fact is we need your help."

"I'm glad to give it."

"You keep working with Sam."

"I will."

"Keep me in the loop. Media inquiries." He said these words
with considerable distaste.

"Army can help you with that. I can give you some contact info."

"I'd appreciate that."

Puller took a business card from his pocket and wrote a name
and number on the back and slid it across. The lawman picked it up
without looking at it and eased it into his shirt pocket.

"I best be heading on," said Lindemann. "Enjoy the rest of your
breakfast."

"I'm sure I will."

Lindemann slid his hat back on and trudged out of the Crib.

As Puller's gaze followed him out, a guy sitting two tables away
caught his attention for one reason only.

He had on a U.S. Postal Service cap.

CHAPTER

26

PULLER WATCHED HIM. The man ate his food slowly, deliberately. Coffee the same. One sip, then the mug went down. Ten seconds, another sip, then down again. Puller's food came. He ate it faster than he had originally intended. The carbs and protein pumped up his energy level. He left cash on the table, not even waiting for the bill. He knew the amount from the night before.

He rose, cradling his last cup of coffee, walked past tables, ignored the stares, and stopped at the postman's booth.

The man looked up.

"You Howard Reed?" asked Puller.

The skinny, sallow-cheeked fellow nodded.

"Mind if I join you for a few minutes?"

Reed didn't say anything.

Puller flipped out his cred pack, badge followed by ID, and sat down without waiting for an answer.

"I'm with Army CID investigating the murders you stumbled onto on Monday," he began.

Reed shivered and pulled his cap down lower.

Puller ran his gaze over him. Too lean in an unhealthy way. Spoke of some serious internal problems. Sunburnt skin. Probably looked ten years older than he was. Stooped shoulders. Body language spelled defeat. In life. In everything.

"Can I ask you some questions, Mr. Reed?"

The man took another careful sip of coffee and set it down, the mug just so. Puller wondered if he had OCD.

"Okay," said Reed. It was the first word he'd said. His voice was hoarse, weak, like he didn't use it much.

"Can you take me through your steps that day, starting with you pulling down the street? What you saw? What you heard? Maybe something you usually see or hear but didn't that day? You follow me?"

Reed slid his paper napkin from next to his empty plate and wiped off his mouth. He went step by step. Puller was impressed with the man's memory and method. Maybe you got that delivering a zillion pieces of mail, covering the same ground, seeing the same things over and over. You'd get a sense if something looked different.

"You ever see the Reynoldses before?" Puller asked.

"Who?"

"The murdered family was named Reynolds."

"Oh." Reed considered this, took his time, and treated himself to another deliberate sip of coffee.

Puller noted the wedding band on the man's gnarled finger. Married but eating his breakfast out at half past five? Maybe that's where the hopeless look came from.

"Saw the girl one time. She was out in the front yard when I was delivering. Never saw the man. Maybe saw the woman once passing by in her car when I was coming through."

"Did you know the Halversons?"

"The folks who lived there?"

"Yeah."

Reed waggled his head from side to side. "Never did see them. Wouldn't have gone up to the house, but I needed a signature for the package I was delivering. Certified mail, return receipt requested. Were they killed too?"

"No. They weren't there at the time." Puller remained silent for a few moments. "What happened to the package?" he asked.

"The package?" Reed's cup was halfway to his lips.

"Yeah, the one that required the signature."

Reed put his cup down and placed a finger against his cracked and dry lips. "I went in the house with it." He shuddered and gripped the laminated tabletop. "Then I saw…"

"Right, I know what you saw. But focus for me please. Package in hand. Then you turned and ran back out. Hit the door, broke the glass against the banister." Puller had learned all this from Cole.

Reed looked alarmed. "Am I gonna have to pay for that door? I didn't mean to break it, but I ain't never seen anything like that in my life. And hope to God I never do again."

"Don't worry about the door. Focus on the package. Was it addressed to the Halversons?"

Reed nodded. "Yep, I remember seeing the name on there."

Puller didn't respond. He just let the man think about it, picture the package in his mind. The mind was a funny thing. Give it time and something fresh usually popped.

Reed's eyes widened slightly. "Now I think about it, it was a C/O."

"Care of?"

"Right, right," Reed replied excitedly. He slid his hands along the tabletop, bumping against his empty plate. He didn't look hopeless anymore. He looked engaged. Maybe for the first time in years, thought Puller.

Puller reasoned, "So it wasn't meant for the Halversons really? It was just sent to their house. Was there any other name on it? The Reynoldses? They were the only ones staying there."

Reed remained silent, his gaze pointing slightly upward as he thought it through. Puller said nothing. He didn't want to break the man's focus. He took a drink of his own coffee, now lukewarm. He performed a long visual sweep of the diner. More than half the heads there were turned his way.

He didn't flinch when he saw tat boy. Dickie Strauss was sitting at the far end of the diner, facing Puller's way. He had a much bigger man with him. The second guy had sleeves, so Puller couldn't tell if the arms were inked in a similar way or not. They were watching him while trying very hard to seem not to. It was pathetic really. Dickie must've forgotten all his military training, thought Puller.

He refocused on Reed to find the man staring at him. "I can't remember," he said apologetically. "I'm sorry. Do remember the C/O, though."

"That's okay," said Puller. "The package? Was it big, small?"

"Size of a piece of paper."

"Okay. Do you recall who sent it? Or where it was mailed from?"

"Not offhand, but I can maybe find out."

Puller slid across a contact card. "Any of those numbers or emails will get to me. Now, do you remember what happened to it? You ran out of the house, kicked open the door."

Reed looked away from his plate. For a moment Puller was afraid the man was going to throw up his breakfast.

"I...I must've dropped it."

"In the house? Outside the house? Sure it's not in your mail truck?"

"No, it's not in the truck." He paused. "Yeah, must've been in the house. Had to be. Dropped it there. I ran out and it wasn't in my hand. See that now. Clear as day."

"Okay, I'm sure it'll turn up. Anything else you can tell me?"

"I don't know. I mean, I ain't never been involved in anything like this before. Don't know what's important and what's not."

"House right across the street? Notice anything funny over there?"

"Treadwell's place?"

"Right. He lived there with Molly Bitner. You know them?" In Cole's report, Reed had stated that he didn't know anybody in the neighborhood, but Puller preferred to hear it for himself.

Reed shook his head. "Naw. Only know the name 'cuz I'm the mailman. He gets lots of biker magazines. Has a Harley. Parks it out front."

Puller shifted in his chair. He didn't know if Reed was aware that Treadwell and Bitner were dead. "Anything else?"

"Just the usual stuff. Nothing that sticks out. I mean, I just deliver the mail. Just check the addresses. I don't really do more than that."

"That's fine, Mr. Reed. I appreciate your time." He tapped his contact card. "When you find out who sent the package, please get in touch."

Puller rose. Reed looked up at him.

Reed said, "Lot of damn mean people in the world."

"Yes, sir, there are."

"Know it for a fact."

Puller leveled his gaze on the man, waited.

"Yep. Know it for a fact." He paused, his mouth working but no words coming out for a few seconds. "I'm married to one."

After Puller walked outside Dickie Strauss and his large friend followed.

Puller had been pretty sure they would.

CHAPTER

27

PULLER JIGGLED the car keys in his pocket, leaned against his Malibu, and waited for them.

Dickie and his friend stopped on the pavement a few feet away.

"What can I do for you?" asked Puller.

Dickie said, "It wasn't a Big Chicken Dinner. And it wasn't a DD."

"Good to know. But if you're lying I can find out in about five minutes. Just a few keystrokes to get a reply back from the Army Records Center. So what was it?"

"A parting of the ways."

"Why?"

Dickie looked at his friend, who was keeping his gaze on Puller.

"It's personal. And it wasn't nothing bad."

His friend added, "And it's none of your damn business."

"So what can I do for you?" Puller asked again.

"I hear Eric Treadwell got killed."

"You know him?"

"Yeah."

Puller eyed the tatted arm. He pointed to it. "Where'd you get that done?"

"Place here in town."

"Treadwell had one just like it."

"Not just like it. Little different. But I used his as a model."

"Why?"

"Why not?"

"That's not really an answer."

The bigger guy stepped forward. He was an inch taller than Puller and outweighed him by about fifty pounds. He looked like a former Division I defensive lineman. Not good enough for the pros but decent enough for four years of college on a full-ride scholarship.

"It's *his* answer," said the guy.

Puller swiveled his gaze to the man. "And you are?"

"Frank."

"Okay, Frank. I thought this discussion was between Dickie and me."

"Well, maybe you need to rethink things."

"I don't see a reason to do that."

Puller watched as Frank pulled his hand from his pockets and balled up his fists. He also saw what was in the man's hand, although Frank was trying to hide it.

"I got two pretty good ones right here," said Frank, holding up his knotty fists.

"No you don't, Frank, you really don't," Puller said evenly as he stood straight and also took his hands from his pockets. Puller had nothing in his hands, but he didn't need to.

"I know you got a gun. Saw it in the Crib," said Frank.

"I won't be needing it."

Frank said, "I outweigh you by forty pounds."

"More like fifty."

"Okay. So do you get the point?"

Dickie said nervously, "Hey, guys, it's cool." He put a restraining arm on his friend. "Frank, don't, man. Ain't worth the hassle."

Puller said, "Your bud is making sense, Frank. I don't want to hurt you. But if what I'm seeing in your body language gets transferred into action, you will get hurt. The only question is how badly."

Frank snorted and attempted a confident grin. "You think just because you're in the Army you can kick everybody's ass?"

"No. But I know I can kick your ass."

Frank's right hand swung, but Puller had already launched. The top of his head hit the other man flush in the face. Puller's skull was far harder than the other man's nose. A stunned 280-pound Frank whipsawed backward, his face bloody. Puller took hold of Frank's left arm, windmilling it back and torquing the limb nearly to the breaking point. He slid a foot behind Frank's left leg and the big man went straight down to the pavement. Puller had knelt along with the falling Frank, cupping his head with his free hand before it hit the ground so the man's skull wouldn't crack.

Puller dug the roll of quarters out of Frank's fist, dropped it on the pavement, rose, and looked down. When Frank, who was holding his broken nose and trying to dig the blood out of his eyes with his knuckles, tried to stand, Puller put a foot on his chest and nudged him back down.

"Just stay there." He turned to Dickie. "Go in the Crib and get a bag of ice. Do it now." When Dickie didn't move, Puller gave him a shove. "Now, Dickie, or I'll throw you right through the window to speed your ass up."

Dickie rushed off.

"You didn't have to do that, you son of a bitch," Frank said through his bloodied hands.

"And you didn't have to take a swing at me with a roll of quarters."

"I think you broke my nose."

"I *did* break your nose. But it was already broken before. It goes off to the left and has the hump in the middle. Probably caught it on a face mask during a game. Doubt it was ever reset properly. And you've probably got a deviated septum too. Now, when they fix you up, they can make all that right."

Dickie came back out with the ice enclosed in a small towel. When Puller looked over, everyone in the restaurant was standing at the window watching.

Dickie held out the ice to Puller.

"I don't need it, Dickie, your bud there does."

Frank took the ice and held it against his nose.

"What in the hell is going on here?"

Puller turned to see Sam Cole pull up in her police cruiser with the window rolled down. She was in full uniform. She parked at the curb and got out. Puller noted that her gun belt didn't squeak.

She looked down at Frank and saw the roll of quarters. She glanced over at Dickie and then at Puller.

"You want to explain what's going on? Did he attack you or did you attack him?"

Puller looked at Dickie and then at Frank. When neither of them seemed willing to speak, Puller said, "He slipped and broke his nose. His buddy got him some ice."

Cole hiked her eyebrows and then glanced at Dickie. He mumbled, "That's right."

She looked down at Frank. "That your story too?"

Frank sat up on one elbow. "Yes, ma'am."

"And what, a roll of quarters just fell out your pocket?"

"Shirt pocket," said Puller. "When he fell. I heard him say something about doing his laundry. Explains the quarters."

Cole put out her hand and helped Frank up. "You better go have that looked at."

"Yes, ma'am."

They slowly walked off.

"Ready to get going?" asked Puller.

"What I'm ready for is for you to tell me what really happened."

"You saying I lied?"

"That guy didn't slip. He looked like he'd been hit by a truck. And that roll of quarters was probably in his fist when he took a swing at you."

"All conjecture and speculation on your part."

"Well, here's some firmer evidence." She reached up and smacked him lightly on the forehead. "You have blood right there. I don't see a cut, so it's probably his blood. That means he took a swing and you head-butted him. I'd like to know why."

"Misunderstanding." Puller used his sleeve to wipe the blood off.

"About what?"

"About personal space."

"You're really starting to piss me off."

"It's not important, Cole. Small-town, insider-outsider thing. If it turns out to be more than that, you'll be the first to know from me."

She didn't look convinced but also didn't say anything.

"I thought we were meeting at the crime scene."

"Got up early, figured you'd be here," Cole replied.

"I had a chat with your boss."

"Sheriff Lindemann?"

"He came into the Crib. I gave him some contact info to help with the media stuff."

"Thanks."

"He thinks very highly of you."

"It's mutual. He's the one who gave me my chance."

"You said you were with the state police before you came here."

"That was his idea. He said if I had that on my résumé, nobody could stop me from carrying a badge in Drake."

"I take it he doesn't make the hiring decisions."

"County Commission. All men. All men living in the nineteenth century. Barefoot and pregnant and in the kitchen just about covers their idea of a woman's role in life."

"I also spoke to the mailman."

"Mailman? You mean Howard Reed?"

"Yeah, he's in there finishing his breakfast. He said he left the package he was delivering inside the house. Dropped it in there, more likely. He said it was sent in care of the Halversons, which means it was probably addressed to the Reynoldses. Do you have it?"

Cole looked puzzled. "There was nothing like that."

Puller gazed steadily at her. "Didn't you wonder why the mailman was at the door in the first place?"

"He told me he was there to get a signature for something. I just assumed..." Her voice trailed off and her cheeks reddened. "I screwed up. I shouldn't have assumed."

"But you're saying the package wasn't found in the house? Reed was pretty sure that's where he dropped it."

"Maybe that's what they came back for night before last."

"Yeah, but your people had all day in there. Why didn't they find the package?"

She said, "Let's go get an answer to that, Puller. Right now."

CHAPTER

28

Two county cop cars were parked, side by side, hood to trunk, outside the two houses. The officers inside the vehicles were chatting when Cole skidded to a stop with Puller right behind in his Malibu. She slid out of the car before it even seemed to have stopped rolling and approached the twin cruisers.

"You two spend all night jawing or actually doing your job?" she snapped.

Puller walked up behind her and noted that the two cops were ones he'd never seen before, which made sense if they were pulling the graveyard shift.

The cops climbed out of their rides and stood at semi-attention, although Puller interpreted far more contempt in their body language than respect for a superior officer. In the Army that situation would have been taken care of in a matter of a few painful minutes, with a months-long penance by the transgressor to follow.

Cole said, "Anything to report?"

Both of them shook their heads. One said, "Saw nothing and heard nothing. Did rounds regularly, but changed up the timing so nobody watching could catch a pattern."

"Okay." She pointed to Puller. "This is John Puller from the Army CID. He's working with us on this case."

This pair didn't look any friendlier than the ones had yesterday. That didn't bother Puller. He hadn't come here to make buddies with anybody. He nodded at the two but then glanced at Cole. It was her show to run right now, not his.

"You two were at the crime scene on Monday," said Cole. "Did either of you notice a package that the mailman might've dropped in the house over there?" She pointed to the Halversons'.

They both shook their heads. "Any evidence found gets logged in," said one of them. "Didn't see any package."

The other said, "If it didn't get logged in, we didn't find it. But we weren't the only ones in there. Lan should know if a package turned up," he added.

Cole snarled, "I should've known if a damn package turned up."

"So maybe there is no package, Sarge," said the first cop in a calm, even tone.

Puller scrutinized each of them without seeming to do so. Still, he didn't have a good read on them. He couldn't tell if their obvious resentment at being ordered around by a woman was also masking something else, like a lie.

He said, "Well, I guess it will turn up or it won't."

Both cops looked at him.

Before either of them could speak, Puller said, "So no activity last night? No cars, no people walking? No kids outside playing hide-and-seek?"

"There were cars," said one cop. "And they all went to their houses and they're all still there."

The other said, "A few kids outside. None came near the houses. And nobody was out walking last night. It was hot and muggy and the skeeters were out like you wouldn't believe."

Puller looked over at the house where Treadwell and Bitner had been killed. "They have any next of kin that need to be notified?"

Cole said, "We're checking into that. The Reynoldses had some besides the wife's parents. We're in the process of trying to contact them."

"Army can help you with that. They'll have info on the colonel's relatives."

Cole nodded at her officers. "Okay, your shift is up at eight. You can go back to work."

The men turned and strode off.

"Attitude like that all the time?" said Puller.

"Well, I basically accused them of either screwing up or

withholding evidence, so I can understand a little attitude. I'd probably be the same. I guess I shouldn't have gone off like that, but I'm pissed that I missed the damn package." She glanced up at him. "Mind if I smoke a quick one?"

"I don't but your lungs will."

"You think I haven't tried to quit?"

"My old man smoked for forty years."

"What got him off?"

"Hypnosis."

"You're kidding, really?"

"Surprised me too. I didn't think stubborn people could be hypnotized. But apparently they're the most susceptible."

"You calling me stubborn?"

"I'd rather call you a former smoker."

"Thanks, Puller. I might just try that."

"So the next step is checking the evidence log and what else?"

"Lan will be here this morning." She looked at her watch. "In about an hour or so."

"And if the package doesn't turn up?"

"I don't know, Puller. I just don't know."

"Reed said he could maybe find out where it came from back at his office. Check the certified mail records. But maybe you can speed that up officially."

"Yes, I can. It would be nice to know what was in a package that was worth maybe one of my men being killed."

He turned and looked at the house. "Were you one of the first responders?"

"No. Two others. Jenkins over there. And Lou, who you met yesterday. The one who talked to the imposter from the Treadwell house."

"When did you get here?"

"About ninety minutes after the call came in. I was way on the other side of the county."

"And the dog was still in the house?"

"Yeah. Why? What does the dog have to do with anything? It didn't bark, I told you that."

"Well, dogs pick up stuff. They chew stuff. They eat stuff they're not supposed to."

Cole looked over at the house, her features stark.

"Let's go, Puller."

She started to run.

29

FORTY MINUTES LATER Puller watched as Cole lifted the edge of the hemming around the sofa the bodies had been on. He handed her a Maglite and she shone it under the piece of furniture.

"Got something," she said. She pulled out a dog bone and two plastic dog toys.

"Seems to be the mutt's hiding place," said Puller. "Anything else?"

She tried to edge farther under the sofa.

"Hang on," he said. Puller lifted one end four feet into the air. Cole stared up at him from the floor. "Now that's using your brain. And muscle."

He looked down. "Bit of cardboard, like from a package."

"And this!" Cole picked up the bit of green paper off the carpet and stood. Puller set the sofa back down.

She examined the bit of paper and handed it to him.

"Looks like the edge from a certified mail receipt."

"Yes, it does. Only where's the rest of it? Do we have to X-ray the dog's stomach?"

"Or maybe the people who killed Wellman took it. They might've figured the dog got the package and hid it somewhere. They looked under the couch and there it was."

Cole looked puzzled. "But how would they know it was even here?"

"They interrogated the Reynoldses. The colonel might've told them they were expecting a package."

"So why didn't they just intercept it? They could've been in the house when Reed delivered the package. They could have signed for it. Impersonated them like that guy did with Eric Treadwell across the street. Reed told us he didn't know any of them. So he wouldn't have known the difference. He just wanted the piece of paper signed."

"But what if they didn't know about the package until later? Until after it was delivered here?"

"I don't get that at all, Puller."

He sat down on the edge of the sofa. "Reed said he was at the door because he needed a signature. That means it's some sort of special mail. But he doesn't say what happened to the package. Why would that sort of package be coming to the Halversons? They're retired. Reed remembered it was actually going to the Reynoldses, but he didn't tell the police that. Only that it was a package requiring a signature. So the killers might have just deduced what we did. Mailman at the door because of a package. What was in the package? They had to find out."

Puller looked out the window. Lan Monroe was just pulling to a stop in front of the house. "Why don't we ask Lan what his evidence list shows?"

"Okay. But I'm telling you I don't think that package is on there."

"Then we confirm it."

Five minutes later they had their confirmation. No package.

Lan looked worried as he surveyed the room. "I never saw anything like that."

"Dog might've eaten it," said Cole, drawing a long look from Puller. "I guess I could have the vet check or do an X-ray."

"It's paper, it probably wouldn't show up, or else the mutt's already digested it and pooped it out," replied Puller.

Cole's phone buzzed. She saw the caller ID and looked surprised.

"Who is it?" asked Puller.

"Roger Trent."

"Your mining mogul."

The phone continued to ring.

"Aren't you going to answer it?" said Puller.

"Yeah, I guess I am."

She opened the phone. "Hello?"

She listened, tried to say something, and then listened some more. "That'll be fine," she finally said. "See you then."

She closed the phone.

"Well?" asked Puller.

"Roger Trent wants to see me. At his house."

"Why?"

"He says he's been receiving death threats."

"You better get going."

"Why don't you come with me?"

"Why? You want some backup on this?"

"Couldn't hurt. And I can tell you're curious about the man. This way you get to see him up close and personal."

"Let's go."

CHAPTER

30

COLE AND PULLER drove to Trent's home in her cruiser.

She said, "I'm taking a shortcut. Cuts off a chunk of time but it's bumpy." She hung a hard right and swung onto a narrow road full of potholes.

It looked familiar to Puller. He gazed around and then saw why this was so.

"What the hell is that thing?" He pointed at the towering concrete dome over and around which trees, vines, and bushes had grown. He'd seen it on his way in here the first night, when he'd gotten lost.

"Folks around here call it the Bunker."

"Okay, but what is it?"

"Used to be some sort of government facility. It was closed up long before I was even born."

"But certainly the older folks in town know what it was. Some of them had to work there."

Cole shook her head. "Nope. No one from Drake ever did work there, at least not that I know of."

"I know the government is a financial black hole, but even D.C. won't put up a facility like that and not even use it."

"Oh, they used it."

She slowed down and Puller focused on the stretch of houses he'd glimpsed the other night. In daylight the place didn't look much different than it had at night. The houses were at least five decades old and possibly older. Many looked abandoned, but not all of them. They stretched over a web of streets, row after row.

They reminded him of military housing. Each one looked the same as its neighbor.

"Are you saying they brought in people from outside the area to work the Bunker?"

She nodded. "And they built all those homes to house them."

"I see there are people living in them still."

"Only over the last few years. Economy cratered, people lost their jobs and their homes. These places are old and haven't been kept up, but when you're on the street you can't be choosy."

"Any problems? Desperate folks sometimes do desperate things, especially when they're in close proximity to each other."

"We patrol it pretty regularly. What crime there is has been just petty stuff. People mostly stay to themselves. I guess they're grateful to have a roof over their heads. County tries to help them out. Blankets, food, water, batteries, books for the kids, stuff like that. We're over here a lot telling them not to use kerosene heaters and crap like that in the houses for heat. And ways to keep themselves safe. Already had one family nearly die from carbon monoxide poisoning."

"And the government just lets you use the housing?"

"I think the Feds have forgotten it was ever even here. Sort of like the end of that movie, *Raiders of the Lost Ark*. One more box in the warehouse."

Puller glanced back at the Bunker. "When did it shut down?"

"Don't know exactly. My mom told me it was sometime in the sixties."

"And all the workers?"

"Packed up and moved out."

"And the concrete?"

"My daddy said that was something to see when they did it. It's three feet thick."

"Three feet!"

"What my daddy said."

"And nobody in Drake ever talked to these folks, found out what they were doing in that place?"

"From what I heard, the government supplied the workers with most of what they needed. And it was all guys, all of them in their forties and single according to my parents. Of course some would come into town on occasion. My dad said they were real tight-lipped about what they did here."

"If they were in their forties back then, most if not all of them are probably dead by now."

"Guess so."

Puller eyed the Bunker and saw the rusted fencing with barbed wire topper that ran around the facility. In between the structure and the neighborhood was a stand of trees. Next, Puller shifted his gaze to a little boy and girl who were playing in the front yard of one of the houses. The boy was running around in a circle while the girl attempted to catch him. They both fell down in a tangle of arms and legs.

"You have kids?"

Puller turned to see her gazing at him. She had slowed the car to a crawl while she too watched the children.

"No," he replied. "Never married."

"When I was a little girl only thing I wanted to be was a mom."

"So what happened?"

She hit the accelerator. "Life. Life happened."

CHAPTER

31

PULLER'S EYE GAUGED IT to be about fifteen thousand square feet with a central block and two wings emanating from that core. It looked like a Parisian cathedral dropped in the middle of West Virginia. The Trent mansion was on the very top of a hill that apparently held no coal deposits, because the land was still intact. The road up was laid with heavy cobblestone-style pavers. A gate awaited them at the entrance to the formal grounds that were enclosed by a six-foot-high wrought iron fence. There was an armed guard at the gate. He looked like a long-retired cop, Puller thought. Fat and slow. But he could probably still shoot halfway straight.

As Cole slowed the cruiser Puller said, "Gates and guards. Man needs protection?"

"Like I said, coal companies are never popular, least at the places where the coal comes out. I'm sure they're a lot more popular where there aren't any mines or lopped-off mountaintops."

The guard must've been informed of their arrival, because he opened the gates and waved them through.

"Good thing we're not here to kill the guy," said Puller. "The rental cop just made it pretty easy."

"He takes his orders from Trent. Like most folks around here."

"You trying to tell me something?"

She said, "I said most folks, not all. And certainly not me."

Up close the house looked twice as big as it did from a distance. A maid in a domestic's uniform opened the front door. Puller half expected her to curtsey. She was Asian and young, with delicate features and dark hair that was tied back in a neat braid. She escorted them along a hallway of immense proportions. It was wood-paneled with large portraits professionally hung on the walls. For a second Puller thought he was actually in a museum. The floor was tumbled marble in a maze of colors. Cole's cop boots clicked on its surface. Puller's combat boots absorbed all the sound of his footfalls as they were designed to do.

He said to Cole, "I thought you said he was rich. I was expecting a much nicer place than this."

Cole obviously didn't appreciate his humor and didn't answer, keeping her gaze straight ahead. They passed a staircase. Puller's gaze slid up it in time to catch a teenage girl staring back at him from the top of the stairs. Her face was plump, her cheeks crimson. Her hair was a tangled mess of highlighted blonde tresses. An instant later she was gone from his view.

"The Trents have kids?"

"Two. Teenage girl and eleven-year-old boy."

"I take it Mom and Dad aren't exactly ready for Social Security."

"Trent is forty-seven. His wife is thirty-eight."

"I'm glad they're young enough to enjoy their money."

"Oh, they enjoy it."

The maid opened a door and directed them inside. She closed the door behind them. Puller could hear her timid footsteps pitter-pattering down the hall.

The walls were upholstered in a dark green fabric. The floor was cherry wood with a satin finish. Two squares of oriental rugs covered parts of it. The chairs and couches were leather. The window treatments blocked most of the light from outside. The chandelier was bronze, held a dozen bulbs, and looked to weigh a ton. A large table sat in the middle of the room with an enormous flower display in a crystal vase resting on top of it. More paintings were on the wall here. They looked old, original, and expensive.

Everything was tastefully done. It had been a careful eye that had coordinated all of this, thought Puller.

"Have you been here before?"

"A few times. Social occasions. The Trents have a lot of parties."

"So they invite the working class to their soirees?"

Before Cole could respond to this the door opened and they turned toward it.

Roger Trent was six-one and quickly eating himself to obese status. His neck was thick, his chin had a twin, and his expensive suit could not hide the width of his waist. The room was cool and yet he was sweating.

Maybe from the long walk down the hall, thought Puller.

"Hello, Roger," said Cole as she put out a hand for him to shake. Puller shot her a glance that she ignored.

Roger?

Trent snarled, "I'm getting tired of this shit, you know that?"

"Well, death threats are pretty serious," said Cole.

The coal baron glanced up at Puller. "Who the hell are you?"

"This is Special Agent John Puller from the Army CID back in Virginia," answered Cole hastily.

Puller put out his hand. "Nice to meet you, *Roger*." He glanced at Cole in time to see her grimace.

The men shook hands and Puller came away almost believing he'd just held a fish.

"Death threats?" said Puller. "How did they come to you?"

"Phone calls."

"Did you happen to record them?" asked Cole.

Trent gave her a patronizing look. "The recording only works if you *don't* answer the phone." He sat down in a chair but didn't motion for them to do the same.

"We can try and trace them," said Cole.

"I already had my people do that."

"And?"

"Disposable phone calling card."

"Okay. How many threats, when did they come, and what phone number were they called into?"

"Three. All around 10 p.m. the last three nights. All on my cell phone."

Puller asked, "You have caller ID?"

"Of course."

"And you answer calls where you don't recognize the number?"

"I have many business interests outside this area and even in other countries. It's not unusual for me to receive such calls and at odd hours."

"How many folks have your personal cell phone number?" Cole asked.

Trent shrugged. "Impossible to tell. I don't give it out freely, but I've never tried to keep it a secret either."

"What were the contents of the threats?"

"That my time is coming up. That they're going to see that justice is done."

"Those were the exact words? Each time?"

"Well, I don't know if that was it verbatim. But that was the gist," he added impatiently.

"But the call said *they're* going to see that justice is done? Meaning more than one person?" asked Puller.

"That was the word they used."

"Man or woman's voice?"

"I'd say it was a man's."

"Gotten threats before?" asked Puller.

Trent glanced at Cole. "A few."

"Like this? I mean was it the same voice?"

"Those other threats weren't by phone."

"What then?"

Cole cut in. "We investigated those. And they were dealt with."

Puller gazed at her for a few moments before turning back to Trent. "Okay. So why do you think they're threatening you?"

Trent rose and looked at Cole. "Why is this guy here? I thought it was just going to be you."

"We're working a homicide case together."

"I know that. I spoke with Bill Strauss. But what the hell does that have to do with my situation?"

"Well, one of your employees, Molly Bitner, was also murdered."

"Again, I don't see a connection. And if she's dead I doubt she's the one threatening me."

"Did you ever meet her?" asked Puller.

"If I did I don't remember. I'm not even sure what office she worked in. I don't get down to that level of employee."

Puller resisted the urge to knock the man through a wall. "You have another office around here?"

"I have several."

Cole said, "Roger, they were blasting on Sunday night at the operation near where the murders occurred. Why Sunday and why at night? You would've had to get a special permit for that."

He looked at her with incredulity. "How the hell should I know? I don't schedule the blasting. I pay other people to handle that.

"Right. Okay. And who would that be?"

"Strauss should know."

Puller said, "Then I guess we'll talk to Strauss."

Trent glared at Cole. "I just want you to deal with my situation, okay?"

"I will look into it, Roger," she said sharply. "But in case you haven't noticed, I'm dealing with a bunch of murders."

He ignored this. "I'm sick of people targeting me just because I've been incredibly successful. It's pure jealousy and I'm tired of it. Hell, I'm the only reason Drake is still around. I'm the only one who creates any jobs here. These losers should be kissing my ass."

Puller said, "Yeah, I'm sure your life is very hard, Mr. Trent."

Trent's features turned dark. "You obviously don't have what it takes to build a fortune. The vast majority of people don't. You have a small number of haves and the rest have-nots. And the have-nots think everything should be given to them without working for it."

Puller said, "Yes, sir. There are a whole bunch of lazy have-nots in the Middle East right now just living the good life off your tax-payer dollars."

Trent's face reddened. "I didn't mean that, of course. I'm a big supporter of our troops."

"Yes, sir."

"Now, if you'll excuse me, I have a flight to catch."

"Flying out of Charleston?" asked Puller. "Bit of a hike from here."

"I have my own jet."

"Right."

Trent walked out, slamming the door behind him.

Puller looked at Cole. "Is he always so cheery to be around?"

"He is what he is."

"Earlier death threats? You checked them out? Did you find who did it?"

"That investigation is closed. And he's right, you really aren't part of this one."

"You asked me to come."

"I shouldn't have."

"Are you that scared of the guy?"

"Don't go there, Puller," she snapped.

The door opened.

It wasn't the maid. It wasn't Roger Trent. It wasn't the teenage girl Puller had spotted earlier. The woman was in her thirties. She was petite, dark-haired, with lovely, delicate features that seemed too perfect to actually be genuine. Her dress was of simple design but the material was obviously costly. She carried herself in a confident manner and her eyes seemed to take everything in.

Puller had seen a pair of eyes like that before.

He looked at Cole and then gazed back at the woman. And then he glanced back at Cole.

Cole said, "How are you, Jean?"

Jean Trent said, "I'm wonderful. How are you, little sister?"

CHAPTER

32

PULLER LOOKED AT JEAN TRENT and then drew his gaze back to Sam Cole. They weren't twins. They really weren't that close in looks. But still, on closer examination, it was evident they were related.

He said, "So Sam's your little sister?"

Trent nodded. "By two years and two days."

Cole said, "But people always think she's the younger one."

"I have regular massages and my own trainer and chef. You go on stakeouts and high-speed chases and eat crap, Sam. It takes its toll."

"I guess it does." Cole added, "So more death threats?"

"What he says."

"You don't seem too concerned," observed Puller.

"Roger travels with a bodyguard. We have more than adequate protection here. He's licensed to carry a concealed weapon and he does. People around here don't like him. But no one has ever actually attacked him."

"If you say so." Puller glanced back at Cole. "You ready to roll?"

"Let's go."

As she passed by her sister, Trent said, "Why don't you come for dinner tonight?" She glanced at Puller. "And why don't you come along too?"

"Why?" asked Cole.

"Roger's going to be out of town and your niece has been asking about you."

Cole looked a bit guilty at this last comment, thought Puller.

Her sister must've noted this too. "Say about eight-thirty? We eat late here."

"Okay," said Cole.

"If you get fancy for dinner, I didn't bring my dress blues," said Puller.

"We're actually pretty casual." She looked at her sister. "Where are you off to now?"

"To see some dead bodies get cut up."

"Have fun."

They walked back to Cole's cruiser.

"How come you neglected to tell me about the family connection?" asked Puller.

"Was it relevant?"

"Who knows what's relevant until it is or isn't?"

"Well, now you know."

"He's about ten years older than her. Second wife?"

"No. He just married late and she married early. Her kids are his kids."

"She mentioned your niece. I saw a teenager on the stairs going in."

"Meghan. She's fourteen. Awkward age for a girl."

"And you said they have an eleven-year-old son too?"

"Roger Jr. He's away."

"Away where?"

"Military academy."

"Trent didn't strike me as the military type."

"He's not. He's far more into private gain than public service. But his son has a problem with discipline and I guess my sister didn't want to deal with it. So away he went to some place in Pennsylvania where they whip you into shape and make you say 'sir.'"

"Not so bad. Discipline is a pretty good asset for life."

"Maybe. But I think they gave up on him too early. He's only a kid. And discipline starts at home. You ship a kid off at that age he probably thinks you don't give a crap about him."

"And do they? Give a crap about him?"

"Not my place to know, really."

"Not close with your rich relations?"

"Who really knows anybody?"

That's more true than not, thought Puller. He said. "So earlier death threats?"

She whipped around, hands on hips. "I told you they were investigated and the case closed."

"I know that's what you told me."

"So why do you keep bringing it up?"

"Because I want to know more than what you've told me. That's generally why I ask questions."

"Well, I don't feel like elaborating."

"Where does your brother live?"

"In Drake."

"What does he do?"

"Generally as little as possible. Is this an interrogation?"

"I'm just trying to understand the playing field here, nothing more. If I offended you, I'm sorry."

His frank manner defused her anger.

"Randy's the youngest. Just turned thirty and sort of lost his way in life. We're hoping he finds it again. Real soon."

"I take it no one sent him away to a military academy."

"Maybe someone should have."

They climbed into the cruiser.

Puller clicked his seat belt. "Any hits on that guy from your BOLO?"

"None. Something tells me he left Drake a long time ago."

She clipped her seat belt across her and fired up the engine. "What'd you do with the laptop and briefcase?" she asked.

"On their way to USACIL via military courier."

"Good place?"

"Best place. You can tell right from the moment you walk in when you see it on the floor."

"See what?"

"The lab's logo. Bought it back in the fifties from some guy for a buck."

"What is it?"

"Detective Mickey Mouse. The guy who sold it was named Walt Disney."

"A crime lab's logo is a cartoon character?"

"When you're that good, who cares what your logo is?"

"If you say so."

They left the Trent mansion behind and headed back to the real world.

CHAPTER

33

Dr. Walter Kellerman had once been a far heavier man but had dropped a lot of weight, noted Puller, when they arrived for the autopsies. He deduced this from his sagging facial skin and his belt having four additional holes cut in the leather to accommodate his shrinking waist.

The bodies had been transported from the funeral home to Kellerman's surgery. It was in a two-room brick building behind his office, which clearly used to be someone's home and was located about a mile from the downtown area. Portable refrigeration beds had been brought in to hold the bodies.

"Is the man sick or eating better?" Puller asked in a low voice to Cole as they slipped on surgical gowns and gloves.

"Little of both. He's walking more, cutting out the red meat, and eating less. They took out his gallbladder and left kidney about a year ago. He knows if he wants to see his seventies he needs to get it together."

"You attended autopsies before?" asked Puller.

"More than I wanted to," she replied.

"Lindemann said the last murder you had was ten years ago."

"They do autopsies for other reasons. Accidents mostly. In coal mining country you have quite a few of those. And car accidents. Have quite a few of those too."

"Okay."

"And if you're wondering whether I'm going to start puking when he starts cutting, the answer is no."

Kellerman had a trim white beard, blue eyes, little hair on his head, and a friendly manner. When he was introduced to Puller he said, "I pulled one stint in the Air Force. Two years in Vietnam, but the GI Bill helped pay for college and I went on and got my medical degree."

"See, Uncle Sam can do things right," said Puller.

"I never regretted it. Makes you stronger."

"If you survive it," said Cole.

Puller noted the body on the steel table with the sheet over it. "Who's first?"

"Colonel Reynolds." Kellerman glanced at the portable cold beds. "I have two trained assistants helping, but it's still going to be a long day."

"We're just here to observe and ask questions," said Cole.

"You're very welcome to do both. I looked over the bodies this morning. An interesting mixture of wounds. Shotgun, small-caliber handgun, strangulation, and blunt force trauma."

"Any idea what was used to kill the teenagers?" asked Puller.

"Probably a hand."

"How can you be sure of that?" asked Cole.

"I'm not sure. He asked if I had an idea. And that's it."

"But why a hand?"

"A bat, metal tool, or other foreign object would have almost certainly left some sort of residue or telltale mark on the skin. Did one post where you could make out the logo of a Louisville Slugger bat on the deceased's chest. But the hand leaves a distinctive mark too. And I found trace embedded in the neck of the boy."

"What was it?" asked Puller.

"Looks to be a bit of black leather."

"Meaning they wore gloves."

"How I see it, yes."

"It's not easy to hit the medulla just right to kill someone," noted Puller. "It's only about three inches long."

"I'd say you were looking for someone with special training. Maybe martial arts."

"Or military," suggested Cole.

"Right. Or military," agreed Kellerman.

He slid down his clear face mask, lifted the sheet from the dead colonel, and readied his instruments.

"Shall we?"

Even with the two assistants' help the seven bodies took many hours to properly autopsy. Puller had boxed up quite a bit of the evidence in special containers, carefully marked, that he would ship down to USACIL. He would include with the packages specific instructions for the lab at Fort Gillem when they processed the evidence. And he would follow up those instructions with an email and a phone call.

Kellerman had left his assistants to sew up the Y-incisions, changed his clothes, and gone home. Cole and Puller walked outside. Puller put the boxes into Cole's car. He had also filled up his recorder with notes on the posts and Cole had taken extensive handwritten notes as well. Yet there was nothing too remarkable revealed by the process.

Shotgun wadding was taken from Reynolds's head and would be compared to find the gauge of gun used. Some of the white material found embedded in his face had not been wadding. Kellerman had theorized it was a blindfold they had made the colonel wear.

"Probably why he didn't try to defend himself or throw up his hands," said Puller.

"He never saw it coming," added Cole.

Stacey Reynolds's torso had been filled with shotgun pellets. The two kids had died from strikes to their necks as they had speculated. Eric Treadwell and Molly Bitner had been killed by .22 caliber shots into their brains. The bullets had come out in reasonable shape and now all they needed was a gun to match them to.

Wellman had been struck on the head hard enough to cause unconsciousness. His life had not been ended by a broken neck. That required a considerable drop that the low ceiling in the basement could not provide. Instead, Wellman had suffered a slow asphyxiation.

Cole and Puller leaned against her car. She slid out a cigarette and lit up.

"Don't look at me like that, Puller," she said. "I just sat through seven bodies being cut up. It's stressful."

"They didn't leave much behind," he said.

"You have any ideas?"

"None that work all the way through right now."

She checked her watch. "Dinner at my sister's."

"Why does she want me there?"

"I don't know, other than you're younger, taller, and fitter than her husband."

"So you're saying she cheats on him?"

"I'm not saying anything, because I don't know. Roger's gone a lot."

"She didn't seem overly concerned about the death threats."

"Roger is not a popular guy. I guess you get desensitized to it."

"She might be, but he clearly isn't. He was both pissed and scared."

"Well, he's the target, not her."

"True."

"I can drop you off at your car and then pick you up at the motel. Give us both time to shower and change. I need to scrub hard to get the smell of death off me."

"I don't think anyone can scrub that hard."

"I'm sure as hell going to try."

CHAPTER

34

PULLER DROVE straight to the post office, which was a few minutes away from Annie's Motel. He arrived right before it closed for the day. He mailed off the boxes via priority shipping to Atlanta and then focused on the young woman behind the counter, who gazed up at him expectantly.

He flashed his cred pack to her. "I'm with the Army's Criminal Investigation Division."

"I know you are," she said back.

"How's that?" he asked.

"Small town. And you're too big to miss."

"I need to find out about a delivery."

"What delivery?"

He explained about the certified mail package Howard Reed had delivered on Monday to the Reynoldses but in care of the Halversons' address.

She nodded. "Howard mentioned that to me this morning when he came in to get his delivery load."

"It's really important that we find out where the package came from."

The young woman gazed behind her. "I really should get my supervisor involved with this."

"Okay."

"But he's gone for the day."

Puller put his big hands on the counter. "What's your name?"

"Sandy. Sandy Dreidel."

"Okay, Sandy, let me lay it out for you. This delivery might be very important in finding out who killed those people. The longer we wait the farther away they get. All I need is the name and address of who sent the package, that's all."

"I understand that. But we have policies and procedures."

Puller suddenly grinned. "I understand that. I'm in the Army. For every policy the post office has, the Army has ten, guaranteed."

Sandy smiled back. "Sure thing. I bet you're right."

"But there is a way to find out the information?"

"Well, yes. We have records."

"Probably just a few clicks of that computer there will tell you."

Sandy looked embarrassed. "Well, we don't have everything in computers just yet. But we have log books in the back."

Puller held out his notebook and a pen. "If you could take a couple of minutes and just write the name and address down here, that could really help us find whoever killed all those people."

Sandy hesitated, glanced over Puller's shoulder and through the window overlooking the street, and then took the items from him.

It took her five minutes, but she returned with the notebook and pen and handed them to Puller. He glanced down at what she'd written and then looked up.

"This is a big help, Sandy. I really appreciate it."

"But you won't tell anybody I did it," she said worriedly.

"No one will ever find out from me."

Back at his motel room, Puller studied the name and address that Sandy had written down for him.

The company name he didn't recognize. The address was Ohio. He did a Google search on his laptop and pulled up the company's home page. When he saw what the firm did he wondered if he finally had a break in this case. If he did, it wasn't that obvious. He phoned the number on the home page but only received a recorded response. The company was closed and would reopen tomorrow morning at nine.

Stymied for the moment, Puller called the hospital where the motel owner Louisa had been taken. He couldn't find anyone who would tell him her condition, but he did purchase a vase of flowers from the hospital gift shop, paying for it with his credit card. On the card he had them write, "Cat is fine. Hope you are too. Your good egg, Puller."

He put the phone down, stripped off his clothes, and stepped in the shower. The Army taught you to wash fast and dress faster, so he was dry and clothed five minutes later.

He was just sliding his M11 into the front holster when he saw it. Someone had slipped a piece of paper under the door to his room.

He immediately checked the window next to the door. He could see no one. The little courtyard was empty of both cars and people. He stripped the pillowcase off one of the bed pillows, knelt down, and used the pillowcase to pick up the paper.

He turned it over. The writing was laser print. The message was straightforward.

I know things you need to know.

There was an address listed.

And then there was one more word printed.

Now.

Puller used the map app on his phone to find the location. From where he was it was a fifteen-minute ride by car. That would probably put him even more in the middle of nowhere than he already was.

Perfect place for an ambush.

Long-range shot.

Or shotgun at close range.

Or ten guys on one. Maybe Dickie and his big friend with the broken nose had decided to get even and would be bringing necessary reinforcements this time.

Puller looked down at his phone. He could call Cole and fill her in. He probably should. He hit the numbers. The phone rang. Went to voice mail. She was probably still in the shower scrubbing death off her.

He left a message telling her about this latest development. He gave her the address he'd been given and then clicked off.

He made one more call, to his friend Kristen Craig at USACIL.

He gave the lady a heads-up on what he was sending and what results he was hoping for from the lab.

"How're things coming on the laptop and the briefcase?" he asked her. "Did you get read into it by DIA?"

"We did," she answered. "But I have to tell you, I'm disappointed so far."

"Why?"

"His briefcase had an old sandwich, a few private-sector business cards, and a couple of magazines. The only report in there wasn't even classified."

"And the laptop?"

"A little porn and a whole lot of nothing else. I mean, he had work stuff on there, but nothing that would have caused the collapse of Western civilization as we know it if the bad guys got hold of it."

"DIA know this?"

"Of course. They're DIA. They had someone come to the lab."

"Porn, huh?"

"We find that on military laptops all the time, you know that. And this stuff wasn't hardcore. Just crap you can watch in your hotel room and not see the title on the bill the next morning. Barely titillating with awful production values. But then I'm not a guy."

"Women have far higher standards. So why all the sirens going off from SecArm?"

"Hey, I'm just a tech; you're the investigator," she said in a playful tone.

He clicked off, pondered this; glanced down at the note, pondered that.

He waited for Cole to call him back. She didn't.

He locked the motel room door on his way out.

He fired up the Malibu, popped the address he'd been given into his GPS, and drove off.

CHAPTER

35

ONE RUSTED, leaning mailbox.

Puller passed by the mailbox and the dirt road that it fronted. Woods on both sides.

He was surprised a place like this had an address that could be found on his GPS. Big Brother really did have all the info.

He parked a quarter of a mile down, got out, and entered the woods. He worked his way back west. He eyed the small house from behind a stand of trees. In the distance he could hear the distinct sound of a rattlesnake warning someone of its presence.

Puller didn't move. He just squatted there, eyeing the place.

There was an old truck out front. The guts of another truck rested on the far side of the house. There appeared to be a garage behind the house. Its single door was closed. The place didn't look like it had been recently inhabited. It wasn't dark enough yet for lights to have to be on in the house, though the surrounding woods threw everything into a jumble of shadows.

No sounds. No people.

He continued to squat, continued to contemplate what to do.

It was apparent that someone who lived this far away from the murders probably had not seen anything. But they might know something. Like the note had said.

So the analysis came down to a possible lead or someone looking to do him harm. Either revenge from Dickie and company, or a counterattack from someone looking to derail his investigation.

He had put his phone on vibrate. It did.

He looked at the screen, answered it in a low voice.

"Where are you, Puller?" Cole asked.

"At the address. In the woods to the east of the house. Where are you?"

"West of it in the woods."

"Great minds. See anything? I've got zip over here."

"No."

"Do you know who lives in the place?"

"No."

"There wasn't a name on the mailbox."

"What do you want to do?"

"Find out why we're here."

"How do you want to do this?"

"How about we keep it simple. I come in from the east and you come in from the west. Stop at the tree line and check back in."

He put his phone away and moved forward. His M11 was out and pointing the way. He assumed Cole's Cobra was doing the same to the west.

A minute later his phone vibrated.

"In place," Cole said. "What now?"

Puller didn't respond right away. He was taking in what he was looking at grid by grid. The Taliban and al-Qaeda had been very clever about leading American soldiers into traps. They could find ways to make something actually very deadly look entirely innocuous. Children, women, pets.

"Puller?"

"Give me a minute."

He took a few steps forward. He called out. "Hello? Anybody in there?"

No answer. He hadn't really expected one.

He took two more steps forward until he was clear of the tree line. But he kept the old truck between him and the house.

He spoke into his phone. "Can you see me?"

"Yes. But just barely."

"See anything on your side?"

"No. I don't think this place is lived in. Hell, it looks ready to *fall* in."

"Ever been down this way?"

"Only going somewhere else. Never even noticed this road before. What do you think is going on?"

"Stay put. I'm going to try something."

He slipped the phone into his pocket and edged forward until he had a sightline on the front porch. He looked up and then down, side to side. Then he looked down again. From his jacket pocket he pulled a scope that he'd taken from his rucksack.

He looked through it, adjusting the optics until he had a clear look at the front porch. He looked up, down, side to side. And then he came back to the down part.

He slipped out his phone, wedged it against his ear. "Sit tight and keep down."

"What do you see? What are you going to do?"

"You'll hear it loud and clear in about five seconds if it is what I think it is."

"Puller—"

But he'd already put the phone away.

He attached the scope to the top of his M11.

He gave one more look around. "Hello, it's John Puller. You asked me to come here. I'd like to talk."

He waited five more seconds. Did they think he was just going to walk right up to the front door?

He lifted his gun and took aim through the scope. His muzzle was pointed at the front-porch floorboards.

He fired three times in rapid succession. Pieces of the decking shot into the air. He heard the ping of metal on metal.

That could only mean one thing. He'd been right. He crouched down.

The front door blew open. The shotgun blast ripped the old fragile wood cleanly. Anyone standing in front of it would have been obliterated.

Anyone being me, thought Puller.

"Jesus!"

He looked to his left and saw Cole staring first at him, then at the large hole in the front door, and then back at him.

"How'd you know it was booby-trapped?" she called out.

"New floorboards in front of the door. They put the pressure plate under it, ran a wire inside the house, and attached it to the trigger on the shotgun that they mounted on something at gut level. Heard my rounds impact the plate." He moved away from the truck. "Still can't figure why they thought I would just mosey up to the door and get my head blown off."

"I'm just glad you're smarter than they give you credit for."

She moved forward too.

Puller saw it and launched. He hit Cole right in the gut, lifting her off the ground. They tumbled back toward the tree line two seconds before the truck detonated. A front wheel landed within six inches of them. Debris crashed down around them. Puller covered Cole with his body. A long strip of rubber landed across the back of his legs. It stung, but did no permanent damage. He would have a welt there, but that was all.

As the flames leapt over the truck, Puller knew he had a second problem. He grabbed Cole by the arm, lifted her over his shoulder, and ran into the woods. A few seconds later, the gas tank exploded, sending a second wave of wreckage sailing in all directions.

Puller set Cole down behind a tree and knelt in the dirt well away from the remains of the truck. He let the debris rain down safely away from them and then peered out from the shield of the tree.

"How did you know?" gasped Cole as she sat up.

"Trip wire stretched between two bushes."

"Someone obviously wanted you dead. Rigged truck, rigged door. One misses, the other one gets you." She looked around and shivered. And it wasn't just because the night air was cooler. "My ears are ringing like a church bell."

Puller wasn't looking at her. He was staring at the destroyed truck.

"You okay, Puller? Did you get hit?"

He shook his head.

"What then?"

"I should've seen that wire long before you hit it."

"But you saw it in time."

He looked over at her. "That's not good enough."

"I need to call a team in to investigate this," she said. "And the fire department. If these woods catch on fire, it'll be a nightmare trying to get under control."

"There's a spool of hose up near the house. If there's still water left in the well, I'll douse the flames."

"What if there're more booby-traps?"

"If I miss the triggers again I deserve what I get."

"Puller, you didn't miss anything."

He ignored this. "Got any bomb specialists on board?"

"Lan Monroe knows something about it. But there's a retired ATF agent who lives outside of town. I can deputize him."

"I'd do it. Need as much expertise as possible on this one."

While Cole called it in, Puller got the hose and sprayed down the wreckage and the flames. Within ten minutes two deputies showed up along with two fire engines. Lan Monroe called and said he was on his way. Cole reached the former ATF agent and arranged for him to come as well.

While the firemen took care of the remaining patches of fire and wetted down the truck remains, Puller got the attention of the deputies and pointed to the house. "I wouldn't go near that sucker right now. What I'd do is find a motorized robot and send it in before anyone with a heartbeat gets close."

Cole said, "State police has one of those. I'll make the call."

After she did that Puller said, "Well, I think we have a dinner to get to."

"You still want to go?"

"Yeah, I do."

"You have any clean clothes in your car?"

"Always."

"Then we can stop by my place and shower. And I can change too. My place is closer to the Trents' than your motel."

They walked back to their rides while the investigation team stood as far away from the house and detonated truck as possible.

When they reached the road, Sheriff Pat Lindemann was leaning against the passenger door of his Ford. He dabbed his face with a handkerchief and spit on the dirt.

"Exciting times in Drake," he said as they approached.

"Too exciting," said Cole.

"You saved me having to get a new sergeant, Puller. I owe you for that."

"I almost didn't."

"What counts is what happened," said Lindemann. He eyed the drive back through the woods. "You're making somebody uncomfortable. They left you the note at your motel?"

"Slid it under the door when I was taking a shower."

"So they're watching you?"

"It appears to be."

"You two have any idea what in the hell is going on here?"

"Not yet," said Cole. "But they just made it personal. So every waking moment of my life is going to be devoted to this, Sheriff."

He nodded, spat again. "Allergies. Never had 'em before." He eyed Puller. "You want some protection from our department?"

"No, I'm good."

"Suit yourself. Well, I best get on. The missus is holding supper for me."

"You take care, Sheriff," said Cole.

After he drove away Puller said, "You angling for the job? He already seems to have checked out."

"He's a good cop. But he's been doing this over thirty years and I don't think he ever expected something like this on the tail end of his career."

As she opened her car door Cole said, "I found out what you did with Louisa over at Annie's Motel. That was really good of you."

"She needed help, so I helped. No big deal. How is she?"

"I don't know. I haven't had a chance to call the hospital. But she'd be dead for sure without you."

"Do you know her?"

"Everyone knows Louisa. Salt of the earth."

"It's nice to help the salts of the earth," replied Puller quietly. "They usually get the shaft."

She put a hand on his shoulder. "I want you to stop beating yourself up about that trip wire, Puller."

"If I'd done that overseas my entire squad would be dead."

"But we're not dead."

"Right," he said dully.

Puller got in his car and followed her out.

CHAPTER

36

AFTER A TWENTY-FIVE-MINUTE RIDE Cole turned down a street in a neighborhood of older, well-kept homes with wide front porches and nice lawns. She pulled into the driveway of a saltbox that had gray shingle siding, a white picket fence, and colorful landscaping. It looked more New England than West Virginia.

He climbed out of his car, got his clean clothes from the trunk, and joined her at the front door.

"Nice place. How long have you lived here?"

"I grew up here."

"Your parents' place?"

"I bought it after they died."

"They died at the same time?"

"That's right."

She did not appear willing to supplement this information.

Puller said, "Looks like it belongs on the rocky Maine coast, though."

"I know. That's why I like it so much."

"You a saltwater girl?"

"Maybe I want to be."

He looked around at the other homes in the neighborhood. "Yours sort of stands out. How come?"

"My dad was in the Navy for a while. Saw the world as a young man. Loved the water. He built this place himself."

Puller touched the sturdy front porch support post. "Handy guy. So how come he came back here if he was an ocean guy?"

"He's from West Virginia. He came back home. I have a few calls to make. You can take the bathroom upstairs. Towels and everything else you need should be in there."

"Thanks."

He found the bathroom, started the shower, stripped off his clothes, and stepped under the water. Five minutes later he was dry, dressed, and out of the bathroom. He bumped into Cole, who was coming down the hall dressed in a long terrycloth robe.

"Good God, you're already done?" she said, staring up at him. In her bare feet he was more than a foot taller than she was.

"You got a thousand guys wanting to take a shower, you can't linger. Sort of built into my psyche now."

She said, "I'm not as fast as you, but I won't be long."

"You want to use this one since I'm done?"

"No, I've got all my stuff downstairs."

"But isn't your bedroom up here?"

She snapped, "You have no need to know where my bedroom is, Puller."

He took a step away from her and looked over her shoulder. "Okay. Mind if I get some water? Getting blown up makes you thirsty."

"Bottles in the fridge in the kitchen."

"Tap's okay with me."

"Not our tap. Use the bottled stuff."

Downstairs he split off to go to the kitchen while she went into the bathroom. He heard the water come on, envisioned her stepping into the shower. And then he stopped thinking about that at all. Business, at least his business, never mixed well with anything else.

The kitchen looked like the galley on a ship; functional, nice use of space, neat as a pin. Navy Dad had obviously carried this theme throughout the house.

Both parents had died at the same time. Must've been an accident, he thought. But apparently Cole did not want to elaborate. And it was none of his business anyway.

He wrenched open the fridge and pulled out a bottle of Deer Park. While he drank it down he looked out onto the backyard.

The grass was cut, the flowers watered. There was a small stone fountain with trickling water. Farther back there was a white garden swing, a fire pit, and a grill under a wooden arbor that was draped with purple-colored vines.

It was all peaceful and soothing and did not match in any way the place he thought Sam Cole would live in. Why, he wasn't sure. He didn't really know the woman.

He stepped out onto the back porch and drank some more of his water.

He closed his eyes and thought back to the trip wire. He hadn't seen it. Not until Cole had almost hit it. And then her shin had grazed it, just enough. By all rights they should have been dead. There had been a delay between the trigger and the detonation. Puller knew why.

The bomber's relay had been poorly constructed. Or maybe he'd just assumed that you tripped over the wire, you'd fall. Couple of seconds of confusion. You scramble back up. Then boom, your head's gone.

In that regard Puller had saved his life and Cole's. But it hadn't been good enough. Not nearly good enough.

I'm not what I was.

I'm not close to what I was.

Not being over there, your senses get dulled. You're a step slower.

He had known the day would come when that would be the case. He'd had no idea, however, how vulnerable it would make him feel. The only solution, really, was to go back over to the Middle East and try to survive.

And I don't really want to do that. Not after six combat tours, getting shot and blown up and nearly dying more times than I can remember.

Does that make me a coward?

A few minutes later he was sitting out on the garden swing when she came outside. Before she'd been dressed in slacks and a blouse with flats. Now Cole had on a light blue sundress with a scalloped front and white sandals with an inch heel bump. He liked the dress better than the slacks.

She joined him on the swing and whisked the skirt across her legs as she crossed them. Her hair was still damp and she smelled of jasmine and lilac. She sat back and closed her eyes.

"Shouldn't we get going?" said Puller.

"I called Jean, told her we'd be a little late." She rubbed her temples.

"Did you tell her why?"

She looked at him. "No. I didn't see a good reason to do so."

"I checked on the certified delivery package at the post office."

She glanced at him. "How?"

"Just asked some questions."

"Didn't want to wait on me?"

"Speed sometimes is crucial. And the post office is only three minutes away from the motel."

He smiled and she smirked in return. "So tell me what you found out."

"It was a firm that does soil testing."

"Why would the Reynoldses be testing soil?"

"I wish I knew."

"And if the dog didn't eat the package, that means whoever killed Larry Wellman came back and took it. But, again, how would they even know it was there?"

Puller finished his water and screwed the cap back on. "Like I said, they might have deduced it the same way we did. They realized the mailman found the bodies. Why was that, unless he had a delivery to make at the house that required a signature? That would be the only reason for him to have come into the house. So what was in the package? They came back to find out. Didn't know what it was, but couldn't take a chance."

"But how would they know we hadn't found it?"

Puller said, "Maybe they're getting some inside info."

"I can't believe I've got someone on my police force that's helping the other side."

"I'm not saying it's a fact. I'm just saying you have to consider it."

"And the bombing?"

"I actually take that as a good sign."

"Meaning you're making someone nervous, like the sheriff said?"

"Yes."

"*If* it is connected to the murders. You ticked Dickie and his big buddy off."

"You think they'd retaliate by trying to blow me up?"

"No. You're probably right." She closed her eyes again and rested her head against the back of the swing. She rubbed her temples again and grimaced.

"I didn't even ask if you were okay," he said in a low voice. "I hit you pretty hard. *Are* you okay? No concussion or anything?"

"I'm fine. You knocked the wind out of me, but it was better than the alternative." She opened her eyes and let her fingers graze his forearm and then remain there. "And I neglected to thank you."

"The light was poor. Usually you can see the sunlight glinting off it. That's why the Taliban and al-Qaeda favored pressure plates and other triggers that were belowground."

"I didn't see it at all." She leaned over and pecked him on the cheek. "Thank you for saving my life, Puller."

He turned to look at her. He thought that he saw a tear glistening in her right eye, but she looked away before he could be sure.

"You're welcome."

She removed her hand from his arm and rose.

"We better get going. I can drive. You leave your ride here. We'll take my truck. Tired of the police wheels right now."

He let her walk a bit away from him before she turned back. With the sunset behind her, Sam Cole looked radiant in her dress. Puller took a moment to admire the view.

"Are you coming?"

He rose.

"I'm coming."

CHAPTER

37

JEAN TRENT WAS DRESSED in khaki slacks, red sandals, and a matching red sleeveless blouse. She was seated in the sunroom on the western side of the house where there was no sun left to shine. She already had a cocktail in hand and asked Puller and her sister what they cared for.

Puller opted for a beer, Cole a ginger ale.

"Wow," said Jean. "You two look like trouble for sure."

"Sorry we're late," said Cole. "We got detained over a case."

"No worries. It allowed me time to have another martini." She glanced at Puller. "You should try one."

Puller ignored that comment and said, "Have you heard from your husband? Did he get to where he was going?"

"He rarely calls me from the road. I'm not even sure when he's going to be back."

"Where's Meghan?" asked Cole.

"Swimming laps in the pool."

"This late?" asked Cole.

"She's trying to work off her stomach. I tell her it's all part of growing up, just baby fat, but the other girls call her names and she hates it."

"I would too," said Cole.

"Roger is large-boned and prone to weight problems. We never had that issue in our family," Jean added, looking over at Puller, who perched on a small settee covered in green-and-purple vine fabric. "Now, if you're any indication, height runs in your family."

"It does," he said.

"Father or mother?"

"Father."

"And your mother?" asked Jean.

Puller didn't answer. He turned away from her and looked around the room.

Jean looked at his waistband. "Do you have to carry a gun to dinner?"

"Regulation. Have to carry it with me always."

Cole said, "Will Meghan be joining us for dinner?"

"Doubtful. She's also starving herself."

"Not good, sis. Young girls are prone to eating disorders."

"I've talked to her until I'm blue in the face. I've had her seen by specialists. They wanted to put her on all these pills, but I put my foot down. We hope it's just a phase that she'll grow out of."

Cole did not look convinced of this. "So it's just the three of us for dinner, then?"

"Probably," Jean said.

"Well, are we or aren't we?"

"I can't definitively answer that right now."

"Great," Cole said disgustedly. "Did I tell you I have enough unanswered questions in my day job? I'm going to see my niece."

"I didn't see a pool in the yard when we were driving up," said Puller.

"It's an indoor pool," said Jean. "We're not sun worshippers here."

"And coal dust might turn the pool water black," said Cole.

Her sister turned to her. "That is complete and total bullshit and you know it."

"Do I?"

The maid arrived with their drinks and Cole took her ginger ale and handed the beer to Puller. She said, "Okay, I'm going. You two can chat about me behind my back."

She left and Jean turned to Puller and clinked her glass against his bottle. "She's a little intense for my taste."

"She's a cop. She has to be intense. And she's a woman, so she has to be even more intense to be accepted."

"If you say so."

"You two are pretty different. Not in looks, but in every other way."

"I wouldn't disagree with that. So why were you two really late? You're not sleeping with her already, are you?"

"Already?" he said in surprise. "She certainly doesn't strike me as the type to sleep around."

"I didn't mean that. And she's not. She's attractive and unattached and you're attractive and I don't see a wedding band on that big hand of yours."

"That doesn't explain the 'already' comment."

"Well, I think my little sister is getting a little desperate."

Puller leaned back and took a drink of his beer. "No, we weren't sleeping together. We were getting blown up together."

She sat up straighter. "Excuse me?"

"Someone booby-trapped a truck at a house we were at. Came a few seconds away from not joining you for dinner tonight or any other night."

Jean put down her glass and stared at him. "You're joking."

"I don't joke about almost getting killed."

"Why didn't Sam mention it?"

"I don't know. She's your sister. You obviously know her a lot better than I do."

She picked her glass back up but didn't take a drink. She stared down at the olives. "I wish she had never become a cop."

"Why?"

"It's dangerous."

"Lots of things are dangerous."

"You know what I mean," she replied in a sharp tone.

"She's a public servant, risking her life to keep the peace. To keep the good citizens of Drake safe. I admire her."

"And you're a soldier, right? A public servant?"

"That comes with the job description, yes."

"Iraq and Afghanistan?"

"Both."

"A young man I had a crush on in high school, Ricky Daniels, joined the Army right after he graduated. He died in the first Gulf War. He was only nineteen."

"If he had come back would you have married Roger Trent?"

She swallowed the rest of her martini. "I see no reason why that's any of your damn business."

"You're absolutely right. Just making small talk until your sister comes back."

"Well, don't trouble yourself. About the small talk. I'm perfectly fine with my own company."

"So why did you want me to come tonight?"

"I don't know, actually. It just struck me as a good idea at the time. I'm an impulsive person."

"Really? You don't strike me as such."

"Well, I am."

"So tell me about the earlier death threats your husband got."

"Why? More small talk? I told you it wasn't necessary."

"No, I'm wearing my investigator hat now."

"It was stupid. Nothing to it."

"Death threats are rarely stupid with nothing to them."

"Well, these were."

"Do you think the same person is making them again then? And should your husband not be worried? Because it's clear he is."

Jean didn't look as confident now. Her hand shook some as she set her glass down. "I'm not sure I'm the best person to answer that."

"You didn't seem all that concerned about it this afternoon."

"My husband is not Mr. Popular. Lots of people hate him."

"Any you know personally?"

"Yes."

"And yet you married him."

She looked at him darkly. "That's right, I did. So what? And he wasn't rich back when I did. He was still struggling to build his business. So I didn't do it for the money."

"Not saying he was. And not saying you did."

"But you were thinking it."

"I'm sure he has lots of other appealing qualities."

"He does, actually."

"Good to know."

"I don't like your attitude."

"I don't have an attitude. I'm just trying to go with the flow."

"Try harder."

CHAPTER

38

COLE WALKED BACK into the room. "Well, Meghan is far more interested in burning off fat than talking to her aunt." She stopped speaking when she saw her sister scowling at Puller.

"Everything okay?" she said, glancing at him.

He said, "Everything's just fine."

The door opened again.

"Randy?" exclaimed Cole.

Randy Cole had cleaned himself up since Puller had seen him last. He had on freshly laundered jeans, a black T-shirt, and loafers. His hair was neatly combed and he'd shaved.

Sam Cole seemed genuinely surprised but pleased.

Jean looked stunned but not unhappy.

Randy came forward and Cole hugged him. "How are you doing, stranger?" she said in a light tone. Puller assumed she was trying to defuse any possibility of tension.

"I'm doing," said Randy. He looked over at Puller. "Seen you at Annie's."

"Yes, you did."

"You the Army guy everybody in town's been talking about?"

"Guess I am."

"I wanted to join up."

"Why didn't you?" asked Puller.

"Failed the physical. Eyes not up to snuff and something in my chest. Probably from breathing all this fresh air my whole life."

Jean said, "Let's head in to dinner."

The dining room was large, paneled in zebra wood with enough moldings, cornices, and medallions to qualify for palace status. They occupied one end of an antique Sheraton table that was long enough to require three pedestals for support.

Randy rubbed his hand over the highly polished wood. "Damn, coal sure pays good, big sister."

"You've never been here before?" asked Puller. He was sitting next to Randy and had noted him looking around in wide-eyed astonishment at the opulent surroundings.

Jean said quickly, "Not for lack of asking. That was why I was surprised to see you tonight. You never came before when I invited you."

Puller glanced at Randy. The Trents had been married all these years and Randy had not come to their house? Then a possible answer struck him.

"How long have you lived in this house?" he asked Jean.

She kept her gaze on her brother. "Five years. Took that long to build the place. Added a lot of workers to the job rolls, I can tell you that."

"Yeah," said Randy. "Hey, sis, why don't you get your hubby to build a couple more of these? Knock the county unemployment down for sure."

Jean laughed uneasily. "I think we have all the space we need, Randy."

"Damn shame," said Randy.

"But you know there's a job for you at Trent if you want it," she said.

"What would that be?" asked Randy. "Vice president? CFO? Chief ass-kisser?"

Cole turned to Puller and said hastily, "Randy and our father worked for Trent Exploration."

"Doing what?"

"Finding coal," said Randy. "And we were damn good at it."

"Yes, you were," agreed Jean. "They found rich coal seams in the most unlikely places."

Randy said, "Daddy never went to college. Hell, he barely finished high school. Then the man went into the Navy for a spell. But he knew how to read a geological report. And he knew this country better than anybody. And he taught me all he knew." He stared at Jean. "And I know it better than anybody now. Even Roger with all his fancy equipment."

"Which is why it would make perfect sense for you to go back to work for him."

"You mean to make him even more money?"

Cole said, "Randy, if—"

Randy cut her off by saying, "Hey, can a man get a drink in this place?"

Cole said, "How'd you get here, Randy? Feet or wheels?"

"I won't be driving drunk, I might stay here overnight. Hey, Jean, you got room for me? I can hang out with the family. Just like old times."

She said quickly, "Absolutely, Randy. I'd love that."

"Well, maybe not. I might have something to do in the morning. Or maybe even tonight."

Puller glanced at Randy, trying to get a read on his pupils. He drew a slow intake of air. No alcohol. He glanced at Cole in time to see her doing the same thing.

Puller said, "You see yourself staying in Drake?"

Randy grinned and shook his head. "Man, I don't see myself staying anywhere."

Cole said, "Randy, you're not making any sense."

Randy nudged Puller with his elbow. "They think everything has to make sense, Puller. I just don't get that shit. Do you?"

Puller sensed Randy didn't expect or even want an answer so he said nothing. He looked around at the two sisters. Then at the brother. What was missing was obvious.

Mom and Dad.

Cole had said they had died.

The house was five years old. Randy had never been here.

He wondered if Mom and Dad had died five years ago.

He looked at Cole again. He started to say something, but it was almost as if Cole could read his mind. Her look was pleading. Puller closed his mouth and looked down at his hands.

The meal was served. There were four courses, and all of them were good. The Trents obviously had not simply a cook but a chef. Puller felt self-conscious as the hired help ladled out the soup and meticulously served every course. But he figured if he'd gotten up and started serving himself it might cause the maids more distress than anything else.

Over an hour later they all pushed back from the table, their bellies full. Randy wiped his mouth one last time with his napkin and finished off his glass of what Puller suspected was a very expensive red wine. When he was a kid his father had taken him and his brother to Provence and Tuscany. While the boys had been too young to drink, even by European standards, their father had taught them about wine. The general had been a connoisseur and collector. It also didn't hurt that he spoke fluent French and Italian.

"Thanks for the vittles," said Randy. "You still swimming in the cement pond, Jean? Keep that girlish figure of yours for old Roger?"

An embarrassed Cole glanced at Puller. "Randy, I don't think you need to play the Beverly Hillbillies act for Agent Puller."

"Oh, it's not an act, Agent Puller. I'm clearly white trash that's got rich relations. But I just refuse to put on airs. Let that be a lesson to you. Never forget where you came from."

"Should I get a room ready for you, Randy?" asked Jean.

"Changed my mind. Got places to go, people to mess with."

Cole said, "Would that include people like Roger?"

Randy stared over at her, his smile deepening but also hardening, Puller thought. Still, it was an infectious smile. Puller felt his own lips tug upward.

"Man's out of town, ain't he? That's what I heard."

"You have sources on his movements?" asked Puller.

"No, I saw his jet fly over Drake earlier."

"Would that include people like Roger?" Cole asked again.

Puller glanced at Cole. She looked about as tense as Puller had seen her. And that included quite a few stressful situations.

"I'm cool, sister cop," said Randy. "Roger goes his way. I go mine. And you folks go yours." He spread his hands to indicate the members of his family. "But I guess your way is the same as Roger's."

"Don't talk about things you don't know anything about," said Jean. "It's a bad habit. Gets folks into all sorts of trouble."

Randy rose, dropping his napkin on the table. "Damn nice visiting with you. Let's shoot to do it in another ten years or so."

"Randy?" said Jean. "Wait. I didn't mean it like that."

But he walked across the room and was gone, shutting the door quietly behind him.

CHAPTER

39

PULLER AND COLE left about thirty minutes later. Puller sat in the passenger seat of the truck and gazed out the window. He was full of questions about the evening, but he wasn't going to ask any of them. It was none of his business.

Cole finally said, "Well, that was a lot of fun."

"Families usually are."

"I'm sure you have questions."

"I don't like people prying into my stuff, and I'm going to show you the same courtesy."

They drove on in silence for five more minutes.

Cole began, "Our parents were killed when a boulder dislodged by a mine blast from one of Roger's operations crushed the car they were in."

Puller turned to look at her. "About five years ago?"

"About, yes."

"And Randy took it hard?"

"We all took it hard," she said fiercely. Then her look and tone softened. "But Randy took it the hardest of all. He and our parents were always close. Especially he and Daddy."

Cole drove for a few more miles in silence. Puller looked around the truck's interior and noted the new vinyl seats and the rebuilt dashboard with what looked to be original equipment. Even the floorboards looked new, with not a trace of rust.

"Did your dad redo this truck?"

"Yeah. Why?"

"Reminds me of the cottage. Did you buy it along with the house?"

"Yes. Paid the money into the estate."

"Is that what Randy lives off? Jean obviously doesn't need the cash."

"Yes. That's how we set it up. Randy needed it more than me."

"I can see that."

"It's funny. No one thought Roger Trent would amount to anything."

"So how did he end up where he is today?"

"I have to admit, he worked hard. And had some vision. And some luck. He worked his way up in the coal business. He's ruthless, arrogant, but he's got a sixth sense for making money. And my daddy and brother did find a lot of coal for him. Even if it's destroying the land."

"But I guess it provides jobs."

"Not nearly as many as it used to."

"Why? Is the coal running out?"

"The coal is always running out. From the first scoop you take. But all mining operations in Drake and a lot in West Virginia are now surface mining."

"Where they basically blow up the mountains to get to the seams?"

"Coal companies will tell you the decision to do surface versus deep mining is based on geology, topography, and pure economics. The lay of the land, depth and configuration of the coal seams, the cost of extraction versus the available profit, stuff like that. The reality is you need fewer workers to do surface mining. Which means more profits to the coal companies. Now, Trent will argue that a lot of the surface mining is covering ground that was already deep-mined. They're just coming back to get what the deep mining couldn't. So it's a second shot and at least some economic activity and jobs are created. And he may be right about that. But it's not a compelling argument when there's no food on the table or a roof over your head."

She stared over at him. "I have no idea if it will turn out to be relevant to the investigation, but it might make sense for you to learn some things about coal country."

Part of Puller wanted to say no. He had little interest in the intricacies of coal mining and he felt the focus on the investigation slipping some. But he could sense that Cole wanted to talk about it. And the Army had drilled into him the value of knowing the field on which the battle will be fought. He found the same to be true for the investigative side.

"Okay."

CHAPTER

40

T WENTY MINUTES LATER she stopped the truck and pointed up ahead. The moonlight was especially strong tonight and Puller could easily see what she was trying to show him.

"What do you make of that?" she asked. The object was a three-hundred-foot-high mound that looked startlingly out of place between two other peaks.

"Tell me."

"That's what's called a 'valley fill.' What they fill it with the coal companies call 'overburden.' That's basically everything they tore off the land: trees, soil, and rock that the coal companies sweep away to get to the seams. They have to put it somewhere. And since West Virginia has a reclamation act, meaning the coal companies have to put the land back close to how they found it, the companies take the overburden, dump it in a valley, hydroseed it, fertilize it, cover it with mulch, and go on their way. Problem is, when they dump the overburden like that they've turned the geology upside down. Topsoil is on the bottom and rock that was on the bottom is now on top. Native plants and trees won't grow in it. So they introduce non-native plantings that are royally screwing up the ecosystem. But they've met the letter if not the spirit of the law and they move on. And this dumping also changes the topography of the land. Rivers get redirected. Flash floods occur. Mountains fall down and crush homes."

"I didn't really see that many folks living around here."

"That's because Trent has bought out entire neighborhoods."

"Why? People wanted to sell?"

"No, they just didn't want to live next to a mining operation where they were blowing up the land. Can't drink the water. Can't wash your clothes outside. And you got health problems spiking on everything from lungs to livers. Randy wasn't kidding when he mentioned his lung problems. He was diagnosed with it when he was a teenager. A precursor to COPD. And unlike me he's never smoked in his life. But he did play football and run track near a coal mining operation. And he's not the only athlete from around here to suffer like that. Quality of life went to shit. Where there were towns and communities, now all you see is one little trailer, or one little house in the woods. That's all that's left. Used to be over twenty thousand people in Drake County. Now we don't have even a third of that. Next ten years we might just disappear right along with the coal."

She drove on, stopping in front of a chain-link fence with warning signs posted on it. Behind the fence was a large metal facility rising many stories into the air. It had long chutes running from it in several directions and at several levels.

"That's a loadout. Where they crush the coal and load it in trucks and on railcars. There's a railhead that runs right up to it."

"They're working late," said Puller as he watched lights flick back and forth from the facility and from trucks rumbling around.

"They work 24/7, like you said. Used to be they knocked off work at dark, but no more. Time is money. And the only thing they have to sell is the coal. Does them no good sitting here. That stuff will go to power the electrical grid. Keeps the lightbulbs and laptops going, as they like to say around here. At least in the coal company marketing materials."

"I take it you hate all parts of it."

"Not all parts, no. It does bring jobs. It does help the whole country because we need the power. But some folks think there might be a better way to get to the stuff than blowing up the land. And at some point the costs do outweigh the benefits. Some folks will tell you we hit that tipping point a long time ago. But if you're not from around here and you don't have to deal with black water in your sink, or big rocks falling on your house, or your kid getting cancer because the air pollutants are off the charts, what do you care? They call us the United States of America, but we're not really united about anything. Appalachia brings the coal to the rest of the country. And when all the coal is gone and West Virginia looks like Pluto, what does the rest of the country care? Life goes on. That's the reality."

"How did your dad feel about it? He sounds like he was a salt of the earth guy."

"He spent a good part of his life looking for coal. I think he stopped thinking about what it was doing to the planet. If he ever did."

"And Randy?"

"What about him?"

"He looked for coal too. Was apparently good at it. Now he's obviously dropped out of life."

Puller paused. "Was he the source of the earlier death threats against Roger?"

She put the truck in gear. "Got one more thing to show you."

CHAPTER

41

Cole pulled her truck to the side of the road about five miles later. She got out, reached behind the seat, and pulled out two construction hard hats. She handed one to Puller.

"Where are we going that we need these?" he asked.

"To see my parents."

Puller slipped the hat on and followed her. Cole had pulled a powerful flashlight from the bed of her truck and turned it on. They walked through the woods down a gravel path that soon turned to dirt.

"Ordinarily you have to get permission, be certified, and also be escorted for where we're going. But screw that. It's my mom and dad after all."

They left the path and crossed a field, where they were confronted by a chain-link fence. Puller was prepared to scramble over until Cole pointed out the slit in the links.

"You did that?"

"I did that," she replied.

They cleared the fence and kept walking. Cole finally slowed when they reached the edge of the cemetery.

"We're obviously going to see their graves?" said Puller.

She nodded.

"Why all the complications?"

"Trent bought the community and the cemetery was part of it. Technically you have to make an appointment now to see your dead relatives' final resting place. But to tell the truth, Puller, and though I am a sworn officer of the law, that requirement just rubbed me the wrong way."

"I can see that. It would've me too."

She led him around the graves until she stopped at a pair of them and shone her light on the markers.

"Mary and Samuel?"

Cole nodded.

"You were named after him?"

She smiled bitterly. "They thought I was going to be a boy. When I turned out to be a girl they named me Samantha and called me Sam. They didn't think they were going to have any more kids, you see. Randy was a little surprise that came along years later."

Puller read the birth and death dates carved in the marble.

"A boulder? Wrong place, wrong time. Senseless."

Cole didn't say anything right away. When she did her voice was deeper, huskier, like the walls of her throat were closing in.

"Could you give me a minute?"

"Sure."

He walked about fifty feet away and started to examine some of the other graves. The cemetery was in complete disrepair. Headstones toppled, weeds and grass thigh high in places, and everything coated in dust. He had noted, however, that Mary and Samuel Cole's headstones sat straight in the earth and there were fresh flowers on the graves, and the grass had been trimmed away. He assumed that was Cole's doing.

"Hey!"

He whirled around when he heard Cole call out. He was next to her a few seconds later.

"Somebody's over there," she said, pointing to her left.

Puller squinted into the darkness. Cole aimed her light in that direction and did a sweep.

"There!" Cole pointed to the figure of a man fleeing to the east. She held her light steady and kept him in the crosshairs. Her mouth dropped.

"Randy? Randy?" she called in a louder tone.

The man was out of range of the light a few seconds later.

"That was your brother?" asked Puller.

"Yeah. I wonder what he's doing here."

"Maybe the same thing you were. At dinner he said he had places to go and people to see. Maybe he meant coming here." He paused. "You want to go after him?"

"No. Let's just leave."

She drove them back to her house. His Malibu was in the driveway. They got out of the truck.

"You want to come in for some coffee? You said it helps you sleep. Jean's fancy dinner didn't include any. She's more into after-dinner liqueurs or teas with names I can't even pronounce. I just want my coffee Maxwell House black."

Puller really wanted to head back to the motel and get some work done. And he almost said that. But instead he replied, "Thanks. Sounds good."

She made the coffee and poured it out in two mugs. They carried it outside and sat on the swing in the backyard. She took off her heels and rubbed her feet.

"No mosquitoes. I'm surprised," he said.

"I spray," she said. "And one benefit of the mining up here is that the skeeters don't seem to like the coal dust and other by-products any more than we do. Plus they've filled in so many sources of water that it's cut down on the breeding grounds."

They drank their coffee.

"I appreciate you letting me vent tonight about my family."

"No problem with venting. Helps to clear the mind."

"But we have seven homicides and a bombing to solve. And to think just last week the biggest problems I had were drunk and disorderlies, a few moonshine stills, and a burglary involving a microwave and a set of false teeth."

"Part of my brain has been working it all through dinner and right up to now."

"And what does your brain say?"

"That we're making progress."

"How do you know that?"

"Somebody tried to kill us."

"So what next?"

"Keep digging. But I have to go back to D.C. tomorrow."

Her face fell. "What? Why?"

"Reynolds worked for DIA. I've got interviews set up there. Angle I have to cover."

"Can't somebody up there do that? Army must have lots of agents."

"They do. They've just decided not to deploy them on this case."

"I still don't understand."

"It is what it is, Cole. But I'll be back soon."

Her cell phone rang. She answered it. Listened and asked a few questions. Then she clicked off.

"That was Sheriff Lindemann."

"And what did he have to say?"

"He's not happy that his peaceful hamlet is now the scene of murders and bombings."

"I can understand that."

"They put the fire out. The house where you were going to has been abandoned for years. No prints on the letter slipped under your door. The explosive used was dynamite and the ATF guy said the detonators on both devices were professional jobs."

"Good. I hate going up against amateurs. They're too unpredictable."

"I'm glad you can pull some good news from all that."

"So no clues? No leads?"

"Not right now."

"Seems hard to believe that someone could get the necessary elements and set two bombs in a place like this and no one notices."

"Lots of explosives up here, Puller. And lots of people who know how to use them."

He finished his coffee and set the cup down on the arm of the swing. He stood. "I better get going."

"Yeah, I guess you better."

"Thanks for the primer on coal country."

"You're welcome. Still beating yourself up about that trip wire?"

He didn't answer.

"You're a strange man."

"I've been called worse."

"I actually meant it as a compliment."

She looked over at the door to her house and then back at him. "It's late. You can stay the night, if you want." She kept looking at him.

Reading her mind, he said, "You know, sometimes the timing on things really stinks."

She smiled weakly and said, "You're right, it does." She rose, took his cup. "Get going. It's late. What time do you want to meet tomorrow? I'll buy breakfast."

"Let's sleep in. Zero-eight-hundred at the Crib."

She smiled. "Juliet."

"Not time for Romeo yet."

She went up on her tiptoes and pecked him on the cheek, her hand pressing lightly against his chest. "Famous last words again."

He climbed into his car and drove off. She waved at him from the front porch and then went inside.

He eyed her in the rearview mirror until he couldn't see her anymore.

He steered his car in the direction of Annie's Motel.

CHAPTER

42

Puller killed his headlights and slid his M11 out.

The lights were on in the motel office. A pickup truck was parked out front. He had planned to check on Louisa's cat. But someone else was in there now.

He crept forward, keeping his weight balanced and his gaze swiveling. It might be nothing, but after nearly being blown up Puller was taking nothing for granted. The bomber obviously knew he was staying here. Maybe he was back for another try.

He reached the truck and made sure it was empty. He opened the passenger door, checked the glove box, and read off the name on the registration.

Cletus Cousins.

The name meant nothing to him.

He left the truck and moved to the little porch in front of the office and peered in the window. The man was short, in his twenties, and carrying a large cardboard box.

Puller tried the doorknob. Not locked. He opened it, his gun pointed at the man's head.

The young man dropped the box.

"Please, God, don't shoot. Please."

His head was shaven. He had a flabby gut, a trim goatee, and looked ready to crap in his dirty jeans.

"Who the hell are you?" asked Puller.

The man was shaking so badly, Puller finally lowered his gun a notch. He flipped out his creds. "Army investigator," said Puller.

"I'm not going to shoot you unless you give me good reason. What are you doing here?"

"My granny told me to come."

"Who's your granny? Not Louisa. She said she didn't have any family in the area."

"She don't. But my granny is her best friend."

"What's your name?"

"Wally Cousins. My granny is Nelly Cousins. We been in Drake our whole lives. Everybody knows us."

"Truck registration says Cletus Cousins."

"That's my daddy. My truck's in the shop, so's I took his."

"Okay, Wally, one more time, why are you here and what are you taking?"

The young man pointed at the box on the floor. It had fallen open and its contents had spilled out. Puller could see some clothes, a Bible, some books, a few framed photographs, and some knitting needles and balls of colored yarn.

"To get this stuff," he said.

"Why? Are you taking it to Louisa at the hospital?"

The young man looked confused. "No, sir."

"What then?"

"Taking it to my granny."

"So you're taking Louisa's belongings to your grandma. And that's not stealing why?"

The young man's eyes widened. "Well, she ain't gonna use it no more. She's dead."

Puller blinked. "Dead? Louisa's dead? When?"

"Yes, sir. Died about three hours ago. And Louisa told my granny she could have this stuff when she passed. Like I said, they were good friends. About the same age and all."

Puller eyed the box again and then lifted his gaze to Cousins. "You don't wait very long around here, do you? Before you start scavenging the body?"

"Don't you know, mister?"

"Know what?"

"Lotta folks around here ain't got nothing. They find out you dead and ain't got no relations, your stuff's gone before you know it. Why you think so many empty houses around here all trashed? So when Ms. Louisa passed on, Granny told me to get myself over here and get this stuff Louisa said she could have before it was gone."

Puller lowered his pistol. "How did your granny know Louisa died?"

"She called the hospital."

"Someone else I know called the hospital. They wouldn't tell her anything."

"My aunt is a nurse there. She told Granny."

"I thought she was doing better."

"I guess she was. My aunt said she looked better. But then the machines started going off. She just stopped breathing. My aunt said that happens sometimes with old folks. They just get clear tuckered out. Tired of living, I guess."

Puller examined the box more closely and saw that there was nothing of value. He eyed one of the photos. It was of two women in their mid-twenties wearing poodle skirts, tight blouses, and pink heels with hairdos so big they looked like a bee's nest on steroids. He flipped it over and looked at the date written in pen on the back.

November 1955.

"One of these ladies your granny?"

Wally nodded. "Yes, sir. She's the dark-haired one." He pointed to the young blonde woman on the left. She had a mischievous smile and looked ready to take on the world. "And Ms. Louisa is right there. They sure look different now. Especially Ms. Louisa, of course."

"Yeah." Puller looked around. "You taking the cat?"

"Naw. Granny got three dogs. They'd eat that dang thing up." He eyed the gun. "Can I go now?"

"Yeah. Go on."

Wally picked up the box.

"Tell your granny I'm sorry about her friend."

"I will. What's your name?"

"Puller."

"I'll tell her, Mr. Puller."

A few moments later Puller heard the truck start up and roll slowly out of the motel parking lot. He eyed the room and then heard the meow. He walked past the counter and into the back bedroom. The cat was on the unmade bed lying on its back. Puller checked the food, water, and litter tray. The cat hadn't eaten or drank much. Maybe it was waiting for Louisa to come back. If so, it would probably be dead soon too. It looked about as old in cat years as Louisa had been in human ones.

He sat on the bed and gazed around. From 1955 and a poodle skirt with the world lying before her to this crappy existence decades later. People taking your stuff before you were even in the ground.

I thought I'd saved her. Couldn't do it. Just like my guys back in Afghanistan. Couldn't save them either. Way it went. Beyond your control. But the Army taught you to control everything. Yourself. Your opponent. What all the training didn't tell you was that the most important things, the ones that actually decided life and death, were almost completely outside your control.

He rubbed the cat's belly, rose, and left.

He popped his trunk, took out the tape, and strung it across the entrance to the motel office after securely locking the door.

The yellow tape was visible from a long way away. Its message was clear:

Do Not Enter.

Next, he eyed the door to his room. His gaze drifted to the spot in front of the door. He looked for wires, a new piece of wood, saw none. He hefted a large rock from the flowerbed encircling the parking lot and tossed it at a spot in front of the door. As it flew through the air he ducked down behind his car. The rock hit and nothing happened. He picked up another rock and aimed it at the door handle. It struck the spot solidly.

Again, nothing.

He pulled from his rucksack a long telescoping pole with grips on the end that could be fixed at virtually any angle. He placed his room key in the grips and played out the pole. He looked around. The place was empty. He seemed to be the only one staying here right now.

He inserted the key in the lock, turned it, and using the pole pushed open the door.

No explosion. No fireball.

He put the pole away, locked his car, and went inside his room. He stood there for a few moments, letting his eyes adjust to the darkness here.

Everything looked just where he had put it. He checked his little booby-traps to tell him if someone had been here. None were tripped.

He closed and locked the door. Sat on the bed. He added up his growing list of failures.

He had failed to see the trip wire in time.

He had failed to save Louisa.

He checked his watch. Pondered whether to make the call.

Cole would probably already be in bed by now. And what exactly did he have to tell her?

He lay back on the bed. His M11 would rest in his hand all night.

His cell phone buzzed. He looked at the number and inwardly groaned.

"Hello, sir."

"Damnedest thing, Gunny," said his father. The old man would alternate referring to Puller as his XO, gunnery sergeant, or sometimes simply "you asshole PFC."

"What's that, sir?"

"No orders from high command and a Saturday night with nothing to do. What say we get together and bang some shots back? We can catch a ride to Hong Kong on a military transport heading out. Know some places. Good times. Lovely ladies."

Puller untied his jump boots and kicked them off. "I'm on duty, sir."

"Not if I say you're not, soldier."

"Special orders, sir. Straight from HC."

"Why don't I know about it?" his father said in a clenched tone.

"Bypassed local chain of command. I didn't ask why, General. It's the Army. I just follow lawfully given orders, sir."

"I'll make some calls. This bullshit has to stop. They try to run around me one more time they'll regret it."

"Yes, sir. Understood, sir."

"Hell to pay."

"Yes, sir. Have a good time in Hong Kong."

"You hang tight, Gunny. I'll be back in touch."

"Roger that, sir."

His father clicked off and Puller wondered if they had stopped giving the man his nighttime meds yet. When medicated he usually was sound asleep by this time, but he'd now called his son twice late at night. He'd have to check on that.

He stripped down to his civvies and lay back on the bed.

Every time he had a conversation like this with his father, it seemed to tear a little piece of his reality away. There might come a time when his father called and Puller would actually believe everything the man said. That he was back in the Army, heading up his own corps, that Puller was his XO, or his gunny, or one of his hundred thousand asshole PFCs.

One day. But not tonight.

He turned out the light and closed his eyes.

He needed to sleep, so he did.

But it was a light sleep. Three seconds to wake, aim, and fire at the enemy.

Bombs, bullets, sudden death.

It was as though he'd never left Afghanistan.

CHAPTER

43

By 0600 Puller was up, showered, shaved, and dressed.

He sat outside on the porch in front of the office and drank a cup of his percolator coffee. No one had broken through the yellow tape he'd strung after Wally Cousins had left.

Eight o'clock at the Crib was eggs, ham, and grits with more coffee. Cole was back in uniform, her femininity buried under polyester, police gear, and regulation black shoes.

"Louisa died yesterday," Puller said.

"I hadn't heard about that," replied Cole, her fork poised halfway to her mouth.

He told her about Wally Cousins's visit to the motel. Cole confirmed that Cousins's grandmother and Louisa were longtime friends.

"I called the hospital this morning and said I was her grandson," he said. "They told me that she died in her sleep."

"Not a bad way to go, I guess."

Better than a boulder crushing your car with you in it, thought Puller.

"She has no family left here, he said. What'll happen to her body? Funeral? And what about her motel?"

"I'll make some calls. We'll take care of it, Puller. Drake isn't what it once was, but we still have good folks here that care, who take care of their own."

"Okay." He took a sip of coffee. "Do folks really have to move that fast around here when someone dies?"

She shrugged. "I won't tell you Cousins was wrong. When folks have nothing they do strange things."

"Like that neighborhood you showed me, next to the concrete dome?"

"I admit some of those folks go scavenging around the area. And sometimes they take things from people who are still alive and kicking. We call that burglary or robbery or grand larceny and they have to pay the price."

"Jail?"

"Sometimes, yeah."

Puller took a bite of eggs. He'd called his SAC back at Quantico and brought him up to speed on all the latest developments. When he'd mentioned the bombing attempt Don White had said, "You've obviously gotten someone excited."

"Yes, sir," Puller had said. But he didn't ask for additional assets. If the SAC wanted to send them, he would. Puller was not going to beg.

He had also arranged to be on a commercial flight out of Charleston later that day. He had to make inquiries at the Pentagon about the late Colonel Matthew Reynolds and he also needed to visit the man's house in Fairfax City. Puller *had* hinted that another CID agent back in Virginia could see to this detail as well as he could, but the SAC made it clear that Puller was the entire show right now, at least as far as the U.S. Army was concerned.

"How long will you be gone to D.C.?" she asked.

"Not sure. Depends on what I find out. But not longer than a couple of days."

"Any word from your fancy lab in Atlanta?"

"Nothing on the briefcase and laptop. They just got the other items. They're good, but they need some time. I'll check in with them today and fill you in on what if anything they've found out."

"How about that soil testing company in Ohio?"

"They open at zero-nine. So at zero-nine I plan to hit my speed dial."

"They may not tell you much without a court order."

"Maybe not. But we can get a court order."

Cole said nothing. She just drank her coffee and looked around at the other patrons of the Crib.

Puller studied her. "You never answered my question about Randy and the death threats."

"I guess you didn't have to be a world-class detective to figure that one."

"Parents killed by Trent. Probably how Randy sees it. He lashes out at the SOB. So he sent the earlier threats. You investigated and found out the source. You dealt with it and don't want to talk about it further."

"That's a pretty good read."

"Okay, now here's the question. Is he the source of these new threats?"

"Don't think so."

"But you're not absolutely sure?"

"I've been a cop long enough to know that anybody can be violent if given the right motivation."

"You want me to talk to him?"

She shook her head. "Puller, that is not your investigation. You are here for one reason only."

"How do you know it's not connected to what happened to the Reynoldses? And that is my turf."

"How could it be?"

"I don't know. That's why we investigate stuff. Will you let me talk to him?"

"I'll think about it. But I don't even know where he is right now."

"How does he support himself? Other than the money your parents left?"

"He works odd jobs."

"Does Roger think Randy's behind the new threats? Is that why he called you directly?"

"Probably," she admitted.

"When does Trent get back into town?"

"I don't know. I don't keep the man's calendar."

"I think this morning would be a good time to go to the office where Molly Bitner worked and ask some questions."

"You really think there's a connection between them and the Reynoldses? I mean aside from them maybe seeing something."

"That's what we have to find out. But for the record, I don't really believe in coincidences."

They both turned to the plate glass window as a pale silver Mercedes SL600 pulled up in front of the Crib. The top was down and the occupants were clearly revealed.

"Speak of the devil," said Puller. "That's your sister driving and your brother riding shotgun."

CHAPTER

44

As Jean Trent and Randy Cole walked into the Crib, heads at every table turned their way. Jean Trent was dressed in a short dark blue skirt, white sleeveless blouse, and three-inch heels, and her hair, despite the open-top ride in the Benz, looked lovely and her makeup was expertly applied. It was a wave of glamour pouring into the Crib that probably left everyone there, from the working class to the office dwellers, slightly lightheaded. It was as though a movie star had decided to breakfast in Drake, West Virginia.

She smiled and waved to folks at various tables. Randy had none of his cocksure manner from the night before. He slouched and studied the floor. He wore dirty jeans, a white T-shirt with an Aerosmith silkscreen, and a lousy attitude on his features.

Puller studied the pair before rising and waving to them.

"Jean? Over here. We have room."

"For Chrissakes, Puller," hissed Cole.

He looked down at her. "You don't want to catch some more family time?"

Jean and Randy headed toward them. Puller got up so Jean could slide into the booth, and then he sat back down. Randy settled in beside his other sister.

Cole said, "Were you at the gravesites last night? Pretty sure I saw you."

"Law against it?" her brother mumbled.

Jean said, "I corralled our wayward brother when I was driving into town. Convinced him a meal with his big sister wasn't a fate worse than death." She eyed him. "And you look like you could use some meat on your bones," she added. "You hardly touched your dinner last night."

"What were you doing at the gravesite?" Cole asked.

"What were you doing there?" he shot back.

"Paying my respects."

"So was I. You got a damn problem with that?"

"Okay. You don't have to get all pissed off."

He looked around. "Can we order some breakfast? I'm hungry." He rubbed his head.

"Headaches again?" asked Puller.

"What's it to you?" Randy snapped.

"Just asking. Maybe some food will help."

Puller raised his hand and waved the waitress over.

After Jean and Randy ordered, Puller lifted his coffee to his lips, took a sip, and set it down. "You really look like you could use a few hours of sack time."

Randy looked across the table at him. "Thanks for your concern."

"No concern. Just an observation. You're a big boy. You can take care of yourself."

"Yeah, well tell that to my sisters here."

"That's what sisters do," said Puller. "Worry. They worry about their brothers. Then when they get married they worry about their husbands."

Cole said to her brother, "I don't even know where you're living. Do you even have a place to stay or are you just jumping from one friend's place to the next?"

Randy laughed in a hollow tone. "I don't have that many friends in Drake."

"You used to," said Jean.

"They've all grown up, got married, had kids," said Randy.

"And you could've done the same," said Jean.

Randy eyed her. "Yeah, Jean, you're right. I could've married me a rich fat woman and lived happily ever after in some big house and drive around in some fancy-ass car."

Jean didn't even flinch. Puller figured she'd probably heard that one a million times from lots of different people.

"I don't believe there're any rich fat women in Drake, Randy," she said. "And if you're thinking of changing which side of the plate you hit from, the only rich fat guy in town is taken."

"Don't we all know that," snapped her brother.

Jean smiled. "Sometimes I don't know why I bother, I really don't."

"Never asked you to."

"Oh come on, Randy. You're laying a guilt trip on all of us. Slinking around town, never know where you are, you show up looking like shit, take some money, and then slink off again. We wait for you to call, and when you do, we make a fuss over you. You came to dinner last night only because Roger wasn't there. And you shoot off your mouth, all your sarcastic little quips that you think are so funny. Poor Randy. I bet you just love it, don't you? Makes up for a life that you just don't have."

Puller hadn't seen that one coming, and apparently neither did Cole. She said reproachfully, "Jean!"

Puller glanced over at Randy, who never took his gaze from Jean. "Keep going, sis, I'm enjoying this."

Jean said, "I saw him wandering down the road like a lost pup. Gave him a ride in my car. I brought him here to feed him. I've offered to get him work. I've offered to help him any way I can. And all I get back for that is shit thrown right in my face. And I'm tired of it."

Her voice had risen steadily to where heads at other tables were turning in their direction and Puller could see folks muttering together.

Cole put a hand on Randy's arm. "She didn't mean that."

Jean exclaimed, "Of course I did. And you would too, if you'd take your head out of the damn sand."

Randy's manner suddenly changed. The grin and the confidence came hurtling back. "Hey, Jean, does Roger pay you each time you screw him? Or does he get a volume discount? And after he slaughtered Mom and Dad, did you charge him double to bang you? You know, to show your anger at him wiping out our parents and not giving a shit?"

Jean reached across the table and slapped her brother so hard that Puller saw her wince from the shock of the blow. Randy didn't show any reaction, even as the skin where she had struck him turned pink and then a dull red.

"Is that the best you got?" said Randy. "All the money has really made you soft."

He stood. "I got things to do. Hey, Jean, thanks for the ride. Or maybe you should thank Roger for me. It's his car after all. He owns it, the house, the business and *you*." He looked out the window at the Benz. "That model's looking a little old, sis. Rog might be looking to trade it in. He's gone so much, makes you wonder. Didn't know coal men needed to fly off on their fancy jets all that much. And despite all your working out and dieting, a little too much alcohol and birthing two kids is taking its toll. Now don't get me wrong. You're still nice-looking. And Roger is fat and ugly. But the rules are different for men and women. They're not fair rules, but they are the rules. And whoever has the gold makes the rules. And that would be Roger. Now you have a good day, big sister."

Randy turned and walked away. As Puller watched he high-fived a couple of guys in one booth and then slammed the door on his way out.

He turned to Jean, who just sat there looking as stunned as she probably felt.

Cole said, "Both of you said things you didn't mean."

"I meant every word I said," replied Jean. "And Randy did too," she added quietly. She looked back out the window, at the car. Puller could see the thoughts running through her mind like frames from a film. Where was Roger right now? *Was* he thinking about trading her in?

Cole reached over and took her hand. "Jean, what Randy said was bullshit."

"Was it?" her sister snapped.

Cole looked down.

Jean glanced at Puller. "What do you think? You're supposed to be a great detective."

Puller shrugged. "I can't read people's minds, Jean. But if your husband cheats on you then you sue his ass for divorce and end up with as much of the gold as your lawyers can get. Since you married him before he struck it rich I assume there's no prenup."

"None."

"Then I wouldn't worry about it. Best advice I can give."

When Jean and Randy's food came the waitress looked around and said, "Is he coming back?"

"I seriously doubt that he is," said Jean pleasantly. "But if you can keep it warm and then wrap it for me, I'll try to find him and give it to him."

"Okay." The waitress walked away.

Jean cut up her eggs and was about to say something when Puller rose.

"Going somewhere?" she asked.

"I'll be right back." Puller had just spotted Bill Strauss sitting at a table in the corner. He walked off.

Jean looked at Cole. "You two sleeping together yet?"

"Jean, why don't you just shut up and eat your eggs?"

Cole wriggled out of the booth and hurried after Puller, who was already standing next to Strauss.

"Hello, Mr. Strauss. John Puller, CID, you remember me?"

Strauss nodded. He had on another expensive three-piece suit with a French-cuffed monogrammed shirt.

"Certainly, Agent Puller. How are you?"

Puller said, "Great."

"Investigation coming along?"

"It's coming," said Cole, as she came to stand next to Puller.

He said, "When do you expect your boss back in town?"

"I'm not actually sure."

"Boss doesn't fill in his second in command?" asked Puller.

"Why do you need to know when he'll be back?"

Puller said, "That's really between Trent and us." He slapped Strauss on the shoulder. "Tell your boss I said hello."

He turned and walked back to Jean's table. "I'll need to talk to your husband again. Tell Roger we'll need to see him when he gets back into town."

She put her fork down. "Why?"

"Just give him the message. Thanks."

He walked toward the door.

Cole laid cash down for their meals, said a hasty goodbye to Jean, and hurried after Puller. He was already outside, where he was looking at the silver Benz.

"What were you trying to do in there with Strauss?" asked Cole.

"Just getting some info. He's the COO?"

"Chief operating officer, yeah."

"How long?"

"Pretty much as long as Roger's been in business."

"Strauss is older."

"Yeah, but Roger is more ambitious, I guess."

"Or at least he's more of a risk-taker."

They started walking back to the car.

"Still heading to D.C.?"

"Yeah. No way around it."

"Think things will start hopping here soon?"

Puller said, "Seven people have already been killed. I think it's been hopping for a while."

45

THEY DROVE OVER in Cole's cruiser to the Trent office where Molly Bitner had worked. Along the way Puller called the soil testing company in Ohio. After being transferred to two different people who could not help him, Puller motioned for Cole to pull off the road. She put the car in park and turned to him.

Into the phone Puller said, "Well, let me talk to a supervisor." He waited another couple of minutes until the voice came on the line.

Puller explained the situation and the person on the other end responded.

"Can you tell me anything over the phone?" he asked.

Puller listened and nodded. He asked for their contact information and wrote it down in his notebook. "Okay. The court order will be coming. I'd appreciate a fast turnaround."

He clicked off and looked at Cole.

She said, "So a court order is necessary? I didn't think soil samples were so confidential. Could they tell you anything?"

"Only that it was Matthew Reynolds who had requested the work done. He paid by credit card. And it was some samples of organic matter that he wanted vetted. They wouldn't tell me from where or what they found. I've got their information here. Can you get the paperwork going on that?"

"I'll see the county attorney today." She put the car back in drive and pulled back onto the road.

"It must be soil from around here, don't you think?"

"I would assume so. But we have to know for sure."

"And why test it?"

"Pollutants," said Puller. "I mean, why else?"

"So that may be what this is about? Pollution?"

"Well, if they came back and killed Wellman to get the report, then yeah, I'd say that might be what this is about. It must be something really serious, though."

"This is West Virginia, Puller. There's a ton of ground and water pollution here already. Hell, we can't even drink the water. People know that. You just have to look around or see the crap in the air to know it's dirty. So I don't see how it would be worth killing seven people to keep secret something that everyone already knows exists."

"That's a valid point. Let's look at it from another angle. Has Trent had run-ins with EPA?"

"There isn't a coal company operating in West Virginia that hasn't had run-ins with EPA and the state regulatory folks. Coal drives the economy here, but there are limits."

"And if you exceed those limits you can get in trouble?"

"Yes," she conceded. "But again, is it worth killing seven people, including a police officer? If Roger had run afoul of some reg he'd have to pay a fine, which he's done in the past. Many times. He has the money to do that. He doesn't have to resort to murdering people."

"What if it was more than just butchering a reg?"

"What do you mean?"

"You told me if people kept dropping dead from cancer that Trent might get run out of town on a rail. Foul water, sickness, maybe kids dying. That could crater his whole company. Cost him everything, including that big house and his private jet. Maybe he goes to prison too, if it's shown he knew about it and did nothing. Maybe they stumbled onto something like that."

Cole didn't look convinced. A few miles passed before she broke the silence.

"But how would the Reynoldses be involved in that? I mean, I can understand Bitner. She worked at one of the Trent offices. Maybe she found out something. Overheard something. Saw something in a file or on a computer screen she wasn't supposed to. But if so, why not just send in the soil sample request herself? Why use the Reynoldses?"

"Maybe she thought someone suspected her. So she used the Reynoldses as a go-between, to shield her own involvement. They're living right across the street. Maybe they spoke, became friends of a sort. They see Matt Reynolds in his uniform. He's official. A soldier. Works at the Pentagon. Sworn to protect his country. They think he can help with all his connections. He agrees to do it. But then someone finds out. They send in the hit team. Take both families out."

"Lot of firepower. It's not like Roger has teams of killers at his beck and call."

"How do you know he doesn't? Union and coal company battles can get pretty intense. He already has security. And Jean told me he carries a concealed weapon. Are you telling me he doesn't have guys with guns on his payroll to handle stuff? Intimidation? Scare tactics?"

"With surface mining you don't really have much union involvement because you don't have miners going underground to get the coal out. So those types of battles don't happen that much around here. In fact, the union hall closed years ago."

"I concede it's a theory we need to work out. Let's hope we can find out something where Bitner used to work. And we can't forget about the meth lab. If this is tied to drug dealers we need to know sooner rather than later."

"The drug angle in my mind is more viable to explain all this then the coal angle. Drugs, guns, and violence just go hand in hand."

"But that doesn't explain the soil sample. Or the Reynoldses' involvement. Or Wellman getting strung up."

"My brain is starting to fry. Okay, let's focus on what's coming up next. How do we handle Bitner's office? What tack do you want to take?"

"Ask broad questions and hope for equally broad answers. We keep our eyes and ears open. Anything in plain sight is fair game."

"Well, if you're right and the company killed all those people to keep some secret, I doubt Bitner's office coworkers will be too forthcoming. They're probably scared shitless."

"Never said it would be easy."

CHAPTER

46

THE TRENT SATELLITE OFFICE was a one-story concrete block building painted light yellow that was reached by a winding gravel road. The parking lot held about a dozen cars and trucks. One of the cars was a Mercedes S550. It was parked in a spot right next to the door.

"Bill Strauss's?" asked Puller as they passed it on the way to the entrance to the office building.

"How'd you guess?"

"The car was parked in front of the Crib. The only other guy in town who could afford a ride like this is Roger Trent, and he's not in Drake right now. Strauss beat us here somehow, probably when I told you to pull over. Or he took another route." He eyed the dilapidated facility. "I would've expected some fancier digs for the company COO."

"The Trent company philosophy is take the money home, not waste it on office space in the middle of a coal mining operation. Even Roger's office at company headquarters is pretty spartan."

"So there's an operation near here?"

"A loadout like the one I showed you last night. And a surface mining op about a half mile north."

"So they blast close to here?"

"Blast close to just about everywhere around here. That's why the population has shrunk so much. Who wants to live in a combat zone?" She gave him a quick glance. "Military company excluded," she added hastily.

"Trust me, soldiers would prefer not to live in a combat zone."

"Who do you want to talk to here?" asked Cole.

"Let's start at the top."

They walked inside, asked at the front desk for Strauss, and were shown back to his office. It was paneled with crudely stained plywood. The desk was cheap, as were the chairs. There were old metal file cabinets stacked in one corner. A ragged couch and dented coffee table occupied another corner. There was another door that Puller suspected led to a private bath. Strauss probably had drawn the line at having to urinate with the hired help.

There was a shiny computer with a twenty-three-inch screen on his desk. This was the only sign Puller saw that modern technology rather than Goodwill inventory had come to the Trent empire. When he thought of the mansion he had been in the night before, he now saw what Cole had meant.

They really do take the money home. At least the head honchos do.

Strauss rose from behind the desk and greeted them. He had taken his suit jacket off, revealing a potbelly covered by his starched white shirt with the French cuffs. The jacket hung on a hook on the back of the door.

His fingertips were yellowed with nicotine and he must've just crushed out a cigarette in the overstuffed ashtray because the air was heavy with smoke. Puller waved his hand in front of him to clear the air, while Cole took several deep breaths. Maybe she was trying to suck in as much of the foul air as she could, thought Puller. Secondhand smoke gratefully inhaled.

"Thanks for meeting with us, Bill," said Cole.

"No problem, Sam. If I knew you wanted to meet with me this morning, we could've done it at the Crib." He motioned them into chairs.

"We'll try not to take up too much of your time," said Cole.

"Right. I understand you had dinner with Jean last night."

"Yes. She invited a few of us over while Roger was out of town."

"Where is Roger, by the way?" asked Puller.

"He's doing business in New York," answered Strauss.

"Business in New York?" said Puller. "I thought the company was a private concern."

Strauss settled his gaze on him. "That's right. Trent Exploration is private. But it's also very profitable in the energy sector. That makes it attractive to all sorts of investors."

"So is Trent thinking about going public?" asked Puller.

Strauss's smile was tight. "I really can't comment on that. And I fail to see how that might be relevant to your investigation." He sat back down and glanced at Cole. "So what can I do for you?"

"As I mentioned to you before, we need to talk to Molly Bitner's coworkers. But before we do, I'd like you to give us a description of what she did here. And how long she'd been working at Trent."

Strauss sat back and interlocked his fingers behind his head. He glanced at the pack of Marlboros on his desk and the stuffed ashtray next to it, but must've decided against lighting up again.

Puller studied the man and his body language as he awaited Strauss's response.

"She'd been here about four years. Before that she worked in another of our offices; the one on the north side of town."

"Why the change?" asked Puller.

Strauss shot him a glance. "We often have workers switch between offices. It's based on the needs of the company and also the desires of the workers. The north office did more work with a surface mining operation near there. This office handles more of the centralized operations, sort of a clearinghouse for multiple sites. I can't give you the exact reason Molly came here because I don't know. It may be that some of her coworkers could answer that question."

"We'll be sure to ask," said Puller.

"And what did she do here?" prompted Cole.

"Filing, answering phones, dealing with orders from the field. Pretty normal stuff. She wasn't in a position to order anything without higher approval. In the business world she would be described as a secretary or assistant office manager, I suppose."

"Good worker? Any problems?"

"As far as I knew we never had any problems with her."

"You notice anything unusual about her over the last several weeks?"

"No. But I wouldn't necessarily. As I said, I knew her, of course, but we had little interaction on a daily basis."

"No money problems of which you're aware?"

"No one was garnishing her wages if that's what you mean."

They asked a few more questions and then Strauss led them to the cubicle where the office manager worked. Before Strauss left them Puller said, "How's your son doing?"

Strauss turned to face him. "Just fine. Why?"

"Just wondering."

"You know you had no right to ask him about his military career. And quite frankly I found your questions insulting to him."

"Sorry you felt that way. Were you ever in the military?"

"No."

"If you were you probably wouldn't have thought they were insulting."

Strauss looked at Cole, scowled, and left them.

CHAPTER

47

THE OFFICE MANAGER was named Judy Johnson. She was a rail-thin woman who had a strong grip and a businesslike manner. Her hair was brown and gray and worn back in twin pigtails. Her face was lined and her eyes a deep caramel and lively. She wore a beige jumper with a white blouse. Her black flat shoes were scuffed.

Johnson told them that Molly had been a good worker. She had come to this office principally because it was an easier commute for her and a slot had come open. She did not have access to all the files at the office.

"Which ones didn't she have access to?" asked Puller.

"Principally the ones kept in Mr. Strauss's office," said Johnson. "There's also a closet in his office. Inside that closet is a safe. They're kept in there."

"I thought it was a private bathroom," said Puller.

"No. We all use the same restroom," replied Johnson.

"And the key to the safe?" asked Cole.

"There's one key for the closet door and one key for the safe. And Mr. Strauss keeps those with him at all times."

"What's so important that you need those sorts of precautions?" asked Puller.

"Well, this office keeps geological reports on the location of coal seams and other related data. Pretty valuable for people if they knew where the coal was located."

"So Trent doesn't own all the land where the coal is?"

"No. They're always looking for new sources and send out teams regularly to hunt for them. If someone could learn where the coal was and buy up the land before Mr. Trent, they could use his own work to their benefit."

"Do you do any soil testing here?" asked Cole.

Johnson looked puzzled. "Soil testing? In what regard?"

"For pollution, things like that."

"We comply with all pertinent environmental regulations," Johnson said automatically. Obviously she'd been well coached on that, thought Puller.

"I'm sure. But you didn't answer the question," persisted Cole.

"We do soil testing all the time," Johnson said.

"Okay, but you just seemed puzzled when I asked the question."

"That was because I thought you were here to talk about Molly. And she had nothing to do with any of that."

"Are records of soil testing kept here?" asked Puller.

"If so, Mr. Strauss would keep them in the safe. But I think most of that work is done by outside contractors and the results are then sent directly to the office in Charleston."

"So I understand Molly and Eric Treadwell were just living together for expenses?"

"That's right."

"Common practice around here, so Sergeant Cole told me."

"Yes."

"How'd they meet?" asked Puller.

Johnson said, "I believe at a Trent company picnic. Eric had come with some friends. He and Molly hit it off. They had both been married before and I don't think either was inclined to do it again. They liked each other's company, and like Sergeant Cole said, it's not that unusual around here."

She paused and played with one of her pigtails. "Now, is there anything else?"

"So were you close with Molly?" asked Puller.

"We were friends, sure."

"Any idea why someone would have wanted to harm her and Eric Treadwell?"

"I can't think of a one."

"Did you ever visit them at their home?" Puller asked.

Johnson looked away before she answered. "Once or twice maybe. We usually met in town for a meal or to go the movies."

"You ever think that Molly or Eric might have a drug problem?"

"Molly? Drugs? No, never."

"So you're familiar with the signs of a drug user?" said Puller.

Johnson hesitated. "I...my son. He's had some...issues with that. I...think I know what to look for."

"So nothing like that for Molly. How about Eric?"

"I never noticed anything like that about Eric. But I didn't see much of him anyway."

"So nothing unusual you can think of?"

Johnson hesitated. "Well, there was one thing. I'm sure it's not important, but it was a little unusual."

"Tell us," said Cole. "We'll figure out if it's important or not."

"Well, Eric came here once drunk as all get out and made a ruckus."

"Did you report it?" asked Cole.

"No. We didn't even tell Mr. Strauss. It was after WVU won the Big East, so we just let it pass. Guess a lot of folks got drunk and partied after that one. And as I recall Molly got him to calm down. He was going on and on about the Mountaineers. Had a WVU sweatshirt on and was waving one of those big hand things. Then he passed out on Mr. Strauss's couch. We just closed the door and let him sleep it off. Molly would check on him from time to time."

"Was Strauss here?" asked Puller.

"Oh, no, of course not. He was out of town."

"So when exactly was that?"

"Last December," said Johnson. "That's when they play for the Big East championship."

"So that was the only time something out of the ordinary happened with Molly here?"

"So far as I know."

They asked a few more questions and then left Judy Johnson to her pigtails and cubicle world.

They spoke to other people who worked in the office. None of them had anything helpful to add. Molly was a good worker. They could think of no reason why anyone would want to kill her.

As Puller and Cole walked back to her car she said, "Not much to go on there."

"We were both in Treadwell's house."

"I know that. So?"

"You see the ring on his finger?"

"I noted it, yeah."

"It was a Virginia Tech ring because we know he went there. And there was a Virginia Tech football poster in his bedroom. Virginia Tech Hokie alums are pretty intense about their football team. So even if he lives in the state, why would he get so excited about West Virginia winning the Big East? Virginia Tech used to play in the Big East. Now they pretty much dominate the ACC in football. So this loyal Hokie alum gets so excited he'd come to this office and basically pass out drunk because the mountaineers kicked ass?"

Cole looked back at the building.

"You mean he really came to get into Strauss's office? To maybe get into that safe?"

"Looks that way to me. Now the question is, did he?"

48

Cole dropped Puller back off at his car.

As he climbed out she said, "Do you think Eric Treadwell got into the safe?"

"Yes. And I think Molly helped him."

"How?"

"Strauss hangs his jacket on the back of the door. Presumably his keys are in the side pocket. I think while Strauss was using the public bathroom Molly snuck in there and took impressions of those keys. Treadwell was a machinist. Easy for him to make duplicate keys. He pulls his fake drunk act and gets to the couch. Maybe somebody goes out to get him something and leaves him alone in the office. He has the keys in his pocket. Molly closes the door and basically stands guard. He jumps up, opens the closet door and the safe, and takes out what he needs. Molly comes in to check on him. Maybe she has some files she's carrying with her. He gives her the stuff from the safe and she hides it in the files. I noted there was a big copier in a pretty secluded corner of the office. Molly makes copies of the stuff there and takes the originals back to Treadwell when she 'checks' on him again. He puts the originals back in the safe and no one's the wiser. They probably knew Strauss wouldn't be in that day. She could easily access his schedule."

"And so what was in the documents?"

"Like Johnson said, geological maps."

"Worth killing people over?"

"Apparently so."

"I just don't get it."

"Right now, neither do I."

Puller watched her drive off and then turned around to head to his motel room and prepare for his flight to D.C. He stopped when he saw Randy Cole come around the corner of the motel.

"Sorry about rushing off this morning," Randy said with a grin.

"No sweat. I think Jean took it pretty hard."

Randy sat down on the front porch and Puller joined him there.

"Don't let that act fool you. She's hard as steel. Harder than all of us. She's probably forgotten all about it by now." He rubbed his cheek where she had struck him. "Yep, hard as steel."

"Guess she has to be, married to a guy like Trent."

"Got that right."

"So you pretty much hate the man."

"He killed my parents."

"I heard it was an accident."

"That's what everybody says."

"You know different?"

"Damn straight I do."

"Can you prove it?"

"He owns this place, lock, stock, and barrel. It wouldn't matter if I had all the proof in the world."

"Come on, Randy. Your sister's a cop. And I don't see her as a big fan of Trent's. If you had proof, she would work like hell to bring him down. Am I wrong about that?"

Randy looked away and his confident demeanor faded. He rubbed his temples.

"Lot going on up there?" said Puller.

"Lot of nothing but pain."

"You really need to see a doctor about that."

"Yeah, right."

"Have it your way. If there is something wrong the longer you wait, the worse it'll be."

"I'll take my chances."

"Suit yourself. Your parents' grave markers are the only well-kept ones in the cemetery. Is that your doing or Sam's?"

"Both."

"Sam told me a boulder dislodged by a mining blast hit their car?"

Randy nodded and his eyes suddenly glistened. He turned farther away from Puller and rubbed at them.

"They were driving over to Jean's. Trent was blasting nearby. Stuff come down right on the road." He paused, collecting himself.

"And they died?" said Puller.

Randy nodded. "Doctor said it would've been pretty much instant, so they didn't suffer. Good thing. It was a while before we found them."

"Who did find them?"

"I did."

"You said they were headed to Jean's? You mean their old place."

Randy nodded.

"Why were they going there?"

"It was my birthday," Randy said in a voice so small Puller barely heard it. "Jean was throwing me a party."

"So they died on your birthday?"

Randy nodded, his head dipping low. "It was a shitty present, I can tell you that. Haven't celebrated my birthday since."

"How'd you find them?"

"When they didn't show up, we tried calling. No answer. Then we split up. Three ways they could have come. And lots of times they close roads up here for work and such, so they never took just one way. We had to cover 'em all. Sam went to one. Jean to another. And I took the third. I took the right one." He teared up again and this time Puller looked away.

"Where was Roger while all this was happening?"

"Back at the house getting drunk." He slowly shook his head. "You know what he told me after he found out what had happened?"

"What?"

" 'Shit happens.' The bastard just told me that. 'Shit happens.' "

"I'm sorry, Randy."

"Yeah," he said curtly.

Puller looked down. "I can see how that might mess a person up."

"I'm good."

"You really believe that?"

"Yeah, I really do. Hell, you can't pick your family. You just got to deal with the one you have."

Tell me about it, thought Puller.

"And Jean? How did she take it?"

"She goes her own way. Does her own thing. She keeps busy. She was as broke up as the rest of us. But she's young and rich and she's got a lot to live for. Family to take care of. Kids to raise."

"And how about you? You got a long life ahead of you."

"You think?"

The way he said it made Puller look at him intently. "You thinking about ending it prematurely? Because if so that would be pretty stupid."

"Nah, I'm not worth that much grief."

"You been sending the new death threats to Roger?"

"Didn't know he was even getting any. How's your investigating going?"

"Guess the whole town's talking about it."

"Pretty much, yeah."

"It's going slow."

"Hard to figure all those people killed."

"Did you know Eric Treadwell or Molly Bitner?"

"No, not really."

"Either you did or you didn't, Randy, which is it?"

"I knew them to say hello. That was about it."

"Did you know them well enough to tell me if they were doing drugs? Maybe dealing?"

"No. I didn't. But I'm not into drugs, so I wouldn't know. My choice of addiction is beer." Randy looked over his shoulder at the motel office. "Nice what you did for Louisa."

"I only did what anybody else should have done."

"One way to look at it. Sam's a good cop. She'll be good helping you on this."

"She already has."

"Jean told me about the bomb. You saved Sam's life."

"I almost didn't. I cut it too close."

"Still a hero in my book. Probably don't tell her enough, but I'm proud of my sister."

"Then tell her yourself. Life's short."

"Maybe I will."

"You want back in your family, Randy?"

The other man rose. "I'm not sure, Puller. Just not sure."

"Well, at some point you have to make that choice."

"Yeah, I know."

He turned and walked off the way he'd come.

Puller watched the man go.

Drake, West Virginia, had turned out to be a far more complex place than he had expected.

CHAPTER

49

THAT AFTERNOON, Puller boarded a commercial jet out of Charleston heading east. He landed at Dulles Airport less than an hour later. He rented a car and checked in at CID headquarters in Quantico to fill in his SAC, Don White. Next, he drove to his apartment and let AWOL out. While the cat was enjoying some fresh air, Puller filled up its food and water dishes and cleaned out the litterbox.

He'd made an appointment with Matthew Reynolds's superior at DIA for the next afternoon. After six full hours of sleep, he woke, had breakfast, ran five miles, lifted some weights at the gym at Quantico, showered, made some phone calls, and finished up some overdue paperwork.

He dressed in his combat fatigues and drove north to the Pentagon in his rental. A special agent from the DIA Office of Counterintelligence and Security met him at the Pentagon Metro exit and they headed into the Pentagon together. Both men showed their cred packs, announced that they were armed, and were given clearance into the building without an escort.

The DIA agent was named Ryan Bolling. He was a compact five-ten former Marine who'd been with DIA for a decade. He was a civilian now, as were all of the personnel at DIA's Counterintelligence and Security.

As they walked along Puller said, "Thought you guys would be a little more hot to trot on this case. Feeling lonely out there all by myself."

"Not my call. I just do what I'm told, Puller."

They walked along Corridor 10 to A Ring and kept navigating

the Pentagon's complex passageway system until they arrived at the home of the J2. There was a large reception area where the executive assistant and the secretaries sat. On the backside wall was the door to the J2's office. National colors plus the flag officer's flag. It was red with two white stars. Puller had been in there once years ago. It was well appointed, with the ubiquitous "I Love Me Wall" that was filled with photos of the flag officer and his famous friends.

The J2 was out of the country. His second in command, the vice chair's office, was to the left. The red flag held only one star. Off to the right was a small conference room where J2, or the vice chair if the J2 was out, would meet for staff meetings. He would also come here every morning at 5 a.m. to preview the daily briefing he would later give to the Chairman of the Joint Chiefs.

Puller had been cleared to speak to the vice chair. She was Army, a one-star brigadier general named Julie Carson and also Matt Reynolds's direct superior.

Before they entered the woman's office Puller asked Bolling, "What's the book on Carson?"

"You'll have to find out for yourself. I've never met the woman."

A few moments later Puller was seated across from General Carson in her office. Bolling sat in the opposite chair. She was tall, trim, and taciturn. Her blonde hair was cut short and she was outfitted in her dress blues.

"We probably could have done this over the phone," began Carson. "I don't have much to tell you."

"I prefer the face-to-face," replied Puller.

She shrugged. "You CID guys must have more free time than the rest of us." She glanced at Bolling. "I'm sure you're thrilled to be babysitting this guy."

Bolling shrugged. "I go where they tell me, ma'am."

Puller said, "Field grade officer? Murdered. Guy was in charge of J23. Oversaw prep of the briefing book for the J2 and then up the line to the Chairman? Minute the guy was identified as DIA a barrage of memos went up the line to you, ma'am, the J2, the Director of DIA, and on up. Even the SecArm is interested."

She leaned forward. "And your point?"

Puller leaned forward too. "Your casual attitude puzzles me, quite frankly."

"My attitude is not casual. It's just that I don't think I have any information that will be helpful to the investigation."

"Well, let me see if I can change that opinion. What can you tell me about Colonel Reynolds?"

"Our career paths crossed from time to time. We were rank equals until the last few years when I started to hit the fast track. It was ironic that I ended up with the star and he didn't. But he wanted to get out and I wanted the star. He was a good man and a good soldier."

"When was the last time you saw him?"

"Friday before he was found murdered. He was leaving early to go to West Virginia. We had a meeting about a matter he was working on, and then he left. In fact, we met in the conference room across the hall."

"Did he seem disturbed or anxious about anything?"

"No, he seemed perfectly fine."

"You say you two had served together at other places?"

"Yes. Fort Benning, for example."

"Know it well."

"I know you do. I checked your record. And how's your father doing?"

"Fine."

"That's not what I heard."

Puller said nothing. He glanced at Bolling. The man did not seem to know what they were talking about.

Obviously sensing that Puller was not going to react to this, Carson changed subjects. "How did a soldier with your combat record and leadership qualities end up at CID?"

"Why not?"

"Best and the brightest are meant for higher things, Puller. They're meant for command."

"Do the best and the brightest sometimes commit crimes?"

She looked puzzled but said, "I guess."

"Then how are we supposed to catch them if the CID doesn't have some of the best and brightest too?"

"It's not a joke, Puller. If you'd gone the West Point route one day you could be sitting here with a star on your shoulder and more to come."

"Stars get to be real heavy, ma'am. I like to stay light on my feet."

Her lips pursed. "Maybe you aren't cut out for command. Too much of a joker."

"Maybe," said Puller. "But this meeting isn't about my career shortcomings, and I don't want to take up more of your time than is absolutely necessary. As you said, you're busy. What else can you tell me about Reynolds?"

"He was very good at his job. He kept the folks in J23 working like a well-oiled machine. The briefings were strong and the analysis underlying them was spot-on. He was retiring and going into the private sector, which was a loss for the country. He was not involved in anything at DIA that could have led to his murder in West Virginia. That about cover it for you?"

"If he was helping to put the briefings together he was privy to some highly classified and potentially valuable information."

"We have a lot of people here who qualify for that distinction. We've never had any problems in this office regarding personnel. I don't think Reynolds would be the first."

"Money problems? Personal problems? Any motivation to sell out to an enemy?"

"It's not easy to do, Puller. My people are looked at six ways from Sunday. Reynolds had no financial problems. He was as patriotic as they come. He was happily married. His kids were normal and well adjusted. He was a deacon in his church. He was looking forward to retirement and carving out a new career in the private sector. There's nothing there."

Puller looked at Bolling. "You guys have any occasion to look at Reynolds for any reason?"

Bolling shook his head. "Checked before I came over here today.

Guy was spick-and-span clean. No basis for any blackmail, stuff like that."

Puller turned back to Carson. "So you knew he was going out to West Virginia?"

"Yes. He told me. His wife's parents were ailing. He commuted on the weekends. It never interfered with his work so I had no problem with it."

"He ever talk to you about anything unusual going on out there?"

"He never talked to me about West Virginia, period. It was a personal family matter and I never asked. None of my business."

"Well, someone murdered him and his family out there."

"Yes, they did. And it's your job to find them."

"Which is what I'm trying to do."

"Okay, but I think the answer lies in West Virginia, not in the Pentagon."

"Did you know his wife?"

Carson glanced at her watch and then at the phone. "I have a conference call coming up shortly. And the J2 is out of the country so I'll be presenting the briefing to the Chairman tomorrow morning."

"I'll try to make it snappy," said Puller, but he looked at her expectantly.

"I knew Stacey Reynolds only through Matt. I saw her at the occasional function. We were friends, but not close friends. That's all."

"And Colonel Reynolds never mentioned that something unusual was going on in West Virginia?"

"I thought I already answered that."

Puller sat patiently looking at her.

"No, he didn't," she said, and Puller wrote this down in his notebook.

"When I was assigned this case I was told that it was *unusual*. I assumed it was unusual because it involved the murder of a DIA field grade officer who had access to highly classified intelligence."

"Thankfully, murders of such people don't happen often, so that I guess it would qualify as *unusual.*"

"No, I think the term was in reference to the fact that we were going light on assets with this investigation. And if Reynolds was not doing anything of importance for DIA and you don't think his murder had anything to do with his assignment to DIA, why would it have been described to me as unusual? Then it just becomes another homicide."

"Since I wasn't the one who described it that way to you, I have no way of answering that question." She glanced at her watch again.

"Anything else you can think of that might help my investigation?"

"I can't think of a one."

"I'll need to interview Reynolds's coworkers."

"Look, Puller, do we really need to go there? I've told you all there is to tell. My people are very busy trying to keep this country safe. The last thing they need is to be distracted by something like this, which has nothing to do with them."

Puller sat up straighter and closed his notebook. "Your friend and colleague was murdered, General Carson. I've been assigned to find out who did it. I intend on accomplishing that mission. I'll need to talk to his coworkers. I'll do it efficiently and professionally, but I am going to do it. Right now."

They had a stare-off, which Puller ended up winning.

She picked up her phone and made some calls.

As Puller rose to leave she said, "Maybe I was wrong about you."

"In what way?"

"Maybe you do have what it takes to lead."

"Maybe," said Puller.

CHAPTER

50

THEY LEFT the J2's office, grabbed a left on Corridor 9, and took the escalator to the basement. The lower level at the Pentagon was a bewildering maze of sterile white corridors that not a drop of sunlight would ever touch. It was Pentagon lore that there were DoD employees from the 1950s still wandering around down here trying to find their way out.

The personnel of J23 were analysts and graphic artists, about two dozen in total, who methodically built the briefing book each week, using intelligence input not only from DIA but also from other agencies like CIA and NSA. Then they would tweak it to the current Chairman's intelligence preferences. It was a PowerPoint presentation set in hard paper and was succinct in getting to the meat of the matter without delay. In the Army brevity was a virtue beyond all others.

The people in J23 were a mix of uniforms and civilians. Thus Puller saw fatigues, old green uniforms, new blue uniforms, slacks, button-down shirts, and the occasional tie. The unit operated around the clock and the perk for the night crew was that they got to wear polo shirts. Reynolds had been the highest-ranking officer here.

Since J23 was housed in a SCIF, or Sensitive Compartmented Information Facility, room, Puller and Bolling had to put their cell phones and other electronic devices inside a locker on the wall outside the entrance. No picture-taking or outside communications capabilities were allowed in an SCIF.

They were buzzed in and Puller eyed the reception area. It

looked like many others he'd seen in the Pentagon. This was the only way in or out, except for possibly a fire emergency exit somewhere in the back. At the end of the corridor was an open bay. Here individual cubicles were lined up and analysts and artists toiled away on the product that General Carson would be poring over tomorrow at 0500. The lights in here were dim. The lights at the cubicles were better. Still, Puller thought, half the people here probably needed eyeglasses after less than a year fighting terrorists from their desks mostly in the dark.

Puller and Bolling showed their creds and were granted access to Reynolds's coworkers, the highest ranking of whom was a lieutenant colonel. There was a small conference room where Puller conducted his interviews. Each person was spoken with separately, a common enough interview tactic. Witnesses questioned together tended to tell the same story, even if they had different information and perceptions to begin with. They were informed by Puller and confirmed by Bolling that Puller was cleared for everything up to "TS/SCI with polygraph" and had a "valid need to know." In the intelligence world those phrases opened many a locked door and mouth.

The coworkers expressed more shock and sorrow over the death of Matthew Reynolds than his commanding officer had. However, they also could not provide any useful information or leads about why Reynolds had been murdered. His work, while classified, did not involve anything that would have led to his death, they told Puller. When he was done he was no further along with his investigation than he had been when he'd entered the building.

Next, he searched Reynolds's office, which had been secured ever since he had left for West Virginia and been murdered. While J23 was technically open storage space, meaning if you put something somewhere, there it would stay safely, Reynolds might still have had a safe in his office. As it turned out, he didn't. Neither could Puller find anything in the man's office that would assist the investigation. It was clean and sparsely furnished, and computer files, which he went over in Bolling's presence, yielded no clues.

He exited J23, retrieved his cell phone from the locker, walked back to one of the main exits with Bolling, and left the DIA man there. He returned to his car in the vast parking lot. But instead of driving off right away, he sat on the hood of his green Army Ford and studied the five-sided building that was the single biggest office space in the world. It had received a sharp punch in the face on September 11, 2001, but had come back stronger than ever.

The Pentagon had started a long renovation of the then nearly sixty-year-old building back in the late 1990s. The first wedge finished, ironically enough, had been the part hit by the American Airlines jumbo jet temporarily flown by madmen. More than ten years later the entire renovation of the building was nearly complete. It was a testament to American resilience.

Puller looked the other way and watched as kids of Pentagon personnel played inside the fence of a daycare center within the Pentagon grounds. He guessed that was what the military was always fighting for, the rights and freedoms of the next generation. Watching little boys and girls sailing down plastic slides and riding toy horses somehow made Puller feel a bit better about things. But only a bit. He still had a killer to catch and he felt no closer to doing so than he had when he had first been given the assignment.

His cell phone vibrated and he slipped it from his pocket. The text message was brief but intriguing:

ARMY NAVY CLUB DOWNTOWN TONIGHT 1900 I'LL FIND YOU.

He didn't know whom it was from, but the sender obviously knew how to contact him. He studied the words for a few more seconds before putting the phone back. He checked his watch. He would have enough time. He'd been meaning to do this when he came back east anyway. And after spending time with the dysfunctional Cole family, it seemed more important still.

He punched the gas and left the Pentagon in his rearview mirror.

CHAPTER

51

"WHAT ARE YOU doing here, XO?"

Puller stood at attention as he gazed down at the man.

"Reporting in, sir," he said.

His father sat in a chair next to his bed. He was wearing pajama bottoms, a white T-shirt, and a pale blue cotton robe cinched at the waist. He had socks and slippers on his long, narrow feet. He had once been over six-three, but gravity and infirmity had sliced two inches off him. Now when he stood he no longer towered over most people, not that he stood that often anymore. The fact was, his father almost never left his room at the VA hospital. His hair was nearly gone. What was left was cottony white, like Q-tips stitched together, and nearly encircled his head, just nicking his ears.

"At ease," said Puller Sr.

Puller relaxed but remained standing.

"How was the trip to Hong Kong, sir?" he asked.

Puller hated playing this fictional game, but the doctors said it was better that way. While Puller didn't put much creed in the shrinks, he had deferred to their expertise, but his patience was growing thin.

"Transport plane blew a tire on takeoff. Never made it. Almost ended up in the drink."

"Sorry, sir."

"Not half as sorry as I was, XO. Needed some R and R."

"Yes, sir."

As his father looked at him, the first thing Puller noted was his eyes. It was also part of Army lore that Puller Sr. could kill you with a look that would induce such a deep sense of shame at your having failed him that you would just curl up and die. It wasn't true, of course. But Puller had talked to many men who had served with his father, and every one of them had been on the receiving end of such a look. And every one of them said they would remember it to their final day on earth.

But now the eyes were just pupils in the head. Not lifeless, but no longer full of life. They were blue, but hollow, flattened. Puller looked around the confines of the small, featureless room, just like hundreds of others here, and concluded that in many important ways his father was already dead.

"Any orders, sir?" he asked.

His father didn't answer right away, and Puller often didn't receive any answer to this question when he came to visit. When the response did come, it surprised him.

"It's over, XO."

"What, sir?"

"Over. Done. Dead and done."

Puller eased forward a half step. "Not following, sir."

His father had hung his head, but now he turned to look at his son. The eyes flashed like blue ice thrown at the sun. "Scuttlebutt."

"Scuttlebutt?"

"You have to pay attention to it. It's shit, but they get you in the end."

Puller now wondered if paranoia had been added to his father's list of issues. Maybe it had always been there.

"Who gets you, General?"

His father waved a careless hand around the room as though "they" were right there. "The people who count. The bastards who call the shots in this man's army."

"I don't think anyone is out to get you, sir." Puller was now wishing he had not come to visit today.

"Of course they are, XO."

"But why, sir? You're a three-star."

Puller caught himself too late. His father had retired a three-star, a lieutenant general. That would have been a career achievement worthy of virtually any person who ever wore the uniform. But Puller Sr. had belonged to that rare percentile who expected to reach the very top of the mountain with everything they did.

It was well known in the Army that Puller Sr. should have gotten that fourth star. The man also should have received something even more coveted: the Medal of Honor. He had earned it on the battlefield in Vietnam; there was no question about that. But in the Army it wasn't just about valor in the field, it was about politics far away from battle. And the fact was, Puller Sr. had ticked off many important people who had a great say in his career path. Thus the fourth star and the Medal of Honor would never be his. And while his career kept advancing after that snub, it didn't do so at quite the same trajectory. When the trajectory flattened, the highest targeted goals were no longer achievable. You would miss them. He had missed them. He did have three stars and every medal other than the one he had wanted above all others.

"It's because of him," snapped his father.

"Who?"

"Him!"

"I don't know who you mean."

"Major Robert J. Puller, United States Air Force. DD. Convicted at court-martial of treason. Imprisoned for life at USDB. They blame me for what that bastard did." His father paused, drew an angry breath, and added, "Scuttlebutt. The sons of bitches."

Puller's face collapsed in disappointment. His brother had been convicted and imprisoned long after their father had retired. And yet he was blaming his son and Puller's brother for his career problems. On the field Puller Sr. had never let the buck of responsibility pass him by. He took the credit and the blame. Off the field, though, it had been another matter. His father had been a finger pointer. He laid blame on the most unlikely of places. He could be petty and vindictive and callous and unfair, brutal and unyielding. These personality traits could also be applied to his description as a father.

Normally, Puller would say something before leaving. He would play out the fiction as the shrinks had requested. As he started for the door, his father said, "Where are you going, XO?"

Puller didn't answer.

"XO!" yelled his father. "You have not been dismissed."

Puller kept walking.

He passed down the hall of the VA hospital that was filled with old, sick, and dying soldiers who had given their all so that the rest of the country could live in peace and prosperity. He could hear his father screaming until he was three hundred feet away. There had never been anything wrong with the old man's lungs.

When he hit the exit, he never looked back.

Family time was over.

The Army and Navy Club was next.

He was back on the hunt.

Where he really belonged.

CHAPTER

52

OLD.

Architecturally impressive.

Efficiently run.

These were the thoughts running through Puller's mind as he walked toward the Army and Navy Club on 17th Street N.W. in downtown Washington, D.C. He nodded to the men working the valet zone as he headed inside. He took the short flight of steps up and looked left and then right. He was in his dress greens. The Army was phasing out the green and the white uniforms in favor of the blue. They were in essence going back to their roots. Blue was the color chosen by the Continental Army during the Revolutionary War to distinguish the colonial fighters from their British redcoat counterparts. And it was also the color of the Union army during the Civil War.

Two big wars. Two big victories.

The military didn't mind building on past successes.

Puller would ordinarily only wear his dress uniform to a special military occasion. He would never wear his rank uniform when interrogating someone. He recalled that when he'd been a sergeant first class, commissioned officers would look down their noses at him while he was questioning them. That no longer happened now that he was a warrant officer. And military personnel lower in rank could have their legal counsel argue that you had intimidated their clients by shoving your rank in their face. So Puller largely stuck to civilian clothes. But tonight something told him to dress up a bit.

To the right was the club's main dining area. To the left was the reception desk. Puller eschewed both and headed up the stairs, taking them two at a time.

He had gotten here early for one purpose. He didn't like other people finding him. He liked to find them first.

He reached the second floor and looked around. There were meeting rooms here and small dining areas. On the third floor was a library where there was a table with bullet holes from being over-turned and used as a shield by American soldiers during a skirmish in Cuba over a century ago.

There was also another establishment on the second floor that caught Puller's eye.

A bar. If you were looking for a soldier off post and during his off hours, you would probably matriculate to a bar.

He looked through the glass doors into the bar. There were four people in there, all male. One Army, one Navy, and two men in business suits. The suits had their ties loosened. They were looking at some papers with the guys in uniforms. Maybe a meeting that had carried over to the bar.

They clearly weren't his mysterious texter.

He next looked around for a surveillance post and found it almost immediately. A restroom down the hall had a small ante-room with an open doorway leading back into the hall. There was a large mirror there. Puller took up position in front of it and found that it made an excellent vantage point for viewing the bar entrance.

Whenever someone came to the restroom Puller pretended to be exiting it. When they came back out, he pretended to be either adjusting his clothes in the mirror or yakking on his cell phone.

He checked his watch.

Seven on the dot.

That's when he saw her.

She was in uniform. He had assumed that from the military time used in the text. Military folks were punctual; it became ingrained by your training.

She was in her early thirties, slender, medium height, with short dark hair framing a nice face. She wore wire-rimmed glasses and a set of dress blues; her official cap was in her right hand. He noted the silver bar on her shoulder denoting her rank as a first lieutenant. There were two types of officers in the U.S. military, commissioned and warrant officers. She was commissioned and therefore higher-ranking than Puller. Her commission came from the President of the United States, while Puller's came from the Secretary of the Army. If he achieved the rank of chief warrant officer 2 he would receive a commission from the President. But in the military pecking order he would still be below the true commissioned officers. They had gone to West Point or ROTC or OCS. He had not. He was a specialist. They were generalists. In the Army the latter ruled the day.

She peered through the glass into the bar.

It took Puller only four long strides to reach her.

"You want to do this in private, Lieutenant?"

She whirled around and it was probably only her Army training that turned a scream into a gasp.

She gazed up at him. Female regulation shoes could have no heel higher than three inches. She had chosen the full three and still looked like a kid next to him.

When she didn't say anything he let his gaze wander to the right side of her uniform and saw her nameplate.

"Lieutenant Strickland? You wanted to talk to me?"

His gaze wandered to the left and he studied her ribbon rows. Nothing there that would knock anyone's socks off, and he wouldn't have expected there to be. The Army's combat exclusion for females limited what they could earn in the field. No blood, no glory.

He saw her gaze go to his rows of ribbons, and her eyes widened as they took in the enormity of his combat experience and military achievement.

"Lieutenant Strickland?" he said again, more gently. "You wanted to talk?"

She met his eye and changed color. "I'm sorry, I wasn't expecting, I mean…"

"I don't like to be found, Lieutenant. I'd rather do the finding."

"Yes, of course, I can see that."

"How did you know how to text me?"

"Friend of a friend."

He pointed to the stairs. "They have some private areas up there."

CHAPTER

53

S**HE FOLLOWED HIM UP** and they found a quiet spot and sat down in worn leather chairs. When she didn't seem inclined to begin the conversation he said, "I obviously got your text, Lieutenant."

"Please, just call me Barbara."

"You can call me Puller. So I got your text." He let this dangle.

"I know you're investigating Matt Reynolds's death."

"Are you one of his coworkers? If so, someone forgot to tell me."

"I'm not one of his coworkers. But I knew him. I knew him well."

"So you were friends?"

"More than that. He and my father served together. He was a mentor and one of the main reasons I joined the service. I was a friend of his wife's too. And I knew his kids. In fact, I babysat them when they were younger."

"Then you have my condolences."

"Was it as bad as...I've heard?"

"What did you hear?"

"That the whole family had been slaughtered."

"Who told you that?"

"It was scuttlebutt. I'm not sure who told me."

"It was pretty bad," replied Puller.

"Okay," she said shakily. She pulled out a tissue and dabbed at her eyes.

"As you noted, I've been assigned to find his killer."

"I hope you do," she said firmly.

"And I need all the help I can get."

"I...I might be able to assist you."

Puller opened his official notebook. "I need to know everything you can tell me."

"It's not too detailed. I knew that Matt and Stacey had been going back and forth to West Virginia to care for her ailing parents. They took the kids too. They hated it, of course. They were away from their friends, spending their summer in the middle of nowhere, but family is family. And Stacey was very close to her mom and dad."

"I'm sure she was."

"Matt commuted there on Friday and came back on Sunday to go back to work on Monday. He did that most weeks."

"I know that. I talked to his commanding officer, General Carson."

Strickland's face flushed at this comment, but she hurried on. "He called me up about two weeks ago and said that he'd come across something in West Virginia that was really puzzling him."

"In what way?"

"He wouldn't go into detail, but from what he said he had stumbled onto something that was really serious."

"Like maybe a drug operation?"

Puller didn't normally like to interject anything into the conversation when questioning a witness, but his gut had told him to do it this time.

She looked at him strangely. "No, I don't think it had anything to do with drugs."

"What, then?"

"Something bigger than that. That involved other people. I could tell that he was a little scared, uncertain of what to do."

"How did he *stumble* on this, as you said?"

"I think he learned about it from someone else."

"And that person had stumbled onto it?"

"I'm not sure. It might have been that the person was already looking into it."

Puller's pen hovered over his notebook. "You mean like the police?"

"No, it wasn't anyone in authority. I'm pretty sure of that. At least Matt never mentioned it."

"Who, then?"

"Well, I think it was like someone working undercover."

"But you just said it wasn't the police."

"Well, don't the police sometimes use civilians in undercover operations, particularly if they have some inside connection to a target?"

"I guess they do. But then you're talking drugs or maybe gun-running."

"I don't think it was that, because I don't think that would have scared Matt so much."

"He had his family out there. He might have been nervous for them."

"Maybe," she said uncertainly.

"He ever tell you a name or give a description of this 'under-cover' person?"

"No."

"Did he say how he met the person?"

"Ran into them one day."

"Why would they confide in him?"

"Because he was in uniform, I believe."

"But if the person were working undercover they presumably would have already been working with the police. So why go to some guy in an Army uniform?"

"I don't know," admitted Strickland. "But I do know that Matt was involved somehow and he was really worried."

"Where are you assigned?" he asked.

"I'm an analyst at DoD."

"What do you analyze?"

"The Middle East, with an emphasis on the border between Pak-istan and Afghanistan."

"Ever been there?"

She shook her head. "No. I know you have. Many times."

"It's okay, Barbara. Some people make good analysts and some don't."

"And some people are good in combat. Like you."

"Would you like to analyze a situation for me?"

She looked surprised but nodded gamely.

"When I was assigned this case I was told that it was unusual. Four bodies in another state, one of them a DIA colonel. Normally, we'd bring the heavy artillery on something like that. Multiple CID agents, tech support, even bring folks up from USACIL. But they sent just me because it was termed unusual. You got any idea why that would be the case?"

"DIA involvement?"

"But General Carson said nothing Reynolds was involved in would have been connected with his murder, so they couldn't have been concerned about that. But the SecArm's office even called down to the lab in Atlanta about the case. They seemed to think it was some hot stuff going on, and more than just the DIA angle. Why would they have thought that?"

"Because someone from DIA told them it was hot stuff and wanted to keep a close lid on it?" suggested Strickland.

"I was thinking the same thing. When I earlier mentioned General Carson your face changed color."

Now Strickland turned pale.

Puller said, "It's just stuff I tend to notice. Don't take it personally. So tell me about the lady."

"I don't know her all that well."

"I think you know her a lot better than I do. Tell me, would Reynolds have confided in her the same concerns he did to you?"

"Matt was a soldier's soldier."

"Meaning he followed chain of command. So he would have told her. And maybe she saw an opportunity to score a victory. An unexpected one that might get her the second star, especially if what Reynolds had stumbled onto had to do with national security matters. Is that plausible? Or am I barking up the wrong tree?"

Strickland bristled. "I think Julie Carson would crawl over the body of her dead mother to make major general."

"So she's that ambitious?"

"My experience in the military is that everyone who gets at least one star is that ambitious."

"So she tells Reynolds to stay on the case. Interface with this undercover person. She smells that second star. But instead Reynolds and his family get wiped out. Now Carson's sitting on a potential bomb. If the truth comes out not only will she not get the second, but the first star might get stripped."

Strickland nodded. "She has to play cover-up. But she told you that Matt's work at DIA had nothing to do with his death. That he wasn't working on anything sensitive."

"What else would she say? He headed up J23. That alone is enough to believe his work got him killed. He helps prep the Chairman's daily briefing. And if someone called Carson on it, she'd just say she was walking the 'need to know' fence. Stonewall me, but count on the fact that Reynolds being DIA will be deemed to be the cause of his death. And she probably is hoping against hope that whatever really got Reynolds killed never comes out. Then she's safe. Otherwise, she's looking at a lot of explaining if it's discovered that she kept the lid on something big in order to score professionally. She went for the home run and popped up to the shortstop."

"It that's true, she's in real trouble." Strickland looked almost gleeful.

Puller said, "My job is to nail a killer, not knock off a one-star from her chosen career path. She might have screwed up, and if she did she might have to pay the piper, but that's not my goal, okay?"

The gleeful look fled Strickland's features. "What are you going to do?" she asked.

"Have a second conversation with a certain one-star," said Puller. "I appreciate your help, Lieutenant."

Strickland again turned pale. "You won't tell her it was..."

"No, I won't."

CHAPTER

54

"WHAT THE HELL are you doing here?"

Julie Carson was not in uniform. She had on jeans and a sleeve-less Army green T-shirt and her feet were bare. Her arms were tanned and muscled. She probably hit the gym every day and ran at lunchtime to catch the rays and keep her body lean, thought Puller.

She gazed up at Puller, who stood on the other side of the door to her condo. In his regulation dress uniform shoes he was about six feet five and the breadth of his shoulders filled the doorway.

"Got some follow-up questions."

"How'd you know where I lived?"

"I don't mean to insult your intelligence, but I'm an Army inves-tigator and you're in the Army. Like looking in the phone book."

"I still don't like it."

"Duly noted. Can we do this inside in private?"

"I already talked to you."

"Yes, you did, and like I said, I had some follow-up questions."

"I'm busy."

"And I'm investigating a murder. Of one of your people."

The door down the hall opened and two young people came out and looked over at them.

"Inside might be better, General," observed Puller.

She glanced at the young couple, stepped back, and let Puller in, closing the door after him. She led him down the hallway. Puller noted the high-end fixtures, oil paintings, and tasteful furnishings in her condo across from Pentagon City Mall that was only one Metro stop from the Pentagon.

"Nice commute for you."

"Yeah, it is," she said brusquely.

They settled in the living room. She'd pointed him to an upholstered chair and she sat on a small loveseat across from him.

On the walls were pictures of Carson with an array of high-
ranking military personnel and politicians. Every one of these
people, and they were mostly men, had probably been instrumental
in her career path. He had noted a similar photo wall in her office
at the Pentagon.

"Nice place."

"I like it."

"I still live like I was back in college."

"I'm sorry," she said bluntly. "Maybe it's time you grew up."

"Maybe it is."

"I'm not sure what sort of follow-up questions you might have."

"Based on new information."

"What new information?" she scoffed.

"About Colonel Reynolds." He stopped and stared at her.

"Okay, I'm waiting, or am I supposed to guess?"

Puller took his time sliding out his official notebook and uncap-
ping his pen. While he was doing that, he was also watching her.
He saw Carson run her eye over his ribbon rows. You didn't wear
your ribbons or medals on your fatigues. But the dress uniform
showed them in all their glory. And she could not help but come
away impressed. Like his SAC had observed, Puller *had* been a
stud in the field. The colored ribbons and bits of metal had never
meant much to him. The actions behind the official awards were
what he remembered. But if the military's display of bragging
rights got someone's attention in an investigation, they were worth
their weight in gold to him.

"You've accomplished a lot, Puller," she said with grudging
admiration.

"Only thing I want to accomplish right now is to find a killer."

"Then you're wasting your time sitting here talking to me."

"I don't think so."

"Get to the damn point. I've got better things to do than this. As I told you, I have to give the briefing tomorrow morning."

"Yeah, I'm kind of surprised you're not still there making sure it's perfect for the four-star."

"That's none of your damn business. And let's not forget which of us has the star. I'm beginning to lose my patience. And just so you know, I've got good contacts at CID."

"I'm sure you do." He glanced up at her photo wall to see the image of the current CID head staring back at him. "And I'm sure they're better than mine."

"So get to the point!"

"Talk to me about what Colonel Reynolds told you about what was happening in West Virginia. Specifically what he was concerned about."

She looked at him in bewilderment. "I already told you that Reynolds didn't talk to me about anything that happened in West Virginia."

"I know. I've got it written down in my notebook. I just wanted to give you the opportunity to correct the record before it becomes permanent."

The two stared stonily at one another.

"I don't like what you're implying," she said.

"And I don't like being lied to."

"You're way out of line."

"What's out of line is giving me false information that will make it that much harder for me to find Reynolds's killer."

"Who told you that I knew anything about this?"

"I'm an investigator. It's my job to find out things."

"If people are saying false things about me, I have every right to know."

"If they're false. But not if they're *true*."

She folded her arms and sat back.

He noted this. Before her posture was aggressive. Hands on knees, torso angled toward his, just begging to tell the truth and get this over with. Now things had changed.

She must've noted his appraisal, because she said, "I helped revise the manual on interrogation techniques, Puller, so spare yourself the embarrassment of trying to read me."

"Would that be enhanced interrogation techniques, ma'am?"

"You know as well as I do that the Army adheres to the Geneva Convention."

"Yes, ma'am."

But she sat still farther back and her eye contact was not as direct. He decided to press his advantage. "Was Reynolds a good soldier?"

"Yes, he was. I told you that."

"And good soldiers follow chain of command?"

"Yes."

"So if I told you that Reynolds had told someone else of his concerns who was not in his chain of command, it seems likely, does it not, that he would have told his direct superior as well? Meaning you? He's the eagle cluster. You're the one-star, as you so clearly pointed out to me."

She crossed her legs, her chin dipping slightly. "I don't know what to tell you."

"Sure you do. The truth will do just fine."

"I can have your ass in the stockade for a statement like that."

"But you won't."

"Why? Because of your old man? He's long gone from the ranks, Puller. So don't try that leverage on me, legend or not."

"That's not what I was thinking."

"Sure it was. Your poker face leaves a lot to be desired."

Puller continued on as though he hadn't heard her. "Actually, I was thinking of that star on your shoulder."

Her features hardened even more. She actually looked like she might jump up and attack him. But to an experienced interrogator such as Puller, he could see just beneath this hard shell the beginnings of fear in the woman.

"Why?" she said. "Thinking of trying to knock it off? Don't even bother. I worked my ass off for it. I earned it."

"Actually, ma'am, I was thinking that your shoulders look broad enough to carry that star and probably at least one more."

This tactic had clearly surprised her. Carson uncrossed her arms and legs and sat forward. She eyed the notebook.

Acknowledging this subtle gesture, he said, "This will all go in the report as though it took place at our initial meeting at the Pentagon."

"Frankly, I didn't expect that sort of nuance from you, Puller."

"Probably most people don't."

She looked down, her fingers nervously rubbing together. When she looked up she said, "You want to go grab a cup of coffee? I feel like getting some fresh air."

He rose. "My treat."

"No," she said quickly. "I think I'll buy, soldier."

CHAPTER

55

THIS SECTION OF ARLINGTON had a million places to get coffee within walking distance. Puller and Carson passed several such establishments, but all were crowded with yakking teenagers and their smartphones and laptops. They passed these and entered one off the beaten path where they were the only customers. The humidity had broken and the air was crisp and refreshing. They sat next to an open window in the café.

Puller placed his hot cup of coffee down after taking a sip and studied her.

Before leaving the condo she'd slipped on a white long-sleeved T-shirt and Nike sneakers. There were lines around her eyes, crow's-feet that were stamped in more deeply than a civilian's. Leading people who carried weapons just did that to a person. Her blonde hair stood out starkly from her tan. She was quite attractive and super-fit and carried herself like she was well aware of both. He knew she was forty-two and had worked her butt off for the one star. He had no desire to derail her career. Everyone was entitled to one professional mistake, and this was probably going to be hers.

"You wear your dress greens well," she said quietly. "Special occasion?"

"Army and Navy Club. Little function."

She nodded and sipped her coffee. "Matt called me about four weeks ago," she said quickly, as though she just wanted to get this over with. She didn't look at him. She kept her gaze on the tabletop.

"And said what?"

"He'd stumbled onto something. That was his word. *Stumbled*.

It wasn't planned. And I certainly hadn't sent him out there on a mission. He was just commuting to be with his wife and kids. His call to me came out of left field."

"Okay." Puller took another drink of coffee and set it down.

Carson said, "He'd met someone who was involved in something. Correction, he met someone who had *found out* something."

"What and who?"

"I don't know the who."

"How did he meet this person?"

"By accident, I think. Anyway, it wasn't planned."

"And do you know the what?"

"It was big, whatever it was. Matt thought it so big that we might have to call in someone on our end."

"And why didn't you?"

Her words came fast. "Because I didn't know enough. I didn't want to pull the trigger on something and have it blow up in my face. This was totally off mission. Not my jurisdiction. Hell, I don't even think it had anything to do with the military. I was out of my comfort zone, Puller, you have to understand that. I had no control over the information flow and no way to verify it. Neither did Matt. He was relying on people he didn't know."

"You still could have gone to the police. Or had him go."

"And tell them what? Matt didn't have enough info either, at least according to what he told me. A lot of it was gut."

"Did he think this person might have been working undercover?"

"Undercover?" she said with genuine surprise. "You mean like a police officer?"

"Sometimes civilians go undercover on their own."

"How often?" she said skeptically.

"Once is enough."

"Well, Matt never mentioned anything like that."

"And what did you tell him to do? Follow up? See what he could find out? You thought maybe this might be an opportunity for career advancement? Outside the normal scope of work?"

"You put things pretty bluntly, but you're right. And the next

thing I knew he was dead. His whole family was dead. Wife, kids…
everybody." Her lips started to tremble. When she tried to pick up
her coffee cup, her hand was shaking so badly the coffee spilled
on her.

Puller took the cup from her, set it down, wiped the coffee off
her with a napkin, and then gripped her other hand.

"Look, ma'am, maybe you didn't play this the best way possible,
but no one can every time. And I know there was no way you ever
intended for any of this to happen."

She glanced quickly up at him and then just as abruptly looked
away. She turned to the side and used another napkin to dry her
eyes. Puller waited until she'd composed herself and turned back
to him.

She said, "Sorry about that, Puller. Generals aren't supposed
to cry."

"I've seen them tear up over the bodies of their men."

She smiled resignedly. "I was talking about *female* generals."

"Okay. When you found out what had happened to the Reynoldses, what did you do?"

"Quite frankly, I freaked. And when I calmed down, the only
thing I could think of was the potential blowback to me. Doesn't
paint a very flattering picture of me, but it's the truth."

"And you figured that the murder of the head of J23 would gen-
erate enough interest on its own? You knew there would be a lot of
backdoor maneuvering from people in slots way above either one
of us. And maybe you dropped some hints that until they knew
for sure what was behind it all it was better to go in light with just
one CID agent, treat it like a normal homicide investigation? See
where the chips fell?"

"I'm not sure my plan was that refined. But I realized as soon as
I said anything that it might come out anyway and I would look
really bad. It's been a hole in my gut ever since."

"I can understand that. But you might have been closer to the
truth than you thought. You said he fell into it by accident?"

"Yes. Matt also said he thought it might have national security implications. I mean, he really did say that to me. I had no way to verify it, but I know he believed it."

"You ever been to Drake, West Virginia?"

She shook her head.

"Well, it's not exactly a hotbed of terrorism, if that's what we're talking about."

"All I can tell you is what Matt told me."

"Fair enough. And someone did kill him because of it." Puller thought some things through while Carson stared miserably down at her hands.

"Don't beat yourself up too hard, ma'am. You were just seeing if maybe you could get something done, something to help the country."

"Let's just call a spade a spade, Puller. I thought I could use this to help get the second star. I was selfish and myopic. And now four people are dead who shouldn't be."

Seven, thought Puller. *Actually seven people are dead.*

"Okay. Anything else you can think of that might help me?"

"Matt did say that he thought whatever it was would happen soon."

"Soon because they were afraid of exposure? Or soon because the plan had been in place for a while and it was time to execute?"

"Probably both, considering they felt the need to kill Matt and his family."

"I'm surprised that he didn't provide you more details."

She said, "He didn't leave any evidence of who the person might be? You're sure?"

"We didn't find much of anything. We do think a soil sample might be involved."

She looked at him with a quizzical expression. "A soil sample?"

He nodded. "The killers may have come back for it, in fact. So it must've been important. That ring any bells with you?"

"Well, he did say that this thing might have far-reaching implications."

"But he never said how?"

"No. Now I wished I had pushed him for more details. I just never thought it would end like this. I guess I should have. The Army teaches you to provide for every contingency."

"We're human, so that means we're not perfect."

"The Army expects us to be perfect," she shot back.

"No, they just expect us to be better than the other side."

She eyed the notebook. "How will your report read?"

"That you were very cooperative and provided me with valuable intelligence."

"I owe you, Puller. I had you all wrong."

"No, you probably had me pegged right. But your aim was a little off."

"Hustling for a star and being a female can add up to a lonely life."

"You've got a big family around you. It's called the United States Army."

She smiled weakly. "Yeah, I guess so. When this is over, look me up. Maybe we can have a drink."

"Maybe we can," said Puller as he closed his notebook and took his leave.

On the way to his car he glanced at his watch. He had one more stop and then he could be back in West Virginia by taking a morning flight.

Unfortunately, he probably wasn't going to make it.

The four men had surrounded him.

CHAPTER

56

"JOHN PULLER?"

The men had materialized in the parking garage near Puller's ride. He noted the twin black SUVs idling nearby.

"What does Homeland Security want with me?"

The leader of the bunch, a small, trim man with curly dark hair and frown lines stacked on his forehead, said, "How do you know we're with DHS?"

Puller pointed at the waist of one man. "He's got the SIG nine." He pointed to another man. "He's carrying the SIG forty cal. DHS is one of the few that lets their people mix and match. Add to that you've got a DHS lapel pin on your jacket. And my final clue was the Homeland Security parking sticker on one of your rides over there."

The man looked around and then smiled. "Good eye. Still need to see our cred packs?"

"Yeah, I do. And I'll show you mine. Army CID."

"Yeah, I know."

"I know you know."

"We need you to come with us."

"Where and why?"

"The why will be explained by others. The where is not too far."

"Do I have a choice?"

"Not really, no."

Puller shrugged. "Then let's go."

The ride was ten minutes. They entered another parking garage, swept down two levels, left the vehicles, and took an elevator up five floors. Puller was led down a hall where every single door was shut and secured with key and combo locks. There was nothing to show this was a federal building, which wasn't unusual, Puller knew. DHS in particular kept ordinary-looking space like this all over the country. But to someone who knew what to look for the place screamed federal. The carpet was government beige, the walls government beige, the doors metal. The government spent a lot of money, Puller knew, but not on the finishes in their office buildings.

He was led into a room and left there at a small table with the door closed and locked from the outside. He counted off five minutes in his head and was beginning to wonder whether someone had forgotten he was there when the door opened.

The man was in his fifties and carried the heft and gravitas of a long government career in a field that did not include paper pushing or staple counting. He held a file. He sat. He rustled through the file and then he finally acknowledged Puller by looking at him.

"You want something to drink?" the man asked. "We got coffee, though ours sucks. We have water. Just tap. The high-end Deer Park perk got whacked last year. Budgets cuts are a bitch. Next they'll be taking our guns."

"I'm good." Puller glanced at the file. "That about me?"

"Not per se, no." He tapped the file. "I'm Joe Mason, by the way." He reached across and shook Puller's hand.

"John Puller."

"That one I got figured out," said Mason. He fiddled with the cuticle on one of his fingers. "How're things coming in West Virginia?"

"Figured that was what this was about. Not all that good, actually. I assume you've been read in?"

"You can call your SAC if you want. Don White's a good guy."

"I will call my SAC."

Mason pulled out his phone. "Let's get the perfunctory shit over with so we can move on to more substantive stuff. Call him now."

Puller made the call. Don White filled him in on Joe Mason of DHS and told Puller to be cooperative with the man.

Puller slid the phone back to Mason and looked at the file again. "So do *I* have to be read in?"

"I was just now thinking the very same thing, Puller."

"And have you reached a decision?"

"Everything I can get hold of about you tells me you're a crackerjack guy. Patriotic to the marrow. Tenacious as a bulldog, you're gonna get whoever you set after."

Puller said nothing, just eyed the man. He wanted him to keep talking. He wanted to keep listening.

Mason continued. "We have a situation out there. Sounds corny, doesn't it? We have a situation. Anyway, the problem is we don't know what the situation is." He looked up from the file. "Can you give us any help there?"

"Is this why SecArm was so interested in the case? Why they only sent me initially?"

"The Secretary of the Army is interested in this case because we are. And while you are the only one currently visible, there are other assets deployed on this. And not just from DHS."

"I understood DIA isn't interested in this."

"I would not agree with that statement."

"FBI in on it?"

"FBI is in on everything whether we want them or not. However, we did not want to overwhelm you with alphabet suits, so I was picked to deliver the interface."

"Okay, there's a situation, only you don't know what it is. I would have thought DHS would have more to do than work on something like that."

"I would agree with you except for one thing."

"What's that?"

"A piece of chatter that NSA picked up two days ago. Want to guess where it was coming from?"

"Drake, West Virginia."

"You got it."

"I thought NSA could only listen to the foreign part of a conversation. That it couldn't listen in or read the emails or texts of Americans."

"That's mostly correct as far as it goes."

"What did the chatter say?"

"Well, it was in a language that one would not expect to be coming from rural West Virginia."

When the man didn't tell him what it was, Puller got a little ticked off and said, "New Jersey? The Bronx?"

"Try again, and head farther east."

"Arabic?"

"Dari. You know it's one of the major dialects spoken in Afghanistan."

"Yeah, that I know. So Afghanistan. Has it been translated?"

"Yes. As follows: 'The time is coming soon.' And that everyone needed to be prepared. And that justice would be theirs."

"And you took that to mean some attack on the United States?"

"That's what I'm paid to think, Puller. And also paid to prevent."

"Why was this chatter so special? People say stupid stuff all the time that leads nowhere. Even speaking in Dari."

"The chatter wasn't clean. It was encrypted. And it wasn't encrypted with some fancy computer algorithm. It was in code. Code that my people tell me was very popular with the old KGB before the Cold War ended. Now we also know that the Taliban has started using old KGB codes to communicate with implanted cells. I guess it harks back to the days when the Red Army was rolling around in tanks there."

"Taliban using a KGB code in Dari coming from West Virginia. Now that's diversity for you. But they broke it?"

"Obviously, or else I wouldn't be sitting here talking to you. Ironically, the old code stuff is coming back into vogue, Puller, because we've gotten so good at cracking computerized encryption. Bottom line, it made us sit up and take notice."

"I haven't seen one turban in Drake. Just a bunch of proud Americans with a little red around the neck. How can you be sure the plan will be executed in Drake? The terrorists could just be hiding out there and the target could be someplace else."

"Other components of the chatter lead us to believe that the target is at least in the vicinity of Drake."

Puller sat back, thought about this. "Well, there's a big concrete dome where a secret government facility operated in the 1960s.

That's probably a good place to start. In fact, it's the only thing out of the ordinary in the place. Other than a bunch of dead bodies."

"If it were only that easy." Mason pulled a sheaf of papers from his file and slid them across to Puller. He said, "We tracked down what that facility was used for. It doesn't really help us."

Puller scanned the sheets of paper. It was a classified document that he was cleared to read. It was dated from the 1970s. He said, "They built bomb components there?"

"Key components. Not the boom part of the ordnance. The concrete dome was put in because some of the material they handled there was radioactive. Back then DoD had money to burn. And there was no EPA. So instead of cleaning up the site the military just covered it over."

"Is it a threat?"

"Environmentally? Who the hell knows? Maybe. But that's not our concern. The report is clear that all materials and equipment were removed from the place. And you're not going to punch through three feet of concrete to see if your Geiger counter goes nuts."

"What if someone were to blow it up, maybe release the radio-activity, if there's any left in there?"

"Yeah, Puller. You'd need a mountain of explosives, a lot of assets on the ground, and you have no way of knowing if there's anything in there to make it worth your while. So they release some radio-activity into the air in Drake? Who cares?" Mason sat back in his chair. "No, the answer has to lie somewhere else."

Puller slid back the papers. "Okay. What else?"

"We know you talked to General Carson."

"She was cooperative."

"Reynolds knew something. That was why he was killed. He knew about something happening out there."

"I just found that out. If you've known for a while it would've been good to know back then."

"Drake didn't exist for me until we decoded that transmission. And that was only two days ago. You're probably way ahead of us."

"Because you're not out there. You left it to me and some local cops. Two days ago was shortly after the murders. They have to be connected. You could have sent a team out here. Why didn't you?"

"Tricky questions, trickier answer."

"I'm used to both."

Mason smiled. "I guess you are. Soldiering is a lot more complicated than it looks."

"The soldiering part is easy compared to all the other crap. Firing a gun straight just takes practice. No practice in the world prepares you for the backroom hopscotch." He paused. "You ever in? You look the type."

"Marines. Didn't do my full time. Got out, went to college, and ended up carrying a gun for Uncle Sam anyway. But I wear a suit instead of the uniform."

"Marines have covered my back many a time."

"And I'm sure you did the same for them. But getting back to your query, the consensus here is to let this thing play out a bit. We bring in the heavy artillery we spook these folks."

"Spooking might not be such a bad idea. Especially if they're planning a second 9/11. But why they would pick Drake after they hit the Big Apple, I'm not sure. The damage potential just isn't the same."

"Which is why we're worried. And if we went in heavy, we figured they'd scatter, regroup, and hit somewhere else just as unlikely and they wouldn't make the chatter mistake again. Their choice of location has us concerned, Puller. It's not a traditional target. It has no replication value. You nail one airport or mall or train station it shuts them all down countrywide."

"But you hit a Podunk, you don't get the same result."

"Which means they know something we don't. This is not on our tactical or strategic grid. We don't have a playbook page on this one. *We're* the ones who are spooked, frankly."

"Your strategy could be playing with the lives of everyone that lives in Drake."

"Yes, it could."

"But since there're so few of them and most of them are dirt poor, I guess that makes it okay?"

"I wouldn't go that far. They're still Americans, poor or not."

"But if this were the Big Apple we were talking about, or Houston or Atlanta or D.C.?"

"Every situation is different, Puller."

"The more things are different the more they're the same."

"An Army guy who's also a philosopher. I'm impressed. Seriously, though, I don't want any innocent citizens to die. But it's tricky. But if it were New York or Chicago or L.A. and certainly D.C., we'd be going in with the big guns, no doubt."

"So Drake is the experiment in evolving tactics?"

"Drake is an opportunity."

"Okay, Reynolds was military and maybe that was enough to make him a target. What about Molly Bitner and Eric Treadwell?"

"Right across the street and all."

"Could one of them have been the one Reynolds *stumbled* onto? That's the word Carson used."

"What makes you say that?" asked Mason.

"From what I can tell they never went anywhere other than the nursing home or hospital, which isn't even in Drake. The only people they would logically come into contact with would be the neighbors on the street. My focus, obviously, is on the only neighbors to end up murdered too."

"I see where you're going with this, and I like the angle. We don't have anything concrete on either of them, but it still might be a promising lead."

"So what do you want from me?"

"To do what you've been doing. Keep digging. The only change will be that you'll report directly to me instead of your SAC. You're going to be our eyes on the ground there, Puller." Mason rose. "I know you want to get back."

"I was going to go by the Reynolds house in Fairfax City, check it out."

"We've done that canvass already. Nothing there. Your SAC can verify that. If you want to go over there, feel free."

Puller didn't hesitate. "I'd rather see for myself."

"Pretty sure you'd say that. You'll have full access. You can go right after you leave here."

"Thanks."

"Now that the prelims are out of the way, fill me in on your investigation."

Puller gave him the condensed version. Mason perked up when he mentioned the probable videotaping of the Reynolds family.

"That sounds ominous," he said.

"Yes, it does," replied Puller.

When he got to the soil report, Mason stopped him. "I'd like to see it."

"Yes, sir."

"Why a soil report?"

"Must've been important somehow."

"And we don't know from where it was taken?"

"No."

"After you go by the Reynoldses' you need to get back to Drake. I'd let you ride on DHS wings, but I don't know who might be watching. Right now I'm not trusting many people."

"Not a problem. I'll go the way I came."

As they walked down the hall Mason said, "Samantha Cole? Asset or liability?"

"Asset."

"Good to know."

"What's your gut telling you about this?"

Mason stared straight ahead. "That it'll make a lot of people forget 9/11."

Mason turned left down another hall.

Puller kept walking straight ahead.

Right now it was the only direction he could go.

CHAPTER

57

PULLER DROVE DIRECTLY to the Reynolds home in Fairfax City. It was in an older neighborhood of modest homes. Reynolds had probably been transferred back and forth from the D.C. area several times during his military career. For those who had to sell their homes at the lows of the real estate market and then buy back in at the highs, it could be rough financially. Puller didn't know Reynolds's personal situation, but he concluded the man was probably looking forward to a fatter paycheck in the private sector to offset all those years of earning far less than he was worth while serving his country.

Two hours later Puller sat in the living room of the home holding a picture of the Reynolds family in his gloved hands. Though the place had already been processed by DHS, he never broke crime scene procedures.

In the photo the Reynoldses looked happy, normal, alive.

Now they were none of those things. He had noted baseball gear in the boy's room and swim and tennis posters in the daughter's room. There were photos of Matt and Stacey during various military functions. And on vacation. Sailing, skydiving, swimming with the dolphins. There were pictures of their children on tennis and basketball courts. The daughter in her prom dress. The son, then just a toddler, hugging his old man when he was in uniform. Puller could easily read the expressions on their faces.

Dad was being deployed.

The son was not happy about it. He was hugging his father tight, trying to keep him from going.

Puller put the photo back where he'd gotten it. He locked the door on the way out. He sat in his car for a while gazing up at a house that had no one left to live in it. It would go on the market, be sold, the belongings dispersed, and the Reynoldses would live on only in the memories of their friends and family.

And in mine.

Afterwards, Puller drove to his apartment and packed a duffel bag full of clean clothes. By the time he got there it was very late. He spent a few minutes with AWOL while he thought through the night's events. He'd changed his return flight to Charleston for the next morning. He'd missed the last direct flight there tonight.

Carson had been more right than she thought and also more wrong. There *was* something big going on. Only she had thought that Reynolds and she were the only ones on the federal side who knew about it. That was incorrect. She had thought she had blown it by not contacting the authorities. Obviously, the authorities *had* known, albeit after Reynolds was dead. The fact that the Reynolds family had been slaughtered did not give Puller much confidence in DHS's ability to cover his back if need be. But for the chatter, they'd still be clueless.

As he stroked AWOL's ears his thoughts turned to Sam Cole. How much if any of this could he tell her? The official answer was simple: He could tell her little if anything. The unofficial answer was far more complicated. He didn't like putting people in harm's way without telling them the lay of the land. He would have a short flight and then a longer car ride from Charleston to think about it.

He checked his watch. He had prearranged this. He had to, otherwise it couldn't happen.

He made the call. He spoke to a line of people and gave the appropriate responses. Finally, the familiar voice came over the line.

"Surprised when they told me you'd set up a call for tonight," said Robert Puller.

"Wanted to catch up."

"It's late on the East Coast."

"Yeah, it is."

"The call's monitored," his brother said. "There are people listening." He changed voices, dropping it deliberately into a deep baritone. "Can you hear us clearly enough, Official Monitor? If not we'd be glad to speak up while we plot the destruction of the world."

"Knock it off, Bobby, they might cut the call off."

"They might, but they won't. What else do they have to do?"

"I saw him."

For the Puller brothers this was not so subtle code. There was only one "him" in their lives.

"Okay. How's he doing?" Robert's voice had quickly turned serious.

"Not all that great, actually. Things tend to wander."

"In and out of the stars?"

"Right. Exactly."

"Otherwise?"

"Healthy. Live to be a hundred."

"What else?"

"A beef he has."

"With whom?"

"Blame game. Still the stars, he thinks. But trajectory shot all to hell."

Puller didn't care if the monitors figured out they were talking about their father. Unless their conversations were deemed to be criminal or inappropriate in any way, this call was confidential. And military careers could be curtailed and even destroyed if it was shown that any part of a prisoner's conversation was revealed in an unauthorized way, particularly when a highly decorated combat vet was on the other end of the line.

"One guess," said Robert.

"Right," said Puller.

"He really believes that? The timing is way off."

"Not in his mind."

Puller heard his brother give a long sigh.

Puller said, "Thought about not telling you."

"As in what does it matter?"

"Something like that. Maybe I shouldn't have told you."

"No, no, you should have, little brother. I appreciate it." He paused. "Working on anything interesting?"

"Yes and no. Yes I am and no I can't tell you about it."

"Well, good luck. My money's on you."

They spoke for another thirty seconds on innocuous matters and said their goodbyes. When Puller clicked off he stared down at his phone imagining his brother being walked back to his cell. Nothing to do but wait for the next day when he would get out of his cage for an hour. Wait for the next phone call from his brother. Or the next visit. Totally out of his control. There wasn't one segment of his life in which he had real input.

I'm all he has left.

I'm all the old man has left.

God help me.

And them.

CHAPTER

58

Early the next morning the jet lifted off from Dulles Airport and climbed smoothly into the sky. Puller drank a bottle of water and spent most of the short hop staring out the window. He checked his watch. Nearly 0600. He had tried to sleep some last night, but even his Army training failed him as his mind continued to whir about as fast as the plane's engines.

The plane landed in Charleston less than an hour later and he retrieved his Malibu from the parking lot. He arrived in Drake in time for breakfast. He met Cole at the Crib Room after calling her on the drive in. He drank two more cups of coffee and had the biggest breakfast platter the Crib offered.

She stared over at him as the mounds of food disappeared.

"Don't they feed you in the big city?" she asked.

He took a bite of eggs and pancakes. "Not this trip they didn't. Not sure the last time I ate, actually. Maybe breakfast yesterday."

She sipped on her coffee and tore a bit of toast off and ate it.

"And was your trip productive?"

"It was. We actually have lots to talk about. But just not here."

"Important?"

"Wouldn't waste your time otherwise. Anything on your end?"

"Got the court order faxed." She slid out several sheets of paper. "And I got the results of the soil testing."

Puller put his fork down and eyed the paper. "And?"

"And I'm not a scientist."

"Let me have a look."

She slid the report across.

As he picked it up she said, "The first two pages are legal mumbo-jumbo basically covering their ass if their report is wrong or they did a test incorrectly, or the results ever end up in court they are one hundred percent not liable."

"That's comforting," muttered Puller.

He flipped to the third page and settled in to read. After a minute he said, "I'm not a scientist either, but while I see terms like apatite, rutile, marcasite, galena, sphalerite, and other stuff I've never heard of, I also see uranium, which I definitely recognize."

"Don't get your shorts in a wad. There's coal in fifty-three of the fifty-five counties in West Virginia, and pretty much where you find coal, you find uranium. But the levels of radioactivity are low. People breathe in uranium particles all the time and do just fine. And the level of the parts per million on the uranium shown on that report means it's naturally occurring."

"You're sure about that? You said you weren't a scientist."

"As sure as I am that coal is more a rock than a mineral. Since it's formed from organic remains it technically doesn't qualify as a true mineral. It's actually made up of other minerals."

"Everyone in West Virginia knows this stuff?"

"Well, not everyone, but a lot of folks do. What can you expect from a state whose official mineral is a lump of bituminous coal?"

He sifted through the pages. "Do we even know where these soil samples came from?"

"That's the hell of it; we don't. It could be from anywhere. The report doesn't specify. I guess they assumed Reynolds would know where he'd taken the sample."

"Well, presumably it's somewhere from around Drake, because I don't think Reynolds ventured much outside of here."

Cole played with a packet of sugar, bending it back and forth until it broke and sent the white crystals cascading down. She swept them onto her coffee cup saucer. "Do you think Reynolds was working on something that didn't involve Drake? Maybe these samples are from D.C."

"I don't think so, particularly after what I found out up there."

"So why don't you hurry your butt up and finish eating so we can leave here and you can tell me all about it."

"Okay, but we need to stop by the police station. I have to fax that soil report to a couple of places."

They paid their bill and climbed into her cruiser parked outside. She drove to the police station and Puller faxed off the report to Joe Mason in D.C. and Kristen Craig at USACIL in Georgia.

Back in the cruiser Cole turned to him. She was wearing her uniform, and her gun belt made this maneuver more difficult than it should have been, but she seemed determined to face him.

"So spill it, Puller, and don't leave one thing out."

"You have any security clearances?"

"I already told you that I don't, unless you count the little certificate I got when I was a state trooper, and I doubt that would impress you federal types."

"Duly noted. Now I know that going in, and what I'm about to say is probably classified and my ass could get fried for telling you."

"Duly noted. And they won't find out from me."

He gazed out the window. "Dickie Strauss and his big friend were in the Crib watching us."

"Along with half the town of Drake," added Cole.

"We still need to run down his tat connection with Treadwell."

"Yes, we do. But right now all you need to do is talk."

"Start driving. I'd rather be on the move when I tell you what I'm about to. And head east."

"Why?"

"Because after hearing it, you might want to keep going until you hit the ocean."

59

It took Puller about an hour, but he brought Cole up to speed on most of what he'd learned while he was in D.C. He did tell her about DHS's interest, but he did *not* tell her that Drake was being used, essentially, as bait for a possible terrorist cell operating in the area. He didn't tell her because Cole would be duty-bound to raise the alarm in her locality. Then it would all be over for Mason and his trying to nail the guys communicating in coded Dari.

Still, Puller had been tempted to do just that.

"Would have been nice to know this stuff a long time ago," complained Cole. "They always play these sorts of games up there?"

"It's not a game to them. It's a fence straddle and they're not sure who to trust."

"I'd last five seconds up there. I don't play well with others."

"You might surprise yourself."

"No, I might shoot somebody. So where to?"

"Crime scene. Got an idea I thought of on the plane ride back."

Lan Monroe was just coming out of the Halversons' residence as they pulled up. An evidence kit was banging against his short leg. He threw up his free hand and smiled as they climbed out of the car.

"Welcome back, Puller," he said. "Glad to see D.C. didn't eat you alive."

Puller looked at Cole and said in a low voice, "You always this discreet with info?"

She looked uncomfortable and said to Monroe, "You finished up in there?"

"Yeah. It's all ready to be released."

She nodded and watched him load his gear in his vehicle.

Puller observed the police car parked out in front. He recognized the deputy named Dwayne. As he continued to watch, Dwayne flicked a cigarette butt through the open car window.

"They're not supposed to smoke on duty but Dwayne is trying hard to quit and he's a real bastard without his nicotine pop. I know that better than most—"

She stopped talking because Puller had abruptly walked off.

"Hey," she called out and followed him.

Puller passed between the Halversons' home and the house next to it. He stopped and eyed the deck built onto the back of the neighbor's house. It was made of pressure-treated lumber long since grayed from the sun and elements. He looked from the deck to the nearby woods facing it.

Cole caught up to him.

"What are you doing?"

"Having an epiphany."

"Is this the idea you had on the plane?"

"No, this is the idea I had five seconds ago."

He eyed the thick glass ashtray that rested on one railing of the deck. It was filled with butts. He wondered why he hadn't noticed it before.

"Who lives in that house?"

"Old couple by the name of Dougett. George and Rhonda, if I remember correctly. I talked to them before when we were canvassing the neighborhood."

"Who's the smoker?"

"He is. When I interviewed them I found out his wife won't let him do it in the house, hence that ashtray on the deck. So what's the big deal about the guy being a smoker? You on a one-person bandwagon to reclaim the souls of all us poor dumb cigarette addicts?"

"No. It's that the ashtray is on a deck that overlooks the woods." He pointed between the two spots.

Cole looked at where he was pointing. "What are you getting at?"

"How old is Dougett? The guy, I mean."

"Late seventies. Bad shape. Overweight, pasty, got some kidney problems, or so he told me when I talked to them. He was TMI on his health issues in general. I guess it's an old person thing. Not enough to fill up their lives otherwise."

"So that means he's up at night trying to pee and nothing is coming out. He gets frustrated, can't sleep, comes out here for a smoke because it's too hot during the day to do it."

"Probably. But he also told me he sits in his car during the day with the engine running and the AC on so he can light up. But so what?"

"Are they home now?"

"Car's in the driveway. They only have the one."

"Then let's put my idea to the test."

CHAPTER

60

PULLER CLEARED THE STEPS up to the Dougetts' front door two at a time with Cole in his wake. He knocked. Four seconds later the door opened and George Dougett stood before them. He was barely five-five and his bloated figure, pale features, wobbly knees, and bent spine bespoke numerous health problems and lots of pain. He looked like he could drop dead at any moment, and probably on occasion wanted to.

"Sergeant Cole," he said. "Back for more questions?"

He sounded almost gleeful. Puller figured the man's life was otherwise pretty dull. Even a murder investigation was probably preferable to doing nothing except sitting in your car smoking and waiting for your life to be over.

"I'm John Puller, Army CID, Mr. Dougett. You mind if I ask you a few questions?" Puller flipped out his cred pack for the man, who seemed even more thrilled by this.

"Hell yes, you can." His voice was sound run over gravel until it got all clogged. He gave an enormous cough that nearly lifted him off his feet.

"Damn allergies, excuse me." He blew his nose into a fat wad of tissues held in one puffy red hand and ushered them into his house.

They followed him down a short hall to a small den paneled with sheets of plywood wood stained dark. The furnishings were forty years old and looked every bit of it. The shag carpet had permanently lost its shag and the shine on the furniture had disappeared probably twenty years ago. They settled into chairs and Dougett said, "I was in the Army. Oh, that was many moons ago, of course.

Korea. Wonderful country. But very cold. I was glad to get back here."

"I'm sure," said Puller.

"You taking care of yourself, Mr. Dougett?" asked Cole.

He smiled resignedly. "I'm old and fat and I smoke. Other than that I'm fine. Thanks for asking." He peered over at Puller. "Damn, you're a fine specimen of a man, son. See you coming at me on the battlefield, I might just surrender then and there."

"Yes, sir," said Puller, who was thinking of how he wanted to play this out. "I noticed you smoke on the rear deck."

"Yeah, the missus doesn't like the smell in the house."

"Where is your wife?" asked Cole.

"Still in bed. Arthritis gets her something fierce in the morning. Rolls out around noon, just in time for lunch. Don't ever grow old, that's my message to you two."

"Well, the alternative isn't too appealing," said Puller. He counted back in his head. "Sunday night. Did you see anything unusual? Hear anything? Like a gunshot?"

"Hearing's not great, son. And Sunday night I was hugging the porcelain. Something the wife made for dinner didn't agree with me. Happens more often than not these days. I didn't go outside. Told the lady here that when she come and asked on Monday. And the missus was asleep in bed. Guess my throwing up all night and having the runs from hell didn't affect her peaceful rest at all."

"Okay. How about late Monday night? Were you out on the deck?"

"Yes. I go to bed late, get up earlier and earlier. I figure I'm gonna be lying for eternity in a box soon enough, so why waste what time I got left sleeping? I like it in the early morning. Got a little cool breeze, see the dew on the trees and grass. It's nice."

"Do you remember seeing anything unusual Monday night?"

He stuffed the tissues in his pocket and rubbed his chin so hard it was like he was trying to polish it. He grinned and pointed first at Puller. "Saw you." He next indicated Cole. "And I saw her. Out on patrol or something in the woods. Well, I guess that was technically Tuesday morning."

"We were looking for somebody. I saw someone run through the woods a few minutes before that. Did you see them too?"

Dougett was already nodding. "I did. Running fast. Knew their way. There's a path back there."

"Mr. Dougett, why didn't you tell me that when I was here before?" asked an exasperated Cole.

"Well, nobody asked me. And I didn't know it was important. And it happened *after* you came by and asked me questions. I sure didn't know it was connected to what happened over at the Halversons'." His voice dropped. "Was it connected?"

Puller said, "Can you describe the person?"

"It was a man for sure. Tall, but not so tall as you, son. Big shoulders. Looked bald. Way he was moving I'd say he was young. It was dark, but there was some moonlight. Fellow had scars on his arm, or else was burned or something. It was all blackened."

"So he had on a short-sleeved shirt?"

"Like a tank top, yes, sir."

"Good eyes," said Cole. "Night, at a distance, even with moonlight."

"Lasik," said George, pointing to his eyes. "I'm old and fat but I got me twenty-twenty at distance, and it wasn't that far away."

"You think he was from around here?" asked Cole.

"Can't say. Like I said, he seemed to know his way through those woods okay. I could maybe pick him out in a lineup."

"Tell 'em the rest, George."

They all turned to see an old woman shoot into the room on a three-wheeled scooter designed for disabled persons. She had on a pink robe and her swollen feet were stuffed into too-small slippers. Puller noted that she wore a pearl gray wig that was cut short. She easily weighed two hundred pounds and looked as unhealthy as her husband. But despite her arthritis she steered the scooter with a practiced hand and rode it right up next to Puller.

"I'm Rhonda, his far better half," she said by way of introduction.

Puller said, "John Puller, Army CID. What 'rest' are you talking about?"

George Dougett cleared his throat, looked warily at his wife and said, "Some other things I saw."

"*We* saw," corrected his wife. She looked at Puller and smiled triumphantly. "I was watching from the window."

"Why?" asked Cole.

"Because my husband sometimes falls asleep outside while he's smoking his cancer sticks. So I watch him to make sure he doesn't ignite himself."

"I have never ignited myself," said George indignantly.

"That's because you have a loving wife of fifty-six years who looks after you," said Rhonda in the tone of a parent to a child.

"And what did you see?" Puller asked.

"It was nothing," said George nervously.

Rhonda snorted. "It sure as hell was something." She pointed at Cole. "Saw that deputy of yours that got killed."

"Larry Wellman? You saw him do what?"

"He was walking around the house, looking at things."

"He was patrolling," said Cole. "That was his job."

Puller asked, "Did you see him go *in* the house?"

"No."

"Was he alone?" asked Puller.

Rhonda nodded.

"What time was this?" asked Cole.

"I'd say between twelve-thirty and one in the morning. George had smoked four cancer sticks, and he milks them for all he can."

"Will you please stop calling them cancer sticks!" he snapped.

"Oh, I'm sorry, Mr. Touchy. George had smoked four of his *coffin nails*, and that usually takes him until close to 1 a.m."

George groused, "Fifty-six years I've put up with this woman. It's a miracle I haven't killed her."

"Keep going, ma'am," Puller said to Rhonda.

"Well, then I went to the bathroom. George will have to pick up the story from there."

Cole said, "Wait a minute, didn't Officer Wellman notice you sitting on the back deck smoking?"

George shook his head. "I was lying on our little glider couch. The back part faces the Halversons'."

"How could you see anything, then?" asked Puller.

"I was looking around the corner of the couch. I could see everything, but it would've been real hard to see me. And I'd put out my smokes by then."

"So Wellman was patrolling. Then what?"

"And then I must've fallen asleep," he said sheepishly.

"See," said Rhonda in a gloating tone. "I went to the can and you could've ignited yourself into oblivion. Cremation on the cheap."

His husband scowled. "I just said I'd already put the smoke out. And you'd like it if I cremated myself, wouldn't you? Then you could spend my burial money over at that casino you like so much."

"Mr. Dougett, if you could focus on what you saw?" prompted Cole.

"Oh, right. Anyway, I woke up and the next thing I seen was the big bald fellow coming out of the house."

"Wait a minute. The bald fellow was in the house?" said Cole. "You never said that."

"I didn't? Well, I'm saying it now. He came out moving fast. He ran into the woods. Then I heard a car pull up. That was four thirty or so. I remember because I checked my watch."

"That was me," said Puller. "I drove up, called Sergeant Cole, and then went in the house. I looked around, found Wellman dead, and then heard Cole drive up." He looked at Cole. "I saw a guy running in the woods, came back out, and that's when I hooked up with you and we went after the guy."

"So the bald guy who came out of the woods must've hung around while you were in the house," said Cole.

"Must have," agreed George. "I saw him take off, and just a few moments later I heard the back door open and you came out. I didn't see where you went after that."

Puller said, "Hid behind the car parked in the driveway."

Cole said, "But Larry's car was taken. How did that happen?

Who did it?" She turned to the Dougetts. "Did either of you see anything about that?"

They both shook their heads.

George said, "That might've happened when I was asleep."

"And I was in the bathroom a long time," said Rhonda. "When you're old," she added, "everything just takes longer."

Puller said, "Just to get the timeline straight, you last saw Wellman patrolling between half past twelve and one. He didn't go into the house. The next you saw was baldy leaving the house shortly before I arrived. I found Wellman dead around five. And he was killed about three hours or so before that, or two A.M. That would be about an hour after you saw Wellman patrolling, and then you fell asleep. But baldy could have already been in the house or come there when you were asleep."

Cole interjected, "That means baldy could have killed Larry and then fled."

Puller shook his head. "But what happened to the car? This guy apparently didn't drive off in it. And if this guy did kill him, why hang around in the woods at all? Why not just get the hell away? It was only because he hung around that I spotted him."

"It's a real head-knocker," added George.

Puller said, "Did you notice if the patrol car was missing when you woke up? Or did you hear a car start up?"

"Neither," said Dougett. "I must've really been out."

"Would you two like some coffee and cupcakes?" asked Rhonda.

Her husband barked, "It's the morning, for Chrissakes, Rhonda. Who the hell eats cupcakes in the morning?"

"I do," she said primly.

"We already ate," said Puller.

"Well, we hope we were helpful to you," said George.

"Do you think we're in any danger?" asked Rhonda in a way that demonstrated she was thrilled at the prospect.

"I've got a gun," said George grimly.

"You've got no bullets for it," said his wife. "And even if you did you haven't fired it in years. Probably shoot yourself before you'd hit anything else."

Cole and Puller left the couple bickering over this point and walked back to the police cruiser.

She said, "So where does that leave us?"

"We've got to find baldy."

"Any thoughts on that?"

"Yeah."

61

As they were driving back through Drake, Cole slowed her cruiser and pulled to the curb. Puller looked where she was staring.

"Roger Trent is back in town," he said.

A black Cadillac Escalade with gold trim sat idling at the curb, a man he'd never seen before at the wheel. Puller eyed the driver closely, his gaze taking in all relevant details and his mind crunching through those observations and arriving at certain conclusions.

Interesting.

Next to the vehicle stood Roger Trent. He was dressed in a suit. Puller noted that it looked baggy and wrinkled, as though the man had slept in it. He had opened the door of the vehicle and was about to step inside.

"Looks like he just walked off the plane," he noted. "Let's have a chat with him."

She pulled to a stop next to the Escalade and Puller rolled his window down. "Hey, Roger, got time for a cup of coffee in the Crib?"

Trent scowled at Puller and then glanced at Cole. "I just had a cup of coffee there."

"Got some things to talk to you about. Won't take long."

"Is it about those death threats?"

"Yep."

"I'll give you ten minutes." He turned and walked into the restaurant.

A minute later Puller and Cole were seated across from him.

They ordered their coffees. The place was about three-quarters full and everyone there kept shooting nervous glances at the trio.

Puller noted this and said, "You come here often? I understand you own it."

"I own just about everything in Drake. So what?"

Puller ran his gaze down the man's wrinkled suit. "You just get back into town?"

"Yeah, again, so what?" He glanced sharply at Cole. "I thought you wanted to talk to me about those death threats."

"We're working on it, Roger."

"Right. Well, you might want to look a little close to home. Just like last time."

"I have. And I don't think that's the source. I wanted to let you know that."

"I'm not sure you're the most objective person to make that decision."

"We think Molly Bitner's murder had something to do with her working at your office, Roger," said Puller.

This comment drew a sharp glance from Cole, but Trent didn't catch it. He was staring at Puller.

"And why do you think that?"

"Soil reports."

"I don't know what that means. What sort of soil reports?"

"You know, the environmental kind."

"I still don't understand."

"Eric Treadwell and Dickie Strauss were friends, did you know that?"

"Not really, no."

"They have the same tat sleeve. Dickie said he copied it from Eric's."

"What does any of that have to do with me?"

"I'm not sure, Roger," said Puller. He took a sip of coffee and studied the man. "How'd the trip to New York go?"

Trent looked startled. "How did you know that's where I went?"

"Bill Strauss told us. He wouldn't tell us why, but he did say that your company was very profitable and investment opportunities were everywhere."

Trent glanced away and Puller saw a small tremor start up in the man's left hand.

"Everybody needs energy," added Puller.

"Right," said Trent curtly. "Are we done here? Because you clearly have nothing to tell me that is helpful."

Cole glanced at Puller. He said, "I guess so. You should probably go home and get some sleep. You look beat."

"Thanks for your concern," snapped Trent.

As the other man rose, Puller did too. He stepped closer and said in a low voice, "I would take those death threats seriously, Roger. But maybe not for the reason you think."

Trent grew a shade paler, turned, and left. A few moments later the Escalade roared off.

As Cole and Puller walked outside, she said, "What exactly was that about?"

"That man is scared. For a lot of reasons. Personal. Business. Why do you think that is? He owns the whole town. Big fish in a little pond."

"I don't know," said Cole.

"Big fish in a little pond," repeated Puller.

Cole got it. "There's a bigger fish in town."

"Could be."

"Who?"

"We find baldy."

"How? You said you had an idea."

"Let me put it another way. We find Dickie Strauss."

"You think he's the guy Dougett saw running from the house?"

"Fits the physical description. Burns on the arm? Try a tat sleeve. And if it wasn't Dickie, it might have been one of his tat sleeve crew."

"There aren't any gangs in Drake, Puller."

"None that you're aware of," he corrected.

"Why would Dickie Strauss have been in that house? And if he was, then that means he killed Larry Wellman. Why would he do that?"

"That's not necessarily so."

"What do you mean? They were both in the house and Larry ended up dead. Somebody had to kill him. He didn't hang himself."

"Agreed."

"So what's your point?"

"Let's just find Dickie instead of arguing. Any idea where he might be?"

She slid the cruiser into drive. "Yeah."

"Where?"

"You'll find out when we get there. I can play things close to the vest too."

CHAPTER

62

THE CONCRETE DOME. Puller studied it as they passed by.

"Maybe Drake should make that into a tourist attraction," he said.

"Yeah, that would be a great draw. Stare at cement for a dollar," replied Cole.

She turned down a street and steered the cruiser into the neighborhood that had once housed people that had worked in the nearby facility. They passed abandoned houses that were starting to cave in, and other homes where people had worked to make them livable. Puller stared at small kids with dirty faces, and skinny mothers who ran after them. He didn't see many men, but figured they were probably out earning a living or at least trying to find work.

He sniffed the air. "Nice aroma."

"We try to get them to take their trash to the dump, but it's an ongoing struggle. And the bathrooms in these places stopped working a long time ago. Most have put in outhouses of some kind."

"Nice life for the citizens of the richest nation on earth."

"Well, those riches must be concentrated in the hands of a few, because we don't have any of it."

"They are," said Puller. "Like your brother-in-law." He looked around. "Those are electrical poles, but those transformers don't seem to be hot."

"People here were trying to tie into them and getting fried. We had the electric company turn this part of the grid off and do a workaround." She pointed to a telephone pole that had some cable running from it down to the ground where it snaked inside some of the homes.

"Telephone service is being tapped into, as you can see. We let that pass. Folks here can't necessarily afford cell phones. But they can still talk to people. Phone company is okay with it. Hell, more and more people don't even have landlines these days. They make their money off cell phones and data usage and stuff like that."

Cole pointed up ahead. "There's our destination."

The place was at the end of the street and far larger than the other homes. Puller stared at the massive overhead doors painted red, though the paint had mostly faded away.

It struck Puller what he was looking at. "A firehouse?"

"Used to be. Hasn't been used for that since they domed over the Bunker. At least that's what I was told as a kid."

"So what do they use it for now?"

The next instant Puller heard the motorcycle start up. Actually, it was more than one motorcycle.

"Harley club," said Cole. "Of which Dickie Strauss is a member. They call it Xanadu. Some of them might not even know what it means. But it helps keep most of these boys out of trouble."

"And Treadwell too? He had a Harley. Is that where the tat sleeve came from?"

"I don't know about the tat sleeve. And no, not everyone in the club has one."

"But it would have been nice to know that Dickie and Treadwell belonged to the same club."

"We just found out that it might have been Dickie that ran out of the Halversons' place. Until then, I had no reason to suspect he was involved."

"But maybe the motorcycle gang was connected to Treadwell's death."

"It's a club, Puller, not a gang. Most of the members are older guys. They have families and bills to pay."

She pulled the car to a stop in front of the old firehouse and they got out. Through the open doorways Puller could see an old fire truck with rotted wheels in one bay, and the ubiquitous fire pole just beyond it. Wooden lockers lined both sides of the wall, and there was old firefighting equipment stacked in piles.

In the other bay were a half dozen vintage Harleys. Puller counted five men inside, two on their Harleys and revving the motors and the others tinkering with their machines.

"How come those guys aren't out working?"

"Probably because they can't find jobs."

"So they just sit around playing with their expensive rides?"

"Most of these bikes are twenty years old, Puller. Nobody's playing with anything. I know most of those men. They work hard. But when there's no work, what do you do? County unemployment rate is nearly twenty percent, and that's folks who are still looking. Lots of people have just given up."

"Do they keep their bikes here?"

"Sometimes, why?"

"You said the people who live here are scavengers."

"Yeah, but they don't touch the motorcycle club stuff."

"Why not?"

"Because the club members help them."

"How?"

"They collect food, blankets, and hire some of the guys to work for them when they have jobs lined up. Most of the club members have special skills: mechanics, plumbers, electricians, carpenters. Like I said, hard workers. They'll go by the houses and fix stuff for the families free of charge."

"Bunch of Good Samaritans."

"We do have them here in Drake."

They walked up the cracked concrete drive to the front of the firehouse. Several of the men looked up. Puller saw Dickie Strauss walk out of a back room, stop, and stare at them. He was wiping his greasy hands on a work rag.

Cole said, "Hey, Dickie, we'd like to talk to you."

Dickie turned and ran toward the back of the building.

"Hey," shouted Cole. "Stop! We just want to talk."

Puller had already moved forward, into the building.

Two guys who'd been working on their Harleys blocked Puller's way. They were both built like fireplugs, older than Puller, with tie-dyed bandanas and overly confident expressions. Their hands were huge and the pronounced cords of muscles in their forearms showed they performed physically hard labor for their daily bread.

Puller held up his badge. "Out of the way. Now."

One of the men said, "This is private property. Let me see your warrant."

Cole said, "Let him by."

Puller had one eye on the fleeing Dickie and the other on the lead bandana.

"I need to talk to him," said Puller. "Just talk."

"And I just need to see your warrant."

"This place is abandoned."

"Does it look abandoned to you, slick?" asked the other man.

Cole was about to pull her gun when the lead bandana put a hand on Puller's shoulder. A second later he was facedown on the concrete floor. His stunned expression revealed that he had no idea how he got there. The other man yelled and swung at Puller. Puller grabbed the man's arm, cranked it down, whipsawed it around, and the man joined his buddy on the cement. When they tried to move, Puller said, "If you get up I will put you both in the hospital. And I don't want to do that. This is not your fight."

Both men collapsed back down and stayed there.

Puller had just straightened up when Dickie's huge friend, Frank, rushed at him from a darkened corner of the building. His nose was bandaged and he had two black eyes from the previous collision with Puller's head. He was holding a long board.

"Payback," snarled Frank.

He was about to swing it against Puller's head when the shot whipped past him and carried a chunk of the board with it. The impact knocked the wood out of Frank's hands.

Frank, Puller, and the other Harley guys looked over at Cole. Her Cobra was now pointed at Frank's crotch.

"Your choice," said Cole. "Do you want kids or not?"

Frank quickly backed off, his hands protectively over his privates.

Puller raced past them and out the rear entrance.

The dirt bike whizzed around the corner and came at him. Dickie had taken the time to put on a helmet, or else Puller would not have done what he was about to.

He pulled his forward M11, took two seconds to aim, and shot out the rear tire. The bike slid sideways, Dickie fell off, and the two-wheeler came to rest about twenty feet from him.

A few seconds later Dickie was yanked up by Puller.

"You could've killed me," shouted Dickie.

"If I'd shot out your front tire, you'd've gone head over bars. This way the only thing you hurt was your ass. But then again, with you, I don't see much difference between that part of your body and your brain, if you actually have one."

Cole rushed up to them and holstered her Cobra. She got right in Dickie's face. "Are you an idiot or what? What the hell kind of stunt was that?"

"I just freaked," whined Dickie.

"Were you really infantry?" asked Puller. "Because First Division has pretty high standards and I don't think there's any way they would've let a screwup like you in the ranks."

"Go to hell!" snapped Dickie.

"Where you're *going* is jail," Cole snapped back.

"What for?"

"Trying to kill a military officer, for one thing," said Puller. "That'll put you in a federal pen until you're middle-aged."

"I didn't try to kill you."

"What do you call trying to run me down with your bike?"

"You were trying to kill me," Dickie shot back. He glared at Cole. "He shot out my tire. Could've killed me."

"Well, I'm sure you gave him a damn good reason. Now tell me why you took off like that. All we wanted to do was talk."

"This guy already beat up Frank. I didn't want him to come after me. He's a psycho."

Cole said, "That's bullshit and you know it. Why did you run, Dickie?"

The young man said nothing. He just looked down at the ground, his chest huffing in and out. There was blood on his elbow from where he'd hit the ground.

"Okay, have it your way." Cole cuffed him and read him his rights.

"My dad will be pissed about this."

"I'm sure he will be," said Cole. "That's your problem. But if you talk it'll go a lot easier with you."

"I'm not saying anything. I want a lawyer. This is bullshit. My dad will sue your ass off."

"Did you kill Officer Wellman?" said Puller. "That'll get you a one-way ticket to life in prison. Too bad West Virginia doesn't have the death penalty."

Dickie's face collapsed and the anger bled out of him like a ruptured artery.

Puller continued. "What would you say if we told you we had an eyewitness who put you at the Halversons' right about the time that Deputy Wellman was killed? And then saw you running away from the place?"

When he spoke Dickie's voice was so low they could barely hear it. "That's not...I'd say that person was nuts." There was nothing behind the words. Dickie looked like he might throw up.

Puller said, "Up to you. But we have eyewitness testimony. And I'm betting you touched something in that house. We'll get prints and DNA samples from you. We've got some unaccounted-for trace at the murder scene and something tells me they'll match yours. Then it's bye-bye to the rest of your life."

Cole added, "And because of the little stunt you just pulled we have probable cause to get those samples."

"And we don't even have to get them from you. Since you were in the military your prints and DNA are on file," said Puller.

"You can't access those for a criminal investigation," said Dickie. "Only to ID remains."

Puller smiled. "So you checked? Interesting."

Dickie's face turned the color of vanilla. "I didn't kill nobody."

"But you were in the house?" said Puller.

Dickie looked around. The Harley guys were clustered near

the back of the firehouse watching them. Frank and the two that Puller had laid out were looking particularly homicidal but made no move to advance on them.

"Can we go somewhere private and talk about this?" Dickie asked.

"First smart thing you've said since I've known you," answered Puller.

CHAPTER

63

DICKIE SAT IN THE BACKSEAT of Cole's cruiser with Puller next to him. The younger man gazed out the window, looking like he was being driven to his execution. Puller studied him, tried to absorb what he was thinking. He could have asked questions, but he didn't. He wanted Dickie to just think about things right now. A guilty person would be building a web of lies to cover his crimes during this time. An innocent person would be anxious, afraid that his words could be twisted. He would be trying to think of the best possible way to convey his innocence. A person who was innocent in some respects and guilty in others would have a more complicated thought process. Puller pegged Dickie Strauss as squarely in that camp.

Cole called out from the front seat, "If we take you to the police station, everyone in town will know in about five seconds."

"Could we go somewhere else, then?"

"How about my motel room?" asked Puller. "You know where that is, right? You've been keeping tabs on me, right?"

"Whatever," said Dickie sullenly.

They reached the motel. Out of Dickie's sight Puller confirmed that none of his intruder traps had been sprung, though from the look on Cole's face he could tell that she knew what he was doing.

Dickie sat on the bed. Cole sat in a chair opposite. She'd taken off the cuffs. Puller stood, his back against the wall.

"Heard you helped Miss Louisa," Dickie began. "That was nice of you."

"Yeah, well she died anyway. So much for Good Samaritans. But we need to focus on you, Dickie."

"How much of this has to come out?" he asked.

"Depends on what it is," replied Cole. "If you killed Larry all of it will come out."

"Like I said, I didn't kill nobody." Dickie's hands were balled to fists. He looked like a little kid, albeit with a tat sleeve. Puller half expected him to drop to the floor and throw a tantrum.

"Well, you understand that we can't just accept your word on that," said Cole. "You have to prove it to us."

Dickie looked up at Puller. "You ever look into my discharge?"

Puller shook his head.

"Like I said, me and the Army, we didn't get on. But it didn't have anything to do with my ability to do my job. I was a good soldier. There's not one black mark against me. I would've stayed in for the full ride if I could have. I liked it. Liked my buddies. Wanted to serve my country. But it wasn't my choice. They didn't want my kind."

Puller considered this. As he gazed at the young man's face the answer came to him.

"Don't ask, don't tell," said Puller.

Dickie's gaze fell to the floor. He nodded.

"The military policy on gays?" said Cole, looking at Puller.

Puller said, "Under DADT you were fine so long as you keep it secret. You don't tell, they won't ask. But if it comes out, you're gone." He looked at Dickie. "What happened?"

"Somebody ratted me out. And there were some pictures of me and some of my buddies. Hell, today, it wouldn't get five views on YouTube. But back then the Army didn't care."

"Your butt was gone?"

"In a second. Said if I didn't accept the general discharge things would get real ugly."

"I can believe that."

"Does your father know that you're gay?" asked Cole.

Dickie smiled bitterly. "Why do you think I joined the Army out of high school? My old man thought it would 'cure' me."

"Okay, so you're gay," said Puller. "That's your business and certainly no crime."

"It is to some folks. Especially around here."

"Well, we're not some folks," said Cole.

Puller said, "Let's get back to Officer Wellman. Why were you in the house?"

"Me and Larry were friends."

Cole sat back in her chair, her eyes widening. "You didn't go there to...? Larry is married with a family. And it was a damn crime scene."

Dickie said quickly, "It wasn't like that. We fooled around some when we were teenagers. But Larry was straight. We weren't going in there to have sex."

"So why did you go to the house?" demanded Cole.

Dickie nervously rubbed his palms together. Puller could see the sweat on the skin, and it wasn't just because the motel room's wall AC unit only managed to move hot air from one side of the room to the other.

"Just wanted to see what had happened."

"Why?"

"Bunch of people murdered. Just wanted to see."

"And Wellman let you in the house?" said Cole. "I don't believe it."

"He didn't."

Cole looked confused. "Then I'm not quite getting this. You want to take a breath and try it again?"

"I called him up, told him I just wanted to take a peek. I could tell he didn't want to do it."

Cole snapped, "Of course he didn't. It would have cost him his job if I'd found out. Your presence there would have corrupted the crime scene."

"But was he going to let you in?" asked Puller.

"He told me to come over. That maybe he could let me see some things they'd found. Some pictures."

"This is unbelievable," said Cole.

Puller held up his hand, his gaze directly on the man. "Keep talking, Dickie."

"So I went over there."

"And killed him?" asked Cole.

"I told you I *didn't* kill him."

"Then what happened?" said Puller.

"He wasn't there. I mean his car was gone. I thought maybe he'd gotten sick, or gotten cold feet. But then I thought, you can't just leave a crime scene unguarded. I watch *Law & Order* and *NCIS*. I know this stuff."

"Sure. You're right. Can't do it," said Puller. "Then what did you do?"

"I tried to call him on his cell. But he didn't pick up."

"What time was this exactly?" asked Puller.

"I don't know exactly. Maybe around four or so."

"Go on."

"I got to the back of the house. The door there was slightly open. I opened it some more. Called out to see if Larry was in there for some reason. Got no answer. I was scared."

"But you went in anyway. Why?" asked Puller.

"I thought Larry might be hurt. He told me to come by and then he wasn't there. I was worried about him."

"Bullshit. You wanted to see the bodies."

Dickie looked up at him, scowling, but then his features relaxed. "You're right, I did. I figured maybe Larry got called off on something else. That's why his car was gone. Anyway, I went inside." He stopped, his face draining of any remaining color.

"You saw them," Puller said.

Dickie nodded slowly. "I'll see 'em in my dreams, in my nightmares till I die."

"Very poetic," said Cole sarcastically.

"What did you do then?" asked Puller.

"I was going to leave. But I heard something, something from the basement."

"What was the sound?" Puller tensed. A lot would depend on the answer.

"Like a squeak, like somebody stretching something."

Puller eased. "Okay. What next?"

I had my knife with me. I called down the stairs. Thought it might be Larry. I didn't want him to shoot me. No answer."

Cole said in an incredulous tone, "So you went down into a basement in a house full of dead people in the middle of the night because you heard a sound? You know, in addition to the crime shows, you might want to take in a few movies like *Halloween* and *Friday the 13th*. You never go into the damn basement, Dickie."

"But you went down there," said Puller. "What happened?"

"And that's when I saw him. Larry, just hanging there."

"Did you make certain he was dead?" asked Cole. "Or did you just turn tail and run, leaving him there?"

"He was dead," said Dickie. "I seen dead guys in the Army. I checked his pulse, looked at his eyes." He paused, then forced it out. "He was dead."

"Then what?" asked Puller.

"I got the hell out of there. I ran out the back."

"And then just kept going?" Puller tensed again.

Dickie let out a long breath. "No. I...I stopped running. I felt like I was gonna barf. I squatted down there in the woods. Maybe ten minutes or so. Got myself together. Then I heard a car pull up. Thought it was maybe the cops. Or..."

Puller said, "Whoever killed Larry coming back?"

Dickie nodded. "If it was, I wanted to see the son of a bitch. Call the cops on him."

"Or her," said Cole. "It could've been a woman."

Dickie pointed a finger at Puller. "But it was you. Saw you go in. Didn't know who the hell you were. But then I saw your jacket. CID. Knew what that was. Larry told me the dead guy was Army. That explained why you were there."

"And then?" asked Puller.

"Little while later heard another car pull up." He pointed at Cole. "You that time. That's when I took off."

"And that's when I saw you out the window," said Puller. He looked at Cole. "Story coincides with what we know."

She nodded and then glared at Dickie. "Would've been nice to know this before. I should arrest you for withholding material evidence."

"And for just being stupid," added Puller. "So were you and Eric friends?"

"I knew him. He was in Xanadu." He held up his arm. "I told you I got a tat sleeve like his."

"When you went into the Halversons' house that night did you know that Eric and Molly were across the street dead?"

"Of course I didn't."

Puller let this answer hang there.

"I was worried about him, though."

"Why?" asked Puller.

"Stuff."

"Stuff got a name?"

Dickie shrugged. "Not that I ever heard."

"Any reason why Eric and Molly would have wanted a soil report done?" asked Cole.

"Soil report? Nope, no reason I know of."

"How about a meth lab?' asked Puller. "Got any 'stuff' on that?"

"Eric didn't do meth."

"Okay, but did he make it to sell? That's the key question."

Dickie didn't answer right away. "I think I need to lawyer up."

"Think or know?" asked Puller while Cole looked at him warily.

Puller pushed off from the wall and stood next to Dickie. "Let's look at this intelligently, Dickie. See how it affects you. Will you take a couple minutes to do that with me?"

Cole said, "Puller, he said he wanted to lawyer up—"

Puller shot her a glance and she closed her mouth. He turned back to Dickie, put a hand on his shoulder. "Just hear me out, Dickie, what do you have to lose? The Army kicked your ass out. Didn't let you serve when I know you wanted to. This is a second chance for you to do something for your country."

Dickie mumbled, "I'll listen."

CHAPTER

64

PULLER SNAGGED A CHAIR with his right hand, swung it around, and set it directly in front of Dickie. When Puller sat down in it, his knees were almost touching the other man's.

"I'll let you in on some top-level stuff, Dickie, but in return, I need some things from you. You're patriotic, right, want to help your country?"

"As much as the next guy. Like you said, I'd still be in the Army serving if they hadn't pulled that crap on me."

"I know. I hear you. I served with gays and straights. Didn't matter to me so long as they could hit the target they were shooting at and had my back when I needed it."

Dickie looked more comfortable. "So what's going on?"

"Trouble's coming to Drake, Dickie. In fact, it's already here. All these people dead, some of them your friends."

"I know that. I know, man."

"But it's not just those people. The Feds think something big is coming here. Really big."

"To Drake?" Cole said, obviously stunned by this news.

Dickie said, "Big like what?"

"If I knew then it wouldn't be such a problem. But I don't know. And if that situation stays the same then we're all screwed, you see that, don't you?"

Dickie nodded. "Yeah, I guess so."

"I knew you were smart. Mechanized guys all have to be smart. Lot of stuff to remember with all the equipment you guys had. I just had to worry about my gun and personal gear. You guys were wheeling around in thirty-ton armor."

"Ain't that the truth. I drove the Bradley. And even the damn Abrams. And I was good."

"I bet you were. Army's loss. Don't ask was a bunch of crap anyway."

"Damn sure was," agreed Dickie.

"So something big is coming. People dead, pieces not adding up. Weird chatter coming out of Drake that federal ears caught. Now what I need from you is some HUMINT. You know what that is, right?"

"Sure. Human intelligence."

"On the ground, here in Drake. You know stuff. You know people. You know folks who knew Eric and Molly. Your old man works for Trent."

"You think Roger Trent is involved in this?" Dickie said sharply.

"I don't know who's involved and who isn't. That's why I need your help. You up for it?"

"What do you want me to do?"

"Listen. Go to places. Sit with folks. Listen some more. Don't make it obvious. Don't play detective. I just want you to do what you normally do, but just do it differently. Listen, pay attention. Something seems weird, remember it, get in touch. Okay?"

Dickie was already nodding. "Okay. Sure."

Puller handed him a card. "My contact info. I assume you know how to reach Sergeant Cole."

Puller rose.

"That's all?" said Dickie. "I can go?"

"You're not doing me any good sitting in my motel room. I need you out there. Give you a chance to serve your country again, even if your country did screw you over."

Dickie rose, looked at Cole, and then put out a hand to Puller.

"Ain't been many folks willing to give me a shot like this."

"I'm not most folks."

"I had you pegged wrong, I guess."

"I guess we did the same to you," noted Cole.

"You need a ride?" Puller asked.

"No, I'm cool."

After Dickie left, Cole said, "And you didn't tell me something big was coming to Drake because why?"

"Because I was told not to. And then I decided to disobey orders."

"What's it based on?"

"Chatter NSA picked up. In Dari. Justice is coming. Whatever is going to happen will happen soon."

"Dari? What the hell is that?"

"Dialect spoken in Afghanistan."

"Afghanistan? You heard that in Drake?"

"Apparently so. At least in the vicinity of. Couldn't get an exact location. And it was encrypted in old KGB code. And it was sent out shortly after the murders. Gotten DHS's blood pressure up."

"What else do you know?"

"Not enough, that's for damn sure. You know one thing Dickie didn't explain."

"What's that?"

"How did he get to the Halversons' that night? Didn't drive. No car out front. He ran into the woods. Escaped that way. Long way back to town."

"That's true."

"Complicated guy. Who would've figured."

"You think he knows more than he's telling us?"

"I think he's caught between a rock and a hard place. He's involved in something that he doesn't want us to know about. But I don't think it's connected to the chatter."

"But I don't know why you recruited him to help us. Especially if you think he's involved in something criminal."

"I've spent most of my adult life reading people. Especially soldiers and those formerly in the ranks. My instinct tells me that Dickie wants to help. I think he went to the Halversons' that night because he suspected something. Or someone. What I think he wanted was just another chance to prove the Army screwed up in discharging him. So I gave it to him."

"Well, if he gets killed that second chance will have come at a big cost."

"Most second chances do. And most of the time they're worth it."

"When he went to the Halversons' do you think he knew Treadwell and Bitner were sitting dead across the street?"

"I think he might have known. I think he probably tried to call and got no answer. I think he might have gone over to their house that night too, but couldn't get in. The place was dark. He couldn't have seen the bodies from the window. And there were no signs of forced entry."

"So what's his connection with Treadwell? Not just the Harley club. He's scared."

"Seven people have been killed. He *should* be scared. Along with everyone else."

65

COLE LEFT TO TAKE CARE of some paperwork back at the station. They arranged to meet later. Puller drove off in his car. Three minutes later he parked and sat there thumbing in a phone number.

The voice said, "Mason."

"Agent Mason, it's John Puller."

Puller could hear the squeak of the man's chair as he presumably leaned back. While the normal world went on around them, Mason was working 24/7 to keep the monsters at bay.

"I'm glad you called. We got one more piece of chatter and some additional intel that have combined to ratchet this sucker up to a new level."

"I thought it was pretty high already. What new stuff do you have?"

"Another KGB code-encrypted piece of Dari. This time they said some shit about Allah the great and good. That didn't get me excited. What did get me excited were numbers."

"What numbers?"

"A date, Puller. They gave us the D-day, at least that's what we think."

"And what was the date?"

"You're not going to like this because I sure as hell don't. Three days from today."

"You said you had other intelligence. Does it at least give us some idea of what they're planning?"

"Yes, the mystery on that score is finally solved. And that's the real scary part. There's a gas pipeline that runs through Drake, northwest corner of the county."

"Okay."

"We didn't think anything of it, really. Pipelines are natural targets, but not that popular because the human damage potential is not that significant. This pipeline supplies natural gas for three states: West Virginia, of course, Kentucky, and Ohio. The pipeline is owned by a Canadian outfit but operated by an American company. Trent Exploration. From what you told me you've had some interaction with Roger Trent, right?"

"Right." Puller thought rapidly. "You think anyone at Trent is involved in this?"

"I'm not ruling out any possibilities at this point."

"But what's the vulnerability of the gas pipeline? And even if they did blow it up, how much damage are we talking about? Like you said, it would be limited."

"The structural damage could be severe, but manageable. And then you'd have disruption of service. Not that sexy for a terrorist. They like body parts hanging from trees, not gas customers complaining because their stovetop isn't working. And there are resources in the area that can respond to any damage to the pipeline and bring things under control."

"Okay, so the pipeline is the target?"

"We don't think it's that simple." He paused and Puller could visualize the man organizing the words in his head. "What's a very popular tactic that the Taliban employs in Afghanistan? You should know this better than most."

Puller did know better than most. "A feint and then the real hit. One bomb to draw in the first responders. Second bomb goes off to kill them."

"Right, only here we believe it's a variation on that tactic. We believe the attack on the gas pipeline is a *diversionary* tactic."

Puller felt the hairs rise on the back of his neck. "So what's the real target?"

"If that gas pipeline explodes first responders from a hundred-mile radius will get there ASAP. That's not guesswork. There are tri-state teaming agreements in place in the event that pipeline goes up in flames. Those resources are committed to that contingency and they can't be stood down for any reason."

"Okay."

Mason continued. "Now, there's lots of forest in that area. It's been dry as hell. You could be looking at a fire that could cover three states and fed by a mountain of gas, at least until they could shut it down. As I said, disruption in power could be severe. Hundreds of thousands of homes are fed by that gas. No telling when they could get it up and running again, especially with a forest fire raging around it."

"That sounds bad, but like you said, not very sexy for a terrorist. Then what's the primary target?" Puller said again. "By definition that has to be worse than the diversionary target."

"Forty miles from that pipeline is a light water nuclear reactor that feeds power right to the national grid."

Puller drew a long breath. "You think that's what they're after?"

"It's the only asset we can see in the area worth their while."

"How would they attack the plant?"

"Right now security seems tight. But we can't afford to find out later it wasn't good enough. But if they can pierce that place, and somehow blow the reactors, it would be devastating. A radiation cloud could cover multiple states within a few days. And with all emergency crews fighting a gas pipeline eruption and potential fire, together it would be catastrophic."

"So beef the security the hell up at the nuke plant."

"We think they have folks on the inside there. That was the separate piece of intelligence I was telling you about, Puller."

"Can you find out who?"

"In three days, probably not. And if we change security in any way there…"

Puller finished the thought for him. "The insider will easily find out, tell his people, and they go early and try to blow it anyway. And the same for the pipeline."

"Right. At some point we have to make that decision, Puller. We have to beef up security at both places. But ideally we nail these bastards before that becomes necessary."

"Necessary? Joe, it's three days."

"I told you it was bad."

"I haven't seen one Middle Easterner in Drake while I've been here."

"Well, I have to believe they're keeping a pretty low profile."

"What do you want me to do? I'm just one more."

"Keep doing what you're doing. Find these guys, Puller."

"And if I don't, in time?"

"Then I have to pull the trigger."

"And they'll pull the trigger too."

"Way it goes. Keep me in the loop, and I'll do the same to you." He paused. "I wish I could send you some assets, but the brass here thinks that might tip our hand."

"Yeah, I know. I do have one local asset."

"Right, Cole the cop."

"No, guy named Dickie Strauss." Puller filled Mason in on what he gotten Dickie to do. "At the very least it gives me another pair of eyes on the ground here. He was a former soldier."

"I'm not thrilled you engaged this guy, Puller. We know nothing about him."

"I didn't have a lot of options," Puller replied.

He could hear Mason sigh. "When are you meeting with him? We don't have much time."

"I can meet with him tonight."

"You got a safe place to do that?"

Puller thought for a moment. "Yeah, I do. Place called Xanadu."

CHAPTER

66

PULLER CLIMBED OUT of his car and walked into the Drake County library. It was a one-story orange brick structure that was architecturally tasteless and had not worn well. He went inside, asked a librarian at the front desk a few questions, and was shown what he needed. While there were a few computers in the library, Puller found himself using the old-fashioned method of looking through newspapers by hand. He covered the time period that seemed relevant to him. What he discovered was nothing, which in itself was significant.

As he was leaving his phone rang. It was Kristen Craig, the forensic tech from USACIL in Georgia.

"Got some preliminaries for you, Puller."

He sat in his car with the air running and wrote down what she told him.

"We did a super-fast rush on the DNA samples you sent. Looking at the exclusions list we found one set unaccounted for. We uploaded it to the FBI's Combined DNA Indexing System. We might get a hit."

"What else?"

"We identified the wadding in Colonel Reynolds's body. It was a twelve-gauge."

"Anything else. Manufacturer?"

"Nope, sorry."

"Okay, keep going."

"The doc up there who did the posts was good. Our guys have

basically validated everything he did. We don't have the bodies down here, obviously, but the guy knew what he was doing."

"Okay." Validation was good, but what Puller really wanted was some info that could help him solve the case.

"We did find something strange on the twenty-two-caliber round you sent down."

"What was that?"

"Well, I had it confirmed by three different people down here, because it's not something you'd expect to find on a round fired into someone's brain."

"Don't keep me in suspense, Kristen."

"It was gold foil. West Virginia is coal country, not gold, right?"

Puller thought of the Trents in the big house. "Well, for some people up here it's apparently the same thing. But gold foil?"

"That's what it is. Just a nearly microscopic bit, but we confirmed that's what it was. Don't know what it means."

"You make any sense of that soil report I sent down?"

"The soil report didn't reveal anything startling. The uranium levels were normal, particularly for coal country. There was nothing else remarkable. If someone was killed because of it, damned if I know why."

"You and me both. What about the stuff from the meth lab?"

"Now that was interesting. You sure it was just a meth lab?"

"It looked like one. It had the stuff you'd normally associate with one."

"Yes, it did, but it also had one item that you wouldn't normally find in one."

"Like what?"

"Tungsten carbide."

"What did you find that on?"

"Some of the bottles, the tubing, and some coils. Enough to where it couldn't be just some trace residue."

"So it might have been on Treadwell's or Bitner's hands?"

"Possibly. We did find Treadwell's prints on the equipment."

"So it wasn't just planted there," said Puller. "That's good to know."

"You were thinking it was planted?"

"No. But I like confirmation of my ideas as much as the next person. So tungsten carbide? That can be used in industrial tools, as an abrasive, in the jewelry trade?"

"That's right. Stiffer and more dense than steel or titanium."

"Treadwell had a ring. Maybe it was made of tungsten and it leached somehow onto his skin."

"It wasn't. We checked the ring."

"He worked at a chemical shop. And he had a Harley."

"Again, that doesn't necessarily explain the presence."

"Anything else?"

"Isn't that enough?" Kristen said.

"You haven't given me any answers."

"I only provide facts. You have to come up with the answers, my friend."

She clicked off and Puller slowly put his phone away.

There was another use for tungsten carbide that he, being in the military, well knew. It was very often used in armor-piercing ammunition, particularly when the material of choice, depleted uranium, wasn't available.

But if Treadwell were making such ammo, there wasn't any other evidence of it in his home. You needed space, and specialized equipment to manufacture it. And money. And many of the components on the list to make ordnance utilizing depleted uranium were ones that the government watched very carefully. How could a Harley-driving redneck who worked at a chemical supply store in nowhere West Virginia manage that? And if Treadwell had managed to do that, why had he been murdered? Maybe whoever he was building it for found out he might have gotten cold feet and was working with the government through Reynolds.

Puller would have to check at Treadwell's place of business to see if they might be missing a quantity of tungsten carbide, if they even carried it. And if so, the case might take on a whole new light. He pondered how this could be tied into what Mason had told him. If the targets were the pipeline and the reactor, that type of ammo could be used to puncture the pipeline and maybe the reactors. If so, that meant Treadwell was tied up with jihadists. And Puller wondered how that was possible. How could folks like that operate in an area like this and no one the wiser?

Then he started to think about the pipeline. Owned by a Canadian company but operated by Trent. Was Trent working with terrorists? Was he being paid to help them carry out this mission? But why would a fabulously successful coal mogul do that? Blowing up a nuke reactor could make all of Trent's coal mines radioactive.

Unless they were paying him for more than his business was worth. And that might explain the death threats. And Trent being so nervous. Maybe he'd had a falling-out with his "business partners."

Puller eased the Malibu from the curb. He had fewer than three days to discover the truth. He knew the odds were long against him. But he had put on the uniform to serve his country. And serve it he would. Even at the cost of his life.

67

THE MERCEDES SL600 was parked in front of Puller's motel room when he drove in around two o'clock. Jean Trent was sitting in the driver's seat. The car was running and the AC was cranked. Puller parked next to the other car and got out. Jean Trent did the same. She had on a sleeveless pale yellow dress with a V-front and a white sweater over top, coordinated pumps, and a white pearl necklace. Her hair and makeup were flawless. The old motel seemed an incongruous backdrop for such glamour.

"Looking for a room at the motel?" Puller said as he walked over to stand next to her.

She smiled. "When I was fifteen I used to clean this place for four dollars an hour and thought I was rich. Sam did the same, but she only got three dollars an hour."

"Why the discrepancy?"

"She was smaller and couldn't work as hard. People around here drive tough bargains."

"I believe it."

"You got time for lunch? Or have you already eaten?"

"I haven't. At the Crib?"

She shook her head. "Another place. Nicer. Over the county line. I'll drive."

Puller thought about this. He had short time to divert a possible catastrophe. Did he have time for a leisurely lunch? Then his thoughts went back to what Mason had said. Trent operated that pipeline.

"What's the occasion?"

"It's lunchtime and I'm hungry."

"Have you been waiting long?"

"Long enough. Guess you've been busy."

"Guess I have."

"How's the investigation coming?"

"It's coming."

"You are remarkably tight-lipped."

"It's an Army thing."

"No, I think it's a cop thing. My little sister is the same way."

"Saw your hubby was back in town. He joining us for lunch?"

Her radiant smile diminished a few watts. "No. He won't. You ready?"

He looked at her fine clothes and then down at his own work ones.

"Fancy place? Not sure I'm dressed for the occasion."

"You look just fine."

She drove the country roads with an expert's touch, hitting the turns and accelerating at just the right moment so the big Mercedes engine was at optimal rpm on the straightaways.

"You ever think of signing up for NASCAR?" he said.

She smiled and punched the gas on a particularly long stretch of road, winding the car up to eighty. "I've thought about a lot of things."

"So why lunch with me, really?"

"Got some questions, hope you have some answers."

"I doubt it. Remember the tight-lipped thing."

"Then your opinion. How about that?"

"We'll find out, I guess."

Ten miles later they crossed into another county, and two miles farther down the road she pulled onto a tree-lined asphalt driveway. Around two curves the land opened up as the trees receded and Puller eyed the sprawling two-story stucco and stone building. It looked like it had been dropped, intact, from Tuscany. There were two aged fountains out front and nearby a small stream with a waterwheel slowly turning. There was an outdoor tiled eating area in an adjacent courtyard. A weathered wooden pergola strung with flowering vines provided a ceiling for this dining space.

Puller looked at the sign hanging over the front door. "Vera Felicita? True happiness?"

"You speak Italian?" she asked.

"Some. You?"

"Some. I've been there many times. Love it. I'm thinking of moving there one day."

"People always say that when they visit Italy. But then they come back home and realize it's not as easy as it sounds."

"Maybe."

Puller looked around at the expensive cars sitting in the cobblestone parking area. Most of the outdoor tables were filled with people as nicely dressed as Jean Trent. They were drinking wine and forking and spooning into elaborate-looking dishes.

"Popular place," he said.

"Yes, it is."

"How'd you come to find it?"

"I own it."

CHAPTER

68

JEAN TRENT CLIMBED out of the car and Puller fell into step behind her as she headed to the front entrance. She stopped and turned to him.

"We're also a B-and-B. Four rooms. And I'm thinking about adding a spa. I brought in a CIA chef, and a professional team to run everything. We're hoping to get our first Michelin star this year. We were cash flow positive after eighteen months. Our reputation has really grown. People come from Tennessee, Ohio, Kentucky, and North Carolina."

"And no coal mines around?"

"This is one of the few counties in West Virginia that has no coal." She looked around. "What you do have is unspoiled land. Mountains, rivers. I spent a long time looking for just the perfect location and this is it. I did business plans and demographic and marketing studies. I wanted to fill a need. That's the best way to build something that's lasting."

"I didn't know you were a businesswoman."

"Probably lots of things about me you don't know. You want to find out more?"

"Why not?"

They went inside and were shown to a private book-lined room where a table for two had been laid out. Puller knew little about decorating, but he saw that the interiors had been put together with an experienced eye. Everything was good quality, comfortable, nothing overdone. He had been to Italy many times, and this was probably about as close as one could come to it in West Virginia.

The server was dressed in a white jacket and black bow tie and attended to them with quiet professionalism. They scanned their menus, but Puller finally let Jean order for him. The bottle of white came first and two glasses were poured out.

She said, "I know you're technically on duty, but I'm especially proud of this Italian Chardonnay and I'd like you to try it."

He took a sip and let it go down slow. "Has significantly more body than one associates with an Italian white."

She clinked her glass against his. "It's called Jermann Dreams, 2007. But an Army man who knows his wines. How did that happen?"

"My father took my brother and me overseas a lot when we were younger. Had my first taste of wine in Paris when I was nine."

"Paris when you were nine," she said enviously. "I was in my late twenties before I even left the country one time."

"Some people never get to go."

"That's true. Now I go every year, months at a time. I love it. Sometimes I almost don't come back."

"So why do you? Come back, I mean?"

She took a sip of wine and dabbed her mouth. "This is my home, I suppose."

"Any place can be your home."

"That's true. But my family is here."

He looked around. "Is Roger a partner in this?"

"No. This is all mine."

"Pretty expensive proposition."

"He didn't bankroll me, if that's what you mean. Bank loans and sweat equity."

"Still, I'm sure being married to him didn't hurt."

"It didn't," she admitted. "So he's back in town?"

"I had a cup of coffee with him at the Crib."

"Why?"

"To talk about those death threats. For the record, I don't think Randy is behind it this time."

She put down her wine. "Did Sam tell you about that?"

"Yeah, she did." He paused. "I guess Roger's business is doing great."

"I'm not really involved in it."

"He relies on Bill Strauss a lot."

"He's the COO. That's his job."

He hesitated, pondering whether to mention the pipeline. He decided that was too risky. Noting her suspicious look, he said, "I'm asking more questions than you are. Sorry, it's just how I'm wired."

"We'll see what we can do about that later," she replied.

Their food came and Puller spent a few minutes digging into it. As he swallowed his last bit of fish he said, "I think you'll get that Michelin star."

Her face brightened. "I appreciate the confidence."

"Not easy to carve something like this out of the wilderness."

She finished the wine in her glass. "Are you plying me with compliments for some particular reason?"

"Just being honest. But you invited me to lunch. You said you had some questions. Why don't you get started?"

"But you only offered opinions instead of answers."

"I can't promise what I can't deliver."

"Would you like some coffee? We get our beans from Bolivia. They've started to turn out great product. A special blend."

"I hardly ever turn down coffee."

"Have you been to Bolivia?"

"No."

"South America in general?"

"Yes."

"Business or pleasure?"

"I don't travel for pleasure. I travel with a gun."

The order was placed and the coffee arrived promptly. It was served in delicate-looking cups with a flower and vine pattern. Puller knew instinctively that Jean Trent had personally picked them. She just seemed the type to want to control things, no matter how small.

"Good coffee," he said.

She nodded and said, "Now to my questions. Well, I really only have one. Based on what you've found out so far, do you think Roger's really in danger?"

"I have no way to know if he is or isn't. I came here to investigate the murders of an Army colonel and his family. I did tell him to take them seriously."

"Why?"

"Just my gut."

"I know you thought I was being very cavalier about my husband's personal safety, but I can assure you that I think about it a lot."

"But also like you said, he takes precautions." He finished his coffee and set the cup down. "Do you have any reason to believe that your husband is in danger? Or that he might be connected in some way to the murders that have taken place?"

"Well, one of the victims worked at his company. But I doubt that Roger even knew her. I can't believe that he has any connection to those people getting killed. I mean, what would be his motive?"

"Don't know. Is Roger involved in any litigation right now?"

"He's always involved in litigation. Usually with the EPA or some environmental group. Occasionally with a wrongful death action because of a workplace fatality."

"So what kind of environmental lawsuits?"

"I don't know the particulars. Generally speaking, surface mining is pretty bad for the environment. You can't quote me on that, but it is. People get upset and they sue. If the government thinks Roger hasn't lived up to his legal obligations or has run afoul of some regulation they come after him. He keeps the lawyers gainfully employed. Why do you ask?"

Puller was thinking of the soil report, but he wasn't going to tell her that.

She said, "Okay, I lied. I do have another question."

"Shoot."

"Why are you really here?"

"I thought that was pretty clear."

"Dead colonel? Off post? I checked you out. You're from the

701st. They could have brought in CID from Fort Campbell. The
701st is special. So why you?"

"You know the military well, do you?"

"My father was in the Navy. Lots of men from around here were
in the armed forces. And like I said, I checked."

"Who'd you talk to?"

"I have my contacts. That's all you need to know. And from what
I found out, it seems that sending someone like you out here sends
a pretty clear message. This is not just a routine murder."

"No murder is routine in my book."

"So you won't tell me?"

"I'm just doing my job, Jean. Other than that I really can't say
much."

She dropped him off at the motel. Puller watched her go until she
disappeared from view. Then he turned and looked at his motel
room. Then his gaze swiveled to his car. He walked toward it.
Stopped about fifteen feet away. Studied it. He moved in a coun-
terclockwise direction around the vehicle. Saw something. A bit of
insulated wire with the copper seam exposed. It was tiny, a few cen-
timeters, but the sun had hit it just right so that it gleamed like a bit
of revealed gold.

He dropped to his knees and then bent his head down. He was
up in a second and moved away from the vehicle. He phoned Cole.

"Got a bomb under my car. Want to get somebody over here to
come get it?"

While Cole hurried there with the bomb cavalry, Puller sat on
the front steps leading up to the motel office and calmly considered
the situation.

Folks sure seemed to love their explosives around these parts.

And now maybe he understood the invitation to lunch.

69

THE BOMB WASN'T as sophisticated as the ones at the abandoned house. At least that was the pronouncement of the retired ATF agent who arrived two minutes after Cole did.

Puller stood next to Cole as the bomb was removed from the car and taken away.

"Didn't have much time," he said.

"What?" asked Cole.

"Wasn't as sophisticated because they didn't have enough time to put it together."

"Who are you talking about?"

"Your sister invited me to lunch today. She was waiting for me here. She insisted on driving. I left my car here. I really didn't know why she wanted me to go to Vera Felicita with her, but she did."

"She took you to her B-and-B?"

"Yeah. Then we got back, she drove off real fast, and I luckily spotted the footprint and the piece of wire. Otherwise, you'd be identifying my remains, if there was enough left of me."

Cole didn't say anything right away. She scuffed the dirt with her shoe, her brow furrowed in thought. "Are you accusing her of being involved in this?"

"I'm not accusing anybody of anything. I'm just presenting facts."

"What reason would she have to kill you?"

"Well, if her husband is involved in those murders and he goes to jail, his company will probably tank and there goes her big house and her fancy B-and-B."

"She built that place with her own money and financing."

"So she says. But that operation must've cost a real chunk of change to get going. What bank would loan her that unless Roger cosigned?"

"But how do you figure Roger being behind the murders? He was the one receiving death threats."

"He *says* he received death threats. We have no independent proof of that."

"That's true," she conceded.

"And I checked something in the local newspapers at the library today. There were no public notices of the blasting for Sunday night. They blasted without fulfilling the notice requirement."

"That's a real big deal, Puller. Nice work."

"So we have gunfire and explosives going off at pretty much the same time. One covers the other. And that mine belonged to Trent. Who had the authority to do blasting without filing the requisite public notice?"

"Legally, no one. Whoever did authorize it is in serious trouble."

"I think we need to find out. And we need to find out if anyone saw someone around my car this afternoon."

"I'll get right on that. But, Puller, I can't believe that my sister had anything to do with it."

"I don't want to think that she did either, Cole, but the circumstances are suspicious."

"They are," she agreed.

She scuffed the gravel with her shoe again. "I'm not sure I'm the best person to investigate this."

"If you're okay with it, I can do it."

"I'm okay with it. But Puller, one more thing."

"Yeah?"

"Yes, she's my sister. But you let the evidence take you where it goes, okay?"

"Okay."

"When are you going to do it?"

"Right now."

CHAPTER

70

Stroke. Stroke. Stroke. Stroke. Breath. Stroke. Stroke. Stroke. Stroke. Breath.

The air was humid, the smell oppressive. You could walk briskly and break into a flop sweat.

Four more strokes. A single breath. Then another quartet of strokes and Jean Trent came up for air after touching the side of the pool for the sixtieth time.

"Working off lunch?"

She jerked around in the water and stared over at the far edge of the thirty-meter pool.

Puller was sitting in a teak chair, his big hands on his thighs.

She said, "How did you get in here?"

He pointed to the wall of glass. "Through that door over there. You really ought to lock it."

"I mean, how did you get on the grounds?"

He rose, came over to her, looked down. "You mean how did I manage to dodge the fat old guy in the rental uniform out there?"

She walked to the steps and came out of the pool and wrung out her hair. She had on a black one-piece. She was trim with good muscle tone.

She might have also just tried to blow his car up with him in it.

"You swim?" she asked.

"Not unless someone I'm after jumps in the water. Wanted to talk to you."

She walked over to a teak chaise longue with a blue cushion with white piping set against one wall. A terrycloth robe was there. She slipped it on and sat down on the chaise.

"What about? Did lunch not agree with you? You seem out of sorts."

He perched on a chair next to her. "I was actually wondering whether I should arrest you."

She appeared startled. "What? Why?"

"Attempted murder of a federal officer."

She sat forward. "And how exactly do you figure that?"

"When I got back from lunch with you there was a bomb under my car. I'm getting tired of people trying to turn me into little pieces of flesh."

"I know nothing about that. And since I was with you at lunch I could hardly have planted a bomb in your car."

"You could have paid someone to do it."

"And why would I do that?"

"That's what I'm here to find out."

"I need to get dressed. I have a dinner to go to tonight. If you want to continue this conversation, we'll have to do it at another time."

"Actually, we'll do it right now."

She stood. "I want you out of my house. Now!"

"And I want some answers. I'm here with the blessing of the police department."

Jean's lips parted but she said nothing.

"In other words, your sister knows I'm here."

"I didn't put a bomb in your car."

"*Under* my car."

"I didn't do that either. What reason would I have to kill you?"

"That's an easy one. I'm here to investigate a series of murders. If you or someone you're connected to is involved in those crimes you'd naturally want me out of the way. So you invite me to lunch. You insist on driving. We come back and I almost go boom. You can see why I'm suspicious."

She sat back down; her confidence seemed to drain away. "I... I can't explain that. I don't know what is going on." When she looked back up there were tears in her eyes. "I'm telling you the truth, Puller."

He watched her, debating the authenticity of those tears. He'd watched lots of suspects cry, from iron-hard soldiers to expectant moms to teenagers who'd lost their way as military brats.

"Just because you say it's the truth doesn't mean anything to me," he said. "So until I find out otherwise, you're officially a suspect. Do you understand that?"

She nodded dumbly.

"And if you have any information that would help me in my investigation, now would be a really good time to share it."

"Information like what?"

"Like why is your husband so nervous. And don't tell me it's about death threats. I've come to the conclusion that that's just bullshit. It happened before, with your brother, and I think he's just using that as a convenient cover."

"Cover for what?"

"He's upgraded his security, Jean. The driver of his Escalade? He's a former Marine."

"How do you know that?"

"Army can sniff Marines out from a hundred miles away. The guy is a pro and he's armed. And he's new, isn't he?"

"Yes."

"It was a good choice. He's light-years ahead of the old fart outside."

"But his security here hasn't really been increased. We still just have the same retired cop outside."

"That's because Roger isn't here right now. So I guess he's less concerned about your personal safety, or that of your daughter. His pro travels with him only."

"What would he be afraid of?" she asked.

"You said he has lots of enemies. But they're just the same old ones, right? How about something or someone new? That would justify the new muscle."

"I can't think of what that might be. As I said, I don't get involved in Roger's business."

"If you keep lying to me, Jean, I will cuff you and haul your ass right out of here."

More tears spilled from her eyes. "I don't want to go to jail."

"Then tell me the truth. You picked everything out at your B-and-B. Right down to the coffee cups. You know about business management. I'm betting you supervised the construction of this house, because judging from the interior decorating at Trent Exploration, that's not Roger's strong suit. So are you telling me you've ceded all knowledge of his business to him? Because I'm not buying it."

They sat in silence for a couple of minutes. The humidity weighed down on Puller. At least the desert had been a dry heat. He watched Jean. He was not going to break the silence. He was not going to get up and leave. He was just going to wait for her to finally crack.

"There are some problems at Trent Exploration."

"Like what?"

"Like missing money. Diverted accounts. Offshore phantom banking relationships. Things that shouldn't be there are. Things that should be there aren't."

"And Roger is aware of this?"

"Very."

"What's he doing about it?"

"Whatever he can, but his options are limited. He made some business decisions last year that required an infusion of capital. A lot of it. The revenues he thought would develop from those business decisions never materialized. The debts are still there. He thought he had money to cover it. But with all the money disappearing he's in a cash flow bind. That's why Roger was in New York, trying to get some financing help. But the banks still aren't lending. They've tried everywhere they can think of."

"And now death threats. Maybe from the people ripping him off?"

"I don't know," said Jean. "I really don't."

"Okay, Trent is a big company, but it's not GE. And it's located in a pretty small town. Are you telling me none of you have a clue or even a guess as to who is stealing the company blind? How about Randy?"

"Randy? Why would he do that?"

"He blames Roger for your parents' death, for one thing."

"Even so, he would be in no position to steal from Roger. He knows nothing about computers or financial transactions. This was done by people who are very familiar with both."

"Maybe somebody he's hooked up with."

"In Drake? I don't think so. The situation is getting desperate, though. Roger and Bill are running out of places to turn."

He said, "How about you? If the company goes under do you lose everything, including the house?"

"Probably. But that's why I've been building up my B-and-B. Not because I suspected Roger was having money troubles, but I... I guess I just wanted to be more independent."

In spite of himself, Puller felt sorry for her.

"So Roger really has no idea where all this financial chicanery is coming from? He's a real smart guy. How does he get ripped off and not know how?"

"It's been driving him and Bill crazy. Their whole lives are tied up in this company. If it goes down, they go down."

Puller said nothing. He just stared moodily off.

Jean eyed the scars on his neck.

"Middle East?"

He nodded.

"Remember I told you about the young man I loved?"

"The one who didn't come back from Gulf One?"

"He looked a little like you."

"Still wish he'd come back?"

"Still," she said.

He looked around. "You wouldn't have all this."

"Maybe I don't have it now."

"Maybe you don't."

He rose.

"You're not going to arrest me?"

"No. What you told me helps, though. I appreciate it."

"I used to be a naturally honest person. Then I married Roger and things changed."

He headed out the way he'd come in.

"What are you going to do?" she called after him.

"Find a killer."

CHAPTER

71

"Hey, Bill, how goes it?"

Bill Strauss had just come out of the Trent office and was heading to his car. Puller was leaning against his Malibu. He'd been waiting out here for nearly an hour.

"Puller? What are you doing here?"

Puller pushed away from the car and walked toward the man. "My job. Got some questions. You have some time?"

Strauss glanced at his watch. "I'm actually late for a meeting."

"It won't take long."

"It can't wait?"

"Not really, no."

"Okay, shoot."

"Blasting last Sunday night. No public notice given. Who authorized it?"

Strauss looked taken aback. "What are you talking about?"

"On Sunday night of last week blasting took place at one of the Trent operations. You have to give public notice. And blasting doesn't usually take place on Sundays. You have to get special permission. The notice wasn't given. Was the special permission obtained?"

"I'd have to check the records."

"Roger said he knew nothing about it. Who at your company oversees that stuff?"

"Technically I do as COO. But I have a lot of duties and I have to delegate. We have people who cover the blasting authorizations and appropriate notice provisions."

"Then they would be the ones I should talk to?"

"They would. Unfortunately, they're not at this office. They work in Charleston."

"Can I get their contact information?"

"Why is this important? Those people weren't killed at the mining operation."

"It's still important. So you'll get me the contact info?"

"Okay," Strauss said slowly.

"Great, I'll expect it tomorrow."

"I'm not sure—"

Puller cut in. "Seen your son lately?"

"No, why?"

"Just wondering. You a member of the Xanadu club?"

"What? No, I'm not."

"I'll let you get on to your meeting."

Puller climbed in the Malibu and drove off. On the way he called Dickie and made arrangements to meet with him that night.

When Puller got back to the motel there was a shiny blue Bentley parked out front, and Roger Trent was at the wheel.

72

"I ASSUME YOU'RE LOOKING for me since there's no one else staying here," said Puller.

Trent had on dark slacks and a white open-collared shirt. A cigar was in one hand. His face was red, the corpuscles around his thick nose swollen. As Puller drew closer he smelled the alcohol on the man's breath.

"You sure you should be piloting that thing around in your condition?"

"What condition is that?"

"One called inebriated."

"I'm not even close. I have a big appetite for everything."

Puller looked at the man's gut. "I can see that. You ever think about Weight Watchers?"

"You've been pulling my chain ever since we met."

"You're a hard person to love, Roger."

To Puller's surprise the other man started laughing. "Well, at least you're honest. I understand you and my lovely wife went to lunch today. At Vera Felicita."

"Her invite, not mine."

"Not saying otherwise. But you accepted."

"Yes, I did."

"Did you have a good time?"

"She's very nice company. Did she tell you what happened afterwards?"

"That someone put a bomb under your car, yes, she did mention that. That's why I came by, to tell you she had nothing to do with it."

"Thanks, that's a big relief."

"I was just thinking that we both have a lot in common."

"Oh yeah, what's that?"

"Somebody obviously wants us dead."

"They're just phoning you. I'm the one getting the bombs."

Trent leaned against his Bentley. "You ever wonder why I haven't moved away from here? I could live anywhere, you know."

"You wife prefers Italy, I know that."

"That's my wife. I'm talking about me."

"Okay, yeah, I have wondered. And I can tell you're itching to tell me. Big fish in a little pond syndrome?"

"Hardly that simple. You see, Puller, I don't have a need to be loved. Far from it. You don't go into the coal mining business to be loved. I like being loathed. It gets my juices going. I love it, actually. Everybody against me. You see, in Drake, I'm the underdog. A rich underdog, the richest in fact. But still the underdog."

"You ever thought about getting counseling?"

Trent laughed again. "I like you. I'm not sure why. Hell, maybe I do know why. You hate me too, but you do it on a different level. You do it to my face, not behind my back like all the others around here."

"Does that include your family?"

Trent leisurely blew a smoke ring and watched it drift upward and then disappear.

From the nearby woods the cicadas started up.

"Probably. Sam can't stand me. Randy is a whack job. Jean loves my money."

"One big happy family."

"But I can't blame folks. Remember, I said jealousy? It's true. I bet you're a hotshot soldier. Probably were in combat in the Middle East. Got a slew of medals."

"You just come up with that on your own?"

"I checked you out. Yeah, I bet it was rough over there. But let me tell you what real combat is like. Business is combat. And to win you've got to be an asshole. No marshmallows make it to the top in business. It's kill or be killed. And if you're not at the top, you're at the bottom. And that's where most people will live their whole lives." He flicked his cigar to remove some dangling ash and then put it to his lips.

"Thanks for the Business 101, Roger. Now why don't you talk to me about your financial problems?"

The cigar sagged in the man's mouth and the mirth-filled look in his eyes vanished. "What financial problems?"

"You checked me out, I checked you out."

"Then your information is flawed."

"Tough-looking Marine you have guarding you now. Where is he, by the way? With death threats I wouldn't be going around alone."

"Your concern for my well-being is touching."

"And I take it the bankers in New York weren't receptive to your cash flow problems?"

Trent threw his cigar down on the dirt and ground it in with his foot. "What the hell did Jean tell you? That stupid bitch."

Less than three days. That's all Puller had. He decided to go for it.

"You have your fingers in lots of pies, Roger. Coal. But you operate gas pipelines too, right?"

"What's that have to do with anything?"

"You tell me."

"Nothing to tell."

"You sure about that?"

"Real sure."

"Being in debt is bad. Treason is worse."

"You on drugs or something?"

"Just giving you some advice."

"Why should I take advice from you?"

"Because it's been given with good intent."

Trent laughed. "You're a real funny guy."

"Not really, no. And if things play out the way I think, you're going to need more than one Marine to keep you safe."

"Are you threatening me?" bellowed Trent.

"You're smart enough to know that the threat won't be coming from me, Roger."

Trent climbed back in his Bentley and drove off.

Apparently Puller had struck out again. He had to hope that Dickie would have something more useful to report.

CHAPTER

73

IT WAS NEARLY ten o'clock when he arrived. The neighborhood was quiet. No one was outside. Puller could hardly blame them. It was hot, humid, and the mosquitoes were out in force. It was a night to stay inside the walls, not frolic outside them.

He steered his Malibu through the network of surface streets, following the path that he and Cole had earlier. He made one more turn and the firehouse was up ahead. No lights on, but he didn't expect there to be. No electricity here. That's probably why they all went home when it started to get dark. The overhead doors had been pulled down. Puller wondered if they were locked too. He stopped his car, got out, looked around, and sniffed the air. A mosquito buzzed in his face. He swatted it away. That would only signal more comrades to come, he knew. He'd trained in enough swamps to understand that.

He locked his Malibu using his remote fob. He'd parked it close to the building. He had decided to keep his car as close to him as possible from now on. He walked up to the overhead door, reached down, and tugged. It slid up easily on oiled tracks. He looked around again, could see no one. Still, his right hand sat on top of his forward M11. He'd grabbed his Maglite from the trunk and popped it on. The beam cut through the darkness as he moved inside.

While he was waiting for Dickie, he wanted to check out a theory.

There were two Harleys parked side by side to his right, their front wheels chained together. To his left was a rolling toolbox with a big padlock. It appeared that the members of the Harley club didn't completely trust their neighbors. Both Harleys had large saddlebags. They had locks on them. Not unheard of, and in fact Puller had expected to find them.

He picked the locks and probed the interior of the bags with his light. In the third bag he found what he was hoping for—a bit of plastic, an edge of duct tape, and a few nearly invisible shiny flakes. In another saddlebag he found a few crumbly brown grains. The shiny flakes were pure crystal meth. The brown flakes were an impure version of meth called peanut butter crank. Illegal drugs were more of a problem in the military than the brass liked to let on. Over the years Puller had seen just about every type of illicit drug there was.

So he had found the distribution pipeline for Eric Treadwell's modest meth operation. The Xanadu bike club put it in their saddlebags and delivered it to their customers. And in impoverished areas where people wanted to forget about their reality because it was so bad, drug dealers had easy prey.

So Treadwell and Bitner had been small-time drug dealers. That wasn't why they were killed, he was sure of that. He would let Cole know about this, but it didn't get him any closer to stopping the terrorists.

He went through the storage lockers on the left side of the wall. Nothing. Mostly filled with stuff from the Harley riders. When he attempted to access the lockers on the right, he found them locked tight. He picked the lock of one of them and found nothing. He did two other lockers and found the same: nothing. He didn't waste time on the others.

He checked his watch. He had gotten here purposely early just in case Dickie wasn't playing straight with him and someone had set up an ambush. He had some more time to kill. He decided to employ it by searching this place. It wasn't out of the realm of possibility that folks who distributed meth could be persuaded to do something far more heinous, even if it meant hurting their country. Maybe folks around here felt their country had already abandoned them, so what did it matter?

There was another room off to his left. He went in there, the shadows devolving to cavelike darkness, for there were no windows in here. It was empty. He backed out, his ears straining for the sounds of anyone drawing near.

He ventured up the stairs. There was a kitchen that looked like it was being used by the club. He opened some cabinets and found cans of soup and cereal boxes.

There was another room adjacent to the kitchen. He opened the door and peered inside, his light cutting into the dark. This must've been the fire chief's office, he thought. Old desk, old file cabinets, shelves, and a couple of rusty chairs. He looked through the file cabinets but they were empty, as were the shelves. He sat down behind the desk and started opening drawers. He found nothing until he dipped his hand farther back in one of the drawers after his light hit on something.

He looked at the yellowed piece of paper. It had the date 1964 on it.

The heading said "FIA." He didn't know what that meant.

He read the body of the document. It dealt with procedures in the event of a fire at the facility. There was nothing in it that revealed to Puller what the facility did. Maybe this had to do with what Mason had told him. About the bombmaking component work.

He eyed something written in the margin. The ink had faded but he could still make it out.

The numbers 92 and 94.

He put the page in his pocket and rose.

He heard the noise as soon as he left the small office.

A motorcycle, coming fast, its engine throbbing. He strode quickly over to a set of windows on the second floor that overlooked the front of the firehouse.

It had to be Dickie. He hit his watch with the light. It was time.

He could see the bike's single headlight stabbing through the gloom. The motorcycle rolled onto the cracked concrete fronting the firehouse. Now Puller could make out more clearly the man's image. Blocky shoulders. Chunky torso. It was Dickie.

The sound of the shot made Puller jerk and instinctively duck.

As he watched, the round hit the rider directly in the head, smashing through the helmet, drilling through the skull and brain and exploding out the other side. The Harley drifted to the right as the rider let go of the handlebars. The man fell off to the left and hit the concrete. He jerked once and lay still. The bike continued on before hitting the wall of the firehouse and falling over on its side, the engine still running.

Puller didn't see this last part. He had leapt to the fire pole and slid down it.

The shot had come from the left. Long-range rifle round. Puller figured the sniper was on the ground somewhere. There was no high dirt here, just houses. The shooter could be in one of them. And there were a lot of them. All empty. Well, maybe not.

Puller eased out of the front entrance next to the still running bike. He bent down, turned it off, his M11 making defensive arcs. He thumbed the number on his cell phone.

Cole picked up on the second ring.

He explained things in three efficient sentences.

She would be bringing the cavalry to his aid for a second time today.

He counted to three and then zigzagged his way to the Malibu. Keeping the body of it between him and where the shot had come from, he unlocked his trunk and quickly snagged what he needed.

Night optics.

And his body armor. The outer tactical vest was a modular soft armor configuration that could stop a nine-mil round. But that wasn't good enough tonight. Puller took a few seconds to slip the ceramic plates into the inserts in the tact vest to bump up his protection level. He powered up his optics and the world was revealed in a sharply defined green. He looked over at the body. The helmet was still on, so he couldn't see the person's face. The last piece of equipment that Puller reached for in his trunk was probably the most important.

H&K MP5 submachine gun. It was the clear weapon of choice by Special Forces for close-quarters battle. Its max range was a hundred meters, which meant Puller was going to have to get a lot closer to his target.

Sniper rifle against close-quarters small arms put the latter at a decided disadvantage. Added to that was the fact that Puller was certain the shooter had a night-vision scope to make the kind of shot he just had. He would have preferred to have his bolt-action sniper rifle. But the H&K would have to do.

Puller put his MP on two-shot bursts and slammed the trunk closed.

He had one bit of recon to do. He got in his car, started it, and drove it in reverse over to the body. He used the car as a shield while he slid out.

He saw the entry and exit wounds on the helmet. He popped open the visor and saw Dickie Strauss staring back at him.

He turned to his left and saw it. The slug was lying on the pavement. He focused on it without touching it.

It was a .338 Lapua Magnum round and Puller's body armor was not rated to stop it. The Lapua also had a range of up to fifteen hundred meters. And with ideal conditions and a little luck, a talented sniper could hit his target from even farther away than that.

He broke all crime scene protocols by doing a quick search of the dead man and retrieving his cell phone and wallet, which he pocketed.

Puller got back in his car and, keeping his head down, drove it forward to the firehouse. He got out on the passenger side and slid the MP5 support sling over his head.

It was time to go hunting.

CHAPTER

74

SAM COLE'S RACK LIGHTS cut through the darkness and her sirens shrieked though the normal quiet. She knew these roads better than just about anyone, but a couple of times she pushed herself and her cruiser so hard that she thought they would both go off the road and into the open air before she plummeted to an early death.

She tore into the last curve and punched the gas when she hit the straightaway. A few seconds later, she saw the firehouse. Pulling to a stop, she pointed her headlights at the body on the concrete. Cole drew her gun and opened her door. She called Puller on her cell but got no answer.

She slid out of the car, keeping the door between her and wherever the shooter might be. She eyed the wrecked bike by the firehouse and then her gaze drifted to the Malibu. She heard sirens in the distance. A minute later two police cruisers pulled next to her vehicle.

She called out, "Shooter somewhere out there."

She saw the deputies open their car doors and duck down behind them.

"Cover me," said Cole.

She had on standard-issue body armor and hoped it was enough. She scooted forward and over to the body. She lifted the visor and stared down at the face.

Dickie Strauss didn't look like he was asleep. He looked like someone had dropped a cannon on his head.

She called out to the deputies, "Fatality." She eyed the holes in the sides of the helmet. "GS to the head. Heavy ordnance."

"Better take cover, Sarge," said one of her men.

Cole scuttled back to the car and took up position behind the door. She eyed her deputies. "Call in backup. I want all roads into here blocked off. Whoever it is, they are not getting away."

"What about the Army dude?" one of her men said back.

Cole looked out into the darkness.

Come on, Puller. Don't be dead. Don't be dead.

Puller had set up a surveillance position next to an abandoned house about five hundred yards from the firehouse. He had come this way following, in his mind's eye, the trajectory of the shot. A moderately talented sniper could nail a target all day from six hundred to a thousand yards away, if he had the right equipment. The Lapua round signaled to Puller that the sniper did indeed have the right equipment.

Police snipers in urban settings typically shot at ranges under a hundred feet. Military snipers operated at distances considerably more than that, since combat was an altogether different beast. Puller had heard the report, so the shot wasn't over a mile away. Military sniper rifles were generally longer than their police counterparts to allow the cartridge propellant to completely burn its fuel load, which reduced muzzle flash and powered up the bullet's velocity. That kept the sniper's position harder to find and increased the odds of a lethal shot.

Puller pondered whether the sniper also had a spotter. If so, it was two against one. He heard sirens in the distance. Cole and her team were almost here. That was both good and bad. Good in that reinforcements were always welcome. Bad in that the shooter now had more incentive than ever to get the hell out of here.

He swept the area ahead, looking for the telltale sign of a laser finder. The devices were great at acquiring targets, but discouraged in the battlefields for the simple reason that they gave away your position. Puller had always relied on his scope and spotter, and compared the height of targets to their images on the mil dot scope. The average human head, shoulder width, and distance from the hipbones to the top of the head could be roughly gauged. If you had that, you could use your scope to find the proper range. Cops aimed for the "apricot," or medulla oblongata, the roughly three-inch-long part of the brain that controlled involuntary movement. You hit that, death was instantaneous. Since military snipers usually aimed at nothing under three hundred meters, they aimed for the body because the torso was a larger target.

The shooter confronting Puller had blurred this dichotomy. Head shot but at over three hundred meters.

Cop or military?

Or both?

If the shooter fired again, Puller might be able to locate his position by triangulation. But if the shooter fired again and hit Puller in the head or torso, the Lapua round would either seriously injure him or more likely kill him.

He studied what was up ahead, empty houses, quiet streets. But not all of the houses were empty. There were cars parked in front of some. He could see low-level lights in some of them. Were they not aware a sniper was in their midst? Had they not heard the shot?

He looked back in the direction of the firehouse. His focus went to the exact location of Dickie Strauss's body. Round impacted, bike kept going. He'd fallen off about three seconds later. Back up the timeline to that. Retrace the trajectory. He looked in the opposite direction. He checked the probable firing line one more time. The only straight sightline. House at the end of a cul-de-sac. Dark, no cars out front. Behind it more houses, but on the next block they were all facing the opposite way.

He listened, forcing himself to ignore the sirens. No sounds. No running, no footsteps.

He made up his mind.

A moment later he was on the move. For a big man he could move with almost no sound. It was both easy and hard. Long legs, less movement to cover more ground. But big men were not noted for being light on their feet. People always assumed someone his size would sound like an elephant coming. Some had thought that right before their deaths.

Puller hoped tonight would be another example of this.

CHAPTER

75

THE SNIPER RIFLE weighed fourteen pounds and was forty-two inches long, almost like a barbell. That was why you fired it mostly in the prone position. He carried it in his right hand. The collapsible bipod at the end of the muzzle was in the closed position. He moved quickly but methodically. One kill tonight. He had no desire for another. Not tonight.

He glanced back over his shoulder. Nothing except the darkness looked back at him. He was twenty feet from the tree line. From there a five-minute walk through the woods. A car waiting, a fast drive. Before the police could set up their roadblocks. He liked this area. Lots of ground to cover and not nearly enough cops to do it properly.

He stopped, turned back.

Sirens, yes, but something else. Something unexpected.

His left hand slipped to his waistband.

"Another inch with the hand and you can get a good look at your intestines."

The man's hand stopped right where it was.

Puller did not step clear of the trees. He had no idea if the other man was alone. He kept his MP trained on the target.

"First, take the rifle by the muzzle and toss it away from you. Second, lie facedown with your hands interlocked behind your head, eyes closed, and your feet spread-eagled."

The man set the rifle stock-first on the ground, gripped the muzzle, and threw the weapon. It landed six feet away, thudding to the ground and spraying up grass and dirt.

"First part done. Now execute step two," Puller said.

"How'd you get ahead of me?" asked the man.

Puller didn't like the question, but he liked even less the tone in which it was asked. Unhurried, earnestly curious, but seemingly unmindful of the consequences of being caught. His gaze swept the field in front of him. Was there a spotter out there? A backup team to ferry the sniper away?

"Lucky triangulation," he said. "Worked to the logical conclusion and double-timed it there."

"Never heard you."

"That's right. Why take out Dickie?"

"Don't know what you're talking about."

"Lapua rounds aren't that plentiful around here, I would bet."

"You can walk away from this, Puller. Right now. Maybe you should."

Puller liked this change in tactics even less. It was like the other man was holding the gun on him. Offering him a free walk.

"I'm listening," he said.

"I'm sure you've already considered it. You won't learn anything more from me. It's not my job to do your job."

"Eight people dead now. Must be a good reason." Puller slid his finger to the trigger guard on the MP5. Once it ventured inside the guard he would fire.

"Must be."

"You talk, there might be a deal."

"I don't think so."

"You that loyal?"

"If that's what you want to call it. I let you get to me. My fault. My responsibility."

"Facedown. Last time I'll ask."

Puller lined up his shot. At this range the man was dead. He braced the MP against his right pec. With his left hand he toggled his forward M11 in a thirty-degree arc.

The man dropped to his knees. Then to his stomach. He started to interlock his fingers. But then his hand shot to his waist.

Puller used his M11 to pump one round into each of the man's arms and then stepped to his left and behind a tree. His muzzle flash had given away his position. He had not gone for a kill shot because he didn't have to. The man couldn't have gotten off a clean shot at him. And now with his arms immobilized he wouldn't be able to even point his gun at Puller. The man had gone for his weapon for perhaps two reasons.

First, he'd wanted Puller to kill him.

Puller had decided not to be so accommodating. He wanted a witness he could interrogate.

Second, he had wanted Puller to fire, revealing his position; hence Puller's sidestep behind the tree.

He awaited incoming fire from another sector.

It didn't come.

His glance shot back to the wounded man, who still lay there, blood gushing out from his arms. No arterial spray because Puller hadn't aimed at that.

He noted a second too late that the man's hand was under him. The shot rang out.

"Shit," Puller muttered as he watched man's torso jerk up and then come back to rest on the ground.

The bullet had come out the man's back. Dead center. Contact kill shot in reverse. Self-inflicted.

Puller had just lost his potential witness. Whoever these people were, they were dedicated to something. Choosing death over life was not an easily made decision. It seemed the man had intended it all along. As soon as he knew he'd been compromised and was near capture.

Puller had relaxed for just a moment. It was almost a fatal mistake.

He blocked the knife with his gun barrel, but the man leveled a blow at Puller's arm with his other hand and the impact knocked his MP5 to the dirt. Puller raised his M11, but a side kick from his opponent sent that weapon to the dirt too. The man came at him again, whipping the knife in different directions to confuse Puller. He was six-two, one-ninety, with thick dark hair, a lean tanned face, and the calm gaze of someone accustomed to killing other people.

But then was so Puller.

He pinned the man's knife arm against his torso, dipped down, and slammed his head into the man's throat. The blade dropped to the ground. Puller pivoted around, gripped the top of the man's head with his right hand, and jerked it to the right at the same time he slammed an elbow directly into the left side of the man's neck.

The man gurgled and blood started to trickle out of his nose and mouth.

"Give it up and you get to live, asshole," said Puller.

The man continued to struggle. He kicked at Puller's groin, gouged at his eyes. That was irritating but manageable. Puller wanted this guy alive. But when the man got his hand on Puller's rear M11 and tried to jerk it free, Puller decided it was better to be alive without a captive he could question rather than dead.

Puller moved fully behind the man, looped one long arm, with the elbow up, around his opponent's damaged neck, gripped his torso with his other arm, and pulled in separate directions. When he heard the man start to scream, he lifted him off the ground, whipped him around, and slammed him into the nearest tree. He heard the spine snap and he dropped the entire load to the dirt. Breathing hard, he stared down at the mess he'd made of a human body. He looked over at the knife. Serrated blade. Worn handle. Lots of use. His blood was supposed to be all over it. He felt not an ounce of remorse.

"Puller!"

He glanced to his right.

He recognized Cole's voice.

"Over here. Keep back. Got a dead sniper and his backup and there may be more. I'm okay."

Ten minutes passed and Cole said, "Can we join you?"

Puller made one last scan of the tree line. "Okay."

A few minutes later Cole and two of her deputies were within his sightline.

"Puller?"

"To your right." He stepped out to show his location.

Cole and her deputies scuttled forward to join him around the dead men.

Puller knelt down and eased the sniper over. "Shine your light on his face."

Cole did so.

The deputy named Lou let out a gasp. He said, "That's the guy who was pretending to live at Treadwell's place."

Puller rose. "I thought it might be."

"How?" asked Lou.

"He matched the description you gave of him earlier. Now we know he's as good at sniping as he is at killing up close."

Lou looked at the other wrecked body. "What the hell did you do to him?"

"I killed him," Puller said simply. "Before he killed me."

"That was Dickie Strauss back there," said Cole.

"I know."

"What was he doing here?"

"Coming to meet me."

Cole looked at the wounds on the back of the man's arms. "Your rounds?"

He nodded. "The guy went for his gun. Thought he was trying to get me to kill him. I didn't. Then he ate his own round. Should have seen that coming. But a guy wants to kill himself and he has a gun handy, not a lot you can do about it."

"Guess not," said Cole curtly.

Puller looked around and said, "Let's secure the crime scenes. Call in Lan Monroe and whoever else you need. Then you and I can go talk."

"What about?"

"Lots of things."

CHAPTER

76

Cole was waiting for him at her house. Puller had made one stop at his motel room and then driven over. She greeted him at the front door and he followed her down the hall to the kitchen.

"You want a drink?" she asked. "I'm having a beer."

"I'm good," he said.

They sat in a back room that overlooked the rear yard. It was hot and humid, and Cole's wall AC wasn't much better than the one in his motel room. He thought he could taste the coal in the air, feel his skin turning oily black by just being here.

She sat across from him, her fingers curled around the neck of her Michelob.

"While you were following up some leads," she began, "I checked out Treadwell's place of business. The only useful piece of info I got from them is that nothing was missing from their inventory. And they had no idea why he would have tungsten carbide residue in his house. They don't carry anything like that."

"So it wasn't work-related?"

"No."

"I found the answer to the meth lab."

"What?"

He told her what he'd discovered at the fire station.

"Damn. The Xanadu club dealing meth?"

"Looks to be," said Puller. "But doesn't really get us anywhere. And we're running out of time."

"What do you mean?"

He told her about his conversation with Joe Mason. About the pipeline operated by Trent. And the nuclear reactor that was apparently the real target. And finally he told her about Trent's financial problems.

When he was done, she put her beer down and leaned back in her chair.

"I'm not sure where to begin," she said. "Jean never told me anything about money problems. And she told you?"

"I think I caught her at a vulnerable moment. And I'm not family. Maybe she just didn't want you to know. Maybe she was embarrassed that she might be poor again."

"Are you hungry? I'm suddenly starving."

"Cole, forget about food. We've got less than two—"

She said in a trembling voice, "I need to make sandwiches, Puller. I...I need to do something normal. Or I'm going to lose it. I am. I mean it. I didn't sign up for something like this. Shit like this is not supposed to happen in places like Drake."

He said in a soothing tone, "Okay. Okay. How about I help?"

They went to the kitchen and made turkey sandwiches with pickle slices on top and chips as the garnish. They ate standing up at the kitchen sink.

"What are you thinking?" she asked quietly.

Puller took a bite of sandwich and followed it with some chips.

"Shooter knew what he was doing. Rifle was first-class, so was his ammo choice. He picked his position well, executed his shot, and nearly made his escape. I had to hustle to beat him and also bagged some luck in the process. And I'm really good at hunting down shooters in pretty much any environment." He paused. "And he still almost got away. And his partner was good. Not as good as me, but really good."

"Modest," said Cole.

"Realistic," replied Puller. "Underestimating or overestimating your ability can be fatal. There are guys out there better than me. He just wasn't one of them."

"Okay."

"Let's assume Dickie, Treadwell, and Molly were in on the meth dealing. I said Dickie struck me as a guy who was stuck between a rock and a hard place. He was dealing meth, which he obviously wanted to keep secret, but he had also stumbled onto something else that was far worse."

"You said he was meeting with you tonight? Any idea what he was going to report?"

"No. Maybe nothing. I was the one who called the meeting."

She popped the fridge and pulled out two bottles of Deer Park. She handed him one.

"A pipeline and a nuclear reactor," she said. "And we have two days. That's nuts, Puller. Nuts."

"It is what it is."

"You have to call in the heavy artillery."

"I've tried, Cole. The guys upstairs aren't budging on this."

"So they're just hanging us out to dry?"

They stood there facing each other across a few inches, but it seemed to Puller like miles. He had served his country most of his adult life. And serving your country, in essence, meant serving its citizens. People like the woman staring hopelessly at him right now. He had never felt so conflicted in his life.

"I don't know what to tell you, Cole. I really don't."

She said, "Well, there's one thing I need to do."

"What's that?" Puller asked warily.

"I need to tell Bill Strauss he's lost his son."

"I'll go with you."

"You don't have to."

"Yeah, I do."

They rose and left together.

CHAPTER

77

T HEY DROVE THERE in Puller's Malibu. The night air seemed even more stifling than it had been during the day when the temperature had hovered in the nineties with a matching humidity level. The spray of his headlights picked up swarms of mosquitoes just waiting for victims. A deer leapt out from the woods on the left about fifty feet ahead of them. Puller tapped his brakes. A few seconds later what looked like a small mountain lion exploded from the brush, cleared the asphalt in two bounds, and disappeared into the woods on the other side.

Predators, it seemed, were out in force tonight.

"It was hotter than this in the Middle East, but no humidity. This reminds me more of Florida," said Puller as he piloted his ride along the curvy back roads that seemed to be the only kind Drake had.

"Never been to Florida," said Cole. "West Virginia is the only place I've ever been. This is my *home*."

He punched the AC button to max and rubbed a line of sweat off his forehead even as her words stung him.

"Let's talk it out," he said.

"This puts me in the mother of all awkward positions, Puller."

He glanced at her. "I know. You're an officer of the peace. A public servant. Protect and defend."

"Right. So what am I supposed to do? Evacuate the county?"

Puller gripped the steering wheel tighter and peered out into the darkness. Cole had been telling him which way to go to get to the Strausses' home, but apparently they were on a long straightaway, at least long by local standards, and Cole had obviously seized the opportunity to voice her concerns.

"You can try, I guess. But without more to go on, I'm not sure how effective you'll be."

"But if you back me up? And the folks up in D.C.?"

"That won't be happening," said Puller bluntly.

"Why the hell not?"

Puller decided to tell her the truth. "They see you guys as an opportunity to write a new page in the playbook and nail some bad guys in the process."

"You mean we're guinea pigs?" she snapped.

"Yeah, you're guinea pigs. The Feds figure if we hit the panic button the bad guys will just pull up stakes and go to another place and do it there."

"But this is my hometown. I was born here. I know the people. I can't just wait around for them to be wiped out."

Puller had been staring at her, but now he looked away.

"Puller? Do you understand where I'm coming from?"

"Yeah, I do. And that means I probably shouldn't have told you."

"The hell you shouldn't have!"

"Bottom line, the Feds are going to do nothing to precipitate this. They want to see it play out. They'll call in the troops at the last minute. It should be enough time to ensure minimal collateral damage."

"*Should* be enough time? *Minimal* collateral damage?"

He interrupted her. "But that doesn't mean that we just have to sit here with our tails tucked between our legs. We can try to solve this sucker before the trigger is pulled."

"But what if we can't?"

"It's the best plan I have."

"You're asking me to decide between my country and my people."

"I'm not asking you to do anything, Cole. I'm just telling you what they told me. I don't like it any better than you do."

"So what would you do?"

"I'm a soldier. It's easy for me. I just follow orders."

"That's bullshit."

"Yeah, you're right, it is."

"So?"

He gripped the wheel so tightly that he could feel it give a little. "So, I don't know."

They ate up more ground in silence. She broke it only to give him the final directions to Strauss's place.

As they neared it she said, "What if I decide to raise the alarm?"

"It's up to you."

"You won't shoot me?"

"It's up to you," Puller said again. "And no, I won't shoot you." He took a long breath. "In fact, I'll back you up."

"You will? Why?"

He looked over to see her staring at him.

"I just will," said Puller. "Right thing to do. Sometimes the brass forgets about that little detail. Right thing to do," he said again.

They saw the lights of the Strauss home up ahead. As Puller turned into the driveway he said, "We can get through this if we keep working together."

She pressed the palms of her hands against the dash, as though trying to slow down runaway thoughts attempting to escape her mind.

He reached over and squeezed her shoulder. "You're not alone, Sam. I'm right here with you."

She turned to him. "First time you've called me Sam."

"I'm in the Army. We're a formal race of people."

This drew a rare smile from her. She patted his hand.

"I'm good…John." She looked at him. "Is that okay? That I sometimes call you John? I know that probably sounds silly with everything that's going on, to worry about something like that."

"It's fine. And it's better than Romeo, I guess."

"Or Juliet," she replied.

78

THE STRAUSS HOME was a little over half the size of the Trents', which meant it was enormous by Drake standards. And by most American standards, Puller thought. It stood within its own five-acre grounds and even had a little gate out front, though there was no guard here as there was at Trent's mansion.

Cole had called ahead and roused Strauss and his wife from their beds. The couple was waiting for them when they rang the doorbell. Mrs. Strauss was a large-boned fleshy woman who had taken the time to fix her hair after being awoken in the middle of the night. She wore slacks, a blouse with the bottom untucked, and an expression that was devastated.

Bill Strauss was dressed in jeans and a polo shirt. He had an unlit cigarette dangling between his fingers. Perhaps Mrs. Strauss, like Rhonda Dougett, did not allow smoking in her house.

They sat huddled on a couch together while Cole explained what had happened. When she came to the gunshot Bill Strauss looked up.

"So you're saying someone murdered him? Killed Dickie on purpose?"

Puller said, "I was there. That's exactly what happened."

Strauss gazed at him. "You were there? At the firehouse? Why?"

Cole answered. "That's not relevant, Mr. Strauss."

"Do you have any leads on the killer?"

"We have better than that," said Puller. "We have the killer."

Both Strausses gaped at him. Bill Strauss said, "You caught him? Who is he? Why did he kill our son?"

"We don't know who he is. And we can't ask him why he killed Dickie, because he killed himself a few minutes after he shot your son."

Mrs. Strauss started to weep softly into her hands while her husband slid a hand around her shoulders. When the woman completely broke down and started sobbing uncontrollably a few moments later, her husband led her off down the hall.

Puller and Cole sat there waiting for him to return. Puller rose after a couple of minutes and started looking around the room.

Strauss came back in a minute later. He said, "I'm sorry about that. But I'm sure you can understand how distressed we both are."

"Absolutely," said Cole. "We can come back another time, if you'd like. I know this is very difficult."

Strauss sat back down and shook his head. "No, let's just get it over with."

This time he did light up and blew the smoke off to the side.

"We're trying to find out who the dead man is. If we do, it could help break the case."

"So you're sure he's not from around here?" asked Strauss.

"Don't think so, but we'll confirm it."

"Any reason you can think of why someone would want to harm your son?" asked Cole.

"Not a one. Dickie didn't have any enemies. He had friends. He had his buddies in the motorcycle club."

"Where did he work?" asked Puller.

"He…uh, he didn't currently have a job," said Strauss.

"Well, where did he last work?"

"There isn't much work in Drake."

"Well, there's Trent Exploration," said Puller. "And you're the COO."

"Certainly. That's right. But Dickie didn't want to work at Trent."

"Why's that?"

"Just wasn't something he was interested in."

"So you supported him?" asked Puller.

"What?" Strauss said distractedly. "We, that is to say, I would give him money from time to time. And he lived at home. He was our only child. Maybe we spoiled him." He paused, drawing a sharp breath and with it more nicotine into his lungs. "But he didn't deserve to be murdered."

"Of course not," said Cole.

"If he lived here," said Puller, "we'll need to search his room at some point."

"But not tonight," said Cole.

"He told me why he was booted from the Army," Puller said. This comment drew a sharp glance from Strauss.

"It was...unfortunate," said Strauss.

"The gayness or the booting?" asked Puller.

"Both," said Strauss frankly. "I'm not a homophobe, Agent Puller. You might think everyone from a small town like this is not very open-minded to such things, but I loved my son."

"Okay," said Puller. "He was a good man. He wanted to do the right thing."

"What do you mean?"

"He was helping us in our investigation," said Cole.

"Helping you? How?"

"Just helping us."

"Do you think that's why he was killed?"

"I don't know."

"My God," said Strauss. "All these people killed in Drake in just a few days. Do you think they're connected?"

"We do," said Cole.

"Why?"

"Can't get into that," she said.

Puller sat staring at Strauss for a few moments, debating whether to take a new tack. Finally he decided time was just running out.

"Did you find out about the blasting approvals?"

In a distracted tone Strauss said, "I called the office that handles it. They checked. The foreman for that operation requested the special permit and it was received. But there was a glitch in the public notice. It didn't go out in time. The foreman didn't get that information, so he blasted anyway. It doesn't happen often, but it does happen."

"Who would've known about the timing of the blast?"

"I knew. The foreman. Lots of people at Trent."

"Roger Trent?" asked Puller.

"I don't know for sure, but if he had an interest he could have found out easily enough."

Cole rose and handed him her card. "You think of anything else, give me a call. I'm very sorry for your loss."

Strauss looked confused at the abrupt end to the interview but rose on unsteady legs. "Thank you, Sergeant Cole."

Puller was the last to get to his feet. He drew close to Strauss. "A lot of people have died, Mr. Strauss. We don't want to see any more corpses."

"Of course not." His face reddened. "You're not implying I had anything—"

"No, I'm not implying anything."

"You think he's lying, don't you?" said Cole as they walked back to the car.

"I think he knows more than he was willing to share with us."

"So he helped get his own son killed? He seemed genuinely torn up about it."

"Maybe he didn't intend for his son to be involved in any of this."

They got into the car and Puller drove away from the Strausses' home.

Cole looked back through the rear window. "I can't imagine losing my child."

"Actually, everyone can imagine it. No one wants to experience it."

"You ever think about getting married?"

Puller thought, *I am married. My wife is the United States Army. And she can be a real bitch sometimes.*

"I guess everybody thinks about it," he said. "At some point."

"It's hard being a cop and married."

"People do it all the time."

"I mean being a female cop and married."

"People still do it."

"I guess they do. You know, if you think Strauss is holding something back, I probably shouldn't have been so quick to postpone searching his son's room."

"We'll get to it, but I doubt Dickie would keep anything of real importance there."

"Well, where would he keep things of real importance?"

"Maybe the same place Eric Treadwell kept his tungsten carbide."

"You really think that's important?"

"It's important because it's inexplicable." He looked at his watch. "Sleepy?"

"No. I feel like somebody hitched me to a live wire. But you should stay at my place tonight."

"Why? I've got a room."

"Someone also tried to blow you up. Twice."

"Okay, maybe you're right."

They picked up her car and he followed Cole to her house. She showed him to his room and made sure he had everything he needed.

She paused at the door as he sat back on the bed and slipped off his Army boots.

He looked up. "Yeah?"

"Why Drake? Just because we have a pipeline and a nuclear reactor nearby?"

"I guess for some folks, that's all it takes."

He dropped his second boot on the floor and pulled his forward M11 from its holster.

"You expecting to live your whole life with a gun in your hand?" she asked.

"Are you?"

"I don't know. Right now it seems like a pretty good idea."

"Yeah. I'm thinking the same thing."

"Puller, if we make it out of this alive." She paused. "Maybe we could..."

He looked up at her. "Yeah, I was thinking that too."

CHAPTER

79

It was one in the morning when Puller found himself in Afghanistan again, in the middle of the firefight that he would win every time, even if he couldn't bring home the men he'd lost. He woke from the dream slowly, calmly. But he woke with something else.

An idea.

There had been a hole. A lead he had not followed up. While he'd been killing Afghanis in the desert, his mind had finally fixated on that hole. And he didn't have much time to get it done. He rose, dressed, and left the house as quietly as he had moved through foot patrols in the Middle East. He had paused only to check on Cole. She was asleep in her bed, a single sheet over her in deference to the heat outside. He left her a note on the fridge, made sure her front door was securely locked, rolled his car out of the driveway and partway down the street before starting it up. And then he was off.

Thirty minutes later he eyed the bleak concrete-block building. There was no security system. He'd already noted that on his last visit here.

He scanned the area one more time and then moved forward. The front door lock took all of thirty seconds.

He moved through the interior. He hadn't used his flashlight yet because he had memorized the interior from his earlier visit. Down the hall, fifteen strides, door on the left. He used a penlight to illuminate the lock while he used his tools to pick it.

Twenty seconds later he was on the other side of the door and had closed it behind him. He stared over at the other door. He tried the knob. Surprisingly, it wasn't locked. He opened it with his gloved hand. The large freestanding safe stared back at him. This would be the trickier one. But he'd brought with him several elements that could be used to defeat it.

He shone his light on the metal face of the safe. It was old but sturdy. He inserted his tools in the lock. He worked with a practiced hand for five minutes. There was a low click, and he tugged on the locking mechanism arm and pulled the door open. It took him ten minutes of searching before he found what he was pretty sure he had been looking for.

He unfolded the blueprints and placed them on the desk. He shone his light over them, going page by page. Then he took pictures of each page, folded the plans back up, replaced them in the safe, cranked the door closed, and made sure it locked properly. Five minutes later he was driving off in his Malibu. He reached Cole's house, carried the camera in, and sat on his bed going through each frame. When he was finished he sat back and thought about it, trying to put things in order. Strauss had had this in his safe. Eric Treadwell and Molly Bitner had designed a plan to get this out of the safe and make copies of it. If he needed any confirmation that they had done so, he had it.

He had brought with him fingerprint cards of both Treadwell and Bitner. Both of them must have been sweating when they'd pulled their little raid at Strauss's office, because the moisture along with their prints had been transferred perfectly to the paper. And it was the sort of paper that would carry latent prints pretty much forever. The matches had been perfect for both Treadwell and Bitner.

This is what they had risked so much for. This was ultimately what they had sacrificed their lives for. The one piece he had not followed up on.

Until now.

Now the question was: Did he tell Cole?

The answer was clearer and more immediate than he expected.

He looked at his watch: 0400.

Ironic. He was going to wake her up early again.

CHAPTER

80

Sᴀᴍ Cᴏʟᴇ ʀᴏʟʟᴇᴅ ᴏᴠᴇʀ, opened her eyes, and nearly screamed.

Puller was sitting next to her in a chair he'd drawn up to the bed.

"What the hell are you doing here?" she said, sitting up.

"Waiting for you to wake up."

"Why didn't you just wake me up?"

"You were sleeping so peacefully."

"I didn't think that mattered to you. You woke me up before from a sound sleep."

"It was nice watching you sleep."

She started to say something and then stopped. "Oh," she said.

Puller looked down.

Flustered, she said, "So you decided to wait and scare me to death?"

"Wasn't my plan, but it sort of worked out that way."

Before she could say anything else he held up his camera.

"You want to take my picture?" she said in a confused tone.

"I want you to look at some pictures."

"What am I looking at?"

"Stay here. I'll make some coffee and we can look at it together."

Thirty minutes and two cups of coffee later, Cole sat back against her pillow. "Okay. What does all this mean?"

"It means we have a lot more digging to do. And not a lot of time to do it."

"And you're sure this is important?"

"It's why they broke into Strauss's safe. And I think it was why the Reynoldses and Treadwell and Bitner were killed. So, yes, it's important."

"But I thought they were killed because of the soil report."

"I did too. But there was nothing on it that would raise any alarm. They were killed because somehow it was found out that these plans had been taken from Strauss's safe. And they also discovered that Bitner and Treadwell had told Reynolds about it. So they had to die too."

"So what happened to the soil report?"

"Remember the pieces of the certified mail delivery we found under the couch?"

"Yes."

"I think the killers planted them there. As a red herring."

"Why? And why not just leave the whole thing for us to find?"

"Then we don't waste any time running that lead down. But if we had thought about it some, it was pretty convenient that they left the green pieces of the certified mail receipt for us to find."

"And Larry Wellman?"

"Was on patrol when they showed up. He had to be silenced."

"Damn, Puller, it makes sense." Her features became troubled. "So they killed Larry just to plant pieces of paper to throw us off?"

"Way I see it."

"And Dickie?"

"In way over his head. I don't think he knew anything about the killings. When he found out, it was only a matter of time. And when I enlisted his help I pretty much signed his death warrant."

She looked at him quizzically. "When did you think of all this?"

"When I was back in Afghanistan."

"What?"

"In my head only," he said. "My brain tends to work faster when I'm there," he added in a low voice.

"I can understand that," Cole said slowly.

She looked at the pictures on his camera. "So what do we do with these?"

"I'm going to download it to my computer and then print out pages. But the bottom line is we need to go there."

"Go there? You mean just to look?"

"No, I mean more than that." He checked his watch. "It's still dark outside. You game?"

"It wouldn't matter if I am or not. We don't have any time to waste. Now get out of my bedroom so I can change."

CHAPTER

81

PULLER AND COLE neared the edge of the woods, knelt, and did a quick scan of what was up ahead. Puller shifted the rucksack on his back from his left shoulder to his right.

He did another look around. They didn't have a margin of error on this and he could afford no mistakes. Dawn was coming.

Cole copied him and did a long look around too.

No lights.

Homes dark.

No cars passed by.

They could have been the only ones left on the planet.

He looked right, left, and then at his target and gave Cole a nod.

They stepped out.

Puller had on his fatigues and his face was blackened. M11 pistols forward and back. His strapped MP5 rested against his chest.

Cole was dressed in black pants and a dark shirt. Her face was blackened like Puller's. She had her Cobra, and a throwaway in a belt holster.

Sweat stained Puller's undershirt. The humidity level was off the charts. The combination of the heat and air moisture was debilitating. He could imagine the people in the old homes with no electricity sweltering in the oppressiveness. Or maybe they felt lucky to have a roof over their heads.

He eyed the dome of concrete. It rose up into the night sky like a solid tumor among otherwise healthy organs. He used metal clippers to cut a hole in the fencing, and a few minutes later he and Cole were next to the tumor.

Cole pulled some pages from a knapsack she carried and they studied them under a penlight Puller had in one of the pockets on his pants.

"We need to get an approximate size on this thing," he said, and she nodded.

While Cole waited where she was, he turned west and stepped off. A hundred long strides later he stopped. He'd been doing roughly four-foot exaggerated pacing. It was difficult in the undergrowth, but he managed as best he could. Four hundred feet. Longer than a football field.

He next stepped off the width of the dome.

Two hundred strides later he stopped. It was eight hundred feet wide. Nearly a sixth of a mile. He calculated roughly the square footage inside and came away impressed. The Feds rarely did anything in a small way, particularly back then when they actually had money to burn.

A large facility. Large enough for what?

The blueprints he'd found in Strauss's safe hadn't revealed that.

The plans had contained a warning from the federal government that no blasting could take place within two miles of the dome. In addition, various spots on the blueprints had been marked with the symbol for danger. There had been no date on the document. There had been no explanatory notes. Puller and Cole had scanned every inch of the plans and still didn't know what the place had been used for.

Clandestine. Top secret. Probably why they picked Drake. Today it was a massive lump in the middle of nowhere.

Puller rejoined Cole. She said, "How big?"

"Bigger than it looks," he replied quietly.

He looked back through the woods at the neighborhood. Late 1950s style. Over half a century old. A lot going on back then in the world.

He turned to her. "What else did your parents tell you about this place?"

"Not that much. There was a siren one time that went off. No one was ever told what happened, my dad said. The police were never called here, that I know of. Sheriff Lindemann's predecessor was sheriff back then. I talked to him about it long after he retired. It was totally out of his jurisdiction, he said."

Puller slipped the paper he'd taken from the firehouse out of his pocket. A fire plan. The numbers 92 and 94 written into the margins.

"So did you figure out what those numbers mean?" Cole asked.

"Maybe."

"What then?"

If it was referring to what he thought it was, this case was about to take on an entirely new and potentially catastrophic angle.

"I'll tell you when I'm sure."

"Why not now? You've been speculating to me before."

"Not like this. I want to be sure. I don't want to cause a panic if it turns out I'm wrong."

She licked her lips. "I'm already panicked, Puller. I mean, pipeline, nuke reactor. How much worse could it get?"

"It could get a lot worse."

"Okay, you officially panicked me right past my maximum level."

He knelt in the woods, listened to the sounds of the wildlife passing close to him. Dawn was breaking. He heard a rattle from a nearby snake. He knew there were copperheads in here as well. The swamps in Florida had been filled with aggressive water moccasins. During the last stage of Ranger training some injuries came from snakebites. Some of his fellow Rangers had been afraid of snakes, but they could never show that fear. One had almost died from a deadly bite from a coral snake, but he'd recovered. Only to die four years later in Afghanistan when an IED had exploded under his feet.

Snakebites were bad. IEDs were worse.

Puller listened, considered their options. His deliberations went fast. He didn't have many. He approached the concrete wall from the back side. He pushed through the thick vines and forest tendrils covering its surface. He touched the rough hide of the thing.

"You sure your dad said this was three feet thick?"

"Yes. He watched them do it."

On a structure this big that would have been an ocean of cement. Only the Feds could have done something like this. It was like building the Hoover Dam in a way.

And for what?

"We have to get inside this sucker," he said.

"Okay, how?"

He touched the smooth surface. Concrete, unlike wood, became weaker over time, especially in elements like these. But three feet allowed a big margin of error for degradation of the material. He stared up the side; it rose nearly ten stories into the air. A few trees were taller than it, but not many. He could climb some of the vines to the very top, but then what?

Three feet. He couldn't hack through that. At least not without people knowing about it. He'd need a jackhammer plus dynamite. He looked down, where the concrete met the dirt. Burrow underneath?

He pulled out a collapsible spade from his knapsack and began to dig. Two feet in he struck something. He removed some more dirt and hit the hole with his light.

"Looks like iron," said Cole.

"Yeah, it does. Rusted but still intact."

He wondered how far out from the perimeter it went. It was probably a good many feet. People who engineered gigantic domes had almost certainly not gone cheap on the other details.

No way under. No way over.

Yet there had to be a way. You didn't build something like this and not provide a back door just in case something happened and you needed to get back in.

Something hit him. "Let me see the plans again."

She handed him the packet. He rifled through several pages before he found the one he wanted. He looked at the writing. It was clear. He just hadn't focused on it before. That was it.

He looked at Cole. "We need your brother."

"Randy? What does he have to do with this?" She scowled. "You're not telling me he's involved in this? First, you think my sister tried to blow you up and—"

He grabbed her arm. "No, I don't think your brother is involved in this, but I think he can still help. We need to find him."

CHAPTER

82

THEY CLEANED UP back at Cole's house and started looking. But finding Randy Cole proved harder than it probably should have in such a small town. Cole exhausted all of her possible places within an hour. She called her sister, but Jean had no idea where he was. They went into the Crib and then scoured the small downtown area, taking it block by block.

Nothing.

"Wait a minute," Puller finally said.

With Cole in his wake he fast-walked to Annie's Motel. Puller started kicking open doors. On the fifth Cole looked in the room and said, "Randy?"

Her brother was lying fully clothed on the bed.

Puller and Cole moved inside and Puller shut the door behind him. He flicked the light on.

"Randy? Wake up."

The man did not move.

Cole drew closer. "Is he okay? Randy?"

"He's fine. His chest is moving up and down."

Puller looked around, then said, "Wait a sec."

Puller grabbed an old bowl off a cracked wooden bureau and went into the bathroom, where Cole could hear water start to run. Puller came back out with a full bowl of water and threw it on Randy's face.

He shot up and then rolled off the bed. "What the shit!" screamed Randy as he hit the floor.

Puller grabbed him by the back of his shirt, lifted him off the floor, and threw him back on the bed.

As his eyes focused, Randy gazed at Puller and then saw his sister staring at him.

"Sam? What the hell is going on?"

Puller sat down next to him. "Bed better than bushes now?" he asked.

Randy focused on him. "Was that water?"

"How drunk are you?"

"Not much. Not anymore."

"We need your help."

" 'Bout what?"

"The Bunker," said Puller.

Randy rubbed his eyes. "What about it?"

"You got in there, right?"

"What?"

Puller gripped him by the arm. "Randy, we don't have a lot of time and I can't waste the time we do have trying to explain. We found a blueprint for the Bunker. On it, it said that there could be no mine blasting within two miles. The only reason they would have put that warning on there is if there had been a mineshaft already there or the potential of one. And they wanted to make sure that no one detonated explosives nearby. Your father was the best coal hunter around. And you worked with him. You probably know this county better than anyone. So is there a mineshaft that leads to the Bunker?"

Randy rubbed his head and yawned. "Yeah, there is. Daddy and I stumbled on it one day. It was already there, of course. We were looking for something else entirely. It was really two mineshafts. We followed the first in and found a second that ran in that direction. Followed that for a while. Daddy figured we were under the Bunker at that point. And he was right. That shaft was probably there from the 1940s, Daddy thought."

"But did you get into it?" asked Puller.

Randy looked sleepy again. "What? No, no, we didn't. At least not at that point. I think Daddy was curious about it. He'd always told us stories about the Bunker. We talked some about getting in there. But then he got killed."

Randy drew a long breath and looked like he might be sick.

"Just keep it together, Randy," said Puller. "This is really important."

"After Daddy died, I went back in there and dug a little more. I found a side shaft. Then I let it be for a long time. Went off on some drinking binges. Started sending threats to that asshole Roger. Then about eighteen months ago I went back in there. I don't know why. Maybe I was trying to finish something Daddy started. That's when I found a way in. Took some finagling and some muscle, but within a couple of months I was in. They might've put that dome over the building, and there was a concrete floor, but the floor had cracked in places, probably where the dirt shifted. Maybe from them dynamiting for coal way off somewhere."

"So you got in. And what did you find?" asked Puller.

"Big-ass place. Dark as a cave, of course. I looked around some. Saw some stuff. Workbenches, crap on the floor, some barrels."

"Barrels of what?"

"Don't know. Never looked that close."

Cole said, "Randy, that was dangerous as hell. That stuff in there could be toxic. It could be radioactive. Maybe that's why you've been feeling like crap all this time. Headaches and all."

"Guess it could be."

"What else did you see in there?" asked Puller.

"Nothing. I got the hell out. Place gave me the creeps."

"Okay, next big question. Did you tell anyone what you found?" asked Puller.

"Nah. What for?"

"No one?" said Puller. "You're sure?"

Randy thought for a minute.

"I might've told somebody, come to think of it."

"Dickie Strauss?"

Randy stared at him. "How the hell did you know that? We

played football together. Used to hang out a lot. I was into the Xanadu thing for a while till I lost my bike to repo. Yeah, I told him. So? What does that matter?"

"Dickie's dead, Randy," said Cole. "Somebody murdered him. And we think it has to do with the Bunker."

Randy sat up straighter, all alert now. "Somebody killed Dickie? Why?"

Puller said, "Because he told someone else about the Bunker. And somebody got inside there too. And whatever they found is the reason all these people have been killed."

Randy said, "So what the hell is in there?"

"That's what I'm going to find out," said Puller.

"So you have any ideas?" asked Cole. "I mean about what's in there?"

"Yeah, I do," replied Puller.

"What?" asked Cole. "Tell me."

Puller said nothing. He just looked at her, his heart beating way too fast.

CHAPTER

83

Even though it was still early in the morning in Kansas, Robert Puller didn't sound particularly sleepy. The younger Puller didn't think his brother slept much in USDB. He was a brilliant guy. And brilliant guys didn't tend to sleep much in the outside world full of demands on their time and intellect. Puller figured they didn't sleep much more when all they had to look at were three walls of concrete and a metal door that remained shut twenty-three out of every twenty-four hours of each day.

"How you doing, bro?" said Robert.

"I've been better and I've been worse."

"Balance is good in life."

"Ninety-two and ninety-four. What do they mean to you?"

"Even numbers."

"Another perspective."

"Give me some context."

His brother sounded engaged now, instead of just curious.

"Pure science. Your area of expertise."

Two ticks of the clock went by.

"Ninety-two is the atomic number for uranium. Ninety-four is the atomic number for plutonium."

"That's what I remembered too."

"Why?"

"Hypothetical."

"Okay."

"What sort of uranium and plutonium would you need to build a nuke?"

"What?"

"Just answer the question."

"What the hell are you involved in, John?"

His brother did not often call him John. To his older sibling Puller was either "bro" or sometimes "Junior"—although lately the latter term had not been used by him very much because it was a reminder of their father.

"Just give me your best answer."

"You need lots of things. Most you can obtain. Others you can build. If you have time and some expertise it's not that hard. What's hard to get is the nuclear fuel for the process. There're only two that exist."

"Uranium and plutonium."

"Right. And you need highly enriched uranium, U-235 or HEU, to make a nuclear bomb. To do that you need a manufacturing facility, big bucks, lots of scientists, and a number of years."

"And plutonium?"

"Should we be talking about this? They're monitoring the call."

"Nobody's listening, Bobby," said Puller. "I made arrangements for this to be private."

His brother didn't say anything for a long moment.

"Then I'd say whatever you're involved in is way beyond a hypothetical."

"And plutonium?"

"You get plutonium-239 mostly from radiating uranium in a nuclear breeder reactor. What you're really doing is scrubbing out plutonium-240, which is abundant in reactor-grade plutonium but which can cause a fizzle when using it as a nuclear weapon."

"But again, tough to get."

"Impossible to get for the man on the street. Who has a nuclear breeder reactor in their backyard?"

"But could you get it?"

"I suppose you could steal it or buy it on the black market."

"How about in the U.S.? How do they make it?"

"The only U.S.-owned gaseous diffusion plant is in Paducah,

Kentucky. But that's used to enrich uranium for fuel in nuclear reactors, totally different process."

"But could it be *highly* enriched by that process? To get it to be the fuel for a nuclear weapon?"

"Paducah is set up to enrich uranium for use in nuclear reactors, not build the fuel for bombs."

"But could a plant like Paducah highly enrich uranium?" Puller persisted.

"Theoretically, yes." He paused. "Where exactly is all this going?"

"How much U-235 would you need to build a bomb?"

"Depends on what type of bomb and what type of method you're using."

"Ballpark," said Puller.

"With a simple bomb design and a Nagasaki yield you'd need anywhere from fifteen to fifty kilograms of HEU or six to nine kilograms of plutonium. If your weapons program is super-sophisticated and your bomb design is perfect you could get the same boom with roughly nine kilos of HEU or as little as two kilos of plutonium."

"So Nagasaki?"

"Yield equivalent to over twenty-one thousand tons of dynamite plus the radiation fallout kicker. That's forty-two million pounds of TNT. Mass destruction."

"And a little more HEU or plutonium?"

"Your results go up exponentially. It's all in your bomb design. You can use the gun method, which is not good at all, although the first A-bomb dropped on Japan used that design. That's basically a long tube. Half your nuclear charge at one end backed by a conventional explosive and the other half of your nuke fuel at the other end. The conventional explosives are detonated, it pushes the fuel down the tube where it hits the other half of the fuel, and you have your chain reaction. It's crude, highly inefficient, and your explosive yield is severely limited. You'd need a tube of infinite length to sustain the chain reaction. And you can only use uranium, not plutonium, because of impurity factors. That's why the industry moved on to the implosion method."

Puller said, "Give me the two-cent tour on the implosion method."

"You can use either uranium or plutonium. You basically use conventional explosives, called explosive lenses, to squeeze the pit where your nuclear fuel is located into a supercritical mass. The shock wave compressing the uranium or plutonium must be perfectly spherical, or the pit material will escape through a hole and you'll end up with what's called a fizzle. You also need an initiator, tampers and pushers, and ideally a neutron reflector to push neutrons back in the pit. The trick is to keep the pit from blowing apart too quickly, before you reach optimal supercritical mass. The longer the fission material is allowed to react, the more atoms are split and the bigger the boom. You can triple your explosive yield without a gram more of nuclear fuel if your design is good."

"What are some of the elements you'd need?"

"Meaning what exactly?"

"Talk to me about gold foil and tungsten carbide."

There was silence for three beats. "Why those two specifically? Do you know that they're present in your case?"

"Yes."

"Jesus."

"Talk to me, Bobby. I'm running out of time here."

"Gold foil can be used in the initiator component. You use a small sphere with layers of beryllium and polonium separated by gold foil. That's placed in the center of the pit and is obviously a critical part of the design."

"And the tungsten carbide?"

"It's three times stiffer than steel and dense as hell and therefore works very well as the neutron reflector. That is to get the neutrons back into the pit to maximize the supercritical stage. Are you telling me that... Where the hell are you?"

"In the U.S."

"How did they get the fuel?"

"What if I told you there was a secret government facility operating in the 1960s that was closed a long time ago and a three-foot-thick dome of concrete was put over it, and the sucker was just left that way? All the workers at the plant were shipped in from outside and lived in a neighborhood right next to it. The workers were never allowed to talk about it with the local folks, and when the plant closed down they shipped all the workers off. Ring any bells? You were net-worked in tight with all this stuff when you were with the Air Force."

"Three feet of concrete?"

"In a dome shape."

"Out-of-the-way place?"

"As rural as they come. Entire population far less than one block in Brooklyn. Facility had its own fire department and I found a sheet of paper in there with the numbers 92 and 94 written on it. And I also found out that blasting for coal was not to take place within miles of the dome."

"They're blasting near there? Are you serious?"

"Yes."

"That's unbelievable. Even if you're blasting miles away, there are bedrock fissures that can be weakened. That could be cata-strophic."

"What about this facility?"

"I don't know. I wasn't even alive in the 1960s."

"But if you had to guess. Based on your experience?"

There was a long sigh. "If I were still in uniform I could never tell you this." He paused. "I could be convicted of treason. But since I already have been convicted of treason, what the hell." He paused again. "In the past I heard of early stage processing and enrich-ment plants that were built in rural America. This was post–World War II when the only thing that mattered was kicking the Soviet Union's ass. These facilities were built to enrich uranium and also work with plutonium for use in nuclear weapons. Most if not all of them were closed down."

"Why?"

"Their techniques were unstable or cost too much. It was an entirely new science. People were feeling their way, trial and error. Mostly error."

"Okay. They close down. They take all their stuff with them, right?" His brother didn't answer. "Bobby? Right?"

"If you took all your 'stuff' with you, would you build a three-foot-thick concrete dome to cover it up?"

"And nobody complained about it? Locals? Folks in government?"

"You have to consider the time, John. The 1960s. The big, bad Soviets. There wasn't a twenty-four-hour news cycle. People actually trusted their government, even though Vietnam and Watergate were about to change that. And since nothing has happened in the interim, I guess the locals just assumed everything was okay." He paused. "Is it right there out in the open?"

"Nothing is out in the open here. And the forest has mostly reclaimed it."

"What do you think is going on?"

"The same thing you're probably thinking is going on."

"You need to get this up the chain of command fast."

"I would, except for one thing."

"What?"

"I'm not sure I can trust my own guys."

"Is there anyone you can trust?"

"Yes. But I need you to do me another favor."

"Me help you? I'm sitting in prison, John."

"Doesn't matter. You can still help from there. CID is behind me on this. They can give you some flexibility even from there. But I really need you, Bobby."

His brother's answer was immediate. "Just tell me what you need."

CHAPTER

84

PULLER DROVE to Cole's house and waited. Then a call came in two hours later. Then after that came the call that Puller had been waiting for. When the military wanted to get something done, it could move with amazing speed. It didn't hurt that the Secretary of Defense had thrown his weight behind them.

Cole sat across from him in her living room anxiously watching. Puller answered the call.

On the other end was a retired colonel in his late eighties named David Larrimore, who lived in Sarasota, Florida. The man was Puller's last best hope because he actually had been an engineer and the military-side production supervisor at the Drake facility back in the 1960s. In fact, according to DoD records, he was the only person left alive who had worked there.

Larrimore's voice was weak but steady. He appeared to have all of his faculties as Puller began talking to him. Puller hoped the man's memory was faultless. He would need every scintilla of information he could get.

Larrimore said, "I guess you're never really retired when you wear the uniform."

"Guess not."

"You related to Fighting John by any chance?"

"He's my father."

"Never had the pleasure of serving under him, but he did the Army and his country proud, Agent Puller."

"Thanks, I'll let him know."

"Got a call from a two-star. I've been out of uniform nearly thirty years and it still scared the crap out of me. He said I was to tell you everything. Didn't say why."

"It's complicated. But we really need your help."

"Drake? That's what you want to know about?"

"Everything you can tell me."

"It's a sore spot, son, at least in my memory."

"Tell me why?"

Puller looked over at Cole, who was staring at him with such intensity that he thought she might stroke. He pressed the speaker button on his phone and set it down on the table between them.

Larrimore's voice floated into the room. "I was assigned to Drake because it was the latest facility the government had in its nuclear weapons development program. I had my degree in nuclear engineering and had been stationed at Los Alamos and also did some work on the Hiroshima and Nagasaki bombs. Now this was the 1960s, so we were way past the A-bombs that we dropped on the Japs in '45, but there was still a lot we didn't know about thermonuclear weapons. The Hiroshima A-bomb used the gun method. Compared to what they do today, that's kindergarten stuff. We were measuring A-bombs that topped out at a .7-megaton yield. The Soviets dropped an H-bomb in the Antarctic called the Tsar. It was a 50-megaton blast, the biggest ever. You could wipe out a country with something like that."

Puller watched as Cole collapsed back in her chair and put a hand to her chest.

"There's a classified file I saw that said the facility was used to make bomb components. There might have been some radioactivity left behind, but that was it."

Larrimore said, "That's not correct. But I'm not surprised there's an official record out there like that. Military likes to cover its tracks. And back then the rules of the game were a lot more liberal."

Puller said, "So you were building nuclear fuel for warheads. To be used in the implosion method?"

"You a nuke head?"

"What?"

"That's what we used to call each other back then. Nuke heads."

"No. But I have friends who are."

"We were working with a defense contractor. Name would mean nothing to you. It's long since been snapped up. And the company that bought it has been sold, and sold, and sold."

Puller could sense Larrimore taking a walk down memory lane and he didn't have time for that.

"You said it was a sore spot for you. Why?"

"Way we went into that area, built that monstrosity, didn't tell anybody what it was. We shipped in everybody from outside the area. We didn't encourage mingling with the locals. And when they did go into the little town there, we had them followed. Just the way it was back then. Everybody was paranoid."

"I don't think things have changed all that much," commented Puller. "Was that the only reason you were sore?"

"No, I was also upset how we left things."

"You mean the concrete dome? Three feet thick?"

"The hell you say!"

"You didn't know that?"

"No. The facility was supposed to be dismantled and shipped away, every molecule of it. It had to be that way because of what we had there."

"It's all still there. At least I guess it is. Under a huge dome of concrete. I don't how many acres, but it's a lot."

"What the hell were they thinking?"

"How come you didn't know about that?" asked Puller.

"I did my job as part of the phase-out. Then I was shipped out to another facility way down south. I was a supervisor on the military side, sure, but the private-sector guys really ran it and the generals signed off on whatever they wanted."

"Well, apparently what they wanted was to cover it with concrete rather than dismantle it. Why would that be the case?"

Larrimore said nothing.

"Mr. Larrimore."

"I'm here."

"I need you to answer that question."

"Agent Puller, I've been out of the service a long time. Shocked the hell out of me when I got the call today. I got a good pension that I earned and a few years left to bask in the sunshine down here. I don't want to lose that."

"You won't lose anything. But if you don't help me a lot of Americans might lose their lives."

When Larrimore next spoke his voice was stronger. "Might have to do with why we shut down in the first place. That's what I meant when I said I didn't like the way we left things."

"Which was why?"

"We screwed up."

"How? Did something go wrong in the diffusion process?"

"We weren't doing gaseous diffusion."

"I thought that's what we were talking about. Like they do in Paducah."

"You ever been to the Paducah plant, son?"

"No."

"It's huge. Has to be for gaseous diffusion. Far bigger than what we had in Drake."

Puller looked at Cole in confusion. "Then what were you doing in Drake?"

"Experimenting."

"With what?"

"Basically trying to make a super nuclear fuel that we could spike our warheads with. Our goal, I suppose, was to obliterate the Soviet Union before they obliterated us."

85

S UPER NUCLEAR FUEL?

Puller stared at Cole. This time she wouldn't meet his eye. Instead she looked distractedly at the floor.

Puller said, "Mr. Larrimore, I found a piece of paper at a firehouse near the Drake facility."

"I know the firehouse well. We had a couple of incidents where those fellers were needed."

"The paper had the numbers 92 and 94 written on it."

"Atomic numbers for uranium and plutonium."

"Right. But the gaseous diffusion method is only used to enrich uranium," said Puller. "You can't use gaseous diffusion on plutonium. You get that from breeder reactors."

"That's right. Capturing a neutron. Getting to P-239."

"But if that document had both atomic numbers that means—"

"We used both uranium *and* plutonium at Drake."

"Why?"

"Like I said, to try and build a super nuclear fuel for weapons. We had no idea if it would work or not. The goal was to use uranium and plutonium in a new bomb design. We were juggling combinations and concentrations of each to see what configuration would yield the biggest boom. In layman's terms, sort of a hybrid between the gun and the implosion method, if you understand me."

"I was told that the gun method was very inefficient and plutonium couldn't be used in that design."

"Those were the obstacles we were trying to overcome. We were trying to beat the communists at their own game. And the name of that game was explosive yield."

"But you said you screwed up?"

"Well, let's just say the science and the design logic were flawed. Bottom line was it didn't work. That was why the facility closed."

"But if they closed the plant surely they would have taken the nuclear material with them?"

"The fact that they covered it with three feet of cement tells me they didn't."

"But why the hell would they leave something that deadly behind?"

Larrimore didn't answer for a few seconds. "This would be a guess on my part."

"I'll take it."

"They were probably afraid it would blow up in their faces and radiate a good part of the country. I can't say I was totally surprised when you said they'd cemented over it. Back then they covered up a lot of stuff, quite frankly. Let it stay where it was. Probably thought it was safer than trying to transport it. You're probably way too young to remember this, but around that time a few incidents happened that scared the crap out of the country. A B-52 that was carrying a hydrogen bomb on one of its wings crashed somewhere in Kansas. The bomb didn't detonate during the crash, of course, because atomic weapons don't work that way. And then we had the plutonium train."

"Plutonium train?"

"Yeah, the military wanted to move some of its plutonium stockpile from point A to point B. Right across the country. Train moved through major population centers. Nothing happened, but the news folks got wind of both the plane and the train. It was not a good time for the military. There were hearings on Capitol Hill and some guys lost their stars. Can you imagine if that happened today? With our twenty-four-hour news cycle? Anyway, that was fresh in everyone's minds back then, especially the military brass. So I guess they said, 'Screw it. It stays right where it is.'"

"And the place they left it was a rural county with not many people."

"It wasn't my call. If it had been I would've done it differently."

"You'd think someone would have revisited the issue."

"Not necessarily. You go out there now and start messing around, the news folks will get wind of it. Then the government has to start explaining. And maybe they were afraid that if they did open the sucker up they wouldn't like what they found."

"It's been five decades," Puller said. "Do you think that stuff, if it is there, is still dangerous?"

"Plutonium-239 has a half-life of twenty-four thousand years. So I'd say you aren't out of the woods yet."

Puller drew a long breath and looked at Cole. "How much of it is in there?"

"I can't tell you for sure. But let me put it this way. If they kept the usual supply on hand that we maintained, and it got out somehow, it could make what we did to the Japs look puny by comparison. I tell you what, whoever made the call to leave it there should go to prison. But they're probably all dead by now."

"Lucky them," commented Puller.

Larrimore said, "So what are you folks going to do?"

"We need to get inside the dome. Any ideas?"

Cole tapped him on the arm and mouthed, "Mineshaft."

He shook his head and looked back at the phone. "Any ideas?" he said again.

"Three feet of concrete, son. You got a jackhammer?"

"We have to do it surreptitiously."

Puller could hear Larrimore take several long breaths.

"You think somebody's going to...?" His voice trailed off.

"We can't afford not to think that, can we? You probably knew that place as well as anyone. Anything you can think of would be more than what I've got right now."

"Can you dig along the perimeter?"

"Iron footings that go out more feet than I can deal with."

Several more long breaths. Puller looked at Cole and she stared back at him. The room wasn't hot, but he saw several beads of sweat on her forehead. One slid down to her cheek. She made no move to wipe it away. Puller could feel the perspiration sheen on his face.

Larrimore said, "Ventilation shafts."

Puller sat up straighter. "Okay."

"Inside of the facility was not a place where you could let dust and other things collect, and we also had stuff in the air that we had to get out. We had about as powerful a ventilation and filtering system as you could get back then. We had ventilation shafts on the east and west sides. The filtering system was massive. It wasn't housed in the facility for a number of reasons. The air would be directed there, filtered, and recirculated inside the facility. Place didn't have any windows for obvious reasons. All self-contained. It could get hot in there, especially about this time of year."

"I'll need to know exactly where those shafts are. And where was the filtering system housed?"

"I can tell you roughly where the shafts were located. It's been over forty years since I've been there, son. Memory's not perfect. But I know exactly where the filtering system was located. And both the shafts bleed directly into it. And those shafts are big. Large enough for a tall man to stand up in."

"Where is the filtering system?" Puller said eagerly.

"Right underneath the firehouse."

Puller and Cole exchanged glances.

Larrimore said, "Figured that was the best place to put it. Always a fire hazard with filtering systems. Anything goes wrong, folks are right there to take care of it. The fire station was manned around the clock. The filtering system was alarmed so they'd know if there was a problem."

"How do you get to the filtering system from the fire station?"

"You been there?"

"Yes."

"You seen the wooden lockers? I'm talking the ones on the right side, main level."

"Yes."

"There's a catch behind a panel on the inside of the locker farthest to the left. You can't tell it's there if you don't know where to look. There's a pressure plate in the inside of that locker. It's located on the left side, top corner. You push right in that corner and the panel will swing out on hinges. Behind the panel is a lever. You pull that lever and the whole row of lockers slides out to the right. Stairway going down is revealed. Nifty piece of engineering. Those stairs take you to the filtering system. And from there you can get to the shafts."

He said, "I appreciate this, Mr. Larrimore."

"Agent Puller. If you're really going in that place, keep a few things in mind. Wear a hazmat suit with the most powerful filter you can find. Bring a flashlight because you'll have no light. The plutonium and uranium cakes are in lead-lined barrels. The plutonium cakes are marked in red with the skull-and-crossbones insignia. The uranium cakes are blue with the same skull and crossbones. We were working in a brand-new field and used our own marking system."

"So they're *cakes*?"

"Right. The 'fuel' term is sort of misleading. The uranium and plutonium look like round cakes. They're both radioactive at the highly enriched level. But plutonium is super-radioactive. The plant workers handled the stuff using robotic arms behind protective shields. Even your hazmat suit probably won't protect you completely against direct exposure. And one more thing, Agent Puller."

"Yeah?"

"I wish you luck, son. You're sure as hell going to need it."

86

PULLER STOOD in front of the cracked mirror in his bathroom at Annie's Motel. He had on his combat uniform and his face was streaked black and green. Forward and rear M11s were in their holsters, rounds in chambers. The MP5 was fully loaded and the discharge set on two-round bursts. He had four extra clips in the cargo slots in his pants. He had to bend forward some to get his full image into the silver-backed glass.

In the Middle East, mirrors had been hard to come by out in the field. Puller had used a jerry-rigged contraption he'd made from a scrap of glass with some goop coated on the rear side to capture the light and thus his reflection. Some of his men thought him more than a little weird for looking at himself in a mirror before going out to fight. Puller didn't care what they thought. He did this for one reason and one reason only.

If he was going to die, he wanted his last image to be of a man in a uniform going off to fight for something worth fighting for. In Iraq and Afghanistan the motivation had been easy. It had mostly come from the guy next to him. Fighting to keep that guy alive. It had also come from representing the pack he was part of, the United States Army in general, with the Ranger as a specialty. In third place had come his country. A civilian would have thought that unusual, that the priorities had somehow gotten reversed. But Puller knew better. His priorities were right in line with most who wore the uniform and were routinely catapulted into harm's way.

His ritual completed, he turned out the light, locked the door of his room for perhaps the final time, and headed to his car. He checked his gear and made sure every item he was going to need was in there. That included a few things that Cole had gotten for him. As he drove off, he thought about when he'd arrived in Drake. It had been days, but those days felt like months. It had been oppressively hot, just as it was now. He could feel the heat and sweat collect inside his combat fiber.

He looked at the motel office, thought of the little room where the tiny woman had sat for God only knew how many years. From poodle skirts, big hair, and probably dreams beyond Drake, West Virginia, to death by worn-out body six decades later. He had met the woman all of two times, didn't even know her last name. But for some reason he didn't think he would ever forget Louisa, if only because he had failed to save her. He hoped he had better luck saving the rest of the people who lived in Drake.

He had been on the phone for several hours and had spoken with several different people up the chain of command. What he had requested was unusual. And there was always resistance from the military when you requested the unusual. But Puller had insisted and the military got its back up even more.

And then Puller had demanded. And added to that demand was the perfectly logical fact that if people died because the military had refused to take proper steps, careers would be lost. And not just his.

That had gotten the right people's attention and Puller's plan was now in place.

He drove right at the speed limit, his gaze dead center on the road. Many switchbacks later he stopped at the rendezvous spot and waited for Cole's headlights to cut the dark. His watch clicked to twenty minutes past eleven and he wondered if she'd had second thoughts, when her pale blue pickup slid in next to his. She got out, leaned into her truck bed, hauled out a large coil of phone cable on a plastic reel, and tapped on Puller's trunk. He popped it and she put the cable inside. She got into the passenger seat of the Malibu.

She had on her leather jacket, a black T-shirt, dark jeans, and boots. He saw the Cobra in its holster. He looked down and saw the bulge of her backup weapon in an ankle holster.

"Caliber?" he asked.

"Thirty-eight shortnose chambering Silvertips." She opened her jacket slightly and he saw the gutting knife inside a leather carrier. "And this for true emergencies."

He nodded approvingly.

She glanced over at him. "You look ready to fight."

"I *am* ready to fight."

"You really think someone will be there?"

"I don't play the odds. I prepare for all contingencies."

"I can't believe my brother told Dickie Strauss about that mineshaft and that's what started this whole thing."

"And that's the reason we have to get into the Bunker a different way."

"Otherwise we might get ambushed."

"Right."

They reached the spot, a quarter of a mile away from the east side of the Bunker.

Puller slipped his rucksack over his shoulder. It was loaded down with a bunch of gear. He looped the phone cable reel over the other shoulder and then lifted out the body armor.

"Put this on. You'll have to crank down the straps to make it fit you. It'll still be big on you, but it's a lot better than naked flesh and bone getting hit by whatever they might be chambering."

"Is it heavy?"

"Not nearly as heavy as me hauling your dead body back."

"Thanks, I get the point. What about you?"

"Already armored up."

He helped her on with it, and after inspecting her from all angles and making a few minor adjustments, they hit the woods.

Cole followed Puller, who moved confidently through the thick trees, finding paths and trails that seemed invisible to Cole until he advanced down them.

She whispered, "I've lived here my whole life and I'd be lost in here in ten seconds."

Puller skirted the hide of the Bunker, walked north till he reached the end of the concrete, and then headed west again. He checked his luminous watch. He was two minutes ahead of schedule. Sometimes on the battlefield being early was just as bad as being late. He slowed his pace just a bit.

When they finally reached the edge of the woods, Puller squatted on his haunches and Cole did the same, coming to a stop on his right.

Dead ahead was the firehouse.

Puller pointed to the right of the structure. "Phone line comes in to that spot. There's a jack in the office on the second floor."

Cole had a thought. "The passageway from the firehouse to the Bunker wasn't on those plans."

"That's right," he said. "It wasn't."

"But why not?"

"For a very good reason. Back door in they didn't want to publicize." He rose. "You ready? Because it's time to do this."

Cole rose. Her legs wobbled a bit, but then regained their steadiness. She swallowed a lump the size of a fist and said, "Let's roll."

CHAPTER

87

THE FIRST PART of the mission went exceptionally smoothly. They entered the firehouse through a back door. Puller noiselessly attacked the lock and the wood swung back shortly thereafter.

"They teach you breaking and entering in the Army?" Cole said in a low voice.

"It's called urban warfare," he replied.

They made their way up the steps to the second floor after confirming that the first floor held nothing that was breathing. Puller spent ten minutes rigging the phone cable into the wall jack. He pulled from his knapsack what looked like an old-fashioned SAT phone the size of a large brick.

"Where did you get that?" asked Cole.

"Army. They never throw anything away."

He attached the cable to ports on the phone. He hit a button on the phone and held it up to his ear.

"We have a dial tone," he said.

"Is your call going to be long-distance?" she said, managing a weak smile.

"The longest," he replied.

They walked back down the stairs and reached the set of lockers that David Larrimore had told him about. These lockers were all secured and looked like they hadn't been touched since the place had closed down.

He shook off his knapsack and said, "Time to dress for the show." He pulled out two hazmat suits and accompanying filtration gear.

"The guy said plutonium has a half-life of twenty-four thousand years," said Cole.

"That's right."

He handed her the suit. She stared down at it. "He also said these suits probably wouldn't protect us against direct exposure to that crap."

"These suits are a lot better than anything he had back in the 1960s. But you can stay here if you want and cover my rear flank. It might actually be a better plan than you going in there with me."

"That's bullshit and you know it." She started to put on the suit.

When they were done she gazed up at him. "We look like astronauts ready to do a moonwalk."

"Maybe not so far from the truth."

Puller broke open the last locker, found the pressure point for the panel, pushed it, and the little door popped open. He felt for the catch. He hoped that after all these decades the mechanism would still work.

He breathed a sigh of relief as he heard a pop and then a slight rush of air and the wall of lockers swung away from the wall. It did so with a screech. The thing probably hadn't been opened since the 1960s. This made him smile. Whoever they were up against had not used this way to get into the Bunker. They'd gone through the shaft.

Cole hit the opening with her light. Revealed was a set of stairs.

"You looked disappointed," said Puller through his mask.

She started and stared up at him.

"Hoping we might not be able to get in?"

"Maybe," she admitted.

"Facing fear is better than running from it," he said.

"What if it's fear you can't beat?"

"Then it might be better to be dead," he answered.

He pulled out two pairs of night-vision goggles. "The place will be pitch black inside presumably, so this is the only way we'll be able to see. Once we confirm we're the only ones in there, we can use our flashlights. I'll show you how to use the goggles. They take some getting used to. And if something happens to me, you'll need them to get out as quickly as possible."

"If something happens to you, it'll probably happen to me too."

He shook his head. "Not necessarily. We have to buck up the chances that at least one of us will survive." He explained how the device worked and then slid it over her head and flipped the eye-pieces down over Cole's clear mask shield. He powered it up and took her through what she was looking at.

"Okay, you're officially night-vision goggle certified."

He powered up his own goggles and slid them down in front of his eyes. He handed her the roll of cable. "Spool this out as we go."

"I got the longest length I could. Think it'll be enough?"

"We have to go with the equipment we have. If it's not long enough, we'll figure something else out."

She nodded.

He led the way down the stairs, his field of vision reduced some-what because of the green that made him feel like he was in a dirty aquarium. But certain details were enhanced beyond what his naked eye could ever pick up.

Puller liked details. They were often the difference between walking out of a situation and being carried out of it.

They reached the bottom of the steps. They were now in a long hall formed from concrete painted yellow. They had traveled half of it when he began to see the filtration equipment. He tapped Cole on the shoulder and pointed ahead. "Filtering station."

She tapped him on the back to indicate she'd seen it too.

The machinery they encountered was large, elaborate, and was probably state of the art for its time. Puller faced next what he had expected to, even though the filter station had not been on the facil-ity plans. A large fan. Twice as tall as he was. This would be a tricky part. At least they didn't have to worry about the thing starting up. He contoured his body to get past it and then helped Cole do the same. They were careful with the phone cable so that it was not against the blades of the fan. The last thing they needed was a cut line and no communication. No cell signal could work from under three feet of concrete. Puller worked the line down to the bottom of the floor so that the only thing it was touching was the base of the fan, which was rounded smooth metal.

They continued on another hundred feet or so. In his head Puller calculated distances and concluded that they were close. He shifted his knapsack to a better position and lifted his forward M11 from its holster. The MP5 rested against his chest and he could deploy it on target in seconds. He looked back and saw that Cole had her Cobra out too.

The inside of the facility was large enough not to be classified as close quarters, but an MP5 was a devastating weapon in virtually all encounters that did not involve long-distance killing. But if there was a sniper in here with the same green glasses Puller had, he and Cole were probably dead.

They made their way through two more barriers, one of which Puller had to dismantle, and then they stepped out into a space that was enormous by most definitions. It was also totally dark. Without the goggles they would be operating blind. They had about three hundred feet of phone cable left. He hoped it was enough. He immediately stepped to the right and took cover behind a long metal workbench. Cole scooted along behind him. The place smelled of mildew and rot. What the concrete bunker above could not protect against was moisture from below.

Puller looked around at the walls of the building. They were high, windowless and built of brick. The ceiling was about thirty feet above him. It was solid, with fluorescent lights hanging from support poles. There were additional floors above this one. The plans had shown that. Probably admin and other support offices. But they appeared to be in the main work area of the facility.

And overlying the entire building was the dome of concrete. Puller felt like he was inside a building that was inside an egg.

"We have to grid-search this place," he said through his mask.

"What exactly are we looking for?"

"Things breathing, fifty-gallon lead-lined barrels, and something that looks like it shouldn't be here."

"And what is that exactly?" asked Cole impatiently.

"Something that looks *new*," he answered. "You go left and I go right. We'll work our way to the center." He handed her a walkie-talkie. "These will work in here. They're not bouncing off a satellite somewhere. But they're not secure either, so someone could be listening."

Thirty minutes later Puller had found them.

He counted the barrels. There were five of them. He couldn't tell if they were lead-lined but he hoped they were. As he drew closer he could make out the muck and mildew clinging to the sides of the metal. He hoped there were no holes in them. If so, he was probably already dead. He drew even closer and used a gloved hand to rub some of the muck off. He was looking at a faded blue label with a skull and crossbones.

Blue meant uranium.

The next barrel in line was the same. He pushed against each with his hand. They were full, or at least seemed to be. The weight could be coming in part from the lead lining. Yet the tops appeared sealed and had enough crust around them that Puller didn't think they had been opened in decades. Two other barrels had red labels and the skull warning.

Plutonium cakes. He pushed. They were full too.

The last barrel in the line had the same red label. Plutonium. But that wasn't what he was focusing on.

The top was off the barrel. He eased a few steps closer. Then, deciding to just go for it, he got so close he was able to look down into it. Lead-lined, yes. That was good. There was no penetration into the lead from the outside elements.

That was excellent.

The barrel was also empty. The plutonium was on the loose.

That was catastrophic.

And then he noted something else. On the concrete floor were six identical rings lined up next to the barrels. Puller knew exactly what that meant. There had been six other barrels here. Uranium and/or plutonium. And now they were gone.

He got on his walkie-talkie.

"I found the stuff. And we got one empty barrel. That used to hold plutonium. And a half dozen missing ones."

The walkie-talkie crackled and Cole said shakily, "I found something too."

"Cole, you okay?"

"I...Just get over here. I'm on the east side, about three hundred feet from where we came in."

"What is it? What did you find?"

"Roger. I found Roger Trent."

CHAPTER

88

TOGETHER THEY GAZED DOWN at the prone man. Puller didn't think he was dead, because he was trussed up. One did not tie up the dead. Just to be sure Puller knelt next to him, stripped off his glove, and felt for a pulse. He gazed up at Cole. "Slow but steady. He's been drugged."

Cole said, "And I found these."

Puller looked where she was pointing. This was the last thing he would have expected to find in here.

They were banker boxes. He opened one. They were full of financial records. Puller sifted through a few files. There was also a baggie filled with labeled flash drives.

"What are they?" asked Cole.

"Looks like financial records. Like I told you, your sister said Roger was having problems. Maybe these records tell a story someone never wants anyone to discover. Along with Roger."

"But who would do that?"

"I have my suspicions."

"Who? I mean—" She broke off because Puller was looking over her shoulder.

He said, "Did you check your entire side over there?"

"No. I was doing my sweep when I found Roger lying on the floor. Why?"

He pointed. "That's why."

Cole turned around and saw what had captured his attention. There was a light coming from the opposite side of the building. A soft green light. It had just come on. In the pitch dark he would've seen it before.

She hustled after him, her Cobra out.

Puller stopped and so did she.

She looked where he was looking.

The box was about four feet long and the same width and looked to be built of stainless steel. It was a nice job, no obvious seams. The metal looked like it had been cast in one piece; a nifty piece of craftsmanship. Puller knelt down next to it, put his gloved hand on the box. Then he took it away.

He looked up at Cole. "Warm."

"What's powering this thing?" she asked. "There's no electrical source in here."

"There's lot of energy in here, Cole. There's probably enough in those barrels over there to power New York City for a thousand years once you ran it through a nuclear reactor."

She stared down at the box. "Is...is this it? Is this a bomb? It doesn't look like a bomb."

"Since when have you seen a nuclear bomb up close and personal?"

"I've seen them on the wings of planes. I watched a History Channel program of the ones they dropped on Japan. They didn't look like a box."

"Well, looks can be deceiving."

"Did it just turn on? I didn't see that light before."

"Neither did I, which means that this sucker just woke up."

She drew a sharp breath. "Does it have a timer? Is it ticking down?"

"You've been watching too many movies." Puller was looking over every inch of the box, trying to find a seam, an indication of a hinge, a break in the metal. He ran his fingers over the top, feeling for anything his electronic-aided eyes had missed.

"So it doesn't have a timer?"

Puller snapped, "Cole, I don't know, okay? I've never been around a nuclear weapon before."

"But you're in the Army."

"Not that part. And the Navy and Air Force control most of the nukes. The infantry are just the working-class guys shooting and getting shot at in all types of weather just like they did two hundred years ago. Biggest weapon I was around was a fifty cal. You can kill hundreds of people with a fifty. This thing can kill tens of thousands, maybe more."

"Puller, if you open that thing won't whatever is in there kill us?"

"It might. But if I don't open it, whatever is in there will probably kill us anyway. Plus a whole bunch of other people."

His fingers stopped probing and held on one spot, six inches from the right side of the stainless steel.

"Did you find something?" she asked.

In answer he picked up his dumbbell-sized phone and punched in a number. "It's time to bring in the heavyweights."

"What if the call won't go through?"

"Then we are screwed, that's what."

She started to say something but he held up a finger. "The phone works." He spoke into it.

"Hey, Bobby. Got time to give your little brother some tips on defusing a nuke?"

CHAPTER

89

ROBERT PULLER had been on standby at USDB for the last two hours on orders directly from the Secretary of Defense. Though the military had many experts in nuclear armaments, Puller had insisted that the only one he wanted or trusted was his older brother. That the man was serving a life sentence for treason made the choice problematic. But when Puller had held his ground against even the four stars, the Defense Secretary had intervened and approved his plan. And even the military men had to concede there were few people in the world who knew more about the science of nukes than Robert Puller.

Robert was alert and also anxious. His brother was sitting next to a nuclear bomb, after all. On an earlier phone call Puller had filled him in on everything that David Larrimore had told him.

"Describe the box to me," said Robert.

"Four feet square. Stainless steel. Bolted to the floor."

"Speak up. Can't hear you clearly."

"Sorry, I'm talking through a mask." He repeated the information in a louder voice.

"Okay, implosion, not a gun device."

"Right."

"Talk to me about the barrels. The empty one was plutonium?"

"Right. At least that's what it said."

"This guy Larrimore have any idea how much plutonium was contained in each barrel?"

"If he did he didn't say. I don't think he ever believed they'd leave the shit behind. And I have to agree with him on that point."

"I'm going to assume that this design is not super-sophisticated, so we're talking at least six kilos and possibly more."

"That barrel could hold a lot more than six kilos even with the lead liners."

"I understand, but the size box you're talking about clearly shows they didn't put the equivalent of a fifty-gallon drum worth of plutonium in there. That would be overkill."

"Maybe they're nuts, you ever think about that?"

"Maybe they are, but I'm only concerned with the science of it."

"Can I take the top off or will I get blasted by radiation from the plutonium?"

"How heavy is the top?"

Puller pulled on it and then tapped it. "Not that heavy."

"So probably no lead lining or other shielding. The plutonium should be completely surrounded by the explosives and a tamper/pusher and maybe another layer or two that will shield you. And we know there's a tungsten carbide neutron reflector in there. That thing is super-dense. You should be okay."

"Should?"

"Best I can do, bro."

Puller drew a long breath and motioned for Cole to step back. She did. He tugged. The lid came up. He was not hit with a blinding blue light.

"John?"

"I'm good. I'm not glowing. I take that as a positive sign."

"Do you see a timer?"

Puller glanced up at Cole, who shrugged and managed a smile behind her mask.

Puller said, "Do they really use timers on this stuff?"

"It's not for melodramatic effect like in the movies. It has a very real purpose. The conventional explosions have to go off exactly at the same time or a hole in the shock wave will be created and the pit will escape through that. Then you get that fizzle, like we talked about before, bro."

Puller poked around the box. He uncovered a group of wires and saw it.

"Okay. Got it. That must be the light we saw come on earlier. This sucker must have an internal power source because there's no juice in here."

"What's the timer at?"

"Sixty-two minutes and counting."

"Okay," said Robert. "Wires?"

Cole was holding a strong light over the box, illuminating it for Puller. His latest-generation goggles allowed him to see clearly even in lighted conditions.

"A bunch," said Puller. "They were covering the timer. Should I try and cut some of them? Maybe it'll stop the countdown."

"No. Chances are excellent that they're booby-trapped. If you're looking at twenty wires, only three of them mean anything. That's a common ruse in conventional bombmaking, and the same rule, we can assume, holds true for pseudo-nukers. You cut any of the fakes it'll probably accelerate the timer to zero and you can kiss your ass goodbye."

"Okay, will not cut wires," said Puller firmly. It was oppressively hot in here to begin with and the hazmat suit made it hotter still. His mask kept fogging up and he would use his forehead to clear it, which didn't work so well, since that was the primary source of the sweat. He finally just ripped the mask off, wiped his eyes with his hands, and put his goggles back on.

"The initiator will be in the dead center of the sphere," said Robert. "That floods the pit with neutrons during detonation. The gold foil that was found at the crime scene was probably used as a layer between the beryllium and polonium as we postulated before. The plutonium will be shaped like a ball around that. The tamper/pusher will be around the plutonium. The pusher increases the shock wave hitting the pit. And the tamper helps hold the pit from blowing apart too quickly to maximize your yield."

"Okay, Bobby, I don't need a lecture on every little thing."

"I guess I'm just trying to make sure I still know what I'm talking about," said his brother slowly.

"Don't second-guess yourself. You know this stuff. You're a genius. Always have been."

"Okay, the explosive lenses form the outside layer. You should be able to see the lenses. Like faces on a soccer ball. They're carefully shaped explosive charges. Almost like a work of geometric art. Do you see them?"

"I see them."

"How many?"

"A lot."

"How are they arranged?"

"Pretty seamlessly."

"No gaps?"

"None that I can see."

Puller heard his brother let out a breath. "Somebody knew what they were doing."

"What the hell does that mean for me?"

"If they manage to compress the chain reaction long enough, the bomb yield will rise exponentially, like we discussed. And from your description it looks like they were pretty sophisticated in their design."

Puller checked the timer. It was at fifty-nine minutes, twenty-seven seconds.

"How do I turn this thing off, Bobby?"

"John, you can't actually turn it off."

"Then what the hell am I doing here?" Puller barked so loudly that Cole jumped and almost dropped her light.

"There's really only one way to do it," Robert said in a calm tone. "We have to screw up the detonation. The lenses are seamless now, but if we throw off the timing of the detonation we can cause a fizzle."

"So how do I do that?"

"We throw off the detonation sequence by adding one of our own."

Puller looked up at Cole in dismay. "So you're telling me that in order to beat this thing we have to detonate it? Is that what the hell you're telling me?"

"Pretty much, yeah," said Robert.

"Shit," muttered Puller. "That's really the only way?"

"If there was another, I'd tell you."

"How about if I just start whacking stuff?"

"Odds are real good you're dead and a mushroom cloud probably goes up over West Virginia."

"I should have let the cavalry come in here, chopper this thing out, and drop it in the ocean."

"They couldn't have done that in an hour. And hindsight is twenty-twenty."

"Maybe they could have gotten in here before it engaged. Stopped the timer from commencing or dropped it in some deep hole."

"Again, hindsight."

"If this thing goes off it's my fault, Bobby."

"Two points, John. If that thing goes off, you won't be around to care. Second point, the person or persons who built that thing are the responsible parties, not you! Now how much time left?"

"Fifty-seven and a half till doomsday."

Puller looked up at Cole and pointed to the way they'd come in. He mouthed two words: *Go. Now.*

She shook her head and gave him a stubborn expression when he pointed to the way out again. When he did it a third time she flipped him off.

"John, you there? What's going on?" asked his brother.

"Nothing. Just a tactical issue that has been resolved. Now when you say fizzle, what exactly are we talking about?"

"Maybe half a kiloton yield, but that's just an educated guess on my part. The concrete dome should help contain most of the blast."

"Half a kiloton?" said Puller. "That's equal to five hundred tons of TNT. You call that a fizzle?"

"Hiroshima got hit with a thirteen-kiloton yield and they only used sixty kilograms of uranium and of that only six hundred milligrams actually reacted; that's about the weight of a dime. I have no idea how much plutonium they've got in this sucker, but we have to plan for the worst-case scenario. There's no way it's as small a yield as with Hiroshima. We're talking gun versus implosion method, uranium versus plutonium. To be safe let's assume it's millions of tons of TNT equivalent. That'll send that concrete dome into orbit and spread radiation over six states or more. And you can pretty much kiss West Virginia goodbye."

Fresh sweat sprouted on Puller's face. "Okay, half a kiloton doesn't sound so bad now. So tell me how to make a fizzle."

"We have to make a premature detonation happen."

"Yeah, *that* I get. How?"

"Did you bring the stuff I told you to?"

Cole looked at Puller as she dug in his knapsack and pulled out one stick of dynamite, wire, blasting cap, and a timer. She had gotten these for him. She handed them to him while he cradled the phone against his shoulder.

"I thought I was going to use this to blow a hole in something. But if you'd told me then that I'd have to use this to detonate the nuke I might not be here."

"Yes you would," said Robert. "I know my brother." This was said in a joking manner, but Puller knew the man wasn't smiling. He was in fact probably trying hard to keep his little brother calm. Trying, if it was possible, to take his mind off the fact that he might be sitting on the equivalent of millions of tons of TNT with a radiation kicker.

"Where do I put it?"

"If you're looking at the bomb head-on, place the stick five degrees to the left."

"Why five degrees?"

"I like the number five, John, always have."

Puller placed the stick in that spot and confirmed that with his brother.

Robert said, "Good. Now you obviously have to set the timer for the stick to go off before the bomb timer. With a nuclear weapon even a millisecond difference in the timing of the explosions is sufficient. Stick detonates, punches a hole in the lenses, causing a series of staggered explosions. The sequential detonations will destroy the sphere along with the compression phase. The pit will squeeze through the created holes and critical and supercritical stages will never be reached. With no pit the plutonium can't be compressed and the entire thing collapses."

"And that's real good?" asked Puller.

"Let me give you the three scenarios as I see them. If we're real lucky we go low-end. That means you just have a dirty bomb with nothing nuclear in the detonation. The most we have is a small boom with some radiation exposure, which three feet of concrete should be able to contain. That would be as good as it gets. The second or medium outcome is the half-kiloton fizzle. It obviously helps that you're in the middle of nowhere covered by three feet of concrete. Collateral damage should be manageable."

"This county is full of a lot of people, actually," said Puller, as Cole stared at him from behind the light she held. "And they're basically having a real shitty life right now. So the last thing they need is a mushroom cloud popping into their misery."

"I'm sorry, John, I didn't know."

"No reason you should." Puller drew a long breath. "And the third scenario?"

"My plan works, but it doesn't work that well, and we still go nuclear."

"And that means?"

Robert didn't say anything for a few moments. "I've never lied to you, John, and I won't start tonight. That means that a large chunk of where you are will be completely vaporized. Like a hundred hurricanes hitting all at once. There won't be anything left for miles. That's just how it works."

"Okay." Puller thought of something. "Give me a few minutes," he said.

"What?" asked his brother.

"This thing is going to go boom under any scenario, right?"

"Yes."

"Then give me a few minutes."

He set the phone down, jumped up, and ran off. Cole rushed after him.

"Puller, what are you doing?"

He reached the barrels, sized them up, eyed where he would be taking them, and decided on the best way.

"Mineshaft is over there. I'm going to roll these barrels into the shaft as far as I can. When the boom hits, if we're lucky, the concussive force will send these suckers deep into the rock and then bury them under tons of crap. It's our only option at this point."

"Better than into the West Virginia air," said Cole.

His muscles straining, Puller tipped the first barrel onto its side and quickly rolled it into the mineshaft. There was a slight downward slope and the barrel rolled on its own down into the darkness. Puller ran back to the other barrels and found that Cole was trying to topple one over too, but her strength was not enough.

"Just hold the light on it," he said. "I'll supply the muscle."

A few minutes later all of the barrels were in the mineshaft. Puller and Cole ran back to the nuke and he picked up the phone.

"I'm back."

"What the hell were you doing?" demanded his brother.

"Putting barrels of nuclear shit in a safer place."

"Oh, right. Good idea. Okay, you ready?"

Puller said, "Do you feel lucky?"

His brother replied, "More to the point, do *you* feel lucky?"

Puller licked his lips and glanced at Cole. She stood there as though marbleized.

He set the timer on the dynamite stick to thirty minutes. That would give them plenty of time to get out of the blast area.

They heard a groan.

Cole said, "Roger is waking up."

Her brother-in-law was indeed stirring.

Puller said, "Go untie him and make him understand that we need to get out—"

"Puller," Cole shrieked. "Look."

Robert apparently heard this. He said, "What's going on?'

Puller didn't answer. He was too busy staring at the nuke bomb timer.

It had just gone from forty-seven minutes and eight seconds to five minutes flat.

Another booby-trap that they had engaged, perhaps by removing the cover.

Puller reset his detonator for the only time he could.

Less than five minutes.

He closed the lid on the bomb and he and Cole raced over to Roger Trent. Puller used his KA-BAR knife to cut the bindings and they got him to his feet and then ran like hell to the filtration shaft.

"John!" screamed Robert Puller's voice from the phone.

His brother didn't answer. He'd dropped the phone next to the nuke.

Now all that mattered was getting out of the Bunker.

But even as he ran next to Cole, both of them propping up Trent beside them, Puller knew one thing for certain.

We're dead.

90

As they raced along a groggy Trent said, "What's going on? Who are you?"

"Just shut up and save your breath for running, Roger," snapped Cole.

They made it through the filtration system far faster than when they had to come the opposite way, even with Trent in tow. They raced up the steps, through the firehouse, and out onto the concrete drive in front. Puller and Cole had no time to stop and shed their hazmat suits. Their sweaty hair was plastered to their faces. They had stopped sweating so much only because their bodies were running low on fluids.

Trent's face was flushed and he was breathing heavily. "I think I'm having a heart attack."

"Keep going!" yelled Puller. He ripped off his glove and glanced at his watch. Nearly four minutes had passed. They had less than one minute. Maybe five hundred tons of TNT. A million pounds. The potential blast radius was far greater, even with the containment dome, than the distance they could run in the next minute, even if they were Olympic athletes. And if it went nuclear, in about fifty-five seconds there would be nothing left of them except vapor.

Cole saw him glance at his watch and noted the expression on his face. Puller sensed her watching and looked over at the woman. Their gazes locked even as they sprinted along.

"Nice working with you, Agent Puller." She managed a weak smile.

"Been my privilege, Sergeant Cole."

They had thirty seconds left to live.

In that time they managed to cover another twentieth of a mile. The dome was clearly visible behind them. Puller didn't look at his watch again. He kept running. He picked up his pace. So did Cole. So did Trent. The fresh air had helped revive him and he had somehow realized that they were running for their very lives.

Puller wondered briefly what the shock would feel like. He was about to find out.

Inside the Bunker the dynamite stick detonated.

Robert Puller's method worked, however. The staggered explosions, off by only milliseconds, allowed a seam to develop in the sphere and the pit shot right through it.

There would be no thermonuclear explosion.

Now it became just a bomb.

But it was a big bomb. And Drake County, with all of its coal mining over the years, had never witnessed a detonation such as this one.

The earth trembled beneath their feet, but they felt that for only a second, which was the length of time their feet were actually on the dirt. An instant later Puller, Cole, and Trent were thrown twenty feet in the air. They slammed into the dirt, and were rolled head over heels by the concussive blast coming from the Bunker. They ended up separated and nearly a hundred feet from where they had last stood. Puller barely missed colliding with the trunk of a pine tree.

Debris rained down from the sky.

Puller, dazed and bloody, slowly rolled over. Somehow his MP5 had stayed with him. The barrel had struck him in the face when he'd hit the ground. His cheek was cut and swollen. Every part of his body was screaming in pain, both from the force of the blast that had hit him and from being thrown all that distance and hitting the earth with wicked velocity. As a chunk of flying concrete nearly took his head off, he spun around and looked back at the Bunker.

It was no longer there. At least part of the top of it was gone. Chunks of concrete were flying through the air. Smoke and mist were rising up through the Bunker's new hole. Part of its side had also been blown out. That must've been the source of the concussive force that had knocked them heels over ass. It appeared to Puller to be a man-made volcano on full eruption.

He heard no screams from the adjacent neighborhood as debris slammed down on the houses. There were fifty-seven people squatting in the old houses that had once been home to the plant employees. Cole had earlier that evening directed her deputies to mass-evict all of them, on the pretense of unlawful trespass. The explanation given was that the law-abiding citizens of the county had had enough. These people were in shelters asleep instead of in these homes, which were now being crushed under a maelstrom of flying concrete and rebar. Right now, it looked like a damn good call.

He didn't know if the stuff belching from the Bunker was radio-active or not, and at the moment he didn't care. He had to find Cole.

He found Roger Trent first. Unfortunately, he had collided head-first with a tree far harder than he was. Half his head was gone. The mining mogul's financial problems, along with his life, were over.

Puller looked frantically around as another explosion rocked the area, sending more debris into the air.

Then he finally spotted her.

Cole was nearly a fifty yards from him. She was struggling to get up.

"Stay down," he cried out. "I'm coming."

He sprinted through the debris-filled air, dodging chunks of concrete that were as lethal as fifty-cal rounds. He was fifty feet from her when it happened. The mortar-sized chunk of concrete hit Cole directly in the head. She fell back to the ground.

"No!" Puller screamed.

He started to run faster as concrete and rebar and things he could not identify hurtled down at him. It was like he was dodging death once more in Kabul or Baghdad.

He reached her and knelt down.

The back of her head was bloody. He saw bits of her skull.

He gently turned her over.

Cole looked up at him. Her eyes were unfocused. Her brain was shutting down.

He reached out helplessly to her.

Her eyes stopped moving and her gaze hung on him for a second. Her lips parted. He thought she was going to speak to him.

She gave one last shudder, one last gasp of breath.

Her eyes grew still.

And Samantha Cole died.

He sat back on his haunches.

Not once had John Puller ever cried over a fallen comrade on the battlefield. Not once. And he'd had many opportunities to do so. Puller men did not cry. That was Rule One.

Yet as Sam Cole left him the tears trickled down his face.

CHAPTER

91

THE FEDERAL GOVERNMENT invaded Drake, West Virginia, with the force of a rampaging army. And in a way, that's exactly what it was at this point.

The Feds shut the town and especially the area around the Bunker down. Every inch of ground was examined by teams of experts wearing the very latest protective gear. Air and ground tests were conducted. Robots ran in and out of ground zero 24/7. The media was kept in the dark throughout. The government had gotten quite adept at that over the years. The official story was that an odd combination of methane gas and some old World War II–era storage canisters had combined to give that part of West Virginia an unscheduled fireworks display.

The air and ground contamination turned out to be far less than feared. No mass evacuation had to be ordered. Sophisticated imaging showed that the barrels Puller had rolled into that mineshaft had been effectively sealed under millions of tons of rock. The government wasn't sure whether they would go in to get them out, or let them remain right where they were. Puller's way had saved them a lot of money in storage costs after all.

Remains of the plutonium pit and the bomb were found and taken away. The cleanup process began and would continue for a while. The government outright lied to the media and the good people of Drake every step of the way, and they did so with a smooth confidence.

John Puller had been ordered by a string of generals and civilian brass to keep his mouth shut. He was a soldier and so he did what he was told.

One day that might change, he told himself. It would just not be today.

Robert Puller was the only man in U.S. history to receive a commendation from his country after being convicted of treason, for his part in helping to avoid a nuclear nightmare. However, there was never any talk of his sentence being commuted. And the commendation was given under the strictest secrecy.

Puller did not attend Roger Trent's funeral. He assumed it would be an elaborate affair, no expense spared by his widow, Jean. And he also wondered if anyone from Drake had bothered to show up. The man had been innocent of any complicity in attempting to create a nuclear holocaust. But that didn't take away from the fact that he was still a mean son of a bitch whose business had raped a region and ruined many a life. And Puller didn't give a damn about any of it.

But there was one funeral in Drake that he did attend.

Puller stepped out of the Malibu dressed in his brand-new dress blues. He cut quite a figure as he helped lift the coffin out of the hearse and carry it to the gravesite.

This was Sam Cole's funeral, and nothing would have kept the man away.

The Cole family was there, including Randy, who had on a brand-new suit that Jean no doubt had bought him for the burial of his other sister. He looked more like a lost boy than a grieving man.

Jean was dressed all in high-dollar black. She looked entirely crushed. As Puller watched her he had to assume it was more for the lost sibling than the dead husband. She was now a very rich widow. But she no longer had a sister.

Samantha Cole was buried in her street uniform—not her dress uniform, but the one she wore every day. They had found a last will and testament that had asked that this be done. It seemed very fitting for the sort of cop she had been. Also buried with her was the Cobra. That was also in her will, and Puller had to respect the lady's foresight and attention to detail. Her cottage she left to her brother.

Puller had earlier gone to her home and put a notice up on the front door declaring that anyone attempting to scavenge anything from the premises would be hunted down by the United States Army and dealt with appropriately and with extreme force if required.

As he walked up to the coffin, Puller felt his throat constrict and his chest tighten. It was hot as hell and the sun blazed overhead. The humidity and heat combination must have been in the triple digits. And all Puller felt was the icy cold of nearby death. He lightly touched the polished mahogany, mumbled a few words that felt wholly inadequate. An inferior Romeo for the fallen Juliet.

Finally, he gathered himself and said, "You were a good cop, Cole. This place didn't deserve you." He stopped talking, trying mightily to keep his emotions from running totally away with him.

He ended by saying. "It was an honor to serve with you."

As they were walking back to the cars after the service, Jean Trent drew next to Puller.

"What really happened?" she asked. "No one will tell me anything."

"Do you really need to know?"

She bristled. "Do I really need to know why my husband and sister were killed? Wouldn't you want to know if you were in my shoes?"

"The truth won't bring them back."

"Well, you're a big help," she snapped.

"I'm just giving you the best advice I can," he replied.

She stopped and so did he.

"You weren't at Roger's funeral," she said.

"That's right, I wasn't."

"But you came back for this, in your fancy duds, with all your medals. Why?"

He said, "Because I owed it to your sister. It's about respect."

"You cared for her, didn't you?"

Puller said nothing.

"Will you catch whoever killed her?"

"Yes, I will," said Puller.

She looked away and her mouth assumed a hard line.

"I don't know what I'm going to do."

"You're rich and single. You can do whatever you want."

"I'm not sure about the rich part. Most of Roger's assets have disappeared."

"You have the B-and-B, and a smart lady like yourself, you probably have some cash stashed away."

"Assuming I do, if you were me, what would you do?"

"You're really asking me?"

"Sam thought a lot of you. And she was not easily impressed. If she thought you were okay, then so do I. And I'd like your advice."

"Move to Italy. Open a restaurant there. Enjoy the rest of your life."

"Really? You think I should?"

"Nothing keeping you here."

"My brother is here."

"Take him with you."

"Randy? To Italy?"

Puller glanced over at Randy Cole. He was sitting by himself on a bench looking like he didn't even know where he was.

"He finally went to a doctor, right?"

She nodded. "He has a brain tumor. It's not one of the ones that's always fatal. The doctors think they can treat it, or at least slow its progression, but we don't know how much time he may have left."

"Then I think you both could use a fresh start. Good luck."

He started to walk away.

She called after him. "Puller, I'm having a reception at the house. I was hoping you could come."

Puller kept walking. He didn't have time for receptions.

He had a case to finish. And he was going to finish it. For himself.

But mostly for Sam Cole.

CHAPTER

92

THE MAN LIT HIS CIGARETTE, waved the match until it stopped burning, and tossed it down on the damp cobblestone street. He was dressed in a dark blue jacket and white linen pants with a hat pulled low over his forehead. His shirt was not monogrammed. It was stained with coffee and a small hole had been burned into the cuff by a cigarette.

It had rained most of the day and the clouds were still puffy with moisture. The air was humid but edged with a chill that made him shiver slightly.

He looked right and then left and crossed the street.

The bar had a neon sign that sputtered with each ebb and flow of the unreliable electrical supply. The door to the bar was battered and pocked with what looked to be an arc of bullet holes. That sight didn't bother him. This was not the first time he'd been here.

He edged through the crowd to the bar. He spoke the language passably, certainly enough to order a drink. Some in the crowd here knew him, at least by face if not by name. The passport he carried was a fake, but looked real enough to allow him to travel here. He had no idea how long he would stay. He hoped it wouldn't be all that long.

He took his drink, gave over his coins to pay for it, turned in his seat, and surveyed the crowd. Most were locals, some were tourists, and still others were probably here on business. He never looked directly at anyone. But he had become adept at noting anyone paying him unusual attention. There was none of that tonight. He turned back to the bar, but he listened for the door to open. When it did, he would turn back around to gaze at the newcomers. It happened twice. Locals and a tourist.

The woman approached him. She was young, pretty, her hair dark, her accent strong but lyrical. He had seen her here before. She liked to mingle. She had never mingled with him before. She usually chose someone closer to her own age.

Did he want to dance? she asked.

No, he told her.

Would he buy her a drink?

No, he told her.

Could she buy him a drink?

He turned to her, dipping his chin low so she could not see him clearly.

"Why?" he asked.

"Because I am lonely," she said.

He looked at the others in the crowded bar.

"I don't see how that's possible. I've seen you in here before. The men are very friendly towards you."

She pulled out a cigarette and asked him for a light.

He produced the match, struck it, and ignited the end of her smoke. He waved the match out and gazed again at her.

She took a puff, blew the smoke to the stained ceiling where a fan with bamboo blades slowly moved the hazy air from one side of the bar to the other. It was hotter in here. He could feel the sweat stain his armpits.

"You are not local," she said in English.

"I know I'm not. But you are?"

"Since I was in the womb. Why do you come here?"

"Why does anyone go anywhere?"

"I have never been anywhere. I would like to get away from this place."

"To get away."

"What?"

He felt the urge to talk to her, he wasn't sure why. Maybe he was lonely too. "That's why I'm here. To get away."

"To get away from what?"

"Life."

"Was your life so bad?"

"Pretty bad. But also pretty good."

"You are not talking sense."

He sat straighter on the bar stool. "It does make sense. If you put it in context."

She gazed at him, obviously perplexed. "Context? What is this context?"

He finished his drink and tossed up his hand, ordering another. It was produced a few seconds later and he drank that down too, wiping his mouth with the sleeve of his jacket. He wiped sweat from his forehead.

"Context is everything. It's truth. It's really the only thing that matters."

"You talk funny, but I like you." She swept one hand through his hair. Her touch, and her smell, awoke something in him.

He thought he now understood why she had come to him in the bar.

He paid for his drink and then for hers.

She kept her hand on his shoulder, and then it dipped to the small of his back. He kept one hand near his wallet, but he was reasonably sure that wasn't what she was after. Well, in a way she was.

Money.

For services.

He had a desire to be serviced.

They left the bar thirty minutes later. They walked back to his hotel. It was only five minutes. It was the best hotel in the city, and it was still a dump. But he was not going to be staying here. Not for long, anyway.

They went up to his room at the top of the stairs. He took off his hat and his jacket and let them fall to the floor. She unbuttoned his shirt, helped him off with his shoes. When his pants were off, she said, "Give me a few minutes to freshen up." He put his hand on her substantial rump and squeezed. She kissed him on the neck. His hand went under her skirt and glided over smooth flesh.

She kissed him again, tonguing his cheek, his ear.

His other hand reached for her breasts, but she was gone. Off to the bathroom. To freshen up. He lay back on the bed, in the dark. The ceiling fan whirred overhead. He watched it, counted the revolutions, then closed his eyes, waited for the bathroom door to reopen, see her silhouetted there. Perhaps naked, perhaps nearly so. His life had changed so much in such a short period of time.

It was both terrifying and exhilarating.

Then a man said, "Hello, Bill. It's time we talked."

CHAPTER

93

BILL STRAUSS SAT UP when he heard the man's voice. His body started to tremble. It was an immediate, visceral reaction that was paralyzing.

He watched as the silhouette came forward. The bathroom door opened, the woman slipped through it and then out of the room, closing the door behind her.

A setup. He had fallen for it.

The silhouette turned to hard flesh.

The man stood in front of Strauss and looked down.

John Puller said, "You're a long way from Drake, West Virginia, Bill."

Strauss just sat there staring upward at the far bigger man.

Puller grabbed a chair, flipped it around, and sat down facing Strauss. In his right hand was one of his M11s.

"How did you know? The fact that I ran for it, I guess?"

"Actually, I knew before then. You're not a good liar. I could read you pretty easily the night we came by the house to tell you your son was dead. At Trent Exploration you were the second banana. But you wanted the bigger house. You were the brains and Roger was the front. Why should he get the lion's share? And you were in the perfect position to rip him off. No one would suspect you, the money guy, because everyone assumed that if the business tanked, you would as well. But that wouldn't be the case if you'd already taken all the cash. And the plans to the Bunker were in your safe, Bill. Not Roger's. That was the clincher. You knew all about the place. And you figured out that Treadwell and Bitner had discovered the plans."

Strauss's head dipped low.

"Focus, Bill, I need you to focus." Puller smacked the man on the shoulder and Strauss looked up at him.

"They killed your son, Bill."

Strauss knuckled his thighs and nodded. "I know that. You know I know that."

"But what are you going to do about it?"

"What can I do?"

"Your run is over. You're going to prison for the rest of your life. But you can make amends. You have that opportunity. You can go out on your terms. That's something."

"No, I can't. I can't do that, Puller."

Puller edged forward, his hand bringing up the M11 slightly.

Strauss eyed the gun. "Are you going to kill me? Is that why you're here?"

"I came a long way to see you. And no, I'm not going to kill you. Unless you give me a reason to," he added.

"I'm sorry about Sam."

"I'm not here to talk about Sam. I'm here to talk about you."

"How did you find me all the way down here?"

"I didn't have to find you."

Strauss looked puzzled. "I don't understand."

"I didn't have to find you because I never lost you. We knew where you were at all times. We followed your path all the way down here, in fact."

"I don't understand. How did—"

Puller stood. "They killed Dickie, Bill. Shot him right in the head. You never intended that, did you?"

Strauss shook his head. "It wasn't supposed to be that way. Never that way."

"Right through the head. Just riding his bike. And bam."

Strauss nearly tumbled off the bed as Puller fired his gun and the slug ripped into the wall and stayed there.

"Shot him," Puller continued calmly. "Blew up his brain. I was there, saw it all. Hydrostatic pressure to the head from a supersonic rifle round. A Lapua round, Bill. It was overkill. They wanted to make sure he was dead. He never had a chance. You never would've recognized your kid, Bill. He had no face left."

Strauss pulled himself back up and snapped, "That was not part of the plan. I didn't know...No one told me that Dickie..." His voice trailed off and he started weeping.

"I suppose you're sorry he's dead," said Puller.

"Of course I am. When you came to my house and told me I was distraught. His mother is devastated."

"But you had no problem leaving her behind," Puller pointed out.

"There was no way to bring her. There was no way to explain to her..." He halted, ground his fists into his eyes, wept some more.

"So you kept the missus in the dark over all of this."

"I've set up an account for her. She would never want for anything."

"Except her husband and son. And since you left her behind, you couldn't know she wouldn't die when the bomb went off."

"I was told...I mean our house was far enough away—"

Puller cut in. "Doesn't it piss you off that they murdered your son?"

Strauss said nothing.

Puller slipped his hand into his jacket and pulled out a photo. "I have the autopsy photo right here. You want to see your kid? See what they did to him?"

More tears trickled down Strauss's face. He made no effort to brush them away. "Wasn't supposed to happen."

"Well, it did happen, Bill. You want to see?" Puller said in a tighter voice. He held out the picture.

Straus recoiled from it. "No. No, I don't want to see him...like that," he said in a hushed voice.

"Somebody did that to my boy I'd want payback. I'd want revenge. I'd want justice."

"I...There's no way to do that now."

"Sure there is." Puller slipped the picture back in his pocket. "Amends, Bill. You can make it right. You can do it for your son."

"I can't. You see my wife. They might hurt—"

"She's already in protective custody. She'll go into witness protection. It's all arranged. All done. All you have to do is the right thing."

Puller sat back down, holstered the M11.

Strauss said, "What about me? Can I—"

Puller cut him off again. "You're going to prison, Bill. No deals."

"So I talk and still get prison?" Strauss said bitterly.

"You get to live. It's a good alternative to not living."

"So you are going to kill me? If I don't cooperate?"

"I don't have to."

"Why?"

"The U.S. government will execute you. For treason."

A few moments of silence went by.

Puller finally said, "I need an answer, Bill. Got wings waiting. Depending on your answer, the jet will take you one place as opposed to another."

Bill Strauss rose.

"Let's go."

Puller stood up and gripped the other man by the elbow.

"Good choice."

"For my son."

"Yeah," said Puller.

CHAPTER

94

Puller's choice of running paths was remote and lonely. He liked to come here to sweat and think, and the former helped him do the latter. And he didn't like other people around while he was doing it.

He inserted the ear buds, turned on his iPod, and started his run. Five miles later he was trotting back to his car.

And then he stopped.

There were six men that he could see. One was leaning against the hood of his Malibu. There were four others providing perimeter security. The sixth man was standing near the rear door of the Malibu. Two black SUVs were parked in front and at the rear of Puller's vehicle, blocking it in.

Puller started walking. He slipped out his ear buds and cupped his iPod in his right hand.

"Hey, Joe, how's it going?"

Joe Mason pushed off from the Malibu. "Puller, haven't heard from you in a while. Thought my orders were pretty clear on that score. You report to me."

"Well, sometimes orders get gummed up by facts on the ground and then they have to be changed."

"Is that right?"

"Pretty much, yeah."

"Well, nobody told me that. And it's always good to hear it from the horse's mouth. That's why I'm here."

Puller drew closer to him. He noted the four perimeter guys close in. They were all armed. And they were all the same guys who had once before surrounded him in the parking garage in Arlington after his meeting with General Carson.

"So you're here because you want a report?'

"That's right."

"Okay. Easy enough. There are three basic points. After Dickie was murdered something didn't feel right so I started doing some digging. And here's what I found. You and Bill Strauss knew each other. You grew up together in New Jersey. I checked. You served together in the Marines. Strauss tried to B.S. me and said he'd never served. But he knew what a BCD and a DD were. And he made his son join up because he thought the Army could 'cure' him of his sexual preference. You don't do that unless you've been in the ranks yourself."

"Okay, so I knew him. I served with him. Lots of Marines out there."

"He didn't last long, just like his son. Dickie got dumped because of DADT. His old man got dumped because he was a petty thief and drug dealer and the Marine Corps just got tired of his ass. The interesting thing is you left around the same time. Now, you had no dings on your record like Strauss, otherwise you never would have gotten on with the Feds, and later at DHS. But I'm thinking that you and Strauss stayed in touch. And when Dickie told his old man about a way into the Bunker that Randy Cole told him about, and what he'd seen when he was in there, Bill called you. He figured with your connections, something good might come out of this. Good meaning lots of money regardless of the chaos and pain it might cause."

"Is that right?"

"Yeah, Joe, it is. You came to Drake on the QT, and got into the Bunker and saw what Randy Cole was talking about. Only unlike him, you figured out what was in those barrels. All those nuke cakes just sitting there. Forgotten. What would the value be? Billions?"

"How should I know?"

"And the file you gave me on the Bunker was legit. At least it was legit as far as the Army cover-up went. It was perfect for you.

The last thing you wanted was anybody snooping around there. So when I started asking about it you just pulled out the report and we stopped thinking about the Bunker as a viable target."

"Keep going."

"Second, you had to build the bomb. Strauss got Treadwell involved to do some of the machining of the parts without telling him what they were really for. He just gave him specs that you gave him. But Treadwell and Bitner got too curious and they made the very big mistake of involving their neighbor, Matt Reynolds. He was DIA. Way too close to home. He had a soil report done. I bet it was taken somewhere around the Bunker. I don't think Reynolds knew there was plutonium in there, but he might have thought there was something toxic that people were after. And if he started really digging, your whole plan might get crushed. So six people had to die, including two kids. Which of your guys did the deed, Joe?" Puller looked around and pointed at one guy. "Him?" He pointed at a second. "That asshole? I doubt you came down to do the honors. Boss man doesn't dirty his fingers. You just watched via video. Shotgunned the parents, bludgeoned the kids. What, didn't have the heart to shoot the kids?"

Mason said nothing.

"And then your guys spotted Larry Wellman on duty Monday night. A rookie. Your men approached him, probably when he was making rounds, near the rear of the house where no one could see. They flashed their creds. Fed gods. Wellman couldn't be happier to help. Put up no fight. Asked no questions. He took your guys inside and they strung him up like a side of meat. You planted your bits of the certified letter there and left with his wheels."

"How were we supposed to get the letter in the first place?"

"It wasn't the real letter. You knew about it because Wellman told Dickie, or else Matt Reynolds told you what he'd done when you interrogated him. It wasn't in the house and we never did end up finding it. You learned the letter wasn't discovered, but you wanted us to go down that road because you knew it would lead nowhere and be a big waste of our time. So you killed a man just in order to plant a false clue at the crime scene."

"Interesting," said Mason.

"Then you concocted the Dari chatter to throw the blame onto guys in turbans that never existed. You never would have drawn attention to Drake, but your hand got called because of the murders. You knew CID was going to be coming out. So you did the chatter immediately afterward and then you had your guys do some more chatter and you gave me the plausible but wrong scent on the pipeline and nuke plant. You told me we had three days when you knew the Bunker was set to detonate in two. Strauss made those death threats to Roger Trent to lay the groundwork for something happening to him because Strauss was going to use this as an opportunity to get rid of Trent and the financial records that showed the embezzlement. So Trent and the boxes were put in the Bunker. There'd be nothing left of either one except radioactive dust. People would either assume Trent made a run for it to get away from the money troubles Strauss had caused, or whoever was sending him the death threats had finally gotten their man. It was a neat plan you two came up with."

"I haven't heard anything that connects me to anything," said Mason.

Puller held up a third finger. "And here's why I stopped *reporting* to you and instead started digging. You were the only one I told about Dickie Strauss working with me. More significantly, you were the only one I told about him meeting me that night at the firehouse. His death wasn't a spontaneous thing. Your sniper was there long before, all set up and ready to go. You were the only one who could have orchestrated that. No one else."

"Not how I recall it," replied Mason. "He said, he said."

"And you killed him because you were afraid Dickie would have a change of heart. He went to the house and found Larry Wellman. He saw the bodies of the Reynolds family. He knew Treadwell and Bitner were dead too. He was scared. I doubt you told him what the real plan was, but when people started dying he knew he was in way over his head. He might have figured working with the authorities was the best way out. But you couldn't allow that. So you had your guy blow his head off."

"So you say. No proof."

Puller looked around at the other men. "You got away with it, Joe. You blew the Bunker. You got your nuke fuel. Roger Trent is dead. The financial docs are ash. So why are you here? Your plan worked."

Mason said nothing. He continued to eye Puller steadily.

Puller edged a step closer to the man. "Maybe that Islamic 'chatter' actually wasn't far from the truth, even though you planted it. Maybe you were hired by enemies of this country to detonate a shitload of fissile material in West Virginia. I think those barrels you left behind were *part* of the bomb. And the folks you're in business with are probably not happy about it not going according to plan. So that's why you're here, to get a little bit of revenge on me. And maybe save your ass from the guys in the turbans. How much did you get paid to attack your own country, Joe? Just give me a ballpark."

Mason cleared his throat. "You don't have it exactly right, Puller. I'm a patriot. I wouldn't do that to my country. I knew what I had there. But I wasn't paid to make it go boom."

"Bullshit!" snapped Puller. "You're no different from the 9/11 maggots."

Mason exploded. "You don't know what the hell you're talking about, Puller."

"Then explain it to me, Joe. Explain how a former Marine turns traitor."

Mason started talking fast. "After all these years at DHS I know my way around nukes. And I knew how to get to the folks I needed to in order to build one. Once you have the fuel, the rest isn't that hard. The government would never admit having left nuke fuel behind. I could sell this stuff and no one the wiser. My big mistake was letting Strauss get that idiot Treadwell to build the reflector and some other components, and that came back to bite me in the ass."

"Nothing you just said makes any difference. You're still a traitor. You left barrels of uranium and plutonium cakes behind in the Bunker. That would have made five or six states radioactive."

"Those barrels were empty. I wasn't leaving that stuff behind. You're right. It was worth billions."

Puller said, "You're lying. I saw those barrels. Those tops hadn't been opened in decades."

Mason grinned triumphantly. "We cut open the *bottoms* of the barrels, Puller. And then resealed them. After we filled them with dirt. See, I provide for every contingency. Just like I did when you accessed the bomb. It triggered a countdown accelerator."

"But it was still a nuclear device. You were still going to nuke your own country, you asshole."

Mason snapped, "I knew what I was doing, okay? We only used a minimal amount of plutonium, enough to give it a little boom and some radiation. And it's the middle of nowhere. So what if Drake, West Virginia, went radioactive? It was already dead."

"It has over six thousand people, Joe."

"A lot more people than that die in traffic accidents every year. A hundred thousand people die every year in hospitals because of mistakes. In that context the collateral damage was pretty damn small."

"But you're intending to sell the nuke fuel to our enemies. They won't detonate in an area that has no people, Joe. They'll nuke New York, D.C."

"Yeah, well, I'm in the process of moving to another country. I'm kind of tired of this one. But you did screw things up for me. I can still sell the stuff, but it'll just be trickier. That's why I'm here. To give you a little payback."

Puller said, "Did you really need the money that badly? To sell out to terrorists? You're scum."

"I've busted my ass for my *country* for over thirty years. And in the next round of budget cuts they were going to let me go. I owed them nothing."

Puller held up a fourth finger.

Mason said, "You said there were only three points."

"I lied. We nailed Bill Strauss in South America. He took off before the Bunker blew, of course. It wasn't like he was going to stay around for the mushroom cloud, although he didn't bother taking his grieving wife. Guy's a real winner. Oh, did I mention that he ratted you and all your guys out?"

Mason blurted out, "That's impossible. I spoke to Bill—"

"Yeah, you spoke to him yesterday and today. I was in the room when you did. FBI recorded the whole thing."

"You're bluffing."

"How else do you think I knew all the details I just told you? I'm a pretty good investigator, but Strauss debriefed us on a lot of stuff. Only way I knew about it."

Mason just kept staring.

Puller said, "So you're basically sitting on a bunch of nuclear material you'll never be able to sell. But then again, you don't need a lot of money in prison. Or if you're convicted of treason, you get lethal injection. Either way is fine with me."

Puller looked around and observed that all of Mason's men were now showing signs of extreme nervousness. That was both good and bad. Good in that nervous men were not as effective fighters. Bad in that nervous armed men did erratic things, and were thus hard to predict.

But even though it was six against one, Puller could sense that they were feeling outnumbered right now.

He looked back at Mason. "You ready to surrender, Joe?" asked Puller.

"I'll tell you what I'm ready for, Puller. And I'll tell you right now."

CHAPTER

95

MASON LOOKED OVER at the sixth man standing next to the Malibu. He waved him forward. The man was in his middle fifties, dressed in slacks and a light windbreaker though the air was warm and there was no breeze. He had a SIG nine-millimeter held loosely in his right hand. He was two inches shorter than Puller but about twenty pounds heavier. He looked rock solid, mean, and ready to kill.

Mason said, "This is Sergei, Puller. He was in the Soviet army. He specializes in pain, creating it in others, that is. He's going to take you somewhere and work on you, show you some of his techniques. He's really the best at what he does."

Puller gazed over at the other man, who looked back at him with a superior expression.

Puller said, "Soviet army? You guys can't fight worth shit. You let a bunch of desert farmers kick your ass in Afghanistan."

Sergei's confident look went away and was replaced with a murderous one.

Mason said, "I'm not sure that was your smartest move, Puller."

"Did I hurt your feelings, Sergei? Were you one of the guys who didn't have the balls to carry a rifle? Did they keep you at the rear to work over the guys who couldn't fight?"

Sergei looked even more unhinged. Which was Puller's purpose behind the taunts. Pissed-off people made mistakes. Puller edged a step closer.

Mason said, "Let me give you the rundown, Puller. We're going to take you to a place where Sergei is going to inflict some real pain on you while I watch. And then we're going to put you out of your pain permanently. I tried to take you out twice before with bombs, but missed both times. But the third time, as they say, is the charm."

Puller swung his arms wide and used this movement to distract their attention from him taking two more steps forward. He said, "So that's the plan? Hope you didn't spend much time thinking up that one, Joe, because it really sucks."

"It works just fine for me. And then I have contingency plans, Puller. I always do. Strauss in the federal bag or not, I'm out of here. And don't even think about putting up a fight. We'll shoot you right here if you do."

Puller shrugged. "Well then, let's get this over with. I've got stuff to do today."

Before Sergei could even bring his gun up Puller struck. His iPod's edge had been filed down to the sharpness of a Ranger KA-BAR knife.

A second later the entire front of Sergei's neck was gutted. The Russian fell back against the car, blood pouring down his chest. Puller grabbed Sergei by the collar, swung him around, and knocked the gun out of Mason's hand. He let the Russian drop to the ground to finish bleeding out. In the next flash of movement he wrapped one arm around Joe Mason's neck, spun around, lifted the man off his feet, and drove his head right through the windshield of the Malibu.

Mason lay sprawled on the hood, his head a bloody, pulpy mess. Puller didn't know if he was dead or not. And he didn't care.

He leaned close to the man and said quietly, "That was for Sergeant Samantha Cole."

He turned to look at Mason's remaining men. They were pointing their weapons at him but seemed frozen by the utter ferocity of his attack.

They wouldn't be frozen for long.

Twenty Army Rangers appeared out of nowhere, in full cammie gear, their MP5s pointed at the four men. Five-to-one kill ratio. The odds of victory for the four were zero.

They dropped their weapons immediately.

As they were being cuffed, Mason pulled free from the windshield, and Sergei placed in a body bag, General Julie Carson emerged from the woods. She checked on Mason and walked over next to Puller. She handed him a bottle of water.

"Figured you worked up a sweat."

"With the run, yeah. And thanks for giving me a little 'alone' time with Mason."

"No, thank you. I enjoyed watching."

"Is Mason dead?"

"No. He has a pulse. It's pretty weak, though."

"Tell the ambulance to take its time."

She smiled. "Roger that."

"Not that we needed it, but I'm assuming you got all that recorded?"

Carson held up a flash drive. "You know how seriously the United States Army takes surveillance. Although, I do think we might conveniently lose the footage of you taking the Russian and Mason out. I mean, who needs to know about that?"

He smiled. "I guess I didn't expect that sort of nuance from you, General Carson."

She returned the smile. "I have a few surprises. And we're off the clock, so it's Julie."

"Okay, Julie."

She watched the men being driven off. "I guess it was all for the money."

"Guess so. The nukes?"

"They're not on the market yet, so we'll get them. That's all these guys have to bargain with to escape the death penalty now."

Puller looked over at his damaged car. "Guess I can't drive that."

"Not to worry. I'll give you a lift."

"Thanks."

"And maybe we can have that drink."

"Maybe we can."

CHAPTER

96

Puller said, "You're a hero, Bobby. You saved a town, probably an entire state."

He was seated across from his brother at USDB.

Robert Puller appeared to be trying hard to hide his pleasure at this statement. It was the first time at USDB that Puller had ever seen his brother wear an expression approaching pride.

"Did they deliver the commendation to you?"

Robert nodded. "A first for USDB. Not sure they knew what to do."

"I bet."

"I'm sorry about your friend, Sam Cole."

"And I'm sorry they didn't see fit to commute your sentence."

"Did you really expect them to? The military does not second-guess itself. That would be tantamount to admitting a mistake, and the military doesn't do that either."

Puller reached across and shook his brother's hand, ignoring the glare from the MP on duty. "You saved my ass."

"That's what big brothers are for."

For most of the flight home Puller stared out the window. When the plane soared over West Virginia the pilot came on the PA. He told them where they were and added that he was from Bluefield, which he declared was the prettiest place in the country. Puller began to read the in-flight magazine and tuned out the man's words.

He picked up his repaired Malibu at the airport and drove to his apartment. AWOL greeted him, and he spent a few minutes giving the cat some attention. He looked out at the tiny courtyard visible from his kitchen window. This made him think, for some reason, about Sam Cole's picture-perfect backyard with its fountain where they had sat together and talked. He touched his cheek where she had kissed him. He wondered if he had been wrong to turn down Sam Cole's not-so-subtle invitation into her bed. But then he finally concluded that it had been the right thing to do at the time, for both of them. Although he had always thought there would be other times with the woman.

But what were the odds, really? That he would have lived. And she would have died. That chunk of concrete could have just as easily hit him. Or a tree. Or a deer. But it had chosen to hit Sam Cole and end her life.

A person could explain it away by saying it just wasn't his time yet. Puller had done it himself after dodging death on the battlefield. Other guys had died. He hadn't. But for him that wasn't explanation enough. Not this time. He wasn't sure why it was different in this instance, but he just knew that it was.

He put AWOL aside and reported to CID at Quantico. He wrote up his reports and talked to the people he needed to talk to. He was told that a promotion was forthcoming that would enable him to jump two spaces in the military hierarchy instead of merely one, an unheard-of opportunity.

He turned it down on the spot.

His SAC spent a long time trying to talk him out of it.

"Other guys would kill for this."

"Then let the other guys have it."

"I don't get you, Puller, I really don't."

"I know, sir. Sometimes I don't get myself."

He had cleaned up his desk, returned a few emails, met with some superiors so they could be "in the loop," and then he decided he was done with the Army for a while. He had leave saved up. He wanted to take it. There wasn't an officer in the ranks who would have denied the request. People who had helped avoid nuclear holocaust on home soil could pretty much do what they wanted.

Within reason.

This was the U.S. military after all.

He went home, packed up some things and his cat, loaded the Malibu, and set out. He had no map, no plan, no destination. It was just a CID special agent on the loose with his trusty comrade, AWOL. The cat rode in the backseat like he was being chauffeured. Puller was glad to play the role.

They left at midnight because Puller preferred roaming in the dark. He found a road heading west and took it. By dawn he had covered over three hundred miles without stopping to even take a leak. When he did stop to stretch and relieve himself, gas up, buy the biggest coffee they had, and let AWOL out, he found he was well into West Virginia. Not Drake, another part. He wasn't going back to Drake. There was nothing there for him, if there ever had been.

He didn't want to see the Bunker again, what was left of it.

He didn't want to see the Trents and the Coles, what were left of them.

He would carry Sam Cole in his memories for as long as he had them. Of that he was sure. Being around her had made him a better cop. And a better person. He would miss her for the rest of his life. Of that he was also sure.

He would come back to the Army and return to his duties catching people who did bad things. For some reason, he felt that he would come back stronger than ever. It was a nice feeling. He believed he owed that one to Sam Cole too.

He opened the door and AWOL jumped back into the car. Puller settled himself in his seat, shifted the Malibu to drive, and said, "Ready to roll, AWOL?"

The cat meowed its approval.

Puller eased back onto the road and then gunned it.

He swept down the road, moving fast, flowing smoothly.

And then he was gone, like he had never even been there.

After all, it *was* true.

You couldn't kill what you couldn't see coming.

ACKNOWLEDGMENTS

To MICHELLE, the ride continues.

To Mitch Hoffman, for helping me to continue to see the light.

To David Young, Jamie Raab, Emi Battaglia, Jennifer Romanello, Tom Maciag, Martha Otis, Chris Barba, Karen Torres, Anthony Goff, Lindsey Rose, Bob Castillo, Michele McGonigle, and all at Grand Central Publishing, who support me in every way.

To Aaron and Arleen Priest, Lucy Childs Baker, Lisa Erbach Vance, Nicole James, Frances Jalet-Miller, and John Richmond, for being with me step for step.

To Maja Thomas, the empress of ebooks.

To Anthony Forbes Watson, Jeremy Trevathan, Maria Rejt, Trisha Jackson, Katie James, Aimee Roche, Becky Ikin, Lee Dibble, Sophie Portas, Stuart Dwyer, Anna Bond, and Michelle Kirk at Pan Macmillan, for helping me hit my highest numbers ever in the UK.

To Ron McLarty and Orlagh Cassidy, for giving superb voice to my stories.

To Steven Maat at Bruna, for taking me to the # 1 spot in Holland.

To Bob Schule, for your eagle eye.

To Anshu Guleria, M.D., for sound medical advice.

To the charity auction winners, Matthew Reynolds, Bill Strauss, and Jean Trent, I hope you enjoyed your characters.

To the Fort Benning crew who were so generous with their time and expertise: Maj. Gen. Bob and Patti Brown, Command Sgt. Maj. Chris Hardy, Command Sgt. Maj. Steven McClaflin, Lt. Col. Selby Rollinson (Ret.), Susan Berry, Col. Sean McCaffrey, Col. Terry

McKenrick, Col. Greg Camp (Ret.), Lt. Col. Jay Bartholomees, Lt. Col. Kyle Feger, Lt. Col. Mike Junot, Lt. Col. David Koonce, Lt. Col. Todd Zollinger, Maj. Joe Ruzicka, Capt. Matthew Dusablon, Chief Warrant Officer 4 Larry Turso, Chief Warrant Officer 3 Jose Aponte, Chief Warrant Officer 2 Shawn Burke, Special Agent Joseph Leary, Special Agent Jason Waters, Special Agent Jason Huggins, Sgt. 1st Class Steve Lynn, Staff Sgt. Shawn Goodwill, Nora Bennett, Terri Panco, and Courtland Pegan.

To Tom Colson, for your CID expertise.

To Bill Chadwell, for taking me through the intricacies of the Pentagon.

To Col. Marguerite Garrison (Ret.), for doing the same.

To Michael Furey, for your valuable help.

To Christine Craig, for walking me through USACIL.

To Bill Colwell and Rear Adm. John Faigle, USCG (Ret.), for introducing me to the wonderful Army and Navy Club.

To Maj. Gen. Karl Horst, for a great dinner and conversation.

To Dave and Karen Halverson, for the use of your last name.

To Timothy Imholt, you know why.

To Kristen and Natasha, because I'd be lost without you.

A special welcome to Erin Race as she joins the Columbus Rose team.

A wish for a great retirement to Lynette and Art, and heartfelt thanks for a job well done.

And last but far from least, to Roland Ottewell for another great editing job.